CHAMELEON

THE DOMINO PROJECT

K.T. HANNA

Author: K.T. Hanna
Content Edits: Jami Nord
Copy Editor: Rebecca Weston
Cover Artist: S.P. McConnell
Layout & Formatting: Caitlin Greer

Disclaimer: This is a work of fiction.
Names, characters, businesses, places, events, and incidents are either the products of the author's imagination or used in a fictitious manner. Any resemblance to actual people, living or dead, or actual events is purely coincidental.

#

For Trevor
Because even at my worst, you love me like my best.

CHAPTER
One

Droves of addicts litter the dirty pavement the closer Bastian gets to Block 63. While Markus navigates the Gerts125 through the human refuse, Bastian scans the streets. He tries to avoid the vacant gazes of the Shined, lost staring at the holes in their veins and the stars in the sky, drool running down their chins to pool on the fetid ground. Shine abuse is blatant in the city's outskirts.

The next shockwave hits sooner than it should. Psionic abilities don't normally awaken violently, but Bastian can sense she's a Rare. At this proximity he no longer needs his wristband's help to pinpoint her, but glances at the beeping indicator to avoid arousing suspicion, before silencing it with a brief jolt of power.

Another shockwave warps the air under their vehicle. Bastian doesn't wait for the transport to stabilize, but steps out as it slows and shades his eyes as Block 63 implodes.

Flames envelop the upper floors of the four apartment towers. Pieces of concrete cascade down the outer walls. Amidst the chaos, he can sense her panic, bewilderment, and—above all—her utter exhaustion. The fact that he's still standing there, that the area around him isn't in flames, means she pulled some of the force back into herself somehow.

Panicked screams and distant sirens make it hard to focus. The thin layer of Shine permeating the mess doesn't help either, and Bastian refuses to think about the potential death toll. The surrounding blocks should be safe as long as the emergency forces can contain the blaze.

Smoke and ash obscure Bastian's vision, and he has to close his eyes to focus. He listens for a moment, picking up her— *Sai's*—incoherent inner diatribe, which leads him to the botanica. The vegetation once protected within has already started to wilt, and the glass walls of the small atrium lie shattered in a perfect circle around the girl.

She sits in the center, blinking tears away as silver power tendrils wind their way through black irises, leaving her eyes unfocused. Blood from a cut on her forehead mingles with dark hair, lending it a dull red gleam in the flickering light. Her flannel nightshirt is tattered. She clutches it as she rocks back and forth. Pieces of glass embedded in her back glitter through the shirt, but he'll deal with that later. Her state of mind is the more pressing matter.

"Sai?" Bastian puts a little suggestion behind it—that she can trust him, that he will help her. He has to be careful, though. Her mind is raw from the awakening blast. She continues to rock back and forth, so he repeats himself a little louder. "Sai?"

She looks up at him and blinks, only tears left streaming down her face. Her mouth opens, but no words come out.

Bastian reaches out a hand and waits for her to take it. For a few moments, her eyes dart wildly. He can sense the turmoil—her instincts telling her to run, her mind urging her to go with him. She slides her hand into his, and he tugs her up.

Markus waits at the end of the street, a scowl on his face as he leans against his door.

"We didn't make it in time after all." He gestures toward the buildings, and his voice carries over the sound of the emergency vehicles as they hiss to a halt next to him.

"Obviously," Bastian says as he motions for Sai to get in the back of the car. A second before the door closes, panic crosses her face, but she sticks out her chin and hugs her chest instead. Her erratic thoughts threaten to break the fragile facade she's holding onto.

"At least we saved her," Bastian says softly as he slides into his seat. "Let's get her to the facility."

Markus grunts as he turns the transport back on. "I still don't believe that young thing caused so much damage."

Bastian shrugs and glances at the girl in the rearview mirror. Her face is mostly hidden by shadows, and her eyes are as wary as her thoughts.

"She did most of it, though some of the sparks ignited the building's filtration system. We're lucky the emergency dampeners still work in this sector or the chain reaction would have spread through the city."

"How can you be so calm? Won't they have your hide for this?" Markus steps on the gas and takes them away from the dregs of the city.

Bastian stops observing Sai long enough to chuckle. "No. I'm psionic, not a fortune teller. I'm only as good as the signals I receive, and frankly the onset of puberty is unpredictable. Besides..." He pauses to watch her twirl her blood-stained hair around her fingers. She counts to ten slowly in her head, loud enough for him to hear, and reminds herself to breathe. Over and over.

Markus prompts him. "Besides?"

"This doesn't happen often. Do you remember a last time?"

Markus shakes his head. "Is she special?"

"Pardon?" It's not like Markus to pry into Bastian's business.

"Can she do something special?"

"Besides blow up an entire block?" Bastian laughs. "Not...not really."

The "not yet" echoes silently in his head. Just a few more years and he won't have to fight alone anymore.

Sweat drips in her eyes, reminding Sai how ineffectual eyebrows actually are. She rolls away from her training partner, defending herself with an ease defined by four years of practice. Being the smallest in all her classes makes her an easy target to pick on, but no one has tried it more than once. She positions her hands to better protect her face.

One more test and everything will be worth it.

But one more test is deceptive. They're all aware of the ones whose minds break. The mutterings and the hollow eyes. The inability to recover that leads to them never being seen again. And those are the lucky ones. Sai's seen the mangled remains wheeled out of the examination areas. Not everyone survives the final examination. Maybe not everyone is meant to.

After decimating a city block and killing and injuring over a thousand people four years earlier, Gerts, Newton, & Williams United Conglomerate will never let Sai forget they own her, that she and everyone else in the training facility live only as long as GNW sees fit.

"Fifty-Two! Where is your head?"

Sai snaps to attention, her train of thought broken, and narrowly avoids Eighteen's punch to her face. She dodges to the side and grabs her opponent's right shoulder with both hands, smoothly bringing her knee up into the girl's stomach.

"That's better." Her instructor, Ms. Genna, glances down at her reader and pokes at the screen before moving onto the next students.

Sai wishes she could read those notes, know something about her fate. As she continues to spar, she feels a desperation that isn't her own. Eighteen's shields are weak, and her fears and emotions trickle through intermittently.

Like everyone else, the girl is scared on the inside but refuses to show it on the outside. It's a pity Sai can hear the panic in her head. The bravado is ruined when half the room can skim your thoughts if your shielding isn't tight enough.

Sai watches her opponent as they circle each other in identical stances—hands up, knees slightly bent, ready to react.

They've sparred numerous times over the last few years. Eighteen was one of the first people Sai used to convince others to leave her alone. This might be the last time she sees her, and the pang of regret takes Sai by surprise.

"That's enough for today." Ms. Genna sticks the stylus behind her ear. "Rest up for your final tomorrow. You'll need it." Her parting grin as she leaves the hall is laced with derision.

Sai stays behind to grab a drink bottle and towel. Twenty-Nine pushes in with a smirk and snatches a water straight out of her hands.

"Didn't see you there..." The false smile doesn't reach Twenty-Nine's eyes, even though they crinkle with the expression. Sai shrugs and watches as the girl turns to leave with the rest of the class. They file out in groups of two and three, friendships they've made and maintained over the years, even as their numbers have dwindled. Sai's never been close to anyone. Not after Block 63.

She knows there are no longer fifty-two people in her class. Many have disappeared over the years, but after the example set when Sixteen asked where someone was, no one let on they cared again.

The scent of lemon lingers in the air as she makes her way through the corridors and back to her room. Her feet make so little noise on the pristine tiles, she can hear the soft whir of cameras tracking her every move.

A murmured mantra leaks from the walls, in the perfect loop her benefactors demand.

For your own safety, please do not leave your designated areas. Report any unauthorized personnel immediately. Remember, the future of GNW depends on you.

Sai's room is sparsely furnished, like everything at the facility. Necessity, not indulgence. The steel bed, desk, and chair have been her home since she arrived. Whether or not she survives tomorrow, everything will change.

With the door closed and the cameras locked out, she's finally alone with her thoughts. They're the only thing not monitored consistently. Sai lies down on the bed and twists a strand of hair around her finger.

"I will not fail. I will succeed. I will not be broken," she whispers to the stark white walls. The words comfort her, even if the memories in her head do the opposite. Sixteen slammed against the wall so hard blood dripped out his ears, nose and mouth. All for asking where his sparring partner went. Older students in previous years carted out of exam rooms in such broken states her mind still can't comprehend.

She clenches her fists and continues her mantra in her head. The faint smell of disinfectant comforts her and helps her drift off to sleep.

Sai rolls over and blinks her eyes open. The lemon scent is gone, and the bed is hard. Pain rips through her abdomen, and she curls into a ball.

"C'mon out, Sai. There's someone I want you to meet."

Shivers convulse her slim frame at the sound of her mother's voice beyond the door. All Sai can think of is the pain in her body and just how much she doesn't want to meet the other person outside.

"Sai-y."

Her mother's tones are velvet. It's the voice she uses whenever she wants something, which is most of the time.

Sai claws her way into an upright position, trying to ignore the throbbing in her temples. She opens her mouth to speak, but thinks better of it. Any sign of acquiescence and her mother will take it as an invitation into the room.

Instead, she pushes herself off the bed and stumbles to the door. Fumbling at the handle until it clicks, she opens it a fraction, only to have her mother push it in the rest of the way.

The woman's pupils are dilated, and her face shows the same Shined-out expression Sai's grown so used to. All of the wonder and love in that gaze are directed at whatever fantasy is playing out in her mother's brain. None of it at Sai.

"What?" Sai keeps her tone flat. Disdain is a waste of energy on a woman who won't notice it.

Her mother smiles, an empty, vapid expression. "You're old enough now."

"Old enough?" Sai fights the urge to double over as another throb of pain echoes through her.

"To earn your keep. To bring in money."

Sai backs up a step, suddenly wary. She's seen how her parents earn their keep. With the moans in the night and the strange visitors who leave at dawn. Very little money filters back to Sai. "Earn?"

She sees the shadow move in the corridor behind her mother and knows even before the person speaks that it's a man.

"Hey, Sai..." He's tall and built, but not clean. Not even as clean as Sai tries to keep herself. His eyes are as dilated as her mother's, and sweat slicks back the hair on his head. The smell of body odor is cloying, and Sai steps back, but not quick enough. His hand brushes her arm and revulsion almost makes her retch.

Despite the pounding in her head and the pain in her abdomen, she has one amazing moment of clarity. She looks down at where his skin touches her own and back to her mother.

"I will never be like you," Sai whispers, fighting the tears and the pain. Taking advantage of the momentary confusion and reactions slowed by Shine, she barrels through the adults, wrenching the door to the outside open.

"Sai!" Just before the door shuts behind her, Sai hears her mother let out a pent-up breath and giggle. "She's not ready yet. Will I do?"

Nothing else follows Sai as she runs around the concrete veranda to get to the stairs. If she can make it to the botanica, maybe she'll be safe. Maybe she can pretend her parents never existed. Maybe she can pretend she's worth the time they've never spent on her.

The grass is cool against her skin, and she clutches her nightshirt around her legs as the pain in her head and body increases. She scrunches her toes and smells the faint scent of the now broken grass stems. The ground shakes lightly beneath her, and Sai frowns, momentarily distracted from her nightmares of what will happen if she goes back to the apartment.

Nausea overwhelms her suddenly, and she clutches her stomach, screaming out in pain before she blacks out.

All she can smell when she comes to is the smoke. Not even the shattered glass embedded in her back registers as she looks up at what used to be the concrete block she lived in. She stares at the flames and the rubble, at the already withering plants around her, and knows with certainty she was somehow responsible.

Sai blinks at the sudden light and pushes the dream to the back of her mind. Today is not a day for distracting nightmares. Remembering her parents' apathy won't get her through the exam.

The dim morning light filters down through the slit in the wall that serves as her window. It's too small for her to even squeeze through, assuming she could reach it in the first place. Not that there's anywhere to escape to outside, anyway.

Dressed in training gear, she heads to the cafeteria. The tension in the air is thick and choking even before she reaches the line. She accepts the mash doled out to her and forces it down, trying not to think too hard about what makes it grey.

No one in the room makes eye contact, not even the friends who left training laughing with each other the day before. Everyone knows what the final exam means. There is no positive spin to put on it.

Her last bite of food threatens to stick in her throat, but she washes it down with water and heads to the examination rooms.

Trainers suffuse the hall and foyer outside, finding the students they're in charge of and metering out supplies. Ms. Genna catches Sai's attention and motions her over. "Student Fifty-Two, enrolled 2350 via GNW United Conglomerate 17?"

Sai nods and clenches her fists at her side, hating her full designation.

"That's the spirit." The sarcasm in Ms. Genna's voice makes Sai cringe inwardly. "Your cubicle will be ready after the first round of examinees enter their rooms. Stay in the waiting area until I call you."

The allocated room is small with a bench encircling a training mat. Everyone sits, eyes riveted to the GNW logo in the middle. If they're anything like Sai, they're imagining the worst possible encounter and figuring out a way through it.

From pieces of thought strong enough to break through the shielding of others in the room, she can tell they know it, too.

No one in this room wants to fail, but the chances of success aren't good. If you owe GNW a debt of gratitude, it's their privilege to keep only the strongest.

One by one, the room empties. By the time her number is called, she feels an odd sense of finality.

Her cubicle is small and dimly lit by a buzzing light. There's just enough room for her to change into the sleek black clothes piled neatly on the bench. She traces her fingers over the subtly strong material and the GNW logo embossed over the shoulders.

As she dresses, a sinking feeling forms in the pit of her stomach. This Sparring gear denotes physical fighting. Though quick and light on her feet, even one direct hit to her head wipes her out.

There is no time for doubt. She's been at their mercy since she was twelve.

Sai squares her shoulders and pushes the door open. She frowns at the tall and lanky man standing there. His dark hair partially obscures some of his face, but the piercing pale eyes catch the light and make her pause. Something about him is eerily familiar.

He motions her over. "Are you ready, Sai?"

She starts as he says her name but masks her shock quickly with a nod. No one in the facility uses her name. It's forbidden. Students are numbers. The familiarity of his voice nags at her, and she has to concentrate on his words.

"You will face single, double, and triple waves of attackers. They will be human, psionic and domino. You know what a domino is, yes?"

"Yes, sir."

He nods and continues. "Human combat requires physical prowess. The psionic waves require that you only use your mind. Against the dominos, you need to combine your combat knowledge of both. After all three waves, you'll face a combination of two or all for the final fight of your test." He waits for a moment, his eyes never leaving hers, and she can't help but wonder why someone so young is in a position to be giving her instructions.

"You will be observed through the whole process. Do not use the incorrect type of force against your opponents, or you will fail." He pauses. "And make sure to stay on your toes. A direct hit from anyone will end you."

Sai blinks at his retreating back. How did he know? She shakes her head to clear the nagging doubt. Three at a time will be the problem, not to mention combining her psionic and physical training. There were few classes on the theory behind it, and fewer still on practical usage.

The GNW doesn't want survivors.

She pushes the thought away as soon as it flashes across her mind. Given the price of her awakening, it's no wonder she's considered a danger. She clenches her fists, determined to make up for her past, to prove her parents wrong.

The door at the other side of the hall opens, distracting her from her thoughts. She stands straight and walks into the examination room. The door slams immediately behind her, and for a second, her body breaks out in a light sweat.

It's dimly lit, but she can make out some weapons scattered around. Sai feels her stomach twist at the realization that the weapons aren't only for her to use, but for her opponents as well. The mundane selection gives her hope. Knives, maces, hammers, and swords, but no distance weapons. Not her preference, but at least she doesn't have to resort to only her fists.

As a gate cranks open on the far side of the room, Sai shakes her head to clear her mind.

She readies herself for attack, hands guarding her face, knees slightly bent, ready to dodge. "I will not fail." The words help soothe her nerves.

Her robust opponent crouches low as he circles her. Darting in, she lands two quick punches to his solar plexus and jaw. While small in stature, she's light on her feet and fires off strong, focused blows. He's clumsier than expected and goes down easily.

She frowns as he's cleared from the room and her next opponent enters. The force of his mind is immediately obvious. Her shields slam up, and she hopes all her practice is enough. She's better than her peers, but against someone this strong, any of them would be dust. His first onslaught takes her by surprise and rattles her head, but she deflects his push back at him and the momentum catches him by surprise. He falls awkwardly onto one of the hammers scattered around the room. The crunch is sickening, and his body goes limp.

Her confusion at his ineptitude is stolen by the iridescent domino as it enters the room. It's bigger than she expected, having only seen them from a distance before. The frequency of colors passing through its system makes her blink as she tries to follow the movements. Her eyes adapt slowly, picking the domino out from its camouflage just in time to dodge the first punch.

Her own speed is barely enough to avoid the flurry of kicks and punches. Sai ducks in once with a lucky punch, barely avoiding the hybrid's left hook. Two more quick punches and she rolls to the corner, crouching in wait for the next onslaught, nursing her hand as a reminder to reinforce her punches with psionics in the next attack.

But it seems she only needs to score a hit on it three times before it backs off and the round is declared won. Her mind swims as the examiners announce she's passed the first round. The opponents were far too easy. Cold sweat drips down her spine. Something is wrong.

The second round of two opponents in each category stuns her, too. Almost as easy as the first victories, she finds herself starting to panic as the unconscious bodies are floated from the room.

When the third round is announced and her opponents revealed, Sai's stomach spasms. These men look brutal, covered in scars. Their forearms are the size of her waist, and they're already armed. This. This is the real test.

There's no understanding in their eyes, just the same gleam she remembers from her parents and the beggars that surrounded her childhood home. The sheer focus of a Shine addict craving their next fix.

Resolve set, she clenches her teeth and attacks first, taking the man on the left by complete surprise. Her kick lands squarely on his jaw, and he crashes to the floor. She grabs his mace, jabbing the butt into his skull before he can make another move. His head lolls to the side. One down. The other two back off, suddenly not quite so confident.

Wary now, they're tougher to fight. She avoids most of their attacks except one narrow miss that grazes her ribs. Heat sears her skin and blood trickles down her side. She sections off the pain and aims for their knees, caps the middle man with the mace in the left knee, and follows through with a sound kick to his other one, barely dodging the right guy in time.

Mr. Right murmurs under his breath, his eyes staring at something she cannot see. She leverages two quick punches directly to his face before jumping back out of his reach and into a crouch to sweep his legs. A second later, Mr. Right lies on the floor clutching his knees and gasping something about coconuts and palm trees. Sai backs away, disgusted, and tries to catch her breath.

She barely has time to take stock of her injuries before the wall opens to float the three humans out and deposit the psionics.

Far more difficult than the previous battle, this one is at least less physical. Suggestion has never been her strong suit, but hours of boredom spent in her room rebuilding her shields gives her an edge. The ability to keep the attacks from directly affecting her mind makes it easier to concentrate on her offense.

She resists the urge to use precious psionic energy to reinforce her physical skills in this stage. Punching them will disqualify her. The stipulation for her to use only psionics on her psionic opponents apparently doesn't extend to their own restrictions.

She forces one of them against the wall in a weak mimicry of Sixteen's fate. The second stumbles as he's about to attack, and she barely deflects it back on him in time. He slumps to the ground. Sai doesn't have time to check if he's breathing, but convinces herself he is.

As she pushes the last one back against the opposite wall, her legs buckle for a moment. Sai holds him still long enough to rest a hand on his forehead and send him to sleep. She stands panting over the three subdued psionics, reinforcing the walls blocking her pain. Her head starts to pound with the effort as they're removed and replaced with three dominos.

The adrium-psionic hybrids are far stronger than any human. Their energy supply never ends, and the way the light refracts off their alien skin makes seeing them difficult, even when they're not attempting to camouflage with their surroundings.

"I will succeed." She takes a brief moment to center herself and extends the shielding she uses for her mind underneath her skin. Her punches hit harder, even though she needs to draw on energy reserves to keep her speed up. Where it was difficult with one domino, it's near impossible with three.

It takes almost all of the energy she has left to keep two of them out of reach while she tries to score three hits on the third. Something brushes her shoulder briefly, and her left arm tingles. She pushes the irritation aside and focuses on hitting the dominos. They won't let her tag them.

Reinforcing her own attacks with psionic strength drains her. With one last desperate heave of power, she flings the first domino into the other two. The weight is heavier against her mind than she expected and the throw goes wild, catching the two remaining dominos at chin height and smashing their heads into the stone wall behind them, temporarily disorienting them. It appears to count.

Sai would laugh but doesn't have any spare energy. She needs to dredge up more stamina for her final round.

She closes her eyes for a moment to regenerate what she can.

The sound of the gate mechanism jolts her out of the mild trance. Three psionics and three dominos emerge. No humans.

Six at once. And none of them an easy out. Her mind is tapped, and she feels an odd sense of peace start to wash over her.

When the dark-haired psionic instigates his attack, she feels it in her gut at the same time she hears the strange hum she now associates with dominos. She closes her eyes to get her bearings and make her decision. Her last hope to survive this hell they pitted her against.

"I will not be broken."

She reaches for the glimmer of power inside her and lets instinct take control.

CHAPTER
Two

An incessant noise rips Sai out of her fitful sleep. Slowly, she flexes her left shoulder. A bit stiff and sore, but otherwise not that bad. Must have only been dislocated. As advanced as medicine has become, it still takes a week or three for broken bones to mend and medi-psi's are hard to come by.

She pushes herself up in bed, one that's exactly like her own, and looks around the stark, white room. Machines beep, and the tiny dots affixed to her body so they can monitor her vitals make her skin itch. Sai scowls at them and winces when her eye hurts. Her head pounds softly, and she ignores the pain in her ankle as she pulls her legs up to her chest and rests her chin on her knees.

The room doesn't smell like lemon, and she finds herself missing it. Overhead the tiny window flickers softly with the lights from outside. It's not been long since her test—about a day if her energy levels are any indication. She concentrates on breathing to calm the churning of her stomach. Her body will heal faster if she relaxes. She has no intentions of facing any more tests remotely handicapped.

"You won't be handicapped, you know."

Startled, Sai looks up, instantly regretting the pain that shoots through her body. The speaker is tall, with dark features, but something about him won't stay with her. As though her eyes just refuse to focus properly on him.

Sai scowls. "Why should I believe you?"

He chuckles and moves to sit down on a white chair next to Sai's bed. "Because I'll be overseeing the next level of your training."

His voice is so familiar she knows she should be able to place it but can't.

"You were the assessor, at my final test," she remembers, at least she thinks she does. Her mind isn't working like she's used to.

He nods, and his piercing eyes never leave her face. She shivers again, wondering if he's waiting for something.

Suddenly he stands and walks toward the bed. Sai shrinks back and gives herself a mental slap for being intimidated.

"I'm Bastian." He smiles. The expression seems forced. "Didn't mean to catch you off-guard."

Sai gapes at him, her mouth unable to listen to her demand that it close. The tugging in her stomach grows violent, and now the weird sensations around him make more sense. "Bastian? *The* Bastian?"

He sighs. "Yes, yes." He waves at her, as if trying to wipe the expression from her face.

"Wait." She sits up straighter, putting two and two together. "You're going to oversee the next round of *my* training?"

Bastian nods.

"Why?" Sai finds herself whispering, almost scared of the answer.

He shrugs and flips a hat she didn't notice before onto his head. "Because you remind me of me," is all he says before turning to her door. He pauses for a second, hand resting on the knob. "Rest well tonight. We'll begin tomorrow."

Sai nods as the door clicks closed behind him. She shakes herself, angry at the slight hero worship she couldn't manage to hide. The whispered stories about the young dean are dubious at best. Even the things that paint him in a bad light only serve to make her more curious. At one stage, she thought him a myth. Suddenly, her training no longer seems daunting and the next day can't come soon enough.

Sai isn't usually a heavy sleeper. The fuzziness in her head when she wakes the following morning leaves her disoriented.

"Eat up, miss."

Sai frowns and focuses on the nurse. "Could you tell me where I have to go after I finish?"

The nurse smiles gently. "We'll have someone down to guide you in about twenty minutes."

"I don't need a guide. Just tell me what building I'm headed to."

For a few moments, the nurse looks at her, eyebrows raised a little awkwardly before she takes a deep breath and pats Sai's arm gently. "Didn't anyone tell you, dear?"

At Sai's blank expression, the woman continues. "You were moved last night. From GNW United Conglomerate 17 to UC Central. You won't know your way around here."

"I'm in the capital city already?" Sai asks.

The nurse laughs. "Mr. Bastian isn't in the habit of sticking around in other cities. His headquarters are here." The woman leaves the room after pointing at a set of clothing left on the side table.

Sai dresses slowly. A low hum seeps into the room, steady in its rhythm. Though she knew she would be moved, she hadn't realized it had already happened. How much did they sedate her? How bad had her wounds been? Why had Bastian not mentioned it the day before?

Because it's irrelevant to the situation, you idiot. You're lucky to be alive.

She breathes deep and focuses her thoughts again, seeking the fleeting calm that keeps abandoning her, and is surprised to hear the familiar soothing sounds of the GNW mantra echo through the room in a whisper.

For your own safety, please do not leave your designated areas. Report any unauthorized personnel immediately. Remember, the future of the GNW depends on you.

The knock at the door interrupts her concentration, and she sighs as she calls out: "Come in. It's open."

Sai isn't sure who she expected to accompany her to her first training session, but it definitely isn't the domino standing in front of her.

She scowls, squinting at the hybrid. "What're you doing here?"

"Domino 12 reporting to collect you."

His gold eyes gleam, the color uniform where the pupil should separate from the iris, and somehow the sclera is so white it's almost silver. She wonders if she looked close enough, she'd be able to see gears twirling in his head, even though she knows he's not a machine. The ability to combine the parasitic metal adrium with psionic DNA has always fascinated her.

Though his hair is a constant auburn, his body keeps changing hues. Everything about him shifts, constantly. Iridescent is the only way she can think of to describe him and even that is inaccurate. His clothing melds in and out with the room making it disconcerting to look at him. The only thing solid about him are his eyes and the faintly etched twelve on his left shoulder. Not one of the dominos from her test.

For a moment he seems to smile at her, and she chides herself for stupid illusions. He's a domino; they don't have emotions.

"Ready," she says in a stiff voice.

He motions ahead and falls into step with her. "After you're finished training for the day, I will escort you to your new quarters." He pauses, as if searching for how to express what he wants to say. Sai tries to stop herself from finding him so fascinating. "They are larger than in other cities."

She marks every twist and turn in the corridors, every nook and cranny she passes, the air ducts, and any exits or hidden doors she can spot. Surviving people who like to pick on someone they perceive as weaker can lead to a whole array of skills.

Seven floors up and a significant amount of floor space over, Domino 12 stops her at double steel doors and knocks two times. The doors swing inward silently and open into a large room with a desk on the far side. The desk itself is situated with its back to three huge windows overlooking the entire city.

Sai can see the tops of the apartment blocks as they stretch out beneath them in the circular style of the city, links of radiating lines that meet at the Central building like a jagged spider web.

The squalor of the outlying blocks isn't visible from here, like refuse shunted to the fringe. The gleam of the city's dome flickers softly in and out of hiding as GNW's plethora of advertisements wink in and out of play.

Bastian stands behind the desk, watching the view. His attire resembles the dominos from her exam—all black. She finds herself inching toward the desk, regardless of how harmless Twelve appeared on the walk up to the office.

"You can go now," Bastian commands without turning away from the window.

The domino nods and turns, leaving Sai and Bastian alone in the room.

For a few seconds Bastian stays where he is, and then he turns around and the subtle flickering lights that illuminate his office wash a strange blue wave over his face. He points to one of the chairs near Sai. "Sit."

She does. He's colder than she remembers. Distant. Perhaps learning under someone like him isn't going to be exactly what she thought.

Bastian paces a few steps, sits on the corner of the desk closest to her, and puts his chin on his hand. "Do you remember me?"

"You gave me my final test." Even as the words come out of her mouth, Sai's certain that's not the answer he wants to hear.

He sighs. "Before that? No recollection at all?"

"Your voice?" she asks softly.

He smiles, so briefly Sai almost thinks it's an illusion.

"You were in shock." His words are crisp and clear as he stands up and turns to sit in his chair. He steeples his fingers and peers at her over his hands. "When you came into your power, I found you. Tracking is one of my lesser skills. Finding other psionics, especially when their powers haven't awoken, is almost impossible. It's good to see you've come this far."

So many unanswered questions pop into Sai's head. She stares at him, not quite comprehending that he found her, followed by the bitter afterthought that perhaps he should not have.

"Don't think like that." His reprimand is quiet, direct, and cuts right through her self-pity. "I was like you once, except I was born into a family who understood. Use what you have with honor and goodness and you'll redeem any guilt you believe you should have."

Sai blinks at him. The words burn into her brain. She clears the frog from her throat before speaking. "What sort of training am I here for?"

This time Bastian smiles at her. There's vindication in the expression. "We're going to hone a few memory-sifting techniques."

Nearing the end of her first training session with Bastian, Sai decides her final exam was easy. Memory-sifting pulls so much energy, it makes her whole body ache. She hurts in places she didn't know existed and her head pounds. As she comes to understand what Bastian meant by honing techniques, she realizes having him as her mentor will be grueling.

Bastian waves a hand at her, "Again."

Barely able to resist muttering under her breath, Sai focuses all her attention back into the bowl of clouded substance, pushing her will into one tiny dart to try and draw the intricate patterns Bastian demonstrated to her twice. Her head spins, her vision blurs, and she has to grab onto the side of the chair closest to her.

"Control," he says, and she can't spare the concentration to glare at him.

She can feel his breath as he moves closer, so hyper-aware is she of her surroundings. When he speaks, the sound is magnified, like it echoes off the inside of her head. "If you're deep inside someone's mind, you have to be delicate."

Her concentration snaps, and the gel-like water explodes up, splashing her face. Sai collapses into an undignified heap on the ground, shakes her head, and tries hard not to glare at Bastian out of the corner of her eye.

"I can see that, you know," he mutters as he flips through some of the readers on his desk. "Get rid of that habit now. Appear impartial. Give nothing away, not even annoyance.

Everything you demonstrate to someone else can be exploited, and I have no use for weak things."

She bristles at being called a *thing*. "You're not a very personable teacher."

Bastian doesn't acknowledge her comment, but continues to scroll through his reader. Sai scowls and wipes sweat off her brow, wishing she had her training clothes to change into. There's a knock at the door, with the same sharpness the domino delivered earlier.

"Three minutes," Bastian calls out softly without looking up from his desk. After a few moments and clicks on a different file reader, he hands it to her. "Study everything on this. Learn it, practice the exercises, and I will see you next week."

"Next week?" Sai doesn't quite understand. If he's her trainer, shouldn't he be spending more time training her?

"I'm not technically your trainer, Sai. No one here can teach you more than you already know, but I can guide you. Your abilities are unique. You're my responsibility by default." He dismisses her with a wave of his hand. "Your training is up to you now. Your strength and determination are your own."

With those enigmatic words and uncanny ability to read through her shields, he swivels his chair around and ignores her. Sai pushes down on the rising panic, knowing he'll hear her. But the old fears nag in the back of her mind. Maybe her parents ignored her for a reason.

Domino 12 pushes the door open as she's dismissed and motions her into the corridor. This time she's more curious about her new home. High concrete walls and marble-tiled floors stretch down every corridor. Even when they rebuilt Middle

America after the Disaster Era, even before it became the GNW United Conglomerate, marble was expensive. Now? It's priceless.

Does being brought to train at Central mean she's worth something to GNW? Maybe it was Bastian's plan all along, from the moment he took her out of the rubble? Is this where she'll prove her parents wrong? She twists her hair so violently she gasps in pain and feels Twelve's eyes rest on her for a moment.

Sai glances at Twelve with unabashed curiosity while she rubs her sore arms. "Do you know anything about subconscious mind-sifting techniques?" she asks impulsively.

His golden eyes narrow for a split second, something she would have missed had she not been watching intently. "Theoretically? Yes."

"I never knew these techniques existed until today."

"Then it is not just theoretical?" Twelve's voice is soft, almost thoughtful. Sai looks at him, surprised at the change in tone. She's never heard inflection in a domino's voice before.

She sighs ruefully and rubs at her muscles again. "Technically. Though it's going to take me a while to get the hang of it."

"You should not rub. Not yet. Soak them first. Reach a relaxed state so you can better work on them."

Sai isn't sure she understands, so she stares at him.

"Soak them. You can't afford to be sore tomorrow." Twelve takes the turn without glancing at the numbering system indicated overhead.

"Tomorrow?"

"I will begin supervision of your psionic and physical combination training. There were horrible inadequacies in your last test. You're lucky you survived at all." He stops abruptly and pushes a well concealed panel, which swings open to reveal a decently sized room.

It distracts Sai from her indignation at the domino's comment. There are two beds, one on either side of the room, with desks and bedside tables next to them. Between them, there's a bookshelf with real books. Sai doesn't think she's ever picked up an actual book.

She walks over and touches the bindings, having only ever read them in digital form before. The paper pages are so soft and feel worn with age. She hugs one to her chest as she turns to take in the rest of her new quarters.

There isn't much color in the room, just enough to differentiate the two beds. One is a grey-lilac and the other a blue-gray. She frowns, not sure which one to pick, and settles herself on the blue one, placing the precious book softly to the side.

The domino waits patiently at the door. "Your belongings have been placed inside the wardrobe. Do you need time to change clothes?"

Sai glances at him, then outside at the light beyond the window, and realizes it's not nearly as late as her exhausted body tells her it is. She double-takes and looks at the window again. It's not a slit up so high it serves no purpose, but a true window. Clear enough to see out if she pulls the cloth aside, even if the view is another concrete wall.

"Just give me a minute."

She opens the wardrobe and pulls out a pair of sweats that match the blue-grey of her bedspread. Apparently she chose her bed correctly, and for a moment she wonders who the other occupant will be. It's a shame; she likes her privacy.

Sai shuts the door tightly behind her, amused that Twelve's back is to her. "I'm ready. Sorry for the delay."

The domino shrugs, an eerily human gesture, not one she expected from him.

"I'm not needed elsewhere for now. It is no imposition."

For some reason she can't help but hear an implied "yet" in his words.

"I will greet you at 0700 tomorrow with a schedule. You will need to be awake by sunrise in order to take advantage of a decent breakfast before I come to pick you up. For now, I am responsible for you."

Sai has to hurry after him in order to keep up and thanks her foresight to keep the twists and turns clear in her head. Each corridor mirrors the next. It would be far too easy to get lost in the maze of concrete and marble.

"This is the cafeteria," he states as the hall opens into a large room. "If you are hungry, we can stay. We are not yet late."

There are only a few people milling around in there; most seem to be passing through. Many identical tables and chairs populate the main part of the room, which sits in front of a large open kitchen. Dispensers line the huge bench between those working and those visiting the cafeteria. So many different varieties of food and none of it, at first glance, appears to be mash. Sai barely stops herself from gaping with surprise.

She looks around the room, trying to catch the familiar smell and where it's coming from when she realizes it's the same as in her old training facility. The light smell of lemon disinfectant. While the cafeteria is much bigger and better equipped, the scent comforts her with familiarity. Sai blinks, suddenly aware the domino is waiting for her answer.

"Not really hungry at all." Although she hasn't eaten since she left the hospital wing that morning, Sai has no appetite. In fact, her stomach is in knots. She keeps them at bay by telling herself advanced training is one step closer to redeeming herself.

"Sai?" Twelve bends down to peer at her face.

His iridescent countenance is almost blinding up close, and Sai reflexively shades her eyes.

He straightens up. "Sorry. I forget myself sometimes." There's a brief hum in Sai's ears, and a moment later, Twelve solidifies. His hair is a deep, auburn red and his eyes remain gold, while his definitively male body appears clad in some sort of leather armor she's certain is adrium conforming to his will.

"Thank you," she mumbles.

"We need to attend your orientation. A few of your year-mates made it to this city. They'll take academic classes with you, but they're not training under Bastian."

Sai grimaces. "They're not my favorite people."

"Regardless, they'll be there, along with Bastian, Zacharai, and Markus."

"Those are important people."

The domino stops for a moment and looks at her, as if he's trying to read her mind.

"What?" Sai asks, trying not to let her insecurity at being scrutinized show on her face.

"You spent the morning training under Bastian, yet you seem surprised by the importance he holds."

She shrugs and looks down at the ground for a moment. "I was in awe of him. Now I'm just in pain because of him. Takes your respect down a notch."

The domino moves on. "Interesting."

They come to another huge room, lined with seats and headed by a lectern. Twelve pushes her toward the side of the room and motions for her to take a seat somewhere. "Others will join you soon. I have duties."

Sai takes a seat, pushes back her exhaustion, and waits, hoping to get some of her questions answered.

About forty minutes later, Sai sits in the same row as three of her classmates from pre-testing. She tries to distract herself by looking at the few others gathered, all around their age, but whom she doesn't know. It's hard to look at her year-mates, and even more difficult to sit with people who know she's from UC 17 and are aware of what she's capable of. Every time she's around them, she feels her humanity slip away. What makes her better than the murderers sent to prison or exterminated? Not a damn thing. Just that some nice schmuck picked her up off the streets and took pity on her.

I said: Stop. That.

Sai looks up, startled, and notices Bastian at the end of the podium talking to two other men. His back is to her, but she knows the voice in her head is his.

City Planner Zacharai isn't as tall as Bastian; in fact, he's a few inches shorter. His dirty blond hair makes the man look like the slimy Shine dealers Sai remembers seeing in the foyer to her building before she blew it up.

The Chief of Law Enforcement, Markus, is the other man. He's slightly taller than Zach, and the wrinkles cushioning his smile make her feel at ease. His dark brown hair is speckled with white and that familiar feeling is there, but again, she can't quite place it.

A woman Sai doesn't know welcomes them and talks about the central facility, giving directions on how to get to where. Sai notes that her former classmates write everything down. Apparently no one gave them a domino to hold their hands through orientation. About to snicker, she stops herself and schools her face into indifference.

Zacharai commands attention when he gets up to the lectern. Maybe it's the cocky smile on his shady face. "We've gathered you here today because you're the only ones in your year to pass the final test well enough to train here at Central. Believe it or not, that's a good outcome. Some years we get none."

The others—including Fourteen, Twenty-Nine, and Thirty-Six, if Sai remembers their numbers correctly—laugh nervously. Sai doesn't.

Zacharai barely glances at them before continuing. "You're each entering different specializations. There is one thing you'll all have in common regardless of what you aspire to be. Paperwork." He holds up a hand as if asking the protest to quiet down, and Sai has to force herself not to laugh at the melodrama.

"Every single action you take, every single mission you're given, regardless of what kind, will require paperwork. You'll need permission forms, supervisory details, requisition forms, and supply lists—all filled out in full and transmitted to your supervisor. And you'll still be required to attend a prescribed amount of schooling per day. Together."

He glances at them all. His muddy-blue eyes rest on her for a brief moment longer than the others. A shiver runs down Sai's back.

"Your department dictates with whom you can talk about your work. Don't speak to anyone outside your department about what goes on there. If you do, there *will* be punishment." He waits, letting the statement sink in. It's no longer difficult for Sai to keep a straight face. "Advanced history, politics, and theory will be part of your lesson package. Keep in mind, we expect a lot from you. We found you, educated you, and gave you a home. You leave the facility only when directed to do so. Your indentured time with us is a way to repay our trust in you."

Sai isn't sure why, but she feels the weight of his gaze on her again and blinks back the fatigue of the last few days, forcing herself not to waver under his scrutiny.

He continues after the weighted pause. "I detest being let down. Don't do it. I'll leave you in Bastian's capable hands."

Zach's retreating footsteps are the only sounds left. Sai shifts uncomfortably in her seat, suddenly feeling claustrophobic in the large auditorium.

Unlike Zach, Bastian holds no reader in his hands. He stands to attention and speaks with an authoritative tone. "This is *my* school. Do what you're told, and you'll probably never see me. Disobey *any* of my rules, and there will be consequences. Learn the rules, and don't forget them. Any transgressions are enforced by me." Bastian waits for a moment, and Sai watches as her classmates pale at his words.

He sounds cheerful when he continues. "Take the worst out of the stories you've heard about me and believe it. If you're really feeling cocky? Go for it. But I'm not known for my patience." Bastian looks at each of them in turn. "I don't like being annoyed. Remember that. Ms. Janni will take you to your first afternoon class. Enjoy your learning experience."

Markus steps up to the lectern with an apprehensive look at the device as he speaks into the microphone. "Sai, please come here a moment."

She gulps, aware of her classmates' eyes on her, and walks up to the podium. "Sir?"

He looks her over. "You turned out well. Much better than that beat-up and vacant-eyed child we picked up a few years ago. Heard you made an impression in your final?"

"Yes, sir." Sai bites the inside of her cheek to keep from scowling at her lack of memory of the last fight.

"You're in the enforcement department. I look forward to working with you if the situation arises."

"Yes, sir," Sai answers quietly. Inside she rejoices at finally knowing what it is she's here to do.

Markus smiles and his dark eyes glitter with the expression. "Better run along to that class now, lass. Don't want to be late for the first one."

Sai dashes off down the path and out of the room, almost colliding with the tail end of her classmates.

"Hey, Sai." Twenty-Nine has a haunted look in her eyes, and Sai finds herself not wanting to know how it got there.

"Hi, Twenty-Nine," is all she says as she falls into step with the other girl.

Twenty-Nine flushes. "It's Nimue." She smiles tentatively, lighting up her pale, freckled face for a moment.

"Sai—but I guess everyone heard that already." Sai smiles back but keeps her distance. Just because they've moved cities doesn't mean anything has changed. Nimue, it seems, has other ideas.

"Sai, this is Kabe." Nimue gestures to Fourteen on her right, which only leaves Thirty-Six on the left. "And this is Deacon."

"Nice to...meet you," Sai concludes lamely. She's met them before, sparred with them before, but never really spoken to them. An awkward silence falls over the group as they walk down the halls.

"What did you think of orientation?" Nimue ventures tentatively, a small smile on her face.

Sai shrugs, not sure how to answer, but Kabe pipes up. "Zach's my mentor. Isn't Bastian yours, Sai?"

"Yes." She doesn't think admitting that will be a breach of her department.

"Really?" Deacon speaks for the first time. "What's he like?"

"I'm not sure yet."

"Didn't a domino accompany you to the briefing?" Nimue's eyes light up. "What're they really like?"

Sai takes a deep breath to sort through all the questions, trying not to let the tension in her shoulders bother her. "They're different than I expected. Very different." They wouldn't believe her if she told them he seemed human sometimes.

When they arrive at their classroom and file in, Sai sits down and shivers as the GNW mantra seeps into her mind on the hour, every hour, like clockwork.

For your own safety, please do not leave your designated areas. Report any unauthorized personnel immediately. Remember, the future of the GNW depends on you.

Like anyone could forget.

CHAPTER
Three

Training with the domino is nothing like the training at her old facility. Sai barely avoids another direct hit and bounces away lightly, trying to keep all of his movements in check.

He moves differently. Fluidly. Even after several sessions, it's all she can do to keep up with his approach. And he's right. If she'd had this type of training before her final exam, maybe she'd remember how it ended.

Domino 12 makes no sound when he moves, as if his body is part of the surroundings. Though he's forsaken the chameleon capabilities and is easier for her to see coming, his body still seems to blend in and out occasionally, disorienting her.

She doesn't see the punch. One moment she's in ready mode, light on the balls of her feet, and the next, she's hunched up on the ground, next to the wall.

Her jaw clicks as she moves her mouth, and everything around her shifts in slow motion. Even her body reacts sluggishly and unlike her own. She blinks, trying to regain her bearings, and starts as the domino crouches down in front of her, a definite frown on his flawless face.

"What happened, Sai?" He cocks his head to one side and glances at his fist. "I pulled the power. I didn't try to hit you any harder than every other sparring session we have had. Are you okay?"

Her first instinct is to shake her head, but with the room still spinning, she thinks better of it. She shrugs instead. "I can't take a hit. Never been able to."

"I see." And for a moment those flickering gold eyes grow distant and he lowers himself smoothly to sit on the ground with her. "This is why you fight so defensively."

"Yeah." Maybe if she holds her head still long enough, it'll all come back together.

"But I've seen you take hits before." Now he sounds confused.

For a few moments Sai looks at him, trying to gather the stray thoughts to answer properly. "You've seen me take glancing blows. I can do those. Absorb some of the impact and deflect the rest, reinforced by psionics. But a direct hit? I'm a goner every time."

The domino watches her for a moment. "We will need to work on that then."

"On taking a hit? Not going to happen. Unless they're smaller and less powerful than me, I guess."

But he shakes his head. "No, on other ways to avoid getting hit." He stands in one fluid motion and reaches out a hand to her.

Sai takes it and rises slowly, her balance still slightly off. "You're odd, Dom." She stops short. The heat rises in her cheeks and she wonders if he noticed.

"I am odd?" He looks sideways at her. "How so?"

"Just... You're not like I imagined a domino would be."

For a moment he's silent, and she realizes the soft, almost lilting hum that accompanies adrium psionics is ever-present now. Then he speaks again, softly. "How did you think we would be?"

"I..." Sai pauses for a moment, juggling the right phrasing in her mind. "I never thought of dominos as individuals...but you're very much yourself."

He chuckles, or at least, she thinks it's a chuckle. The sound echoes faintly. "I believe this is a good thing."

"Yeah." Having reached the middle of the room, she readies her stance again.

"Why did you call me Dom?"

Sai blinks. She's been calling him Dom in her mind for several days now. "I don't like numbers. We had them at the training facility. No names. No identifiers. Just numbers. You feel like much more than a number to me."

This time he smiles. "Thank you."

Her head clears slowly after a hit, but even so, she can see the slight modifications Dom is making to her stance to help her avoid getting hit. It's engrossing and she doesn't realize time passes so quickly until the timer on the subcutaneous wristband beeps.

"Dammit. I have to go, Dom."

He relaxes his stance. "Hurry up. He's not patient today."

Sai has fifteen minutes to make it from the defensive training room over to Bastian's private offices. It normally takes just short of that, and today is laundry day. There'll be piled up washing carts hovering everywhere. She glares at the slightly itchy spot on her wrist, as if it's the band's fault she didn't have the foresight to schedule herself five minutes ahead of time.

Used to her routine after a few weeks now, she's realized one thing: It's hard enough to train with Bastian on a good day, but on one of his bad days, which in her experience seem to far outweigh the good, it's even less fun. Maybe his bad days are his normal days?

"Department of Enforcement, my ass," she mutters as she dodges through a series of four laundry carts lined along the hallway leading to Bastian's office. It's not the first time she's wondered why on earth, with all their technology, they haven't figured out a better way to take care of laundry.

She glances at her wrist as she raises her fist to knock. Two minutes early. Perfect.

"Come in."

Of course he knows she's there. He always knows.

"I'm not god," he says as the door closes silently behind her, humor obviously sour.

"That's definitely bloody true," she snaps at him. "There's nothing benevolent about you."

She clasps her hands in front of her mouth, unable to believe she let that slip out. "I'm sorry, Bastian!" she gasps and bows her head.

His footsteps draw closer, and he raises her head with a finger. She's never seen him so close before. Blue—he has startlingly blue eyes. Just for a moment they're there, and then he steps away. "You're irritable today."

Sai waits for him to finish.

"Talk to me. You're not going to train well if you're this worked up. You've been doing so well with outer control lately, I started to think you wouldn't slip again. What is it?"

"I don't get the point," she says slowly, trying to find the right words.

"And?" The letter opener in his other hand resembles a dagger a little too much.

"I..." *Here goes.* "I'm learning how to do things with and without my psionic abilities, but I can't seem to get the hang of this controlled and detailed sifting. What's the point of training me in what I can't do?"

His expression is calm, as always. He sighs. "You really are difficult. Do you know that? Most people simply do as they're told. They like being a part of the bigger picture, of something larger than themselves. Why do you rebel?"

"It's not rebelling, it's needing to understand...sir," she adds the last word belatedly.

"A need to understand?" He twirls the letter opener through his fingers. "There's a lot you still won't be able to understand, Sai. But give it a few months and I think everything will become clear. For now, can I ask you to trust me?"

Sai pales and takes a step back. She's made it all the way here without trusting anyone. Bastian might have pulled her from the rubble, but that doesn't mean he doesn't have his own agenda.

"Will. You. Stop. That." His irritation is palpable. "Who the hell taught you to shield? You're inept. You scream your frustrations to anyone with enough talent to know how to listen and half of those who don't." He grabs her hands and holds them to her head with his own. "Watch how I do this. Close your eyes and follow what I do."

He guides her through every step, every building block, and demonstrates ways Sai never realized she could shield. Everything she's known up until now seems rudimentary and insufficient. He deftly weaves the blocks together, putting force and cohesion behind them until a much more secure wall surrounds the private parts of her mind. She notes the subtle reinforcement he uses and the repetitious way he shows her until she understands and works with him.

"There," he says, leaving cold air to rush in where his hands no longer contact hers. "Now, when you scream, only you should hear."

"But you can still find them, right?" She opens her eyes and knows the answer even before the incline of his head and wonders where the letter opener disappeared to.

"Shall we?"

Sai nods and steps away from the desk a little lightheaded. All these new, refined techniques drain her energy much faster.

Mind-sifting technique control is like playing with mirrors in a fun house, only without the mirrors or the fun. The gel-like liquid, apparently meant to replicate how sifting through actual memories feels, is gloppy and difficult to control. If not careful, it only shows what the reader wishes to see instead of what is actually there. And if really not careful, it just splashes goo everywhere when the control snaps.

But, if she tries really, really hard at controlling the sift, she should be able to...

"Oh. Wow." Bastian's voice is breathless. Sai cracks an eye open to see an intricate web of beautiful designs, even prettier than the ones Bastian had demonstrated, suspended within the liquid.

"You did it!" He's beaming. "I wasn't sure anyone else would be able to."

"Wait—you didn't know I could do that?"

He shrugs and makes notes on a little reader in his palm. "How could I? I'm not you. No matter what some people think, I can't just jump in and take your body for a test drive. You're a Rare. You have to be able to do some of the things I can, right?"

Sai glares and projects a thought toward him.

"Stop being childish, Sai," he says without looking up. "You outgrew that when you killed and maimed over a thousand people."

"Screw you, Bastian." She pushes herself away from the desk, fists clenched, chin raised. "I'm fully aware I should be dead. Maybe next time something in me awakens, I'll do the job properly and take myself with it instead of being rescued by some pity party to have it held over my head for my entire life."

He walks over to her and reaches out to grasp her shoulders, pulling her closer. "That's the fire you need, Sai. Hold onto who you are no matter what anyone tells you. It's the only real thing we all have. Let your pride make you stronger." He releases her abruptly. "How's your stomach?"

She blinks. "I'm fine."

"Not now! Do you have a strong stomach? Do you throw up easily?"

"No?"

"Good. Come here tomorrow after dinner. I think you're ready for displacement."

"Let me guess—you're not going to explain it to me until I get here tomorrow, are you?"

"Maybe." Bastian grins for a split second. "You never know with me, do you?"

Her body threatens to collapse, and her muscles ache. If she doesn't get back to her room soon, into that wonderfully small tub to soak out the aches, Dom will never forgive her in the morning.

"I'm going to bed, Bastian. Stop guinea pigging me. Give me something solid so I don't worry I'll blow us all up."

"Maybe."

She heads toward the door, limping slightly, focusing on her progression. Sai fails to hear Bastian and is startled by his sudden appearance beside her.

"What would you do if razor-tooth rabbits escaped?"

Sai blinks at him again. "Those weird experiments gone wrong? The fanged little menaces?"

He nods.

"I'd kill them, I guess?" She's still trying to understand what he's saying.

"Why?"

She looks at him, her eyes trying valiantly to close. Unless the rabbits stop biting long enough for her to use one as a pillow, Sai really doesn't care. "Because everything I've ever heard about razor rabbits involves them being dangerous and vicious, a pest that needs to be put down."

Bastian raises an eyebrow. "So not because you knew the information yourself, but because someone told you the information was true?"

"Well, yeah. Why would anyone lie about something like that?" Sai has no idea if her answer is even close to right.

He holds her gaze until she begins to squirm. "Good. Maybe it's starting to sink in."

Sai glares at the yellow glob on her white ceramic plate, impersonating the scrambled eggs she thought she was getting. The glob stares back at her, probably smiling. She sighs and clamps down on a fork full of the substance, chewing with renewed animosity.

"It's still better than what we used to eat." Nimue slides into the seat next to her.

"True." The girl has a point. Sai plays with the rest of her food and glances at her classmate, resisting the urge to move away. She's dangerously close to invading Sai's personal space. The clock over the serving line lets her know there's still twenty minutes until seven. She sighs. "Today is going to be a long day."

Nimue glances at her. "Oh?"

"Things to study, beatings to dodge. The usual." Sai dismisses the inquiry in her usual fashion. She's not one to open small talk with many people. No one has ever proven they can be fully trusted, which is why Bastian's question still nags at the back of her mind.

"Sai?"

She looks up from her mangled breakfast and pushes it away in disgust before responding. "What?"

Nimue blushes and tucks a strand of dark brown hair behind her ear. "I'm glad you got out. There were rumors about your test. I'm just glad you made it."

Sai studies the girl's face, seeking any sign of insincerity before answering. Being stuck in the facilities means everyone has at least something in common: an awakened psionic ability. Most psionic users can tell if you're lying. As far as she can tell, Nimue isn't, but then, maybe that's her specialty.

"Thanks. I'll see you in class." She pauses, not sure what prompts her to, then takes a deep breath and gets it over with: "I'm here around this time every morning, if you're bored."

It's not a question because Sai doesn't have time for an answer she's not even sure she wants, but as she turns to leave the hall, Nimue's smile is oddly satisfying.

The satisfaction carries her all the way back to her room where she retrieves her reader, unlocking it by simply picking it up in her banded hand, before hurrying to Ms. Janni's class. As usual, she's the first to arrive and flips through the information she summarized the previous evening with a frown.

There's so much glossed over in the junior division. Maybe they save this part of the past for when children are mature enough to handle it. Glancing over her notes, Sai notices the time on her reader and frowns. Janni is late.

Mildly annoyed, Sai gathers her things and turns to leave the classroom when Nimue's head pops around the door frame. "Sai!"

Sai blinks and looks to the left of the classroom door where Nimue and Kabe lean against it. Deacon isn't anywhere in sight.

"Yes?"

Kabe grins. "We have the morning off. Janni has meetings or something"

Sai shrugs and follows them out into the nearly empty hall. "I was going to get a head start on some of the homework." She glances mournfully at the reader hugged against her chest. "I need all the head start I can get."

Nimue laughs, but it's missing some of the edge of old. "You were never bad, Sai."

"Maybe not, but it takes me a lot of effort to accomplish what everyone else seems to manage easily. My parents never sent me to school before I attended the facility." The words come out bitter, even to her own ears.

Nimue's smile fades, and she pats Sai's shoulder awkwardly. "Sorry. I never knew."

"I never told anyone."

"You can pick my brain any time." Kabe grins and falls into step with them. "What do you want to know?"

She glances at him, fighting back the feeling that there's some hidden motive, and sighs. "I just don't get the whole GNW as a government thing."

"Easy." He seems pleased with himself and clears his throat. "The government couldn't handle their prisons, and so the private sector took over. They couldn't handle the medical experimentation that flooded the hospitals, and so the private sector took that over, too. And when the government could no longer handle the situation between the Damascus and the uprising and virtually abandoned the people, the private sector had to step in again for the good of everyone."

Sai nods, twisting a strand of hair with her free hand. "Yeah, I get that...but why didn't people fight it?"

"Without GNW, the Psionic Wars could have gone on indefinitely. Without them, society as we know it might not even exist today," Nimue says with a smile and a nudge of Sai's arm.

"Yeah." Sai fights off the shiver climbing up her spine. The hallways are cold.

Nimue grins. "You can pick my brain, too! Though I'm usually only good with math."

Sai smiles back. "I like math. It's mostly logical. Mostly."

The other two laugh, and for once, Sai wonders if everything has to have an ulterior motive.

Her last discussion with Bastian weighs heavily on Sai's mind. Displacement doesn't sound nice.

Not only were her classes cancelled, but her session with Dom was called off at the last minute and he won't be back for a few days, which leaves her with a large gap in her afternoons. Maybe she'll be able to convince Bastian to take the time slots.

The steel door is already open when she arrives. Glancing at her wrist, she realizes she's too early. There are other voices, ones she doesn't recognize, coming from within the room. Sai has never really considered herself a snoop, but an open door, with voices speaking inside...

Don't even think it, Sai.

She almost scowls from behind the wall at him, but realizes at the last second he'll probably see it and admonish her again. So, instead, she lets herself slide to the floor and begins to work on her shields. She starts slowly, building them up and deconstructing them exactly the way Bastian showed her. Every time she rebuilds, she weaves a bit more of herself into them, more of her will and determination, in order to cement the underlying willpower that is their foundation. She makes them tighter and more impenetrable, far better than they ever were during her time in the junior division. She begins to treat it as a game: knocking them down as fast as she can and building them up faster, tighter, and more stable.

As she repeats the exercise, it draws her in, taunts her to build better shields, to pull on more power. To see if, and when, she might reach her limit. There's a strange tug in her gut she's only ever felt once before, during her exam just before she blacked out. But this time, it feels good.

Something touches her shoulder, and she flinches, pulling herself back while pushing forward with a burst of energy—all in the blink of an eye. The feeling in her gut vanishes abruptly and her vision clears as she shakes her head. She sees Bastian still leaning over, surprise on his face for an instant before he masks it.

"You didn't answer when I told you to come in." He dusts invisible specks off his clean black coat. "You shouldn't let yourself feel so comfortable in unsecured territory. Anyone can walk down this hall." He motions her into the room and closes the double door behind them.

Sai feels her cheeks flushing. She's never lost awareness so acutely before.

"Though..." He pauses as he reaches his desk. "I do commend you for working on your shields. They're coming along."

"I had nothing else to do." The comment sounds lame even in her own head.

"Are you ready?"

She laughs nervously. "Would it make a difference if I said no?"

He shakes his head and pulls an old metal cage out from underneath his desk. In it is a strange brown rabbit. Or, as Sai looks closer, a razor-tooth rabbit. Its odd red eyes stare at Bastian intently. She blinks, the conversation from the previous day still making no sense in her head.

"Razer-Rab, if you want their cute and cuddly name. Accidental fusion in one of the testing laboratories just before the Psionic Wars. Someone thought it would be a good idea to keep a few of them on hand for testing purposes. I'd commend them, but I think I read somewhere they ate them in a lab blackout."

He pulls an old-fashioned needle out of his drawer with a tiny bottle of serum and begins to siphon it. "I do believe the latter incident is what caused the labs to revert back to some manual locking mechanisms. Can't trust computer-driven ones when blackouts are abundant, can you?" Without even looking at it, he reaches in and grabs the rabbit by the scruff of the neck, ignores the sharp fangs aiming for the artery in his wrist, and stabs it with the syringe, injecting the rabid animal.

After about twenty seconds, it stops snapping its jaw and lies there, perfectly still.

"What are we doing?" Sai takes a step toward the desk, curious despite herself.

"You are going to displace his heart."

Displace. Force out. Sai looks at him in disbelief. "Say what?"

"I know you've studied basic human anatomy, as well as that of multiple lower life forms. You are going to attempt to make his heart cease. To force it out of rhythm. To end its life using psionics."

"You want me to kill the rabid bunny?" Sai asks, a little clearer on why he asked her about killing them the previous day, but only a little.

"I *could* ask you to experiment on humans, but that might get us both in trouble." Bastian's eyes lock on her own as he waits for her answer.

"I've never heard of it."

"Because it's not general practice, nor is it a common ability. Actually, so far, I'm only aware of one who can do it."

"You?" Sai isn't sure why she asks, but she has to know for certain.

"Yes, me."

It's the first time she's heard a raw emotion of any type in his voice. He sounds almost sad. Sai resists the urge to reach out and touch his shoulder, to say something she knows will sound banal, like *sorry*.

"And you want me to try because?"

His clear blue eyes bore through her for a moment. "Because you're a Rare. Not having encountered many others, our limitations and diversifications aren't known. This gives us a chance to find out things we may not be aware of about ourselves. The things we're capable of."

That tiny bit of information is more than Sai thought she'd get from him, even if the exact definition of what a Rare is still escapes her. It's a piece of his confidence, a link to someone other than herself. In that moment, Bastian seems a lot younger than she thought. The weight of the world is gone from his shoulders, and in its place are the vast possibilities for what he might be.

"I can...try?"

"Good." The mask is back, as if it never went away in the first place. "Come here, and I'll guide you through what you need to do. If you lose the thread, stop me, and we'll go in again. Got it?"

"Got it."

It's strange with another person in her head. Sharing even a part of her thought processes feels like an invasion of privacy, but his movements are gentle and precise. It's easy to follow his lines.

Bastian shows her how to flow into the animal, beyond its physical walls, to the sinews and veins that run through the entire system. The beauty of nature's finest computers—a living, breathing thing.

She balks at first. Though Sai understands what it is Bastian is guiding her to do, it's not something she's ever contemplated. For her, all the time spent in the facilities has been trying to get away from taking lives, trying to make up for it. Until now.

It's painful to attempt, even though she knows these animals are beyond reason. They can't be kept as pets and breed like wildfire if not kept in check.

Every time she gets a little bit closer, but can never quite seal the deal. Sai wipes her hand over her brow, startled to see the moon high above the dome outside Bastian's window. The only other source of light is the flickering screens as they flit through their sponsored messages.

"I'm sorry," she whispers, the tiredness makes her voice raw. "Just one more try?"

Sai doesn't even wait for Bastian's response before diving in again, this time determined. Making her way past tiny bones and minuscule vessels to the heart, she closes her eyes at the brief flare of light inside her and wrenches, willing it to cease being.

Something hot and wet drips down her face as she opens heavy eyes to blink the tears away. Only, it's not tears—it's rabid bunny guts all over the desk, the carpet, and herself.

"Oops," she says and slides to the ground, unable to stop the hysterical laughter from spilling out. She killed it, exploded it. Exactly what she never wanted to do again. The giggles won't stop, and the goop sticks to her hands.

Bastian is there with a few wet towels to clean her up, and she blinks in the sudden light that bathes the room. As she dabs the blood away, punctuating the macabre with a streak of laughter she can't quite tell is her own, Sai watches Bastian clean up the rest of the office. It takes him but a few seconds. His eyes closed, a wind picks up, making the end of his jacket flap softly, and all of a sudden the mess is gone. She wonders idly if he was just showing off. Her laughter dies and he hands her a glass of water.

She clutches it gladly and gulps it down, only to start coughing immediately. "What the hell is that?"

Bastian raises an eyebrow. "Vodka."

"You gave me alcohol?" Sai splutters. No amount of twisting her mouth will clear out the taste.

"You looked like you needed it. I know I did after my first—and mine was the mistake of a very bad mood." He reaches into the fridge built into his desk. "Here—water better?"

Sai nods, enjoying the slight warmth of the vodka spreading in her system regardless of her disdain for the substance. "Thanks," she mutters.

Bastian shrugs. "You're what? Seventeen?"

Sai shakes her head. "Not quite, I don't think. I've always guessed at my birthdate."

He watches her for a moment, and Sai wishes she could push hard enough to read his mind the way he does hers. "Well done. You need more finesse. In case you ever need to use this." His voice holds a hint of bitterness.

"Why would I need to... I mean..." She stops without asking the burning question she doesn't want the answer to.

He glances at his watch. "Let's just say, another offensive defense is always good to have."

She nods dubiously. "How did you clean that up?"

He glances at her and shrugs. "Party trick. Maybe I'll show you one day."

Sai glares at him or tries to. Somehow, she feels like it's not as effective as usual.

"It's late. Go and sleep. You'll need it. Domino won't be back for a few days, and you'll have your first mission coming up soon."

"Wait—what? Mission? I'm still a student."

"True, but like I said, you're a Rare and I need you to do what it is I don't have time to. I'm just glad you didn't turn out to be all fanfare and nothing else."

"Now I'm confused." Sai stops and plants her hands on her hips. "What exactly is a Rare? You act like I should know the specifics."

Bastian blinks at her. "Rare. You have an ability, affinity, power—whatever you want to call it—far stronger and more in-depth than others. Rare."

"There aren't many of us then?" Her voice trails off and she feels momentary regret.

"Clearly, at least not many that make it here. Now go and get some sleep. Get up in the morning and do what you do. I'll see you here after your classes. You have preparations to make." His tone means the end of the discussion.

For some obscure reason with Bastian, her fate stings. Sai doesn't like being indebted to anyone, but what she likes even less is this need for his approval.

A scowl on her face, regardless of anything Bastian might try to tell her, she stalks out of his office without looking back.

CHAPTER
four

The heavy steel doors close silently behind Sai. Bastian can still hear her stomping down the corridor. *So young.* He sighs.

"Do you think she is too young?" An elderly man steps out from a previously concealed doorway and tilts his head in Sai's direction.

"She's no younger than I was when I got thrown into this, Mathur." Bastian turns back to his desk and rummages through the contents, fighting a scowl.

"Even when you awoke at fifteen, Bastian, you were never young. She lacks your finesse."

"I noticed that." Bastian surveys the area to make sure he hasn't missed any stray intestines. "She also lacks reason to take a life. According to her, she's lucky to be given a chance to redeem herself. We drill that mantra into their heads from day one. Add hints of suggestion behind the words and it governs their morality. After so many people fell victim when her power asserted itself, I don't think she ever thought to take a life again. If only I'd found her in time..."

"There was nothing more you could do. Do you worry this will break her?" Mathur walks further into the room, steps hesitant as he chooses his footing. His shoes make a slight shush as he moves.

"If she's going to break, she'll break no matter who is responsible. I need her. I can't do this on my own anymore. As much as we want to pretend otherwise, we're balanced precariously. Sooner or later, I'll get found out." Bastian flops back into the chair and looks at the ceiling. His head pounds, his body aches. He knows he's been pushing himself too far, but in this case, there is no one else he can trust. Not yet.

"You are really going to do this?"

Bastian nods. "Are *they* ready?"

"They are already dying, Bastian. All of them. And those are the only volunteers I can give you."

Bastian closes his eyes and nods, sealing off the sadness he feels, and lets the mask fall over his face to hide every emotion he's ever felt. It's better that way, harder for him to slip up. "Thank them for me?"

"There is no need. They understand. You are going to kill yourself if you are not careful, you know. One day you will misjudge the dose, and you will lack the power to retaliate if you are discovered."

"That's a lot of maybes. I'm careful." Bastian avoids eye contact with the doctor. "Besides, I can't afford to slip up, can I? If I do, we'll be back where we started."

Mathur smiles tightly and shifts his weight to the other leg. "We are all grateful for everything you do."

"And do they know you're here?"

"No one knows I am here."

"Not even Mason?"

Mathur shrugs. "Your brother was busy."

"My brother is always busy!" Bastian finally looks at his old mentor. The grey hairs have overrun the black, and wrinkles smile where laugh lines once did. Bastian sighs. "You senile idiot. You're too old and valuable for this cloak-and dagger-business. I would have made it out tonight."

"Your rooms are secure."

"Not as secure as my mind. And that damn leg of yours doesn't do us any favors." He takes a deep breath and counts to five. Ten takes far too long. "Don't surprise me again. I almost killed you this afternoon."

Mathur smiles at him kindly. "You are too frazzled. You need a vacation. You are older than your years."

"And where would you have me go?" Bastian asks dryly. "I'll be fine. I'll go take one of those fantastic relaxing baths Dom is always trying to push on everyone."

At the mention of the domino, Mathur's expression clouds over, and Bastian kicks himself for being so cold. "Sorry. I can be an ass at times."

The old man shrugs and averts his gaze, the twinkle gone from his eye. "How...is... he? How are they doing?" The question is hesitant, as if he really doesn't want to know, but can't stop himself from asking.

"Dom is doing spectacular, but then you know he always does. The others? Well..." Bastian shrugs. "The others aren't your prototype. They're not Dom, and they don't have his sense of self yet. He's working with Sai. Hopefully he can protect her when I send her out on her first missions. She's stronger than you'd think."

"You would not have risked so much if she was not."

"Good point." Bastian glances at his watch. "I have to make sure to keep her away from Zach, though."

Mathur coughs. "Does Zach suspect?"

Bastian shakes his head. "I don't believe so. She hadn't fully recovered strength from her final exam when he saw her. Now I just have to keep her out of reach."

"Not just her. What about you?"

Bastian chuckles at the thought. "I highly doubt it." He leans back and suppresses a sigh. "How's the antidote coming?"

Mathur shrugs his shoulders and fiddles with his glasses. "So-so. Needs more testing, but with enough luck and your continued support, we should succeed sooner rather than later."

"Thank you, doctor. That's very reassuring." Bastian's words drip with sarcasm as he glares at his friend for a moment. "You should go soon if you want to make the time-window. Harlow's security tweaks are far superior to her father's. The blackouts don't last as long."

"I know. I just wanted to see Sai for myself." Mathur starts walking toward the side door. "I trust the shipment will still be delivered?"

"On time, my friend." Bastian picks up his personal reader, balancing the light adrium device in his hand. The warmth seeps into his skin, and he frowns, distracted, effectively dismissing the older man. "On time," he mutters to himself and the now-empty room.

Bastian glances at the clock on his wall and the numbers glimmering through the skin on his wrist from band beneath. Both are in sync. The odds of only one of them malfunctioning is slim enough, but both of them at the same time? No chance. That leaves only one choice. She's late. If there's one thing Bastian hates, it's tardiness.

The knock at the door is tentative. No, not tentative—tired.

"Come in," he mutters automatically, and the doors swing in on his voice imprint command.

Sai teeters at the threshold to the room. Her dark hair is knotted and stands out at frizzy angles from her head. Black soot clings to part of her face.

"You've never been that good at chemistry I take it?"

He watches as she fights a scowl, which seems to be her automatic response to most things.

"It's Nimue who's bad. When she said she was good at math, I don't think it included chemistry. I have no idea how that girl made it through her final test. What'd she have to do? Groom a puppy?"

"Pretty much," Bastian says before turning away and picking up another cage from behind his desk.

"What?" Her tone is incredulous.

"Did you think all psionics are as violent as you, Sai?" His tone is bland, and he studies the effect his bluntness has on her. She'll have to get far better at hiding her reactions to things. Right now she cracks easily under pressure. If she needs a reason and a cause, he'll hand her both on a silver platter.

"I'm not violent!" More indignation. Her moods are far too erratic.

"You are a tad. You excelled at every single fighting class you took. You disabled six fully trained combat men—three psionics and three dominos. You should have been dead, but you're not. Nimue would have died in the second wave. She's an empath. Stick around her and maybe you'll end up feeling happier and less sorry for your poor self."

He winces inwardly at the expression on her face. Sometimes he's aware that what he says to people can come out a lot harsher than he intends. It's a drawback of cultivating an unapproachable facade. "She's not unique, though. There are many levels of empath out there, and to read through shields, she needs skin contact. You have abilities inside you no one has even tapped into yet. So, let's find some more, shall we?"

She runs her fingers through her hair, working out knots in exasperation, and eyes the cage on his desk with distinct skepticism. "Do I have to kill that, too?"

"No. I want to take a different approach after yesterday's mess."

"Fun." Her voice falls flatter than her usual quip. Bastian sighs softly and steps over to look her in the eye.

"I know you don't want to kill. You think you've done enough of that for two lifetimes. I'm here to tell you that, no matter what we want and what we think we're incapable of, there may be a situation that arises where your life is more important to you than the person standing over you. If I weren't to teach you this, to teach you to try and access the abilities you have and use them in defense of yourself or others, how good a teacher would that make me?"

"You said you're not a teacher." There's that stubborn set to her jaw. A myriad of colors pass over her face, reflected from a sudden pop-up triggered just below his window. Red streaks linger longer in her hair, reminding him of all the blood she already has on too-young hands.

"Touché, my dear, but I am your guide." He points to the cage. "Today, we're going to do the reverse. Have you heard of a medi-psi?"

Sai scrunches up her brow in thought and answers tentatively, "Uncommon. The creator of the dominos was one?"

"Ten gold stars."

"Cut it out," Sai grumbles. "Your point?"

"The point." Bastian mulls the words over in his head, trying to figure out how exactly to say what he wants to. "The point is there aren't many medi-psionics. Those of us capable of manipulating body structure, organs, diseases within a body for healing purposes are far and few between. It's probably a good thing there aren't many healers, considering the fact that— logically—you can also do the reverse.

"Since you've already demonstrated an awkward ability to harm, let's see if you can heal. It might not always be a direct correlation. You may be better at harming than healing or at healing than harming. But we'll have to find out. Any questions before we start?"

She nods, and the words that follow are hesitant. "Are we... Can you... Can you do this, Bastian?"

He smiles, the first genuine smile he's had in a long time. "I definitely can, though I won't tell you which way my finesse lies until after we've figured out yours, deal?"

"Deal." Sai smiles back.

Bastian runs his hands over the rabid bunny—as Sai prefers to call it—in awe. The tumor is gone. If it weren't for the horrible nature of the beast that requires its termination anyway, it would probably go on to live a very full life.

Just his luck Sai is more gifted in healing than harming. It makes him wonder what happened when her powers awoke. Did they do the reverse of what they meant to, or did she inadvertently try to heal everyone and have it backlash? She's so lucky to be alive. When power leaks into the eyes, it usually doesn't stop before the user is dead.

The way she sees inside a patient is instinctive and beautiful. A shame, really. Though she's powerful enough to kill someone, her trauma runs too deep and blocks that skill. If her triggers set off panic, there's a likelihood it could backfire catastrophically. She'll have to rely on psionic-enforced physical training for defense instead.

Bastian smiles to himself. He's not even sure *he'd* like to run into her in a dark alleyway.

"Speaking of dark alleyways..." He glances at his watch and suppresses the sudden rush of adrenaline he feels at the time. Regardless of how often he does it, the possibility of being caught always brings him back to his childhood. Every ten days. Like clockwork.

There may be certain liberties his position as dean of the facility has won him, but he still needs to be careful. Securing his office is of tantamount importance, and he's learned not to rely on GNW systems.

His own net of psionics weaves through and around every part of his office. This is his own backup source of power, and it's here he can set alarms attuned only to himself to alert him of any unwelcome guests. After years of practice, it doesn't take long to close his eyes, concentrate, and activate its awareness.

The well-camouflaged side door offers up a hidden passageway. Mathur got in through the path that leads to other parts of Central. It's only safe to traverse during the brief blackout windows twice a day. Once the grid blacks out, his time begins. With Harlow's recent tweaks to the GNW security, tonight's trip requires more haste on his behalf to make it back in one window.

"Do it right the first time," he mutters to himself, following the path down to the shaft where he lowers himself into the narrow opening. It's not a straight drop, and it's slightly difficult for him to navigate with the ladder-like footholds carved into the wall. It makes him wonder how Mathur manages it with his prosthetic calf.

The climb always seems longer than the few minutes it takes, at least on the way down. When he heads back up, he'll feel the strain for days. He glances beyond the wall-shield that blocks the passage from view to the corridor and eyes his watch. Counting down in his head he steps out next to an automated laundry cart. Three lefts, and he drops behind the next door and presses for the handle.

There's a rarely used chute next to him, and he carefully extracts a discreetly wrapped bundle from the opening before climbing through the door. Hefting it lightly to check it's all there, he clips it into his jacket and picks up his pace. It's always there, right on time.

The ground in the tunnel beyond is uneven. He checks the time again and waits for a count of five before stepping out to the low rumble of a multi-transport somewhere in the sky lane far above his head. Only the best transport systems for those in the low-numbered blocks. Banal chatter filters down to him, fading as he makes his way along the path until he hits a damp section, signifying the change from the central "good" blocks of town to the outlying bad.

After many twists and turns, he finally pushes the last heavy wooden door open to reveal a lively but stale beer-smelling establishment. It takes his eyes a while to adjust to the dimly lit surrounds. "Hi, Garr, how're you doing?"

The lady behind the old wooden bar beams at him. Pretty lines define the softness of her expression, but he knows hard lines replace them when the smile fades. Though the seats are worn and the bar surface is scarred, it's cleaner than most other places on the verge of the outlying districts.

"Here," she says and grins, serving three people their orders at once, grey-streaked hair plaited efficiently down her back. "Let Merl get your coat."

Which is perfect. The man takes the coat and artfully pockets the package under it, somehow making it appear far smaller than Bastian knows it is. "I'll have a beer, thanks."

"Preference?"

"Whatever you recommend, Garr." He smiles back at her. She'd worked with Mathur and known his mother when he was a child. Those ties bind harder than any GNW have ever given him. He shakes his head to keep from thinking about it. "Just one for me tonight."

She eyes him as she pours ale into a surprisingly clean glass mug, given the appearance of the bar. "Short trip this month?"

"Necessarily."

"At least you're legal now, eh?" Garr grins at him and pushes the glass across the counter.

He takes it from her and chugs down the drink, setting the mug back on the counter with a bang. "Like anyone was going to try and stop me before."

Garr laughs, and for a moment he wonders if maybe his mother sounded like that before the injury. "Careful. If the higher-ups find out what you're doing, they'll slap one of those tracking chips in you before you can blink."

"There are ways to work around that." He shrugs and stares at the mug for a few moments.

"Bastian?" Garr leans closer than he likes, closer than anyone else would be allowed, to get his attention.

"Sorry. Just thinking." He shakes his head to clear the thoughts, and she serves a few more people while he drains the last of the drops from the cool glass before turning back to him. "You mind, right? Be careful out there. She'd have my hide..."

"No, she wouldn't. Sarah would skin Mason's hide for letting father's position fall to me instead of him. We both know that."

He can see the brief shadow pass over her face. Her shoulders sag in defeat. "Just take care of yourself."

"I learned how to from the best, Garr." He reaches over and squeezes her hands briefly before reaching for the coat Merl is handing back to him. "Till then."

The trip back is less dangerous. Getting caught coming in from a drink in town is nothing compared to leaving the facility armed with ten pounds of pure Shine. Less dangerous perhaps, but just as tiring. So much in fact he almost misses the window to get back into the passage to his room and reset his own alarms before the lights flicker back into consistent brightness. One day Harlow will fix it completely, but for now, power flickers are mostly easy to rely on.

He looks around to find everything exactly how he left it, and nothing disturbed his net in his absence. Something nags at the back of his mind, but he pushes the loneliness aside and drops into his chair, determined to go through a few of the reports on his desk and see if he can uncover any more potential incidents.

Scouting for potential psionics can mean a lot of different things. They flounder without someone to guide them. The facility is as much for the psionics' benefit as for GNW to profit. Their intentions are noble—on paper, anyway. It allows Bastian to subtly recruit and try to find Rares or at least to try and find them before they trigger that excess power so he can hide them because Zach finding them usually results in their disappearance. So far Bastian's success rate has been low. Some of the GNW board believe he's too young to be given so much responsibility and power, but none of them like getting their own hands dirty.

He flips through some of the scouting reports, head beginning to ache as he dismisses the ones that don't meet his criteria. A glance of violet light refracts off the one personal effect on his desk—a photograph of his mother. She was beautiful, and yet all he can remember about Sarah is the damaged husk they left behind.

His gaze lingers, and the anger boils inside at the tarnished memories of her. Nothing can ever make up for the mistakes made in the first tier of the Domino Project, but it's not too late to alter psionics' treatment under GNW. What disasters the previous government concocted, the privatized company cleaned up. Now when GNW creates disasters, Bastian is their janitor.

It's almost dawn. He puts the photograph and report reader down and walks to the window to stare out, toward the edges of the dome. The cities are beautiful works as far as architecture goes and practical, supporting many people off very little. But Central is larger than most. The rules are made here, and grids originate beneath him, wandering in and out of sectors like a trailing spider web. With a touch of thought suggestion, peace—and anything else—is always possible.

He splays his fingers against the glass and watches the heated outlines as he moves his hand lower. There's never enough time to accomplish everything he needs to. Not even these six years clawing his way up after his powers awoke is enough.

CHAPTER
Five

Sai taps her foot softly as she waits for Bastian to finally give up torturing her with boredom and speak.

"About this mission..." Bastian frowns briefly at the reader in his hand.

"Mission?" She suddenly finds her breath short and chest tight. "You were serious? I've only been here a couple of months!"

"You're an enforcer. We're not a large division, in case you haven't noticed. I don't care whether or not you're a student, the experience is necessary." Bastian stops for a moment while Sai processes his words. When she nods, he continues. "In short, we're sending you on some basic missions. You'll deal with them and return home."

She fiddles with her fingers and runs all her arguments through her head. "What exactly does this entail?"

"You can try to talk to them, or you can force them to stop their disruptive behavior. Your choice."

"Easy for you to say," she mutters under her breath.

"Once you do a few of these, it'll become easier for you. Trust me. It's better than the alternative."

That response earns him a scowl. She can sense him brushing the shields she's put up and stares back smugly. Which, in hindsight, probably isn't a good idea, considering the force he slams into her shielding right after. Despite shaking like a leaf, her shields hold. Small victories. She's been taking them for longer than she can count.

"Alternatives in this place are not always what they seem." Dom's voice interrupts her train of thought.

Both Sai and Bastian turn toward Dom, who shrugs at them. "We need to get your things ready, Sai."

Bastian dismisses them with a wave of his hand and is back at his desk before they leave the room.

"Do you think he's okay?" she asks in a subdued tone.

"Okay?" Dom sounds confused. "How would he not be okay?"

"I forget sometimes..."

"Forget?"

"That you're not completely human." She blushes a little and looks away.

"That's probably classified as a compliment where I come from."

For a second, Sai blinks at him before bursting into nervous laughter. "Good one, Dom. Good one."

He pushes the door open when they get to the room and starts going through her things. Three weeks ago, this would have angered her, but she's grown used to him now. At least she'll be packed properly by the end of it. The backpack he emerges from the mess with is so compact Sai raises an eyebrow in disbelief.

"You're sure that's enough?"

"We're only going to UC 8. We won't be gone more than two nights. I have faith you can accomplish your task well within the prescribed time limit."

"We have a time limit?"

Dom looks up at her, his makeshift eyebrows liquid in their upward movement. "Of course. Most things need time limits. I believe we have seventy-two hours. We leave this afternoon before sundown. You're excused from classes today. I suggest you try and rest."

The door clicks behind him before she has a chance to ask anything further. "Fantastic," she mumbles.

"Come on, Sai, you're going to be late." Nimue urges her to follow, her own schoolbooks hugged to her chest. *"You can't be late for this."*

"I know. I know." Sai strips off her nightclothes and pulls on those Dom laid out for her. *The tights are constricting, as are the tiny shorts and candy-striped tank. Without a second thought, she grabs her backpack and chases Nimue down the hall, wedge-heeled shoes echoing on marble slabs.*

"Here we are."

She can hear Nimue's voice, but not see her. The garden is dark, filled with eerie rotting trees. Vines hang low, obscuring her view, but a white pulsing light shines through the gaps, hinting at something inside.

Sai pushes forward, getting tangled in the vines and scratched by tiny thorns she didn't see on them before. They knot in her hair and cling to the parts of her thighs and chest exposed to the air. She struggles, rips them away, and gasps in shock as they fall from her skin, shriveled and dead. There are burn marks on her everywhere they touched.

She clutches her chest, feeling alone and vulnerable, and blinks as the light in the middle of the hidden clearing becomes fainter to reveal Bastian and Dom.

"Here's your mission," Bastian says, and she can feel his smile in her head. The insane one no one should ever have to see.

"Mission?" She hears herself croak out the word.

"Mission." Bastian reinforces the statement by dragging Dom up by his hair. The body hangs limp, but his eyes are open. "Stop his heart, Sai. You can do it. You were born for this."

She whimpers. Unable to tear her gaze from Dom's pleading eyes, she screams as Bastian uses his mind to pull her toward the body, hurtling her at the heart just before everything explodes in a sea of red.

"Sai!"

She shuts her eyes and screams once more, ripping the tangled vines away from her body. Something shakes her by the shoulders, and she fights it with all her might until a resounding slap rings in her ears and she feels blood rushing to redden the vacated spot.

Sai opens her eyes to see Dom standing there, looking at the hand he used to hit her. He's in one piece and fully functional. She crosses the short distance in an instant to fling her arms around his neck.

"You're okay. You're here. We're here!" she mumbles into his smooth, cool shoulder.

"Yes. I am here." He disentangles himself from her and sets her gently back on the bed, handing her the clothes from the top of her dresser: dark blue sweats and a grey tank top. Sai grabs them and eagerly begins to pull them on before she realizes Dom is still there and glares at him. He turns around as she finishes getting dressed. She can't help the flush that rises in her cheeks.

"You had a nightmare?" he asks with his back still turned.

"I guess." She finishes pushing her long hair up into a ponytail before speaking again. "I'm ready now."

"It is okay, you know." He turns around, grabs her backpack, and proceeds to the door. "You won't come to harm. I'll be near you." He pauses for a second, his hand at his ear, a distant look in those golden eyes for a moment as he briefly cocks his head to one side. "I won't let anyone harm you," he finishes before ushering her out of the room.

It's not far to the transport area. Just more cold white floors and concrete walls with occasional windows interspersed. "What were you doing back there, Dom?"

"Which part—slapping you?"

"No, no." Sai waves that away with a rueful grin. "I know why you did that. I mean, where you hold your hand to your ear and listen for a second. You do it fairly often. Do you have a headache? Can you get a headache?"

"I'm not sure." He purses his lips for a brief moment. "I've certainly never had one, though recently others have complained to me they feel interference. The finger to my ear allows me to hear the others clearer. Focuses the range. Our connection has been fuzzy lately."

"Connection?"

"To the other dominos. Something similar to our own intranet—for communication purposes."

Sai nods at him. "Interesting."

"Yes." Dom looks at her oddly for a moment. "Yes, I believe that's an accurate description."

The dock attendant ushers them through to their craft. Dom checks over the controls and nods to the man, allowing him to leave.

"Watch out for Exiled patrols," he calls on his way out the door.

Domino doesn't acknowledge the warning as the man leaves the hold. Sai is forced to ask for an explanation. "Exiled patrols?"

"The Exiled live past the outskirts of the cities, scattered along in different camps." He continues speaking as he tweaks the controls. "Remnants of those psionics exiled during the wars. None of them came back when it ended twenty-odd years ago. They're a known cause of unrest, directly and indirectly."

"Why can't you deal with this?"

Dom studies her for a moment. "You deal with situations because, unlike me, you are human. Psionic, too, but you *are* human. Most people don't take kindly to...things." The last word is spoken with such distaste it surprises Sai.

"You're not a thing, Dom," she says quietly.

"I know that. You know that..." He shifts the gears into position and maneuvers the clunky vehicle to spin. Hover was one of the most surprising additions to technology post-disaster era. It took far less of their precious fuel to generate power and, unlike old-fashioned combustion engines, didn't set the filtered air on fire.

"Then those who count know, right?"

Domino nods and pauses to look at her. "Thank you. I should apologize that *Mele* is currently not ready for use."

"*Mele*?"

"My transport. She's like me." A smile plays at the corner of his mouth as he maneuvers the vehicle into the lanes of traffic speeding past. "It'll take a few hours to get there. There's a file in your bag on the trader we're visiting. UC 8 lies on the outskirts and undertakes trading on a regular basis. Often with, 'shady people' I believe the term is. GNW usually overlooks certain aspects of the trades because they do acquire things that are of utmost necessity."

"But?" Sai prompts him.

"But not everything is, and trying to trade pure Shine to anyone not within the United Conglomerate is punishable."

"It should be," Sai replies hotly. Images of half-eaten food rescued from trash cans when her parents forgot to feed her dance in front of her eyes.

Dom considers her for a moment. "He's lucky they're sending you and not Bastian."

Sai blinks her mind back into focus. "Why would they send Bastian?"

Dom raises an eyebrow, this time mimicking the human gesture in an eerily perfect way. "How else do you think someone so young is in the position he's in?"

"I thought he was born into it." Sai can hear the bitterness in her voice. Her own childhood is a black mark on her memory. Born poor to Shine addicts. Until she blew up her home, Sai never even tried to imagine living in Central.

The lower your block number, the higher your station. Working up isn't an option, not from that far down. She tries not to stare out the windows at the flashes of substandard living that pale even against her own past. Soon they'll be on the sky lane and coast most of the way to their destination. It's difficult to push down the growing excitement, and she fidgets. Never having been on a sky lane before, Sai's only ever seen them in pictures or heard about them. Checkpoints that allow the hovercraft to travel at a higher altitude as long as they keep to the height dictated by the adrium-enforced steel towers that track the vehicles.

She notices Dom watching her. "Sorry, what did you say?"

"I said, Bastian might have been born with station, but he was barely eighteen when his father died. He had to fight to take his inheritance." Dom swerves to avoid a human crawling out onto the road, clutching at a piece of paper as it flits out of his reach. Anger and wonder war in his eyes as the elusive and empty packet escapes his grasp. Shine addiction and the hollow realities it creates. Sai tightens her fists.

"You haven't answered why they would send him." She tries to unclench her teeth, but her words end up coming out angry anyway.

"They only send Bastian when there's no more hope, when eradication is the only option. He's far too busy for little tasks now, which is why he's been spending time with you."

"Eradication?"

"You've heard the rumors about the Eliminator?"

Sai nods at him.

"Well, you've been training with him for almost two months."

Something inside Sai goes cold, and she begins to sweat. "I thought that was some scary story they told the kids at the facilities."

Dom shakes his head. She clamps down her shields and refuses to glance out the windows. All she can think of is how close she's been working with Death himself. If she ever steps out of line, they've got her right where they want her. She would disappear without a trace.

Try as she might, she can't bring herself to hate him.

Sai isn't used to the respect she's shown upon their arrival in UC 8. She follows their eyes and notices why. Her clothes, she realizes belatedly, have the GNW Eye embroidered into them. Its letters swirl together with the same metallic effect the dominos have.

The inn they spend the rest of the night at is comfortable, more comfortable than any bed she's ever slept in, although the eggs in the morning look suspiciously like the ones she argues with on a daily basis back at the facility.

After breakfast, they make their way to the Enforcement Offices. The head of law enforcement in the city greets her. Dom says his name is Artold. She can't help notice the severe lack of regard Dom receives from everyone, but doesn't let it get in the way of her job. Control, just like Bastian taught her. She reinforces her shields, puts a neutral expression on her face, and allows Artold to lead her into their offices.

"McDearny is one of our finest traders, ma'am," the man assures her as he reaches across his desk for a reader.

Sai interrupts him. "I've read the reports and seen the recorded evidence. If more has come to light in the last twenty-four hours, I'd be happy to view it. Otherwise we're just wasting time." Her heart is in her throat, unused to such authority.

"Sorry, ma'am." Artold blushes with embarrassment. "This way, if you'll follow me. We have him in the holding cell."

Holding cell? She finds herself glancing at Dom, seeking some sort of help, but people have moved in front of him, ignoring him, and it irks her. "Excuse me, I need my partner up where he can help, thank you." She manages to say the whole sentence without a single nervous stutter. If only her parents could see her now.

"Of course." Artold motions people to make room. "We detained McDearny early yesterday morning. He's ready for your questioning."

"Thank you. We can take it from here." What would Bastian do? How would Bastian phrase things? Constant questions run through her mind. Sai waits until Artold gets the hint and backs himself and his dithering crew out of the area.

Sai lets out a pent-up breath and eyes the lone figure on the concrete bench in the cell. Its metal bars gleam black in the dim light—another remnant from before the meteors fell. The observations calm her before she speaks. "Do you know why I'm here?" she asks, her tone soft with genuine curiosity.

The man nods, probably because he can't speak without pain considering the bruises and swelling all up the side of his nose, lips, and cheekbones. She watches him and sees the wariness in his eyes, the distrust in the hunched shoulders, and the way he's pulled himself back so far it looks like he's trying to sink through the wall.

And she bets that, if she listens, he's screaming silently in his head.

She sighs. "You were caught trading Shine over the GNW United Conglomerate's protected borders."

"Isth wathn't illegal." He mouths the words distinctly, wincing with each syllable.

"The trading of Shine between two legally licensed facilities or individuals is not illegal, McDearny, but people from outside the UC are not licensed in any way. They fall under street trading." It's not like they were visitors from other continents. Tourism after the Disaster Era has been shaky at best. Anyone outside the borders are Exiled rebels. Even the smallest child knows that. She shakes her head and he starts to speak frantically.

"Hesh had ishd!"

"He had...identification?" The man nods, relief on his mangled face as he realizes she understood him. "This wasn't mentioned in the report."

McDearny scowls—at least, she thinks he does. It's hard to tell.

"I see." So it had been mentioned when they caught him but conveniently left out of the actual report. She glances at him.

"You realize there's only one way I can know if you're telling the truth, right?"

He nods at her again, his eyes bright and clear, trying to hide his fear. She unlocks the cell door with Dom close behind and kneels in front of the man. A memory sift without touch is possible, but she prefers eye contact if it's an option.

His mind is open to her, as open as anyone she chooses to visit. Carefully she leafs through his memories, shying away from the beatings received so recently, and finds the identification. He's correct, but he isn't. What she sees is someone making him believe the person he was trading with was sanctioned to do so. The man can't be blamed for not possessing a dormant gene. At least that would have afforded him minor protection from being duped. She records it herself to file into the report on the way home and stands, releasing McDearny's mind.

"You're free to go." She touches the cuffs binding his wrists, unlocking them with a thought, and steps away as they clatter to the ground. Even without looking at the man, she knows there's fear in his eyes. Mind and memory-sifting are part of why the GNW keep such a tight rein on psionics, even though not everyone can perform it.

"Reimburse him." She gestures to Dom and rubs her temples for a moment, staving off a reaction headache. Bastian may have drilled her in techniques, but she last truly used it while she was still Fifty-Two. Just like everything else, the less she uses it, the more it tasks her to do so. While the practicing made mind matter seem sluggish, the real thing is like a million goopy balls firing at your head and you have to catch and hold onto the right one. She makes a mental note to practice more.

Her head is already pounding, and she closes her eyes for a moment to lean against the cool wall. The reaction headache shouldn't be too bad as long as she can get her hands on...

Dom nudges her shoulder at that exact moment and holds out his hand, dropping two tiny clear pills into her own.

She smiles at him and takes the offered water. "Thanks. I don't want to stay here longer than necessary." She scans the holding area and shakes her head, pushing the images of McDearny's beating out of her mind. "I think they were just excited to find someone not Shined out." She sighs and looks away from Dom, her own memories warring for attention in her mind.

"I know. We'll have to warn the captain for not adhering to protocol." Dom's voice is softer than usual, like he's being considerate of her head.

"Can we wait a few minutes?" Sai massages her temples slowly.

"Of course." Dom grabs one of the readers out of their packs. "I'm not a monster, you know."

"Why, Dom, did you just crack a joke?"

"Me?" He blinks at her. "Not capable. Sorry."

If Sai didn't know better, she'd swear there was a twinkle in one of his golden eyes. She tries to breathe deeply and let her calm facade take over again. How Bastian manages to stay so collected on a regular basis is beyond her.

"I'm not cut out for this," she mutters before opening her eyes.

"You're perfectly cut out for this."

"Thanks," she says dryly, not meaning it at all. "All right, call him in."

Artold is ushered in and stands at ease, facing them.

"I wonder—do you not have a psionic on staff?" Sai remains seated, not confident enough of her energy levels to stand.

"Yes, ma'am."

"Then why didn't you use them?"

He seems confused. "Excuse me?"

"Why did you ignore the broker's claims of seeing valid identification?" Sai finds her patience far thinner than she realized. She just wants to get out and away from people who act first and don't think at all.

"There were no agents registered to buy the substance yesterday. The clinics are meticulously controlled. We oversee the coming and going of all quantities in their prescribed formats."

"McDearny does not have access to this database, correct?" Artold shakes his head, and Sai continues. "And so, it would be perfectly acceptable of him to take identification shown to him at face value and simply think he was making a legitimate trade?"

"Well, yes, but no one was..."

"I'm aware the ID wasn't real, but the point is McDearny couldn't know that. You should have had his memories checked instead of wasting our time by dragging us here to discipline a man who didn't deserve it. Nor did he deserve the beating he very clearly got at the hands of your subordinates." She holds her hand up at his protest. "Don't dig the pit deeper than you already have."

At his bewildered expression, Sai taps her head. "Got it all, right in here." She glances at Dom, who hands her a reader, and peruses the document he's prepared, more grateful than ever that she's not alone. "I think this sums it up. You'll be reprimanded and the replacement of the goods we reimbursed the broker for will be taken out of any bonus you receive up until it is paid for. I suggest you patrol your city borders better and pay more attention to the laws that govern us all."

Artold bows his head, sweat beading his brow. The man knows he got off lightly. Sai can tell it in the way his heart beats fast with relief.

"Thank you," he says and the words are probably the most sincere he's ever muttered.

She ignores him and stands. "We'll be on our way now. I'd say it was nice meeting you, but I'd be lying. Instead, let's hope we don't meet again soon." She turns away from the man, following Dom as he guides her out of the enforcement headquarters of UC 8.

Sai holds her head high and makes sure every step she takes is full of the confidence she borrowed from observing Bastian. Not until they're inside the transport does she let her knees give way to the weariness she feels inside. She's surprised how soft the carpet in the transport is and is only distracted from its texture when Dom closes the door behind him.

"Are they all that easy?" she asks without looking up.

"No. Usually they're a lot more involved than that."

She twists a piece of dark hair around her finger, studying it intently. "I see." She falls silent, trying to sort out the thoughts in her mind.

"You did well, Sai," Dom says.

She looks up at him. "I felt like a fraud. Like they'd know at any given moment I'm just a sixteen-year-old punk who's nervous as hell."

He cocks his head to one side and watches her for a moment. Sai chalks yet another movement up to his human side. "You mimicked Bastian."

Sai can feel the heat rising in her cheeks, and glances away.

"Very good call," is all Dom says before moving to the driver's seat. "Home, then?"

"Yeah," Sai says, lying back on the plush pile of the floor carpeting. It feels warm and safe. She closes her eyes. "Let's go home."

The floor is harder than expected underneath her when she opens her eyes, and for a few seconds she panics that everything was a dream and she's back on the streets where she's been all along. She relaxes as soon as Dom speaks.

"We're almost there. I thought you might want to get the sleep out of your eyes."

She grins and pulls herself upright, ignoring the dull throb in her head from the mind-sifting. "Forget human, Dom. Now you're showing your feminine side."

"Sometimes, Sai," he mutters, imitating one of her tones perfectly, "you can be downright insulting."

She closes her mouth to keep from gaping at him. "Adaptive? Lightning speed, I say."

"I wish that were true." For a moment a shadow settles over his expression, and he fidgets. "I was born this size. I've been adapting for a long time."

He has a point. She watches him intently for a moment. From the smooth lines of his reflective skin, only a mimicry of the human version, down to the silky fingers that grip the console tightly. The realization hits her out of nowhere and she whispers the words. "You can be anything, can't you?"

His hands settle and the tapped beat stops. "I can be anything, within reason, that my mind feels comfortable with."

At first she says nothing, but chews on her lip a bit as thoughts race through her head, and then she smiles. "I'm just glad you're you."

When his lip quirks up at the corners, Sai stretches and goes into the small back compartment to change into a fresh set of clothes, stopping for only a second to admire the insignia. She feels the transport stop and frowns as she comes out of the cubicle. "That was cutting it close."

Dom moves from the pilot seat and shrugs his shoulders. "You almost overdid it. Common sense dictates that unless it's a case of extreme emergency, I let you sleep. As no rabid rabbits tried to attack us, I decided you were in no imminent danger."

"Rabid... He *told* you?"

"No one tells me anything. I don't know what you mean."

As she follows Dom out of the transport, she decides that dominos are not fair creatures at all. No one should have such control over their facial expressions. It's inhuman.

He stops when they get back to the main corridor and frowns for a second.

"We're a day early. He told us to report back immediately." He takes the left-hand corridor instead of the right.

Sai is silent all the way to Bastian's office, mulling things over in her head as she follows Dom. She wants to make sure she gets her wording perfect. There are so many ways the situation could have been misread, but she's certain she was meticulous and has Dom to back her up if there's any question.

Dom stands at the twin doors and frowns again. He steps back a foot and places his right hand on the door. A brief shimmer surrounds it and a faint hum echoes in her ears, after which the door swings inward, reminding Sai that dominos have an affinity for metal.

He takes three steps into the room, before stopping abruptly.

"Dammit." She hears him swear under his breath, something she's sure he's never done around her before.

"What is it?" she asks, pushing panic down.

"Nothing. We should come back tomorrow."

"What?" Sai extends her senses, trying to catch a glimpse of what might be wrong and blanches. Bastian is there, but he feels wrong, ill. "No." She pushes against Dom. "We have to help him."

"You can't help him right now."

"Be damned if I can't!" She raises her voice and shoves at him both physically and mentally, catching Dom off-guard. Sai walks past him, focused on where her head says Bastian is, not on what she can see. Her path takes her through something she never realized was a doorway and into a room that must be Bastian's private quarters.

The bed is huge and dark, covered in crisp white sheets. Tangled amidst them is Bastian, tossing and turning, sweat beading his brow.

"How on earth could he tell me to come back tomorrow?" Sai murmurs as she drops her backpack and rushes to the bed, momentarily forgetting her awe and the fear the majority of people hold for its occupant. All she sees is her teacher, sick, needing someone. Anyone.

"He deals with this every quarter, Sai." Dom is already behind her, standing back, clear of both her and Bastian. "You don't want to be here if he wakes up."

"Why on earth not? What could possibly happen every three months?" She reaches out to brush his forehead with her hand and recoils from what she finds. "No..." She stumbles back, tripping and falling, her graceful balance lost for a few moments. "Why would he do that?"

"He has the GNW physical every quarter, Sai..." Dom says quietly. "I didn't think. He's not to be disturbed for a few days around this time."

"There's no physical in any of the codes that require him to dose up!" She's angry at everything, but most of all for allowing herself to care. The powder and the childhood that paid for it flash through her memories.

"Dose up? He..." Dom pauses for a moment and touches his fingers to his ear, pressing in a short, precise rhythm. The gleam in his eyes changes to silver, bleeding out of the pupils and irises to become one with the sclera. "He doses down, Sai. Don't you understand?"

"No..." Bastian's voice is hoarse and unexpected. "She doesn't understand because all she's ever known is the abuse of Shine by people it was never intended for." He moves in bed, wincing, until he's sitting up against the headboard. His tan face is sallow and sweat beads his forehead, but his eyes are frighteningly bright when they meet hers. "I'm sorry, Sai."

"You asked me to trust you," she accuses him, pointing a finger as if it will help release her anger. "I... How could you?" The tears in her eyes can't be real. She never cries.

"I'm not your parents," he says quietly, his voice strong with conviction. "I'm not going to wallow in my own imagination and leave you to fend for yourself. I won't sell the food supplies for money to get a bit of stash. And I won't whore myself, or you, out on street corners so I can spend just five more minutes wishing I was nowhere near you."

A sob escapes Sai, and she covers her mouth with both hands.

"Am I next?" she whispers, unable to keep her voice steady.

"No. Sai..." Bastian tries to move and sags with lack of energy.

But she shakes her head as her past assaults her memories, and she raises her voice to drown out the sounds in her head. "Did you do this to me? Save me when I should have died? Gave me a chance when I didn't deserve to live? Gave me hope that I could redeem myself and eventually be free of some of this guilt—all to trick me and make me like *them*? I won't do it! I won't! It's everything I hate. *You're* everything I hate!"

"You don't mean that, Sai." Dom tries to reach out for her, but the silver of his eyes, so much like her own, scares her even more.

"The hell I don't!" Decorative tiles splinter against the walls, some crashing to the marble floors. "What's the silver, Dom, huh? Is that how you react to that dust? Is that a domino hyped up on Shine, number twelve?"

Dom's gaze hardens; the silver turns to steel. "That substance is caustic to my internal workings, but you know that because you've studied it."

Sai glares at him, fists clenched to her sides. "You're not supposed to act human either, and you do. How the hell do I know what you can and can't ingest?"

"Sai, it's not how it appears."

"It's not?" She laughs and puts her hands on her hips, tears ignored as they stream down her face.

"No, it's not." Bastian still sounds weary. "I power down for a reason, but I don't think you're up to listening to it tonight."

Even his eyes look tired, but Sai dismisses it. It's even easier for Shined-out people to lie. "You'll be lucky if I ever feel like listening."

"We'll continue your training tomorrow." His facial expressions close off in a clear dismissal, and Sai grabs the opportunity.

"Yes, *sir*." She snaps before turning to leave the room, yelling over her shoulder. "Don't follow me. I no longer require an escort."

The thoughts in her head won't leave her a moment of peace. All those childhood memories she thought were buried come catapulting back. Her mother and father spread out on the floor, each with a partner of their own, Shine as payment. Scrounging on the streets for food. Begging, borrowing, and stealing. Clothing herself in whatever rags she could find.

As she leaves, she screams. Her mind reaches out, lending her strength, and pulls the twin steel doors behind her as she goes. The loud bang, followed by the buckling of the wall, startles her. She can't help feeling vindicated.

The aftermarket street brand of the drug harms every human it touches. How did she ever think GNW could be a home? She's a prisoner here, indentured to serve them until she pays off her debt, unless they tire of her beforehand.

Redemption is a stupid goal. With as many people as she killed, no matter how inadvertently, she'll be stuck with these Shine-mongers for life.

CHAPTER
Six

"Let her go, Dom." Bastian pushes himself up against the headboard and winces. "She's not ready to listen."

Dom glances at Bastian and back to the door. His shoulders sag.

Bastian hears his office doors boom loudly, followed by the sound of rending metal. He groans. "That's going to be expensive. Good to know what triggers her destructive abilities."

Dom turns and squints at Bastian. "You did a number on yourself this time."

"Heavy psi-eval today. Had to make things convincing. It's not meant to be my strength." Bastian gestures to Dom's silver eyes. "You shouldn't tap offline for too long. They'll notice if you keep doing that."

Dom shrugs. "It's okay. We had a few whiteouts today."

"You know what they'll do if they realize what you're capable of, right?" Bastian looks at his friend, concern furrowing his brow. When Shine hits his abilities hard, he doesn't bother wasting energy on maintaining a stony facade. The muddiness of his brain. The strange mist that tries to invade his vision. And the weird constriction of his psionic access, like a chokehold that tightens the more he's dosed.

"I know what they'll *try* to do and what I *can* do. And I'm pretty sure who'll win." Dom's tone of voice is grimmer than Bastian's used to. "I'm not the concern, though. You are. How hard a hit did you take?"

Bastian grimaces, fully aware of the lecture he's about to receive. "A full third."

"You dulled a full third?" Dom's tone is flat.

Reluctantly, Bastian nods.

"A third isn't as bad as a half. But you're going to regret this one for days." Dom sits on the bed and pulls the reader out of the backpack. "You realize that's why they don't usually take a psionic off the drug once they put them on it, right? The backlash is dangerous. I've seen you do a quarter and go out drinking the next day. I wouldn't expect a third to lay you this flat. So what aren't you telling me?"

Bastian sighs. "Fine. Forty-five percent. Okay? I dulled down forty-five percent. Zach was my testing partner. There's no way he wouldn't notice. They only run these compulsory psi-evals every two years. I don't have to be this drastic for the next test. Besides, they won't throw me into the grids. I'm far too valuable."

Dom crosses his arms and taps his foot. "You've been doing this to yourself far too long. I worry about you. I can't babysit you both."

"You know why." Bastian smiles despite his tiredness.

"Your father's logic made sense. Disguise your power level and make sure you were there to take over once Mason left."

Bastian scowls. "One of the few times my father made any sense. Let's not bring Mason up. What's done is done."

Dom shrugs, his movements a bit more liquid than a human. "I may have helped you with this initially, but it doesn't mean I can't caution you."

"You're like an old woman, Dom." Bastian laughs and cringes at the pain in his head.

"That's the second time I've been told that today," the domino mutters, and a muted sheen passes briefly through his form.

"Second?" Bastian laughs again, and this time ignores the pain, watching his friend carefully. "I'll talk to her tomorrow. Hopefully, she'll listen."

"She'll listen," Dom states with certainty. "You realize she has nightmares constantly, don't you?"

Bastian can't bring himself to meet Dom's eyes.

"You shouldn't bait her like this. She's not ready for the brunt of it yet. Right now, you can't tell her everything she'll want to know. You have less than a day to come up with a valid excuse she'll accept for now."

"How astute of you."

Dom scowls. "Make sure you book me into that meeting. I won't want to miss this."

Bastian pulls the sheets tighter to fend off the sudden chill and wonders if his friend realizes his speech patterns are humanizing. "Enough about me, Dom. When's your bi-yearly? It has to be coming up."

"Several weeks. It's okay. I can seal my mind off easily enough. You just need to snap me out of it when they're done." Dom smiles tightly. The expression never sits quite right on his face. "Don't worry—I'll give you plenty of notice."

"Not sure what I'd do without you anymore."

Dom shrugs and throws the reader at Bastian. "Good thing you should never have to figure it out."

He touches his fingers to the side of his ear again and presses a short sequence. His eyes glaze momentarily, and then the gold bleeds back in. As he leaves the room, he tries to smile again.

This time Bastian can see the inherent sadness in it.

When the alarm sounds, Bastian twists instinctively to turn it off, groaning in pain at his aching body. It takes him longer than usual to get out of bed and dressed for the day, and his head still feels muddled, which means recovery from this dose of Shine is going to take longer than he anticipated.

His thoughts are so foggy it's a wonder he makes it into clothes at all, and he shambles toward his office, a cup of coffee clutched in his hand like a lifeline.

Bastian gasps involuntarily at the sight of his office doors. Sai's reaction had been pushed to the back of his mind in order to allow any type of sleep at all. Placing a hand on the wall, he grimaces. She didn't just damage the doors, but the walls as well.

Quite a feat, given that it took a team of dominos and psionic-masons to fuse them into place.

Not that Bastian blames her for being pissed off, but he needs to figure out a way to contain and channel that anger or Block 63 might happen again.

Aside from the doors, which pose a huge gap in his otherwise perfect shielding, every other aspect of his psionic defenses appear to be intact. A good thing considering his vulnerability when he's not at full strength. He's grateful he stored enough to tide him over.

The one thing he can't afford is an accidental overdose. Ending up in the testing facility isn't an option. Just the thought of numbly fueling the psionic suggestion grids is enough to make him shiver.

"Lost in thought?" Dom gingerly picks his way past the debris of the door.

"Never lost." Bastian walks over to his desk and picks up the reader on it before collapsing into his chair and continuing to mutter. "Perhaps sometimes partially misdirected, but never truly lost."

"Semantics."

Bastian raises an eyebrow at Dom. "Droll, definitely droll."

Dom ignores the quip and leans a hand against one of the doors. He frowns a bit as he concentrates. Bastian watches in fascination, and the adrium in Dom's form shimmers briefly as the parasitic and psionic components merge. Their almost flawless marriage validates the theory that the meteors of the Disaster Era caused the psionic gene to emerge. There's a subtle hum in the air, so soft and vibrant it sounds alive. Bastian shivers before he can suppress it, uncomfortable with the intimacy of the repair. The dominos affinity with metal makes a strange sense, but he's never seen any of the others singly exhibit this type of power.

The hum stops.

Dom squares his shoulders and studies the door. "Stop trying to analyze me. You know it doesn't work," he murmurs as he touches the steel once more. A resounding metallic clang reverberates through the room as the huge hunk of metal shifts back to the way it was before. Satisfied, Dom stands back. "There you go. Give me a day or so, and I'll be able to take care of the other one too. But you'll have to get a mason to repair the walls."

"You never cease to amaze me," Bastian says, fingering the report he's yet to read in his hands.

"You and me both."

Bastian glances at the reader again, filled out perfectly with meticulous phrasing and care. Dom probably wrote most of it for her. "Do you think you could fill me in on everything in the report—and those things not *in* the report?"

"That lazy?" But Dom heads over to the desk anyway. "You realize your office is extraordinarily large?" He glances over at the training area. "Was it necessary to have that in here?"

Bastian shrugs. "Means I have to move around less. And no, I'm not lazy. Today, I'm tired."

Dom seems a little embarrassed, the iridescent shades of his skin working in tandem with the sparks in his eyes to produce an oddly red hue. "About last night. I apologize. I wasn't thinking."

"She was bound to find out eventually anyway. Nosy little bugger. It may have been preferable at a later time, but it is what it is." He points at the report. "Summarize."

"They wasted our time by not using their own enforcement psionic to scan the accused's memory. He was telling the truth when he said he'd seen a valid ID. Valid in appearance anyway. From the record Sai made, it appeared to be one of the rehab facilities."

Bastian motions Dom to continue.

"He made the trade following guidelines. Artold didn't believe it because he didn't see anyone on his list and assumed the trader was lying. Sai reimbursed the trader for the inconvenience to his work, as well as for the injuries caused to him by the enforcers in UC 8. Then she reclaimed the money from Artold's future bonuses until that amount was paid back."

Bastian smiles as a small shot of relief briefly lessens his pain. "And she handled this all without help?"

"You know they don't give my kind the time of day, Bastian. Did you really have to ask?"

"I suppose not." He glances at the recorded image Sai plucked from the trader's mind and frowns. The Exiled are getting sloppy. That operative wasn't half as professional as he should be. "She held up under their scrutiny? Maintained a professional attitude?"

"She imitated you."

"Oh?" Bastian is flattered and wary at the same time. Imitating him isn't making her own persona. Imitations fall apart under pressure. "Might have to break her of that habit sooner than later. The quality of the render she plucked from his mind is almost as clear as what I get." Everything would be so much easier if there was a psionic ability handbook. Poking through her head full of tricks was beginning to feel like Russian roulette. He hopes the gun points at the intended target before she goes off.

Sai is more volatile than he realized. Bastian can't lie to her, not when he needs her to trust him. He needs her to believe him and *want* to work with him, instead of rebelling against anything he has to say because of her views on Shine usage.

"It's early. She's excused from classes today due to her late return last night?"

Dom nods.

"Let me know when she's in her rooms and we'll deal with it then."

Dom raises an eyebrow, mimicking one of Bastian's bad habits. He's getting better at it. "When she's in her rooms? You want to talk to her there?"

"If we leave her alone, she'll wallow. There's no way she'll end up coming here of her own accord." He stands up and starts pacing around his office.

Dom follows silently. After a few steps, he nudges Bastian's arm. "What are you doing?"

"I need to move."

"How're you going to talk to her about this?"

Bastian sighs. "I haven't a clue."

"You could tell her about you?"

"It's too long, far too convoluted, and almost too fantastical to believe." Bastian pushes his hair out of his eyes and makes a mental note to trim it as time allows. "She doesn't need to know a lot about me. What she needs to know is that I have valid reasons for using Shine and I'm not about to abandon her."

"Makes sense."

"Of course it does."

It's not even possible to explain the whole situation. He needs her allegiance to GNW to carry over until he can give her enough leeway to question things for herself.

"I can't tell her everything. But by the time we see her this evening, I can guarantee I'll have figured out some way to get her to listen to me and give me a chance. I have to."

"I know you have to." Dom's voice is soft. "You'll let me know if there's anything I can do to help you convince her, right?"

"Yes." Scenarios war in Bastian's head. "You know, there might just be something you can do, but it'll require a disconnect for you..."

Dom pauses for a moment, and a ghosting of colors ripple underneath his appearance. "Consider it done."

The knock on the half-repaired doors takes Bastian by surprise, and he refrains from pulling on his coat. Dom isn't due to arrive for another half hour.

"Deign." Bastian doesn't look up from tying his boots. He's long since preferred the antiquated footwear style. The modern ones that seal like a vacuum around his calves are far too confining.

"What did you do?" Deign picks her way through the entryway, distaste apparent in her tone.

Bastian shrugs. "A training mishap with my protégé."

Deign's brown eyes narrow. "I warned you about choosing her."

"You've warned me about a lot of things, Deign." He takes a deep breath. The woman always puts him on edge.

She smiles, the same predatory smile she wears in board meetings, and taps the side of her almost too pointy nose. "I took a lot of chances letting you take over from your father when you were barely eighteen, Bastian. You should heed me more, or I might take it away."

There are probably a lot of responses she expects, but Bastian laughing is not one of them. She scowls at the hearty sound. "You find this funny."

"Slightly, yes." He crosses his arms and looks her in the eye. Her height is, as usual, accentuated by old-fashioned heels so high she is almost level with him. Sometimes he wonders if it's difficult to balance on the stiletto ends. "You might have been able to take it away when he died suddenly three years ago or even shortly afterward. I've cemented my reputation since then. You know too many people fear me to go against me now."

The line on Deign's brow furrows, briefly exhibiting the faint wrinkles she tries to hide. She flicks her dark-brown hair over her shoulder, in a subtle show of irritation. "Watch your tone with me, Bastian. I've had people exterminated for less."

The *I know* sits on the tip of his tongue, but Bastian chokes it down. This isn't one of the battles he should choose. So, instead, he nods.

She leans in, the long fingernail on her pointer finger dragging down the shirt on his chest. "After all, you really should know best, shouldn't you, dear boy."

Her words stab like icicles all the way down his back, and she smiles, the corners turning up like a Cheshire cat as she deliberately licks her lips—once. With his attention on her, she exits the room with a flounce to her step. Bastian can't help shudder at the implications in the reminder that Deign is indeed the director of GNW.

Bastian flicks the collar of his coat up to ward off the withdrawal chills. The rate his body burns Shine has increased.

"Do that thing before we enter her room? I don't want anyone overhearing." Bastian motions pressing with his fingertips

Dom nods.

The rest of the walk is spent in silence. The soft swoosh of their steps makes him feel like he's hunting his student. Right now Bastian's happy he requested Sai not be given a roommate. Hopefully she'll feel more at ease in her own environment.

Just before they reach her room, Dom whites himself out from the domino connection, and his eyes change hue.

Bastian raises his hand and knocks, ready for the tentative probe that comes his way and even her indignation. The door opens just a crack.

"What do you want?"

Bastian feels her temper rising and chooses his words carefully. "I thought you might be more comfortable if we talk here."

The door closes and he hears a chain slide across. Resourceful of the girl to find an old latch for a tiny bit of added security, even if most people in the facility could just force it open.

She opens the door, gestures for them both to sit on the lilac bed, and curls up with her knees against her chest on her own.

Her eyes dart between them and she frowns. "There's almost no trace now..." The result seems to confuse her.

"Precisely." Bastian splays his hands against each other and studies his fingertips for a few seconds while he gathers the thoughts in his head, before looking back up at her. "You know your histories, correct?"

"Of the Psionic Wars?" Sai's words are clipped, and the scowl hasn't disappeared.

Bastian suppresses the sigh in his throat and clings to his patience. "And everything that came before them."

She fidgets and switches position on the bed. "You know I did well in my history class, Bastian."

Patience has never been Bastian's strength, though. "But did you really listen, Sai? If you had, you wouldn't be acting like a child."

"A child?" She clenches her fists and takes a deep breath. "I haven't been a child for a long time."

"My point exactly." He waves his hand to dismiss her protest and holds it up in a stop gesture. "Give me a chance to explain. I promise I didn't save you just to destroy you four years later. I don't have that sort of time to waste."

She glares at him, but doesn't say anything.

"Shine is a drug conceived by the brains behind Gerts, Newton & Williams Pharmaceuticals during the Psionic Wars. It was created to control psionic abilities. To limit us. To make our abilities more manageable." He waits for a moment and watches the immediate reaction. How her mouth parts slightly. The shock on her face as she fights against the truth. "Shine doesn't affect psionics except to diminish their abilities."

Sai shakes her head, then clutches her knees and leans forward. "But it affects people without an active gene?"

He smiles, lips thinly pressed together. She's so damn perceptive. "Heavily. They never intended it to go live on the streets. If there are no psionic abilities, it attacks the imagination centers of the human brain. The original drug can only be made in the lab, but there was some experimentation with a synthetic version that somehow got out. And now there are so many shoddy Shine producers, GNW can't contain it."

"Wait—they use it to control *us*?" She shivers and shakes her head. "Will they control me? Have they already done it?"

Bastian shakes his head. "It's not like that. They only control what people ask them to—"

"Ask them to?" Sai interrupts him incredulously.

"Families who don't know what to do with children who've awakened. Not everyone wants these abilities."

Sai slumps down, and the air whooshes out of her.

"Or people who they deem dangerous." He catches her gaze for emphasis. "Like me."

"But you're not..." She pauses, looking away for a moment before meeting his eyes again. "Surely they wouldn't do that."

"Only because I don't let them gauge me without Shine."

Sai's eyes open wide as it dawns on her. "Because you're a Rare?"

"Exactly."

Sai opens her mouth a couple of times only to sigh in frustration.

"What's wrong?"

"What do they do with the volunteers, with the people who don't want to be psionic?" She almost whispers the question.

He meets her eyes steadily. "Research."

"Would they do that to you? To us?"

Both Bastian and Dom nod.

"So if they find you out, you'll end up a research ...volunteer? What about me? Will I have to hide, too?"

Bastian smiles at her, relieved at her reaction. He can't lie to her, and she knows that. "Not at all, if I can help it. Shine was made with good intentions—it's just escalated out of control. As long as we're not a threat, we're GNW's greatest asset."

"And that's why only the strongest survive the final exam?" Her shoulders shake a little as she asks the question. "Because assets have to be strong?"

Bastian only hesitates a moment before nodding. "Exactly." He reinforces his smile and hopes the bitterness doesn't leak into his words.

Sai returns the smile tentatively. "I think I'll work on my shields."

"Good." Bastian stands. "Any more questions before I head out?" His knees threaten to buckle, but he wants to show her his Shine consumption isn't a big deal.

"The Exiled are the bad guys? Our enemies?"

Bastian pauses for a moment, choosing his words carefully. "How many people died in the Psionic Wars?"

She contemplates for a second. "Thousands upon thousands."

"Exactly. Regardless of original intentions, the Exiled helped start the war, and GNW finished it. As far as GNW is concerned, there is no greater threat."

"I thought so." Sai sets her jaw. "Thank you."

Bastian nods at her and leaves the room with Dom in tow.

CHAPTER
Seven

Sai stares at her sparse and tidy room. She's not used to having a whole day off. Normally even her weekend afternoons are spent sparring with Dom.

She goes over her personal shields again, building and rebuilding around her mind, tightening the mortar. It's like constructing a tightly woven brick wall, so she's not sure what else she should call it. Every time she practices the exercise, she improves her defenses.

Recently she added outer defenses to the routine in the same way she builds walls for her mind. They're not nearly as secure as they should be. Nothing like Bastian's office protection. That's a different type of reinforcement and requires a whole other level of concentration—concentration she can't find right now.

Regardless of how much she tries to distract herself, all thoughts center back in on Bastian the night before. She should never have let him get that close, but he'd just made her so very angry and scared.

Sai looks at her fingers and flexes them while she fits the last brick in the protective shield around her room. Perfect.

Bastian was still a little weak when he visited. Maybe she could help him. Perhaps what she's learned healing and shielding-wise will be of use in his recovery. Maybe even help others, normal people like her parents were.

With an energetic push up from her bed, she throws the door open, only to find Nimue there with her hand raised, about to knock on the now-open door.

"Nim?" Damn, had she really made her shields that tight? Sai checks, only to find Nimue is a tightly sealed block. "Are you okay?" she asks since the older girl hasn't moved.

Nimue blushes a little. "Sorry. I wasn't expecting the door to open."

"You seem shell-shocked." Sai waits and realizes it's probably rude not to invite someone into your room. "Want to come in?" She wonders if her reluctance shows.

Nimue smiles, and Sai's stomach twists as the guilt starts to boil. How much can it hurt to be polite?

She motions for Nimue to sit on the spare bed while she takes a seat on her own, knees pulled up to her chin. "What's up?"

Sai's never really understood the mechanics of friendship and chatter. Until recently, she and Nimue hard hardly exchanged more than a few words. The other girl always had her own group of friends to hang around with and generally appeared to have a lot more fun than Sai ever did. Most people treated her like a leper, but Nimue had always smiled, always been upfront about how she reacted.

"Not much." Nimue sits down on the bed with a frown and pats at the mattress. "Who *is* your roommate?"

"I don't have a roommate."

A sound like tiny cascading bells echoes through the room as Nimue laughs. "Lucky!"

Sai rocks a little, wondering why she doesn't have one. "Yeah..."

For a few moments Nimue is quiet. She chews on a few strands of her dark brown hair. "I've always admired you, you know."

"You have?" Sai's tone is dubious despite her effort to sound neutral.

Nimue takes a deep breath and continues. "They used to call you a monster, but all I ever saw was someone who woke badly."

"All I ever wanted was to be normal." Sai says the words so softly she's not even sure she said them out loud.

"Normal?"

Sai shrugs. "You know. Not psionic."

To her surprise, Nimue laughs again, but this time the sound is more bitter than Sai ever thought it could be. Chills run down her back.

"Normal isn't what it's cracked up to be, Sai. My family was *normal.*" Nimue spits the word out like it's tainted.

Sai stares at the girl, unsure of how to respond.

"Sorry." Nimue leans back and takes a deep breath, her brow momentarily furrowed with shadows Sai can't begin to fathom. "No one in my family is psionic. They didn't know what to do with me, so when I awoke they gave me away."

"Gave you away?" Sai isn't sure it's wise to let her know that, in order to be given away, someone had to sort of care where you ended up.

"Gave away. Swapped for a couple of years' worth of my father's wages." Nimue looks down, and for a moment before she wipes her cheek, Sai is certain she sees tears.

"Did you know I woke badly?" Nimue's voice is soft and tinged with sadness. "Worse than the majority of those people we schooled with, anyway. I maimed my babysitter and killed my cat. We were never sure how."

"Maimed?" Sai can't help herself.

"Sent her insane. She's never been the same. They keep her at Saint George's back in UC 17." Nimue worries at her fingernails. "After that, GNW took me off my parents' hands. I haven't seen them since."

Sai pauses for a moment, watching the other girl for her reaction. "I guess there are two sides to normal then."

"You think?"

Sai nods, a half-smile spreading across her face at the veiled sarcasm in the other girl's voice.

Nimue's shoulders drop as she continues. "I can make people feel better. Soothe their fears and worries. Make them feel like everything is fine. Deign says I'll fit in well here. Maybe I can make up for things..."

"That's a feeling I know all too well." Sai speaks softly, schooling her expression. Nimue is mentored by Deign? Talk about landing the higher-ups.

"I get so lonely around here. Even if they weren't really my friends, I miss having people around me. Here...I feel alone."

Nimue pulls her arms together, clutching her knees while she studies the floor.

"I never really notice, to be honest. I like keeping to myself."

"Yeah." Nimue looks straight at her. "You always did."

"Self-sufficient, that's me," Sai quips.

Nimue glances back down at the floor. "I wish I could be. Sometimes I feel so dependent."

"You never came across that way, Nim, ever." Sai leans back and stretches out her legs. "Tell you what. We could have breakfast together if you like? Lessen that loneliness early in the morning to hold you through the day?"

It's a generous offer for Sai to make, and the way Nimue beams is an amazing reward. Maybe the worry in the pit of Sai's stomach is indigestion.

"I'd like that. Thank you." Nimue stands up and smoothes down the purple track pants that are part of her training uniform. They fall loosely on the lanky girl. "I've taken up enough of your time."

"It's okay." Sai ushers her out of the room. "I'll see you tomorrow," she shouts over her shoulder as she switches focus and jogs to Bastian's quarters, a million questions inside her head.

Sai cringes at the sight of the doors when she arrives at Bastian's rooms. She steps carefully around the twisted one, wondering how the other got fixed so quickly. Bastian is bent over several glowing panels in his desk, dark hair falling over his eyes. It's the first time she's ever seen him without that coat, if she doesn't count seeing him in bed the previous night. Her cheeks flush.

"You know, I have one good door again. The least you could do is knock," He says without lifting his head. "Dom is busy regaining energy so he can fix the other one."

She interrupts him, curious. "I didn't think dominos had to regenerate."

"Not generally. This type of ability is different." Bastian pauses, his fingers flying over the panels. "I'll get the masons in to fix the rest."

"Those walls are stone?" she blurts out, before clapping her hands over her mouth.

Bastian finally looks up. "Some, and a mix of concrete interspersed with metal reinforcements." He watches her for a few seconds before continuing. "What're you doing here? I don't remember scheduling you."

"You didn't." Now that she's here, she can't bring herself to say what she wants to. Surely he's thought of fixing his Shine hangover through healing before. It's stupid to think she can help him. "Sorry. I shouldn't have come."

"Sai. Stop." His voice has that commanding quality to it, every bit as forceful as usual.

She stops and glowers at him.

"Tell me why you're here. You're not the sort of person to jog this far in order to say hi and leave."

"It was stupid of me. I..." She takes a deep breath. "I thought I might be able to help you."

"With?" He raises an eyebrow, waiting.

"Getting over that hangover." She wiggles her fingers for emphasis.

"Oh," he says and settles back into his chair, a thoughtful expression on his face. "That's an interesting thought. This dose seems to have gone sooner than I thought it would, but we could try it next time."

"It might be worth a shot." Sai kicks the toe of her shoe against the ground and tries to avoid his eyes.

"It's not a bad idea. It's a good one, just ill-timed right now. We can try next time."

She looks over at him and nods, pushing down the anger at the need for a next time. "I'll be going, then."

"Wait." He reaches forward and picks up one of the shining screens on his desk. The reader glints, reflecting the light from the windows. "Well done on your first mission. We're cutting things a little close lately. You'll be expected to do more fieldwork than I anticipated. I should know your next assignment in a day or two."

"In the next day or two?" Sai takes a step back. "I'm still a student, though. What if these people realize I don't really have authority?" What if they see through her pretense? What if they know making decisions terrifies her? What if she screws up? What if ...

"Stop it. Dammit, Sai. Get that chaotic thought process under control." He rounds the table and grabs her shoulders. "Regardless of how well you build those shields, they crumble when you stress. You're broadcasting distress to anyone with half a psionic gene. Control it!"

Sai pulls away, still able to feel the heat of his hands on her skin. "You're hot!"

Bastian shrugs. "I have a high basal body temperature."

Dom strides into the room, glancing at the doors as he passes them. "You really ought to shield better. You're audible from the halls."

Bastian's expression grows distant for a moment, before returning to normal. "Done. Don't think we're through, Sai. You should have the confidence. You aced guidelines and theory."

She glares at him. "I didn't ace it. I worked my butt off!"

"You know what the rules are and about enforcing them. Speaking of which..." He motions to Dom.

"As of tomorrow, you have physical target practice with me."

"Target practice?" Sai looks between them. "Why?"

Bastian raises an eyebrow in what appears to be mock-disbelief. "You honestly think defense is good enough? Just being able to defend yourself won't suffice. Sometimes you may need to go further. For the safety of yourself and others, you might have to terminate your target. If you can't act as a situation warrants, you're worthless in your position as an enforcer."

Sai balks. "What if I'd been required to do something like that yesterday?"

"That assignment was never going to be any real danger." Bastian waves her away. "Begin training with Dom tomorrow at 0800. Attend your classes in the afternoon."

Sai knows a dismissal from Bastian when she hears it and straightens her shoulders.

She turns to Dom. "I'm sorry about what I said the other day, Dom. I was angry. Don't hold my words against me."

He glances at her, an odd tinge to his golden eyes. "I would never hold your fears against you. Remember that."

Sai nods and leaves the room. Some days, she doesn't understand either of them.

Sai almost drops her tray of food when she turns to search for Nimue in the cafeteria and notices her sitting with Kabe and Deacon. Despite having classes with them for a couple of months now, she still doesn't feel comfortable chatting to people.

"Morning, guys," she forces the greeting out as she squeezes in next to Nim.

"Morning, Sai," they chorus around mouthfuls of food, and Sai can't help but smile.

Deacon glares at his tray. "We should get to sleep later than this."

Kabe laughs around the bread roll he's trying to cram into his mouth.

"Deacon doesn't sleep very well." Nimue smiles and bites her own roll.

He grunts at them both and concentrates on his food again.

"Got training first thing." Kabe leans back and stretches his arms out. "You're pretty lucky, Sai, you get to miss class a lot."

"Not really." She pushes her food back and forth on her plate. "I might get to avoid sitting in class, but I still have to do the work. And without class, it's a lot harder."

"Your mentor sends you out on assignments that take days?" Deacon asks incredulously. "I heard Bastian was harsh..."

Sai laughs. "He's not that bad, but I never have a dull moment."

Nimue makes a face. "Dull moments are sometimes nice."

"What, and stare at your four walls?" Kabe pats her on the back. "It's okay, Nim, we understand."

"So what if I like some alone time?" Nimue replies a little hotly.

"Who doesn't?" Sai mutters.

"See?" Nimue says triumphantly. "It's a girl thing. You two wouldn't understand."

They all laugh, and for a few moments, it's easy to pretend they're normal teenagers about to start a day of school. The feeling wears off as they say their goodbyes and go their separate ways.

Sai shuffles back to her room, going over the conversation in her head. The feeling of acceptance doesn't last long. Her skeptical side steps in to start questioning motives. She pushes the door to her room open and locks it behind her.

The hair rises on the back of her neck, and she turns quickly. "Dom!" She glances at the clock and frowns. "I thought we said 0800?"

He shrugs and leans against the bathroom doorframe. "We did. I'm early I thought I'd wait for you."

She nods with some relief and chides herself for allowing the moment of unwariness. It could have been anyone who had a weird affinity with the doors in the facility. "I should have noticed you were there when I opened the door." Sai dives into her closet to find the appropriate gear, popping her head out again when she realizes she hasn't a clue what she needs for the morning. "Sparring? Lifting? Running?"

"Something good for all three will do nicely." He leans back, stretching his arms out to prop him up.

"You're strange today, Dom," she says from inside the closet.

"What? Apart from being a domino?" His tone is mildly amused.

She shrugs and shoves some things into her backpack. "Every time I think I've figured you out, you evolve and come up with an entirely different response."

"Evolve?"

Sai glances over her shoulder to see him pursing his lips, although the expression doesn't quite work on his face. Despite taking on skin tone, there's a sheen to him. Sometimes he almost seems beautiful. She laughs at his thoughtful expression. "See?"

"I think I do." He stands up and flexes his hands. "Shall we?" he asks, but doesn't wait for her to answer before opening the door.

She mimics his walk behind his back and laughs again. It's the first time she's actually looked forward to training of any sort. Maybe this whole Enforcer deal isn't so bad after all.

Air expels from her lungs as she lands on her back with an undignified grunt. Whoever built the gym obviously lied when they said the floors were padded. She swears every landing finds a new piece of concrete poking through.

"Come at me like you mean it, Sai."

Dom's unending patience and inhuman endurance will probably be the end of her. She takes a few deep breaths and stands up, clutching the blade in her left hand. Being the one to initiate the attack has never been one of her strengths. She runs at him with full force. The only sound she makes is the whisper of her feet on the thinly padded ground.

Yet, she finds herself disarmed, rolled, and thrown to the ground—again. "How..." She rasps in a breath. "...the hell..."

Another breath, this one more painful. "...do you keep doing that?"

"You took self-defense. You know perfectly well how to do this. In fact, if my information serves me..." He pauses, a grimace spreading over his face as he drops to one knee. One hand shoots out to balance himself.

"Dom?" She scrambles up and runs to his side, though she doesn't dare touch him.

He doesn't respond. The hand not supporting him is raised to his temple, motionless. Like a statue.

Sai takes a step back, her blade slightly behind her. He's not moving, and she can see each muscle defined in iridescent beauty, shifting through every color it can find. For once, it even reaches his face. She watches, fascinated, as Dom blends into the color of the room, barely visible, and then back out to the opposite end of the spectrum. He's never lost form in front of her like this before. Slowly, she backs up to the wall.

Just as her brain convinces her to fetch Bastian, Dom's body shudders. His color solidifies and he shimmers, taking on the human appearance and complexion he always wears around her. Sai feels her cheeks grow hot as she wonders if everything about a domino can be molded and refined. But it's a brief thought she pushes away in embarrassment. It's none of her business.

Dom's eyes flicker open, whirring in a pinwheel of color until they finally rest on gold. The pain fades from his face, and he pushes himself upright.

"Dom?" she asks softly, not wanting to startle him.

It takes a second for him to pinpoint her. He pulls his hand away from his ear and studies his fingers for a few moments.

"Did I..." His vocal chords are skewed, and the sound comes out hollow and metallic. He clears his throat, a nasty scraping sound. "Did I hurt you?" His face scrunches up, furrowing his brows.

She steps back toward him. "No. You just...stopped."

"Anything else?"

"You...rainbowed."

"Rainbowed?"

"Yeah—that thing where you get all domino-naked and take on every hue possible." *And hurt my eyes,* she wants to add but doesn't. He'll have enough on his mind.

"Damn." He says the word so softly it sounds oddly unlike him.

"Are you okay?" She steps a little closer wanting to reach out and wipe that strange and un-Dom expression off his face.

He looks at her and straightens completely. "Yes, I'm fine. That was just...unexpected. It happens."

"I've never seen it happen." She crosses her arms and stares at him.

"Despite your abilities, Sai, you don't know everything." They're some of the harshest words he's ever spoken to her. "Which is also why we need to keep practicing this until you get it. Stance!"

Sai groans as he readies his stance and beckons her to try and take him down.

Sai limps down the hall and picks up a sandwich on the way to her room. If she's calculated correctly, she has about an hour to get to her bed, power nap, shower, and jog to her class. As long as the hot shower does its job on her aching muscles, it should be enough to get her through the rest of the day.

Every happy thought she had of cuddling a pillow for twenty-five minutes vanishes when she rounds the corner and sees Nimue sitting on the floor outside her room, back propped up against the door.

The girl scrambles to get up as she sees Sai approaching and smiles shyly. "I didn't see you around at lunch, so I thought maybe we could walk to class together?"

Sai takes a deep breath. "Sure. You'll have to excuse me while I shower though." If nothing else, she'll be able to get a good soak to sooth the aches. At least she managed two successful runs at Dom in the end.

Nimue nods as Sai unlocks the door and follows her into the room. "Make yourself comfortable," Sai says, not expecting Nimue to follow her into the bathroom or to pull down the toilet seat lid to sit on. While far larger than anything she had to herself in UC 17, the bathroom isn't made for two people at the same time.

Sai draws a blank. "It'll take a while..." she says lamely.

"That's okay," Nimue says. "Gives us time to chat."

Sai strips inside the shower cubicle. As she reaches out to drop her clothes down onto the floor, her fingers brush Nimue's when the other girl reaches to take the clothing from her. Sai jumps back, smacking her spine into the cold shower tiles, and forces herself to calm down.

Nimue calls out cheerily. "I'll pop these in your laundry bag."

The water is cold when Sai turns it on but heats up quickly. She tries to dismiss the rising claustrophobia. Usually, she can deal with the shower, but with Nimue sitting not three feet away from her, the cubicle feels inhumanly small.

She can hear Nimue chatting brightly on the other side of the shower door. About her breakfast and morning class; about her wish that they could have pets, although she's not sure what would be easy to obtain. The girl talks about shopping, clothes, and faculty staff Sai doesn't even think she's heard the name of. But most of all, Nimue just doesn't shut up.

Sai continues her shower, lathering herself under the hot water over and over again, until she glances at the time. She could be scolded by Resource Allocation for using as much of the precious water as she has, but Nimue's still in the steadily shrinking room with her. Close enough to touch. Far too close.

Her hands fumble for the taps, and she twists them off simultaneously. She clears her throat quietly and raises her voice so she can be sure Nimue will hear her. "Have to get out now, or we'll be late. Shouldn't take me too long."

"Sure," Nimue says. She hears her get up from her seat.

Sai's about to let out a sigh of relief when the shower cubicle door slides open, and Nimue hands her the towel. She snatches it away from the other girl and wraps it around herself. For an empath, the woman has no clue at all. Sai clenches her fists and bites her lip.

An almost inaudible gasp of breath, and the other girl's face pales. "I'm so sorry." Nimue backs away and the door closes behind her.

Sai waits a few moments before she lets herself breathe again. Maybe her shielding exercises have been more effective than she realized. Nimue may not originally have noticed the discomfort. Something about empaths lingers in the back of her mind—something about touch—but it escapes her grasp.

Her legs aren't just hurting when she steps out of the shower; they're shaking, barely able to hold her up. She never lets people get physically close to her. Not unless she's sparring, and then it's different. She's not vulnerable. Up close people can see the scars on her back where the cement and glass fragments dug into her skin. They can see the evidence of what she's done, of the things she has to make up for.

She wraps the towel tighter and breathes deeply again before opening the door to her room, kicking herself for forgetting to grab her change of clothes before taking the shower.

Just as she thought, Nimue sits on her bed, staring at her hands. She looks up at Sai when the bathroom door opens.

"I'm sorry. I didn't think. We all used to share our bath times back there. I never stopped and thought that you didn't join us. I didn't mean to..." Her words trail off, and she gazes out the window.

Sai forces a smile. "Perfectly okay. I'll grab a change of clothes, and we'll head to the class together." She grabs her things out of the closet and ducks back into the tiny bathroom again, shutting the door firmly behind her.

Throwing her hair up into a ponytail, she walks out, ready to go. She makes an effort not to limp as she leads Nimue out of the room.

"I'm really sorry, Sai."

"It's okay," Sai lies because Nimue really does seem uncomfortable. "I'm just not good with people and small spaces."

Nimue sighs. "I should have noticed that. I'm really sorry." For a few moments they walk in silence, until they reach the classroom and Nimue stops at the door for a second. "I'll try to explain later if I can."

Sai blinks at the words as Nimue turns her back and takes her seat. Kabe and Deacon wave in their direction before going back to their books.

Ms. Janni pops her head into the room and looks around. She catches Sai's eye and motions her to come to the door.

"Your domino is otherwise occupied," she says and hands Sai a letter. "I have to witness you opening it—so...open it."

Sai pulls out a dark blue card. For a moment, it appears to be blank, but after a few seconds, silver script appears on it. Despite herself, she's impressed. She watches as the words form, idly wondering if she has the same psionic skill.

Debriefing after class for assignment. Departing at 20:00 hours.

She sighs, ignoring the expectant expression on the class coordinator's face. Sai's joints ache in silent protest, and it's all she can do not to fight down a whimper of pain.

She just hopes Nimue will keep the explanation for when Sai gets back in a few days.

CHAPTER
Eight

"But Dom!" Sai rushes to try and catch up with him.

Dom ignores her as he carries both their packs down the hall to their hover-transport. He throws them inside and looks at her, as if he'd like to throw her in, too. She hurries to get into the vehicle before he can pursue that line of thought.

He climbs in after her, continuing to ignore her.

"I'm not ready for this. Mediate? I've never mediated anything in my life. I'm not calm enough to mediate." She stifles a yawn and pushes past the pillow-covered benches in the middle of the cab.

"Mediate is more code for 'beat them until they give into your way of thinking,' Sai."

"Oh." She glances at her hands. "How many people are we talking about?"

If she didn't know better, she'd think he sounded impatient. "You only have to deal with the head of each faction."

"I didn't think we had gangs anymore," she mutters.

His shoulders stiffen ever so slightly, and the tension escapes just as quickly as it arrived. "These are subsidiaries of GNW. They play a role in one of our major food manufactories. Let's just get them to agree to another decade's worth of signed contracts."

She grumbles and stretches, trying to displace the fatigue that won't leave her alone. "Why don't they just get you to do it?"

He swivels around to her, no expression at all on his face. "You *really* haven't figured that out yet, Sai?"

She shakes her head.

"You're human. Psionic or not, you're still human. I'm not. If they were considering wiping out both subsidiaries, they'd send in a unit of dominos so fast you'd miss it if you blinked. But they want them to stay operational, so they send you. Being human makes you ten times more trustworthy than the dominos no one understands."

"They produced enough of you. How can they do that and not understand you?"

"Good question. Get back to me when you have an answer." He fiddles with some dials as he guides the craft into the traffic stream.

She sits and blinks at him for a few seconds as the soft whirr of the GNW 335 fades into her awareness. The ship is compact, with room for holding cells in the back, and a black rubbery substance covering the floor that looks like it might be meant to hide blood. It's so quiet inside, the lack of noise is amazing. She glances at her notes, trying to redirect her focus as she wiggles into the co-pilot seat.

"Hear each of their sides and decide what's already been pre-decided upon for them. Got it."

Dom adds nothing to her thoughts, and she still doesn't grasp what she needs to do. Economics was her weakest subject. She yawns again and lets her eyes rest.

When she comes to, the cab is dark. A wave of panic hits her and she reaches out with her mind, sighing in relief as she realizes Dom is there.

"You really think I'd leave you sleeping in the transport?" He sounds amused.

"Not really. But it's dark and I don't think we're moving."

"You are correct on both counts."

"Why aren't we moving?"

"Control point," he says softly, and she watches with adjusting eyes as he ducks his head to check under the visor. "Set up to make sure illegals aren't being smuggled into the outer UCs. The official highways are patrolled."

"We're on the outskirts?"

He twists in his seat to look at her. "Did you not hear a word Bastian said last night?"

"I listened. I was just confused." She purses her lips. Crossing her arms, she glares pointedly at her wrist with the barely detectable band on it and back to Dom. "You forget I've never really had the chance to explore outside the schools."

Dom turns to watch things outside the transport before answering again. "In order to get to UC 21—which is where we need to be for this mediation, just in case you missed that as well—" She scowls at him in the dark. "—we need to cut across empty land, not directly under GNW control. When we return to the official highways, they need to check we didn't pick up any undesirables along the way. Understand?"

I'm not a child is on the tip of her tongue, but Sai realizes that's probably how she's been acting since getting dragged into this on such short notice. "Sorry, Dom. I didn't mean to be difficult. Do you have the file?"

"In there." He indicates the backpack at her feet. "I knew you'd need it in the end."

She opens the bag to retrieve it, but Dom's voice stops her.

"I wouldn't read it now. We're about to be inspected, and until they release us from their net, we're not going to have power enough to light your reader, let alone power this transport. Just sit tight and let them do their snooping. We're in a vehicle bearing insignias. They don't generally stay too long on Bastian's transports."

"Is this *Mele*?" Sai squints and tries to look around, eager to understand this vehicle Dom seems strangely fond of.

"No. *Mele* is currently indisposed." And as his voice trails off, the boarding begins.

He's right; it's short—takes all of five minutes, but they are five very long minutes. Men stand at the door, suited up in what appears to be a thin layer of armor. They click out a series of sounds with their tongues, and the misshapen human forms move into the vehicle.

Sai crinkles her nose at the strange dried meat smell that follows them, like the meat was left too long before being cured. Their bodysuits move in a strangely alien way, as if it sticks to their skin and rips off with a soft pop every time they take a step. Every few strides result in a squelch that reeks faintly of feces, rather like a momentarily opened sewer, as they linger around the rear of the transport.

Almost before she realizes it, Sai reaches out tentatively with her mind before pulling back in revulsion. Not even full contact and she wouldn't get closer. There's little resembling humans under those disguises.

The three creatures return to the men standing by the door, bowing their heads ever so slightly. An odd sort of lapping sound drifts back to her, almost like they're panting. Once stationary, the three armored humans talk in a series of odd grunts to Dom and get him to sign a tablet before they leave.

The lights in the cabin flicker back on, and she can feel the energy grid Dom spoke of kick back in as they start moving again.

"What were they, Dom?" Sai asks, shuddering at the memory of the black shiny holes where their eyes should have been.

"They call them Hounds. A little insane, but they sniff out what needs sniffing out. Once the Damascus were disabled after the Psionic Wars, Hounds were relegated human handlers. There's great hazard pay for the job." Dom smiles tightly and clenches the wheel in his hands.

Sai opens her reader and makes a mental note: Research the Psionic Wars in more detail than they were taught in class.

The blood on her knuckles is sticky. She's glad it's not her own. Sai bounces on the balls of her feet, dodging her opponent's sloppy left-right combinations until he leaves too big an opening for her to resist.

She draws back her arm and focuses her mind, briefly, on hardening the outer layer of her skin. Her fist connects with the side of her opponent's face, and the burly blond man's eyes finally roll up in his head as he falls to the floor to join the slighter, dark-haired man she knocked out a few minutes earlier.

Sai tries to stop bouncing, but the adrenaline is still rampant. Her hands hurt. She watches warily as a figure detaches himself from where the other spectators, the underdogs of the two companies, stand and observe.

It's not until she realizes it's Dom on his way over that she starts to relax and let go of the haze she's lapsed into. She nudges the blond guy with her toe and sighs. It didn't go anything like she'd planned in her head.

Sai had envisioned it going something like:

Hi, I'm from Central Enforcement. What seems to be the problem? Followed by demands which she would mediate and calmly explain were impossible.

Instead, her face now smarts where the first punch took her by surprise. If these people wanted to do business with their fists, who was she to say no?

Dom hands her a damp rag to clean her hands, and she stretches her jaw while she does so. She's lucky her instinctive jump back spared her taking the punch square in the face, thanks to Dom's recent training to help her avoid hits. Though, she probably retaliated more forcefully than she intended. His collarbone would *eventually* heal. It might even forecast the weather for him.

"How long do you think they'll be out?" she asks, pressing the cool cloth to her cheekbone.

Dom reaches down and takes their vitals. He shrugs as he stands up. "They're large men. Give them a few hours."

"Great. I don't even know what their demands are yet. The least they could have done is leave me with those." She gestures in the direction of the onlookers. "Those guys are never going to be willing to talk to us about whatever it is these guys want."

"True." Domino takes a few steps toward the group and watches them back up a couple of steps in response. "I don't suppose scaring it out of them would be a good option either?"

Sai fights a smile at the wistful tone in Dom's voice. "Probably not, but we have a couple of hours to waste, don't we?"

Dom nods and Sai steps forward, hands up in a calming motion. Personally, she thinks it looks like she's trying to do some sort of ancient dance, but it seems to have the desired effect because the crowd all take the step or two toward her.

"Excuse me." She figures it a good idea to be polite. After all, she must seem intimidating considering she beat the living snot out of the two guys on the ground. "I'm here to check over the contract for Yearn and Dawson Industries. I was hoping someone here would give me a final list of requests for the new contract, but..." She glances at her hands and shrugs. "I seem to be empty-handed."

She hears someone snicker and takes that as a good sign. "I'd be most obliged if anyone could help me in that regard."

Someone small in stature gets shoved out of the crowd. It's a child, an adolescent. Not much younger than herself. The papers in his hand catch the slight breeze and fight against his grip.

Sai takes a step forward to reach for the papers, grabbing them by the edge just as she hears loud shouts and a twang. The papers rip from the child's hands as Dom tumbles into her and the boy, rolling them both to the side.

"Dammit, Dom. That hurt."

She tries to stand up, but the pain in her side won't let her.

Domino looks at her, his strange eyes stalled in a hue she's never seen, a color she doesn't have a name for. "I'm so sorry."

Sai checks over the child, but the boy stares at her, eyes big as saucers. She follows his gaze to the bloodstain spreading around her lower left side. Mangled feathers attached to a shaft stick out of her stomach at an odd angle. She feels around her back tentatively and cringes as she encounters the sharpened point.

"Dom, get the guy." She gathers the papers in her hands and shoves them at the boy. He sits there, his eyes never leaving her wound.

"Dammit," she mutters through clenched teeth, starting to feel a little light-headed as Dom takes off to the crowd. At the edge of her vision she sees them wrestle the man to the ground, but Dom will deal with that.

She takes a deep breath and focuses on her body. A rabid bunny is one thing, but when her own body is leaking blood, the situation is completely different. The crossbow bolt is crudely fashioned, and she can feel rust flakes falling off the shaft and into her body when she concentrates on it. It's not going to be easy to get out, and she needs to move fast.

She calms herself, blocks out the pain as best she can, and tries not to think about the next step as she snaps the fletching off the back of the bolt. An involuntary gasp escapes her throat. Biting down on the pain and need to panic, she hears Dom's footsteps approaching and sighs in relief.

He crouches down next to her. "You need me to help?"

"I can't reach to pull the shaft out from behind, and pulling the tip back through the front will tear muscles." She says through clenched teeth. "Grab the arrow tip and yank it out so I can start the healing process. On three."

Dom nods and braces one hand against the middle of her back, the other gripping the section of shaft protruding from the wound. "One... Two..." he counts and then pulls.

A scream tears from Sai's throat, and she fights another wave of dizziness. A black haze intrudes on her vision and she banishes it by gulping in air.

Dom hasn't moved, and she gladly rests against his arm so she doesn't have to prop herself up. Bastian made sure she knows her body's own pathways over and over, but there's nothing like a sense of immediacy to make her forget.

Another deep breath and she begins the arduous task of pushing out the unwanted fragments and cleaning the wound from the inside out. Each little chip needs to be worked toward the exit, and the only ones she has are the entry and exit wounds. The effort leaves her gasping, but there is no time to rest.

Next, she moves onto the clipped vein leaking sluggishly into the wound. Her head spins, and she grounds herself with the contact Dom provides, as she encourages the healing process.

She takes another deep breath and turns to the muscles and tendons that were grazed by the tip, inordinately glad none of them were severed. The darkness threatens to overwhelm her again, but she draws on her reserves to make sure they meet their deadline.

With the insides repaired, she can finally turn to the entry and exit wounds. Flesh is just cosmetic, and not as important to Sai as it might be to others. A serviceable knit is all she needs until they can get back and let her apply some of the medi-kit tech in the transport.

Sai draws on reserves and pushes further, a distant pulse from deep inside drawing her on. She finishes closing the wound and sags back against Dom's side, gasping for air.

"I'm done," she whispers, sweat beading her forehead. Willpower is the only thing keeping her eyes open.

She heaves herself into a standing position with Dom's help and glares at the comatose bodies on the floor. "Get them into the holding cells. I need to lie down."

"Sai?" Dom takes a step after her as she stumbles to get her things.

"Later, Dom. Just get it done so we can deal with this and go home."

"I'll get the backpack."

Barely holding onto consciousness, Sai doesn't argue. She accepts Dom's help back to the transport. He's enlisted a couple of the spectators to help lug the bodies. Apparently his saving one of their children means they no longer find him to be a total monster. Several others huddle around a man with his hands and mouth bound. Sai can only assume he is the one who shot the crossbow bolt.

When they arrive at the transport, Sai eases herself gingerly into the passenger seat. She watches as Dom sets the holding cells up and maneuvers the men into them. The cells aren't large by any means. One folded-down seat. Enough to stretch out on if you're not too tall. They're sufficient for their purposes. Oddly, made of a strengthened adrium mix, they remind her of the rabid-bunny cages.

Her eyelids droop for a few seconds. The sound of Dom thanking the men for their help and assuring them he believes they weren't in league with the shooter or their bosses lulls her closer to sleep.

And then Dom is shaking her shoulder. "Sai, don't sleep. You're in shock. You need to stay awake for now."

She blinks up at him. "I'm so tired. Just a few minutes?" She can see he's about to give in, but something talks him out of it.

"No. Stay awake. I'll prepare some of your rations while you use this." He hands her one of the dermal-knitting lasers from the medi-kit. "Then you can eat and nap until they wake up. The passenger side can be reclined fully and should be more comfortable than sitting like you are. I can stand watch."

Sai nods and holds out her hand for the food, but even that's too much effort to do for long. Dom places a bowl in her lap and her head clears a little as she starts to replenish much-needed energy. "Thanks, Dom. Much better."

"Stick with me," he mutters as he digs around in the things they brought back on board. "If you can manage, you might want to arm yourself with their list of demands."

Sai sips at her tea and glowers at the notes in her hands. "They should feel lucky that I'm not dragging them back for Bastian to take care of."

"It's your assignment and your garbage to take out. Would you really have the guts to drop them on Bastian's doorstep?"

Sai closes her eyes in resignation and fatigue, knowing she really doesn't have to answer that question.

It's already dark when Dom wakes Sai. "They're coming around. You beat them better than I thought. It's been over twelve hours."

"Seriously?" Sai asks, rubbing her eyes with the back of her hand. She knows she's stronger than she looks, especially when she uses psionic skill to reinforce her physical abilities. "I didn't think you meant it when you said to beat it out of them..."

"Neither did I."

"I didn't pull my skill."

In the dim light she swears Dom smiles. "I know," is all he says before slowly un-dimming the lights. "They're all yours, my dear." He mock-bows at her before he sits down at the pilot console and activates the recorder.

Sai picks up the notes the boy held and walks over to the cells, pushing her pain to the side. It's bearable as long as she doesn't move too quickly. She drags her blade along each bar with loud metallic clangs and waits as two of them clutch their heads and roll into sitting positions. The man who shot her doesn't stir. "Good evening, gentlemen."

They don't answer her and focus their gazes on the floor. There's only hard black rubber to look at, but they seem to find it fascinating.

"Did you really think that because I'm small I'd be a pushover? Central takes your situation far more seriously than that." She waves the pages in front of them. "These, or so I'm told, are your demands. Give me a reason I should bother to study these in light of how you *greeted* me."

The blond one—Yearns, if she remembers correctly—clears his throat. "Our families have served GNW for over twenty years. We're proud of our accomplishments and legacy as a company.

But our profits are a shadow of what they should be. GNW regulations demand too much of our supply and keep too much of our profit from what they acquire."

Sai raises her eyebrow. "You want more money? From GNW?"

Both men nod.

"Do you realize there are at least thirty other companies we could acquire produce from? They'd be more than happy to take less in payment than you do because of the volume and consistent profit that it means for them, their families, and their employees."

Dawson gulps and casts his gaze toward the floor again, finding something in the depth of the rubber he can engross himself in. Yearn, on the other hand, sets his jaw stubbornly, crosses his arms, and stares at her.

Sai faces him directly, ignoring the throbbing in her side. "Greed isn't a pretty quality in anyone, Mr. Yearn. You take the protection and the trade routes GNW provide you with. I know you make good profits despite your claims because I have your financial reports on hand. The real ones."

She waits for that piece of information to sink in and watches his shoulders sink. "I'm still trying to figure out why I shouldn't just renegotiate your contracts by giving them to someone else, especially since I now have to investigate why one of your employees wanted to shoot me."

Yearn's complexion turns positively gray. "We had nothing to do with that! He did that out of his own frustration."

She glances at Dom, who nods almost imperceptibly. "That might be what saves you."

Her body starts to shake ever so slightly. Bravado can only take her so far. Sai claps her hands. "What do you say we sign those contracts you were sent three months ago, and we're good to go for the next decade?" Both men nod, their shoulders slumped and heads down. "See, I knew you'd understand. Dom, could you get the contracts?" she asks in a sugar-sweet voice, eyes never leaving their three guests. "The altercation will go on file. Your friend will accompany us back to Central and be dealt with accordingly. We've got you on the list now." She taps her temple and turns around to open the hatch.

It's cool outside, with the chill of the approaching winter soft on the air. For a moment it takes her breath away—that she's hurt, that she's here, that it's been over three months since her final test. But then she closes her eyes and counts to ten, letting some elusive calm sweep over her. Pretending to be in control and actually *being* in control are two entirely different things. Not to mention the shaking in her legs and the effort it's taking to keep her body upright.

Sai tries to ignore the pain in her side. She still doesn't understand how she missed the tell-tale signs of a shooter, but it's very different in reality than it is in a theory.

She listens to Dom ushering the men to sign and then releasing the two from their cells. It's difficult to block the sound out and focus a sliver of her power on checking the wound. Sitting down isn't an option because it's seen as a sign of weakness, but the paranoia she has about having healed a serious wound requires she recheck it and leaning against the hull is the compromise.

Being outside feels more vulnerable, but she waits until the men are escorted away from the transport before entering the cabin again. Dom finishes reverting two of the holding cells back to their original form and leaves the third visually blocked off from them. Sai can't help the sigh of relief at not having to watch the sleeping man on the ride back.

"I'll have your bed ready in a few, Sai. You can sleep on the way home. You need it."

Shaking her head, she sits down on one of the smaller single seats behind the driver, facing toward the benches he's making into the bed. She puts her hands under her butt to ward off the sudden chill. "I don't want to. I'll sense them all over those cushions..."

Dom looks up at her and frowns. He reaches out a hand to feel her forehead. "You're warm. Are you sure you're okay?"

She bites her lip and glances away. "No, I'm really not. If they'd have combined their attack, there's no way I'd have knocked them both out cold. One day someone will call me on my bullshitting, and I'll be exposed. They'll realize I'm nothing more than a kid posturing as an enforcer, and all hell will break loose."

"Don't be silly." He kneels down, taking one hand.

"I couldn't even keep this from happening!" Sai knows the tinge of hysteria in her voice is bad, but the wound has shaken her.

Dom shrugs. "Not many people would have been able to. If you're posturing, you're doing fine. Being so harsh all the time will turn you into a female Bastian. How am I supposed to deal with two of you?"

Sai gapes at him and laughs despite herself, cringing at the ache in her side.

"Let me see." Since it's not really a question, she leans to the side as he gently lifts up her shirt. He draws in a breath, a hiss through his teeth. "May I?" he asks softly.

She has no idea what concerns him, but nods anyway, closing her eyes tightly. A soft humming starts in her head as soon as Dom's hand touches her skin. It's accompanied by a beautiful warmth that overrides the pain. She feels so safe and so calm she gasps with surprise.

"Did I hurt you?" Dom asks, but the warmth continues.

"No." Sai is afraid to move. After a few minutes, the humming stops and the warmth subsides. Her side feels almost as good as new. "What did you...?" She looks down at him in amazement and, for a moment, thinks he's beautiful. His gold eyes glow softly and there's a shimmer of incandescence around him, like his camouflage is fading.

"Once something is tentatively healed through psionics, I can encourage it." He smiles and stands up, his hand lingering on her shoulder for a moment. "You'll feel extremely tired soon. We should get you comfortable."

"I'll sleep in the passenger seat if that's okay. I don't want to sleep where they were."

Dom holds her gaze for so long she starts to feel a little dizzy, and then he nods. "You'll be safe up front."

Sai smiles and barely settles down in the seat before complete exhaustion overtakes her.

The shiver down her back wakes Sai up at the roadblock to get back into the cities north of Central. Sai sits upright and turns around, noticing Hounds leaving their transport and giving Dom the go-ahead.

He glances at her before pulling back into traffic. "Sorry about that. I was hoping you'd manage to sleep through them. How're you feeling?"

"Insatiably curious about what a Hound is."

"You're feeling like yourself again then." Dom checks a few of the switches on the console, the cameras, and settles into cruise. He leans back and looks at her, crossing his arms. "A Hound is a failed version of me."

"Say what?"

"Well, not me, but the Domino Project, which initially began decades before the wars. They were the first attempt at making the perfect disposable killer but are far more animalistic than intended. Bound by blood to their handlers, they're currently used to sniff out illegal substances and people."

Sai scrunches her face up, trying to figure it out. "They're related to dominos?"

"Not exactly. They experimented with their sense of smell and hearing, their shell or skin. Don't let one rub up against you. Their skin is abrasive and noxious. Hounds were a part of the process before they thought to introduce the adrium compound into the mix, before they figured out we could synthesize it. Even before the Damascus."

Sai shudders at the mention.

"If the Damascus were operational right now, the Hounds wouldn't be handled by humans, regardless of blood ties."

"Why?"

Dom shrugs. "No one knows. When the Damascus were created, the Hounds' loyalties shifted immediately. Since the

Damascus have been in stasis for the past two decades, the Hounds are less dangerous." He pauses for a moment, his expression darkening. "There's nothing we can do about it anyway. Not about any part of the project."

"You make it sound like you regret being..." Sai stops on the word, not sure how to phrase "being created."

"Sometimes I believe there are instances where humans shouldn't play god, even if I'm the result of one of them."

Sai leans back, slightly confused by Dom's demeanor. No emotions flicker across his face, and his almost reflective imitation of skin dulls for a brief moment.

"Make sure you've filled out your report of the incident in full. We'll deliver our guest to Markus and head straight over to give Bastian the report. He should feed you. Assignments are rolling in. We'll be on our way again shortly."

Sai balks at the information, as well as the complete change of subject. "Do I get time to heal?"

"Maybe."

"You're kidding, right?"

Dom glances sideways at her and shrugs again. "I really wasn't created to kid, Sai."

CHAPTER
Nine

Waiting, especially sitting down alone at a table in one of Central's nicest restaurants, has never been one of Bastian's strong suits. He glances at the menu, sure of his order since before he walked through the door, and eyes the stained glass at the entry as it opens.

Zach raises his hands in defeat and sits down, oblivious to the patrons surrounding them. The deep blue of his suit matches perfectly with the plush velvet of the antique chairs and the brown accents in his tie complete the look. "The woman doesn't know what she's doing, Bastian. She's running this company into the ground."

Bastian glances at his watch, suppresses a sigh, and reminds himself again that Zach likes to be the center of attention always. "I take it you mean Deign? Again?"

Zach blinks and reaches for the glass of wine delivered

stealthily by their attendant. The crystal sings softly as he swirls the liquid. "Who else would I be talking about? Are you paying attention to me, Basty?"

No, Bastian thinks as he pushes himself upright. He clears his throat before speaking softly. "So you're saying the unforeseen profits we've had since Deign took over eight years ago would be much higher with you in her place?"

Zach glares at him and rolls his eyes melodramatically. "Listen, Basty. You don't have the drive I do." He glances at Bastian with unconcealed pity in his eyes. "After all, you've never really cared about the politics of it all. Not since your old man..." He grins and changes the subject. "I've always excelled where it counted, and you sort of drifted along and succeeded in your own way. Not that the jobs you, uh, *do* aren't extremely important." Zach daintily avoids naming Bastian's real purpose. Sitting in one of the most popular restaurants in Central, with its remnants from earth long before the Disaster Era, it's probably best to avoid anything indelicate. "The school needs you. But apart from that, it's nothing that the people depend on now, is it?"

Bastian waits for the lecture to continue, hating the dulling taste of Shine on his tongue. It mixes strangely with the cabernet, giving it a bitter aftertaste. The only reason Bastian ever has to be wary of Zach is his friend's ability to sense psionic strength. He picks the people who fuel the psionic grids overlaying the cities. Zach is the reason Rares are so scarce.

He allows his gaze to drift around the old-fashioned decor. Almost everything at Riccardo's is old, and if it isn't, it's made to look like it. The prices can only be afforded by inner-city Central inhabitants, of course, but then again, most things are...

"The city agencies I run have become extremely profitable. It's not all her doing," Zach continues, a slightly whiny undertone poisoning his words.

"And I 'take it my graduates who provide fuel to the suggestion grids don't contribute either?" Bastian doesn't rely on volume to drive home his point.

Zach pales for a moment but covers it with a grin. At some stage, the server miraculously refilled his drink. "How *is* the student body doing?"

Bastian leans forward and takes another sip of his own drink to stave off the horror he constantly feels at so many young lives lost. "You should know. You helped select the final examinations."

"Point being, I thought only specific candidates were supposed to make it." The smile is gone from Zach's face.

Bastian leans back and shrugs, sealing the mortar of his shields tighter. The young girl inconspicuously serving their meals reminds him of Sai. "We were bound to be surprised one day."

Zach chuckles, but the expression doesn't reach his eyes. "I'm only sorry I couldn't be there."

"And is Kabe measuring up to your levels of sneakiness?" Bastian makes sure his tone is light and inoffensive.

Zach barks out an arrogant, self-assured laugh. "He can try to meet my standards." He winks at Bastian before downing his glass in one shot. "You even found an empath for Deign for once. She'll be good for the grid. Empathy is always the best way to direct any type of suggestion."

"It is, isn't it?" Bastian pops a bit of salad into his mouth. The taste is almost lifeless, and he wishes that for once he visited this place when he didn't have to dull his senses.

"Of course! You know it. You placed her there. And they all thought you were too young to take over."

Bastian raises an eyebrow as he takes another tasteless bite of his food.

"I'm not sure quite how you managed it, old friend, but people in this school fear you. Good for you. 'Rule with an iron fist,' our fathers always said, eh?"

Sometimes Bastian wonders why Zach wasn't drowned in the bathtub as a child. His arrogance leaves him oblivious to anything that doesn't directly affect him. Full of good intentions GNW might be, but reverting government back to inherited positions was one of their major flaws.

"We're going to have to do something about the Exiled. I heard your girl was shot."

Bastian nods, sips his drink, and tries not to tighten his grip to the point he breaks the glass. Dom didn't mention Sai was shot in their last communication. Bastian doesn't like being the last to know. "I don't believe it was the Exiled."

Zach shrugs. "We'll know for certain when they deliver the man to Markus."

"Of course."

Zach watches Bastian for a few seconds. "I've been getting a trickle of information, but nothing solid. You'll take care of it when I have something substantial, of course?" He asks the question carefully, shifting his gaze to the wine in his hand. Asking someone to eliminate a likely human problem is always awkward.

"You know I will. Anything for the greater good."

"You're a good man, Basty. You've always had that outer

calm." He pauses for a second, lips pursed, and then shrugs. "I'm not sure how you do it."

"Because I have to." It slips out before Bastian can stop it. He smiles tightly to lighten the mood. "Comes from losing my mother at such a young age." It's not a lie. That exact moment is when his entire life's purpose fell perfectly into place.

"Sarah would be proud of you." Zach downs the rest of his drink and glances at his watch. "Must go and entertain Deign. Have to make sure her new little brat doesn't accidentally brush against me when she takes my coat. Poisonous little thing, that one."

Bastian raises an eyebrow. "You know the touch has to be prolonged, right?"

"You never know." Zach grins. "Thank your girl for me."

Bastian stands and shakes hands with his oldest and worst friend. "I'll see you soon, Zach."

"Don't be a stranger, Basty. You know where I am."

Watching as he leaves Riccardo's, Bastian wishes Zach hadn't always been as fickle as he is. Perhaps they could have had a true friendship instead of...this.

Bastian hears them coming down the hall before they knock on his door. "Come in," he says, unable to stave off the exasperation.

"What's up, boss?" Sai's greeting is over-bright. "You sound annoyed."

"You're spies? More like elephants in disguise."

"Can't be." Sai lowers herself into a seat. "Elephants have

been extinct for a hundred and seventy-five years."

Bastian glances at her, not sure if she's serious or not. Her pupils seem unnaturally large, and he raises an eyebrow at Dom.

"She's tired and stressed. You sent us into an ambush."

"Not my intention." Bastian stands up, walks over to lean on the edge of the desk, and crosses his arms. "I heard you got shot."

Sai closes her eyes and pulls at a strand of her hair, twirling it around her finger so tightly it probably hurts. "I got shot. Dom saved me. Would have hit me in a place I couldn't stop the bleeding fast enough if he hadn't knocked me out of the way."

Bastian looks back at Dom. "That bad?"

Dom shakes his head and motions for him to be quiet. It's difficult not to push, but it means Dom will talk to him later about it.

Bastian tries a different approach. "The culprit?"

Sai shrugs. "Some disgruntled employee who acted out of rage after I...rebutted Yearns and Dawson's arguments. He's with Markus now."

"Food is ordered. I've read through the file you sent ahead. Frankly, Sai, you don't seem well." He lowers his voice with the last, unable to keep the concern from it.

"Thanks, boss." She waves at him, eyes drooping, and focuses on her hands. "I don't like these assignments. I'm not the person I pretend to be. One day, that'll be dangerous."

"Do you know why I send you, Sai?"

She looks up at him, as if he'll give her all the answers. "No."

"I send you because I know that, if it comes down to it, you *can* be dangerous. There are a lot of people who can pretend. Perhaps even some that can act it out. But when all is said and done, if you get into a pinch, I can count on you to *be* the dangerous element you're pretending to be. Even if you're scared at first." He pauses and watches her bite her lip and turn away from him.

"Sai, you were born with this ability for a reason. Just like I was." He kneels and turns her chair to face him, pretending not to see the tears decorating her face. "Just like Dom was created for a reason. Do you understand?"

She nods and raises her chin, setting her jaw.

"There it is," he says and stands again. "I thought you'd lost the spitfire in you for a second."

"You wish." She laughs weakly, but at least it's a laugh. After a moment she sighs and looks up at him again. "You mentioned food?"

"Oh, I thought with all this feeling-sorry-for-yourself, you might not be hungry." He pretends to press the communications panel on the desk.

"No!" She reaches forward and stops him. "I'm starving. Transport rations are horrible and the healing took it out of me."

"Don't worry. I'm not canceling. Dom might kill me."

She leans back in her chair, watching him warily. "You're in a good mood tonight. I'm not used to seeing you like this."

"My killjoy. I'm in a good mood because I got to see someone today I haven't seen in a while and am not sure how much I'll get to see of him in the future." There's a resounding knock at the door. "Perfect timing. That would be our dinner."

Sai's expression is blissful as she bites into food she's likely never tasted before. Even though the fare is less extravagant than what he ate for lunch, Bastian enjoys watching her experience it. It's amazing how much of an impact a simple roasted sandwich can have on someone unused to good food.

Bastian tries hard not to think about the animals bred and raised in concrete shelters in the outer areas of the UCs, past even where Sai grew up. They have to provide meat to the populace somehow, but if he thinks about it too much, he'll revert to only eating the consumables in the hydroponic shelters.

Sai smiles in contentment as she finishes her last bite and pats her waist. He often forgets her origins. Life below the poverty line and in the training facility hasn't given her palette much of a range.

"Take my guest quarters for now. You leave shortly after midnight, so you may as well sleep here. Dom and I will plan your next assignment while you do. You need to be as rested as possible."

"Fine." But she smiles as she heads to the other side of the room.

"To the right, not the left," he calls as she almost wanders into his room. The slight hitch to her step is worrisome.

"Oops."

Bastian pushes his hair back and stares hard at Dom. "Are you going to tell me how the hell she got shot at on such a routine mission?"

"It wasn't exactly routine, Bastian. They jumped her from the moment we walked in and had no intention to negotiate. What they didn't count on when they were told a woman was coming to mediate for them was that she'd kick them back into last century."

"Hundreds of years and we still have chauvinistic pigs. She gave as good as she got, though?" Bastian can't help but smile.

"Better. One hit glanced off her face, and she almost gave the guy a concussion with one punch in retaliation. Admittedly, she did pack her punches with skill. Her speed and ability to reinforce her strength with psionics are what make her lethal."

"The shot came after?"

"Just as the crowd was warming to her. They even sent in a kid with the demands." Dom shakes his head and avoids Bastian's gaze for a moment.

"What?"

"If I hadn't been trying to save the kid, too, she wouldn't have been hit at all."

"Tell me..." Bastian pauses, thinking of the best way to phrase it. "If you hadn't saved the kid, would the mob have tried to kill you both?"

"I can't say with certainty," Dom admits.

Bastian pushes the point. "But you know they wouldn't have dismissed the death of one of their children, don't you?"

"That seems extremely unlikely. Even if the culprit was one of their own, they were appreciative of him being saved."

"That's it exactly. Don't blame yourself, Dom. She's fine." Bastian waits for his words to sink in. "And you caught the culprit, right?"

"No." Dom grimaces and puts his head in his hands as a ripple of emotion passes over his frame. "I spent too long making sure she'd be okay, and they caught the culprit."

"Not too long. She's alive, and the child is alive. Those are both very good things."

"Then why do I feel so..." Dom searches for a word. "Guilty?"

Bastian eyes his friend, weighing exactly what to say. Dom is still developing, taking on pieces of what he can be. "Because you're far too human for your own good. Might want to block out that emotion from your connection before the others go insane trying to process it."

"Human emotion *can* be a weakness." Dom's eyes grow distant for a while before he blinks them back to normal. "She gets under your skin."

"Sai?" Bastian glances back to the door into the other rooms. "She does a bit, doesn't she?" He clears the table off and puts the trays back on the cart outside his door. "I'm due to make another drop this weekend. I'll meet Mathur, make the delivery and verify the next step. We need to set things in motion before you go for your lab visit. I wish we could avoid you having to go in."

Dom hesitates for a moment. "I actually think I might need a check-over at the moment. I've been having occasional blackouts."

Bastian doesn't look up, but flicks through a few files as they come in. "You always have blackouts. That communication channel has always worried Mathur."

"Not blackouts of sound and communication. Blackouts of myself...where I lose my sense of self and of control over anything. Sai said I rainbowed."

That draws Bastian's attention. "Sai saw one of these?"

"While we trained. It didn't last long, but I'm not the most comfortable thing to be around when I can't control my appearance." Dom turns away, an uncharacteristic sag to his shoulders.

"Rainbowed doesn't sound like a good thing. I'll bring it up with Mathur and see what he thinks."

"Thanks." Dom finally sits down again, but manages to appear uncomfortable while doing so. Bastian can't help but chuckle.

"By the way..." Dom leans back a little, taking a reader off Bastian. "We need a nicer transport. Give the girl a break. Spoil her a bit while you can. You'll owe her enough soon."

"Fine." Bastian rummages in his desk and throws a tiny chip at Dom. "Take mine. I'll take care of the electrical registrations. Just be nice to it. Took me forever to get a GNW-4 class transport."

"Nice." Dom seems satisfied.

Bastian watches in fascination as the adrium closes around the chip on Dom's wrist. "*Mele* still not ready?"

A pained expression crosses Dom's face. "No. I should have known better than to allow her to be piloted by anyone but me."

"That bad?"

"Not completely. She just needs time to regenerate. The vast majority of her construction is adrium. In a very real sense, she's partially sentient. Her reserves can fuel through me. Our components were made to work together. She'll be ready soon."

"Good." Bastian stretches and cracks his neck. "Briefing time. Sai has three assignments we need done in the next ten days. I don't have time for them and hope you can keep her safe enough to get through them unscathed. If you need to, step in, understood?"

Dom nods and looks at his own copy of the commands as they start organizing their transport route.

The GNW board of directors meets at least twice a week depending on the time of year and the agenda they need to cover. Bastian dreads the days with a passion, and not just due to the need to tone down his levels with Shine.

Deign sits at the head of the table to his left. The irony of sitting at her right hand never ceases to amuse him. She waits patiently, toned legs crossed while she studies her nails. Bastian tries to ignore the flickering lights through the large boardroom windows. The view of the advertisement interface from here never fails to irritate him.

Zach takes his place opposite Bastian. Markus files in and plops himself down next to Bastian with a brief friendly smile. Davis, the lead on the current leg of the Domino Project and head of the scientific research division, saunters in with his trusty sidekick Selwyn. They barely glance at Bastian. It's difficult for Davis to squeeze his portly figure into the chair next to Zach, but he manages eventually.

Harlow follows closely behind them and takes her seat next to Markus with a curt nod. She's in charge of security and intel, with a hand in all the computerized systems throughout GNW. Her dark brown hair is twisted neatly up on her head, and her eyes constantly change between blue and green, depending on which facet of the security system her implants are interfacing with.

Markus leans over and interrupts Bastian's train of thought. "I've got the culprit locked down. How's Sai?"

"Well as can be expected."

"Adapting well?"

"Better than anticipated."

"Excellent." The older man claps Bastian on the shoulder and smiles.

Harlow's assistant, Lourd, nudges Selwyn to the side of the room and the small station usually reserved for them. He glares at her, but apparently thinks better than to argue and takes his assigned place with a scowl on his face. In the meantime, the military coordinator Jameson files into the room, closing the door behind him. It's hard for Bastian to forget that half of these people opposed his taking over his father's role a few short years ago.

"Great." Deign pushes herself to a standing position, not a crinkle in her freshly pressed suit, and taps the table lightly to activate the interface screens. "We have a long agenda today." She glances down at her section of table as notes flash through to her.

"Thank you, Bastian, for renegotiating the produce treaty. Let your student knows she's appreciated."

Bastian bows his head politely.

"I need department budgets by next week's meeting if you haven't already turned them in." Again she smiles at Bastian. He squirms a little, despite efforts not to. Being efficient is part of his nature; he doesn't do it to outshine anyone.

"What we need to discuss today are ways to counter the Exiled threat spreading through our cities." Her tone is grim and all movement in the room stops.

Harlow clears her throat. "I'm initiating a damper field around the cities to identify non-GNW citizens. It works in conjunction with bracelets and chip implants."

"We've also increased patrols around the perimeters of each city," Markus says in his quiet, commanding voice. "Identifiers will pulse through checkpoints more frequently, and thanks to the recording Bastian's protégé took of the false IDs used to circumvent security, we have a better idea of what to search for."

"How do you plan on seeing through the forgeries?" Zach

asks, crossing his arms and smirking.

Bastian suppresses a sigh, and Jameson butts in. "Genetically. All patrols will have at least one person with the dormant psionic gene."

Markus nods and continues his explanation. "I'm coordinating with Bastian to ensure full suggestion through the grid so citizens check twice when an ID is scanned for high-risk purchases. If we suggest those are more suspect, they will think it."

Deign nods. "You need to be stricter with the suggestion grid anyway, Bastian. I've had news of some murmurings in the further blocks. Clamp down on that. A populace who thinks they're happy *is* happy."

Bastian nods and reminds himself to breathe. It's not the first time since she backed his tenure as dean that he's done Deign's work for her. "I'll revise the thought influence divisions and have them for you next week."

"Fantastic." Deign smiles and carries on with the meeting. The rest passes in a blur.

It's not until he walks the halls back to his rooms that he has his first run-in with the girl he assigned to Deign. She barrels into him just shy of his quarters and ends up grabbing at his arm, clutching it as if to keep her balance.

"I'm so sorry, Mr. Bastian. I didn't see you."

He looks into those insincere eyes and follows her body down to where she's clutching his gloved hand.

She moves away at the scrutiny, blushing slightly.

"I believe what you need, Nimue, is prolonged physical contact, which my gloves do not allow. A nice ruse, but you forget I know what you can do because I picked you and sent you into Deign's care. If you'd like, I can remove this..." He slowly, deliberately never breaking eye contact, removes each finger of the soft leather gloves that used to be his father's. He holds out his bare hands to her. "...and we can really see who's stronger?"

Nimue pales and backs up a few steps.

"Or else, you can make sure you don't pull this stunt again on me or any of mine. I'll leave you to run back and wish your dear mentor better luck next time."

Nimue takes the chance to nod once, murmuring under her breath, "Thank you, Mr. Bastian," and sprints off down the hallway.

"Damn," he mutters as he puts his gloves back on. "She chose the second option."

Bastian sits in the smoky tavern's back room pretending to take part in a pokshu game. His cleverly woven guise will make even the hardiest psionic believe that's what he's doing and discourage their attention at the same time. While illusions might only be good for stationary implementations of confusion, they're ideal for the current situation.

Trying to illusion a moving target on the other hand... Bastian chuckles and earns an odd look from Mathur.

"Amused?" the older man asks, a well-worn card flying from his hand.

"Too often for my own good." Bastian sighs and glances at the card. A fisher king? He wracks his brain for the rules. It's been far too long since he played, and he's exhausted.

Mathur grins slyly, and Bastian knows the man is aware of

his card predicament. "You seem tired. For how young you are, you should have more of the exuberance, my friend."

"Your jokes really aren't going to work on me today, old man. I don't have the energy to laugh." Bastian takes a sip of the freezing cold ale Garr is so good at providing and places a meteor card on the table. If he remembers correctly, it trumps most things. He's not stupid enough to be seen in the same tavern he was on the last drop, but Garr owns most of them in the far blocks of cities under one name or another. Makes organizing meeting places easier.

He wonders what it would have been like to grow up a normal selfish teenager who didn't give a crap about his parents or how he got what he wanted in life. Kind of like Zach. The thought is a bitter one and leads to dark places he knows he should currently avoid. Dwelling on the past is never productive. He's already missed most of whatever Mathur just said.

"Can you repeat that?" Bastian stifles a yawn. Mathur's slight accent always lulls him.

Mathur's brows pinch. "How often are you dosing, Bastian?"

"Too often. I've had some close calls and a surprise visit. Not sure how much longer I can keep this up."

"Just be careful. If you do it for too long, you will get sick or lose control. We do not need them to deem you dangerous and place you down in that damned research lab."

"I get it, believe me I do." Bastian pauses for a moment to pull his facade into place. It's so much easier to close himself off in the short run. "I've been getting it ever since Mason decided his place was better with you."

Mathur smiles sadly. "Mason did not think he could keep up the pretense as you do. And you have to know he was probably right."

Bastian glares at the glass in his hands and his few remaining cards, aware the meteor only prolonged the inevitable. Mathur always wins. "Doesn't mean he should have abandoned me to Father's fate. It was hell to hold onto what was ours."

"But you did." Mathur pats his hand.

"Only because I made myself indispensable." Bastian can still taste the bitterness inside. He takes a deep breath, done with that topic for now. "We're almost there. I think Dom will help Sai be ready by the time we need her."

"Are you sure this will work?" Mathur sounds dubious.

"Sai is complicated. With each of these missions, she'll figure more out about the stark reality." Bastian takes a breath and sips the beer again. "Information about the Exiled is starting to circulate. The first elimination will be directly after she returns from her last mission. With the right push, I can make her listen. Once there's a question in her head, Sai won't let go of it. Passion and anger are her triggers. Without them, she doesn't have the strength we need from her." He glances at the hand on the table and scowls, throwing the remainder of his cards down.

"And with them?" Mathur prompts, unable to hide his grin at victory.

"With them?" Bastian turns the glass in his hands. "She could be my twin."

"Perfect." Mathur starts to stand so they can leave, but Bastian stops him.

"One more thing before you go." Mathur eyes him warily and sits back down. "Dom is having blackouts."

Mathur leans forward, listening intently. "They always have blackouts. He is not in sync with the others' communication centers and that idiot Davis does not know any better."

"It's not just communication blackouts. He has moments of interference, causing him to lose control and become rainbowed, as Sai calls it."

"He loses his ability to maintain the chameleon phase?" Mathur's eyebrows raise and a shadow lingers over his eyes.

"From what he told me, yes."

"That should be impossible." Mathur sighs and buries his head in his hands for a few seconds before looking back up. "Dom is my pride and joy. I never intended to create more just because he lived for so long. I am certain my directions were not followed properly when they created the rest in my absence." The old man runs a hand through thinning hair. "The only thing I can think of is that it is something in the others. The communication channel is a remnant left over from the Damascus stage of the project. Dominos should not need it. Dom should be having no problems; in fact, he should be constantly adapting, taking on human traits, habits, and appearances."

"He is." Bastian reaches out and grabs his friend's hand to try and soothe him. "You'd be surprised. He seems to have grown attached to Sai. She views him as a person and calls him Dom, too. I think you'll like her when you finally meet."

Mathur's eyes grow distant. "You think? I have ruined enough young lives. I do not want to ruin anymore."

Bastian stands up and starts to put his coat back on. "Stop feeling sorry for yourself, you silly old coot. You've saved more lives with your research than it's possible to count. When Ebony is ready, I believe you'll save a lot more. But once that happens and people have a defense against the suggestion grids, I hope you're ready for the war we'll have on our hands."

The old man stands and clasps hands with Bastian, a proud smile on his face. "More than ready."

"Good. That makes two of us."

Bastian doesn't expect to find Deign waiting outside his door when he gets back. He's relieved he didn't choose to make it an unsanctioned outing. Luckily, she doesn't have Zach's uncanny ability to sense power, so there's no need to frantically dose himself.

"Deign," he says, inclining his head in greeting. "What gives me the pleasure?"

"Me." She has a snarky smile, whether she's being nice or not. Her height doesn't bug him as much as she'd like it to, and she stands behind him, watching over his shoulder as he opens his door, and follows him in.

"You finally got the entrance fixed?" she asks, though he knows she's fully aware of it since the masons were paid out of GNW funds.

Bastian sighs softly, glad he has nothing out on his desk she could possibly want to peek at or play with. Deign is one of those annoying people who wants to touch and try everything. Physical touch empaths are too tactile for his tastes.

He leans against the desk and watches as she makes the rounds of his room. Never one to hurry if she doesn't want to, Deign will get around to telling him why she's graced him with her presence once she's good and ready.

"So." She stops, hands on hips. "You scared my protégé, you

know?"

"Then perhaps you had better see to her training. She's as obvious and amateur as a bull in a china shop—pardon the cliché."

"But she's *my* protégé. Show her more respect." Deign's tone is dangerous, but Bastian doesn't feel like playing games so he glares at her.

Deign tries the pout approach, her lips faintly glossed with something to give the appearance of volume. "It's to hone her skills."

"Get her to hone them elsewhere."

This time Deign laughs. "But you know that's futile. If she can get through your shields, she can get through anyone's. And I'm willing to bet your surprise student is close to as good as you."

Bastian raises an eyebrow at the subtle mention of Sai. "Really?"

She waves her hands in mock-defeat. "Fine, fine. I'll tell her to stay away."

He counts to five again and paces his words. "Deign, I don't have time for this. Why are you really here?"

"Why wouldn't you have time for this?" Her haughty tone almost snaps his patience.

"The school doesn't run itself. There was a reason I ended up here. I recall you jokingly telling the directors it was due to my insomnia that I should be in this position. That, young as I was, I'd been working the ropes with my father for years already." Bastian resists the urge to check the time, to fidget, to fling something against a wall. "Honestly, Deign. What's wrong?"

Her eyes crease, making the fine lines around them visible.

It's easy to forget she's over ten years older than him. Considering her status, she's never had any peers. Most people, like Zach, want to stab her in the back and take her inherited power.

"Nothing's really wrong. I just..." She pauses, and for a few moments she's the vulnerable young woman he remembers over a decade ago at her parents' funeral, when a freak accident placed her into her father's seat.

Deign looks at her nails and draws herself up with all the self-importance she can muster. "I just wanted to congratulate you on training your student well. She's done GNW proud, despite initial plans for her. Make sure I meet her."

"Definitely." Not if he has any way to prevent it. "Anything else?"

Her eyes flicker toward the door to his bedroom and back. She shakes her head and laughs. "Why on earth would there be?"

"Just let me know, Madam Director," he mutters softly as she turns on her heel. She's one of the stronger women he's met in this world, even if that strength is misguided.

Deign stops at the door and turns back to him. "There wouldn't be anything you'd like to get off your chest now, would there?"

Bastian forces a tight smile. "Not right now."

"Don't let me find out from anyone else." And with those enigmatic words, she's gone.

Bastian sighs and punches his desk softly. She knows something. Or knows that she should know something and is fishing for it.

CHAPTER
Ten

Sai throws herself on one of the couches as Dom lowers the hatch on the transport. "Last one. Finally."

He reaches over and hands her three readers. "Go over your reports while we head home."

Sai grits her teeth and stares at the assignments in front of her. Three, in ten days. There were no inns like in that first misleading mission, just this transport. It was almost too silent without the constant mantra ringing in her ears. She hadn't realized she'd grown so used to it.

"You know..." Sai pauses for a few seconds and watches the front window as they pass the steel mills. "...a lot of people out there hate us. Hate GNW. I always thought everyone knew we were all working toward a better future. They taught us everyone was happy. Maybe I'm just imagining things."

"I'd say you're being perceptive."

"Great." She heaves herself up off the couch and wanders to the passenger seat, plopping herself down. "Do you think we did okay, Dom?"

He glances at her for a moment. "I think you did well. UC 19's gangs shouldn't flare up again anytime soon. The enforcer's attitudes toward the people in UC 27 will never be as bad as they were again. And the traders in UC 13 obviously heard about your success in UC 21. It's all been you, Sai. Remember that and have some well-deserved confidence in yourself, okay?"

She's glad it's dark up front, so he can't see her blush. "You never sound confident."

"No." He corrects her. "I never sound proud. I am always confident. I know exactly what I'm capable of. Because I can do most everything, I have reason to be confident. The one thing I will never be is human. Regardless of my brain functions, my thought processes, and a large amount of my genes, people will always view me as something alien, and that is something I'm not confident about."

Sai purses her lips and looks at him. "Just because you're part-adrium doesn't make you an alien. You're one of the most human people I know."

She can see him smile in the dim light and leans back, echoing the expression.

Sai yawns as the sun starts to crest the horizon and melts the frost lingering on the ground. She leans forward when she spies Central in the distance.

"Happy?" Dom asks her softly.

"Right now?" Sai nods. "Content. They haven't called another mission in. I'm heading back to the closest thing I have to a home to see the people who're the closest to family I've ever had. Now if only I didn't have homework galore to catch up on."

"It's all part of it."

Sai glares at him for a moment and then sighs in resignation. "I know. It doesn't mean I don't wish they'd make an exception. Or give me a practical instead of all of the written."

Dom doesn't answer, but she's quite sure he laughs softly.

She squirms in her seat to get a good look at him. He's gripping the steering wheel far tighter than usual. "Do you think Bastian will want to see us?"

"Definitely. Training and debriefing, not to mention I'm sure we'll be sent out again soon."

Sai frowns. "What's wrong?"

"Nothing... I'm sure he'll see us."

She reclines the chair and spends the rest of the journey studying the ceiling, wondering what it is Dom isn't telling her.

It's a strange feeling to wake up in her own bed. For the last two weeks, she's woken up on hard surfaces to Dom doing something or other in the cabin. Making rations for her, gently waking her. It's odd not to have him around.

She feels lonely, something she wouldn't have noticed several months ago. As she rolls out of bed, she groans and reaches around for her clothes. The place is just as impersonal as it was before she left. It shocks her to realize the transport feels more like home than her quarters.

Except for the shower. She missed feeling clean, and the transport's steam version doesn't have enough power to make it a long-term alternative.

It takes her longer than usual to get dressed. She's fully aware the four hours immediately after she grabs breakfast will be spent under Ms. Janni's keen eyes while Sai proves that she learned her studies just as well on the road.

The tirade running through her head is interrupted by Nimue standing directly in front of her on the way to the breakfast line. "Sai, do you have a moment?"

If Nimue's still in the cafeteria, then they're not late for class. Nimue has never been late a day Sai has known her, and she looks worried, so Sai relents. "Sure. Let me grab breakfast first."

"Thanks. I was hoping you'd be here." Nimue falls silent as they choose their food and skillfully weave in and out of the almost-full room to a table at the back. "It's a little early for the boys," she mutters, taking a seat.

Sai drops down on the chair opposite and starts playing with the bagel on her plate. "What's up?"

"I rarely get to see Kabe and Deacon, and you're always gone. They keep you busy."

"That's the understatement of the decade." Sai can't help the sour pout to her lips. It's a sore point.

"I thought..." Nimue bites her lip, her eyes cast downward. "I wanted to apologize for making you feel uncomfortable before you left last time."

Sai's shoulders tense, and though she feels hungry enough to wolf down the bagel, her stomach churns. "That's perfectly fine. Never been fond of people touching me—of people in general, really." She laughs. "I like people less in small spaces, too."

"I just..." Nimue's eyes brim with tears, and for one horrible moment, Sai thinks the girl will cry. But Nimue squares her dainty jaw and sniffs it back. "Having Deign as my mentor is a lot of pressure."

Sai mulls the words over for a few moments before responding. "That whole empathy-reception-through-touch thing?"

If Nimue's surprised, she doesn't show it. Instead, she sighs deeply and nods, biting down on something so non-descript Sai's never had the courage to eat it before.

"You were my strength test. To see if I can break through shields like Deign can. I didn't know how to go about it, so I just..." Nimue shrugs helplessly.

"Shh," Sai looks around, worried that Nimue might be treading dangerous department ground. Her anger at the incident leaks away replaced by concern for her friend. "Don't worry about it. I get it, trust me. We all have to do things we never thought we would."

"So true."

For a few minutes they eat in companionable silence before Nimue breaks it again. "Thanks, Sai. I really didn't want to lose the one friend I have."

Sai grins. "I'm still here. I just have proximity issues."

Nimue ducks her head, a smile on her lips. "I'll respect that in the future."

"Excellent." Sai swallows the last piece of the decidedly stale bagel and stands up. "But I don't foresee a future if Ms. Janni has killed us both."

It turns out Sai didn't need to worry. The tests are easier than expected or else her frantic studies paid off. Basic Disaster Era questions, right down to the meteor showers that delivered the adrium compound and its connections to the origins of the psionic gene. Even given the stark reminder of the meteor's effect on the earth's atmosphere, Sai manages to leave the room with a skip in her step.

"It doesn't get better," she murmurs to herself as she reaches Bastian's doors and knocks.

Bastian and Dom are discussing something quietly as she comes in and look up briefly to acknowledge her. With a shrug, she heads over to the training area and warms up. Her whole body feels revitalized. Sleeping in a real bed did wonders.

"Sai?" Dom calls her over.

She laughs and heads into the main section of Bastian's office. "Yes, sir!"

Bastian continues to leaf through a few of the readers on his desk, pulling them to the fore and frowning while he speaks. "Steer clear of your year-mate, Nim...Nimel? Something like that? Don't let her touch you."

"Nimue," Sai answers automatically. "Why?"

"She's a crafty little empath and much like Deign. They require prolonged skin-to-skin contact to read through shields."

"I know."

Bastian finally looks up at her, and she allows herself to feel small victory at the eyebrow raised in surprise. "You know?"

Sai shrugs. "We've talked about it. It's all sorted. She won't try it again."

This time Bastian's eyes narrow. "Try it again?"

"Don't worry. She's a friend, and she's a bit lost here." The moment the words are out of her mouth, Sai knows they're true. It's strange how she doesn't feel lost. Her parents never thought she'd amount to more than them. Slowly but surely, Sai feels like she has a place. Just as she makes her self-realization, her stomach grumbles.

"You're hungry." Bastian goes back to his readers, and Sai fights the warmth she feels creeping in her cheeks.

"What have you eaten?" Dom asks her.

"A bagel for breakfast."

Bastian laughs, still focused on his work. "You know, Sai, you're a great protégé. I rarely need to think of things to punish you with."

"Because I'm a good student?" Sai asks.

"Because you're amazing at punishing yourself. There's food in my quarters—go get something."

Sai heads toward the almost imperceptible opening on the wall and picks her way through Bastian's quarters, seeking the kitchen. She lets out a low whistle.

The kitchen has everything and more. She pulls open the fridge to find a few large packets of processed meat. She grabs one of them, eyes a loaf of bread, and pulls out some mustard. Piling them all on a plate, she heads back into the office, snagging a glass of water on the way.

They both look up as she walks out.

"Thanks," Bastian says as she plops everything onto the table.

"For?" she asks as she piles the sandwich high. The bread is dense, better for prolonged storage, which makes it easy to stack.

"You brought all that out here for you, didn't you?"

"Yes."

Bastian sighs and watches her for a moment as she builds an impressive tower of bread, meat, and mustard. "You haven't been feeding her enough, Dom."

"You have no idea."

By the end of the first sandwich, Sai decides it's not much fun to have people watching her eat. "So," she says, pushing back from the desk. "Need the debriefing?"

"No." Bastian gestures to the food and raises an eyebrow in query. "Dom filled me in. Both your reports cover everything I need."

Sai pushes a freshly made sandwich toward him and rolls her eyes. "Why am I here?"

"That would be your next mission," Bastian says around bites of food.

She blinks her eyes. "You're kidding. I only just got back. How am I supposed to finish my studies at this rate? Do you want an illiterate enforcer?"

He watches her for a second, stops chewing, and wipes his mouth. "You're hardly illiterate. You're a Rare—automatically a special case whether or not you want to be. You just have to work harder than the others."

"Shouldn't being a Rare mean I don't have to work harder?" She sits back in her chair and glares at them both. "Tell me what I have to do this time, but I swear if I get stabbed, shot, or punched in the face again, I'm not going to be responsible for losing my cool and taking everyone with me."

The instant the words are out of her mouth, she regrets them. Flashes run through her head. Of her mother and the man who made her skin crawl; the botanica shattering and tearing at her flesh and clothes; the inferno she turned the apartment buildings into.

"Sorry," she murmurs, her throat husky with the tears she's holding back. "I didn't mean that."

"That's the point, though, Sai." Bastian pushes himself away from the desk and stands up. "Those are threats you can fulfill. Your control is so much better than it was. We're going to have to move the next step of your training into overdrive."

"This is about training?" Sai asks, slightly confused, still trying to push the unwanted memories out of her head.

"In a roundabout way. We need to speed up your learning curve. There are a few things we're going to have to determine before you go on your next assignment." Bastian won't meet her eyes.

"We know who, but not the when or where. Only that it's soon," Dom explains to her.

Sai isn't sure she likes the answer or the strange avoidance. "What's the plan today?" she asks

"Today," Bastian says as he strides over to the training section, "I'm going to teach you how to use phasing in a covert way."

"Covert? As in sneaky?" she asks, stopping abruptly about five feet from her teacher. "Why?"

"I need to teach you how to actively attack someone." He still won't look directly at her.

"Why?" she whispers again, taking a few steps closer without realizing it. "Why on earth would I need to know that?"

"For your next assignment," Dom breaks in matter-of-factly.

She shakes her head, not sure she understands them. "Someone's going to attack me so I have to defend myself?"

"You shouldn't be surprised. You've been attacked once before." Dom moves over to her right-hand side. "But your next mission is an elimination."

"Elimination?" The word tastes foreign on her tongue.

"Someone GNW considers a threat. If they live, they could topple everything it's taken decades to achieve." Dom's tone is logical. Calm.

"But you said..." She turns to Bastian, hating the anxiety in her own voice. "You said if I used what I have in a good way, that I can redeem my guilt. How is this a good way?"

Bastian studies the ground. "You're talented in many of the same ways as I am. Eliminating those who stand against your benefactors—isn't that a good thing?" he asks, a distinct sadness in his tone. "You said if they escaped and were dangerous, you'd kill the razor rabbits."

"You're sending me to kill razor rabbits?" She struggles to keep the vague hope from her voice.

Bastian finally focuses on her. "No, it's just an analogy. I didn't think I needed to spell it out."

"Well, now you don't have to!" Sai pushes the panic down, back, away from where it can get at her. "Dom's already done that for you. Just like he always cleans up your mess."

Bastian flinches for the first time Sai's ever seen. "I deserved that."

"You saved me so I could be used as a weapon? Fantastic. Let's have at it then. Let me *redeem* myself, Bastian." Her words cut, and she means them to. She'd like them to do so much more. Fear rises in her, and she locks it away.

She throws herself into practice. Phasing requires extreme concentration and coordination, exact destinations, and a mind map of where you're going. Covering short distances in a jump enhanced by psionic abilities, to the extent people think you blinked in and out of thin air, takes a lot of energy.

Phasing into a wall is usually fatal and best avoided.

It was a trick she discovered when she was in the training facility to get away from prying eyes and minds that wouldn't leave her past alone. Now, she practices to use it as a weapon.

Every time she phases, she realizes that her parents were right. Maybe if she'd let the visitor in, she'd never have killed so many people, or be expected to kill again. She ignores the looks on Bastian's and Dom's faces.

Each jump drains her a little more and brings Bastian a fraction closer to being satisfied with her performance. There is no sadness. There are no friends. There is no self.

There is only duty to those who let her live.

Sai lies on her back, staring at the ceiling, but as usual it doesn't have much to say. She throws and catches a jagged little ball in her hands. It's taken a while and a certain blend of psionics, but she can catch it without a scratch by reinforcing her skin. Bastian calls it fine-tuning.

A tear runs down her cheek, and she scowls as she wipes it away. There's no time to feel sorry for herself. It's not her life to live, nor her choices to make. Even Nimue was only trying to find a foothold to ingratiate herself to her own mentor.

Everyone who matters knows who she is. Why did she ever, ever think it was as simple as redeeming herself?

For your own safety, please do not leave your designated areas. Report any unauthorized personnel immediately. Remember, the future of GNW depends on you.

She wants to shout at it for interrupting her thoughts, but the words come out plaintive and resigned. "Shut up. Shut up..."

Everything around her, from the walls to the clothes on her back, was given to her at the sufferance of GNW. They forgave her wiping out one of their blocks in exchange for her servitude. Simple. Logical. It all makes perfect sense. As fond as Bastian occasionally appears to be of her, everything is clear now. He is happy with her progress. It takes a load off his shoulders.

She catches the spiked ball again and closes her eyes, going over every word of the previous day's conversation again.

Sai is a Rare. Her specific talents make her more lethal than the others. Like she didn't know that already.

It's probably a very good thing there aren't more of them, even though she can't help wondering why. Surely not every Rare dies during their awakening?

She sighs and turns over, grabbing her pillow and hugging it, fully aware of the self-pity she's dancing so precariously on the edge of. How is she supposed to deal with preparing herself to kill someone? How the hell does anyone deal with that?

She sits up and punches the bed. Anger is the only way she can motivate violence, and it's not her natural instinct. Given the choice, Sai prefers to be left alone, to be invisible and go around talking to and harming nobody. It's why she fled from her parents' apartment. It's what started this whole mess.

She was perfectly fine being alone in the facilities until Dom and Bastian stuck their noses into her life and pretended to give a crap.

"Dammit!"

She stands up and throws the pillow on the ground. Blood trickles out of her left fist, and she sighs. She forgot she was still clutching the ball.

A bit of exertion, and the pain stops; a few minutes more and the marks are faint, receding even as she watches. She smiles. Healing is a neat trick, and one she's getting better at. No matter what else happens, at least healing will be a positive in her life.

Maybe a jog will make her feel better. She glances at her watch and realizes it's later in the day than she thought. Everyone will be inside at classes or training. With the news of her latest assignment, she begged off contact with other people in order to mentally prepare. Bastian seemed only too happy to comply. Maybe the slight compassion proves him human after all.

It's been two days since they told her. Two sleepless nights. Too much adrenaline. Too many thoughts warring for space in her brain. Far too many memories begging to break down the shoddy barriers she's erected against them. Lock the past away and forget about it. Better to spend time with the one person she can trust—herself. How had she ever thought these two were any different than the Shined-up idiots who bore her into the world?

She grins as she pulls on her shoes and does a few stretches. It feels good to move. For a moment as she closes her bedroom door behind her, she stops and stands perfectly still, tracing over the corridor routes in her head. Then she takes a deep breath and sets off. If she mistimes any of these phases, it's going to hurt badly.

"No pain, no gain," she tells herself. Her laugh is slightly hysterical, even to her own ears.

One phase. Three steps. One phase. Two steps. Another phase—barely avoids people. Four steps to regain her composure and push the laughter to the back of her throat. It's better than any drug they could give her. Endorphin rush. The speed she phases around the building is amazing, until Dom catches her mid-stride as she drops out of one.

"Dammit!" She glares at him, jumping back only to stumble slightly. "You scared the crap out of me."

"You shouldn't waste energy like that."

"I..." She takes a breath and her legs almost buckle beneath her. "I need to sleep. I can't sleep, Dom." Her words are soft and her eyes start to feel heavy. He moves in to help her.

"Don't!" she snaps at him. Regardless of how tired she's feeling, no one can touch her. No one is allowed to get close and make her feel. Not even Dom. "Don't touch me."

She wonders if it's hurt she can see in his eyes, or just another shade of color. He nods, and she realizes that while he might not touch her, he'll follow her back to make sure she gets to her room.

Sai doesn't even say goodnight as she closes the door and collapses thankfully onto her bed.

"Should have done that days ago," she murmurs as her head hits the pillow.

For the first time she can remember, Sai doesn't dream.

CHAPTER
Eleven

Bastian is flipping through his reader when Sai walks in. She barely looks at him as she walks to a spot in front of his desk. Shoulders back, head high, she stands to attention. She's been trying not to think about today for the last week. Knowing you're supposed to kill someone and having to actually do it are two entirely different things, but neither are things Sai wants.

Her efforts at keeping a distance between Bastian and herself don't work like she'd hoped. He closes the space between them, his eyes locked onto her. "You have to remember one thing."

She glances at him, her expression schooled into indifference. The cold impenetrable wall he'd tried to get her to master since the beginning has finally cemented.

"These missions have a greater purpose. However much your own morals might tell you what you're doing is reprehensible, you have to realize your targets pose a very real threat to GNW as a whole."

She nods. As much as she's distanced herself from him, it's nice to hear a justification from someone else. It makes her feel less like a monster.

Bastian watches her for a few seconds more and shrugs slightly before reaching into one of his pockets and pulling out a reader. "This is his dossier. His work touches on aspects of chemical warfare, and it seems to have gained sympathy with the cause in UCs 20, 21, 22, and 25. His name is Franklin Jarvs."

Sai looks up at him sharply. "He's not tagged?"

"None of the Exiled are tagged."

"How?" Despite herself, she's curious. Most people are tagged at birth, and the information is stored in the bands beneath their skin. Thanks to her parents leaving the hospital before Sai was registered, she was only tagged when enrolled in the training facility. She's always hated the stark reminder.

Bastian frowns. "They're not born in the UCs. Why would they be tagged?"

She shrugs and waits for him to continue.

"Franklin will be traveling between these cities. The only time we can pinpoint with a narrow enough window is between UCs 22 and 25. It will be far easier for us to sideline him and complete the mission during that time."

Sai nods and accepts the dossier as she blinks back the burning behind her eyes.

"I expect you to have read and understood this by the time you reach your destination."

"Is that all, sir?" Despite the catch in her throat, she refuses to let her expression give.

"No. I have some advice for you. It helped me. I hope it'll help you." Bastian pauses and takes a deep breath. "Lock down your shields. Make sure you don't leave yourself open to hear a dying man's thoughts. Sometimes they can be confusing or psionically trapped. If you're really that morbidly curious, make sure there is no way for them to get a foothold in your mind." He pauses as if waiting to make sure she processes it. "Understand?"

Sai nods. "I understand perfectly, sir."

Bastian's jaw clenches, like he wants to say something else, but Dom enters the room and stands by the entrance. "Everything ready?"

Dom nods.

"You'll be taking a speed transport. The only one of her kind. Less comfort than last time, I'm afraid." He smiles at her apologetically.

"I'm about to kill someone. Comfort isn't the foremost thing on my mind." Her words are tinged with bitterness despite her best efforts. She makes sure her tone is even before speaking again. "If that's all, I need to pick my things up from my room."

"Fine." Bastian waves her away, looking more irritated than she's ever seen him. "Oh, and Sai?"

"Yes?" She pauses at the door, Dom already swinging behind to follow her.

"Next time I have to send Dom to stop a phasing marathon that you've decided is a good idea just because you can, I'll have some much better ways to make sure you exhaust yourself, instead of letting everybody bear witness to one of the best kept secrets I have."

The threat hangs in the air for a moment, and Sai finds it

difficult to swallow.

"Of course, sir," she answers and leaves the room.

Sai drops her backpack onto the ground in the cabin of the new transport and gapes. Bastian certainly wasn't kidding when he said he was sorry the standard of comfort would be less than on previous assignments.

A holding cage takes up about a third of the craft. There appear to be no conversion possibilities. The front two seats are the usual type—one pilot and one passenger chair. There are two tiny middle benches between those and the cage. The small bathroom in the rear has a convertible shower-toilet cubicle.

Sai puts her hands on her hips, barely noticing the strangely familiar humming beneath her feet. "This is going to be impossible."

"The passenger side reclines," Dom says as he climbs into the vehicle.

"That won't be necessary." Sai closes off her expression and pulls back again. Small talk isn't necessary. Nothing but her duty is necessary.

Dom stands in the doorway, arms crossed. "Are you really going to keep this up with me? When it's just us?"

She can't hold his gaze for long and makes looking away coincide with moving to the passenger seat. "I need to study the dossier," is all she says before turning her back on him.

He's not supposed to be human. So why can she see hurt in his eyes? The dossier stares back at her from the reader's dull screen, hiding any answers it might possess.

It's easy enough to tell herself she can keep up appearances. It's easy enough to be cold and distant when she can leave thirty minutes later and let herself recuperate. But it's going to be a challenge to be unfriendly for the few days allocated to this mission.

There was a time it would all have been easy. She'd have grabbed a reader and leaned back to read a book, not caring whether or not she might hurt someone's feelings in the process. After all, that's how she survived in the training facility.

Sai cringes as she hears Dom prepare the transport for launch. It's hard not to notice him as he moves about. The tight quarters means he brushes against her back or arms on more than one occasion during the preparation, and she knows her shortness of breath isn't only related to claustrophobia.

"Might want to buckle in."

"Why? I've never had to do that before," she grumbles, wrestling with the harness in strangely warm comfort of the seat.

"I'd say just trust me, but right now it'd be redundant." Dom doesn't even glance at her. He swings the steering around abruptly before shifting the gears and easing the vehicle out.

Sai gasps in surprise, momentarily forgetting Dom's snarkiness. The transport moves so smooth and fast, she's shocked. There's no way anyone will catch them in this if, for some reason, they have to make a run for it.

Her stomach clenches, and her temples pound. The overwhelming feeling of self-doubt gnaws at her regardless of the confidence placed in her.

She sits in her chair, watching clunkier transports and pieces of the city she's never seen before fly past. Block after block of identical concrete tower complexes, just like the ones she grew up in.

She leans forward and places her hands on the glass, trying to get a closer look. Not just similar, exactly alike. Sets of four concrete monstrosities with a brief glimpse of green between them as they pass by. She hasn't been to visit a botanica since she obliterated hers. She hasn't dared. Advertisements flit in and out of her vision as they race past.

Sai closes her eyes for a second, and the memory washes over her. The fire around her. The crashing. The devastating realization of what she had done. That painful, empty feeling in her gut. The throaty whispers near her. The silhouettes that danced on the edges of her vision clamoring to get rid of her—until he came and took her hand.

Despite everything else, Bastian has been there for her. He'd saved her, regardless of his motivations. And she knows she would be dead without him. He'd chased away the demons, and they'd retreated, scared of him.

Whether it was the police or some other agency, her neighbor, or the strange silhouettes hovering at the edge of her memories—anyone else would have put the world out of danger and done away with her. A normal person would have. But Bastian wasn't normal.

Neither was Dom. Sai yawns. Behaving distant and controlled takes a toll on her energy. Perhaps letting the new wall down isn't going to kill her.

The chair is clingy and somehow conforms to her position. Being restless isn't helping either. She switches her position around until she finally finds a comfortable spot facing Dom.

Screw it then, she says to herself and relaxes for the first time in days, her eyes watching him as she drifts off into the nap waiting to claim her.

It's not a long nap, but she feels refreshed when she wakes from it and glances down to realize she's been clutching Dom's hand.

"Ack!" She jerks back in embarrassment and looks up at him in horror.

"You're awake." He flips a few switches, moves a few dials. "I was beginning to need it and didn't want to wake you."

She sits back and crosses her arms to gauge him. "Are you serious?"

"Partially. I really..." He glances over at her and shrugs. "...didn't mind at all."

She feels her face flushing and scrambles to pick up the dossier that fell from her lap while she slept. It takes long enough to retrieve that the color drains from her face.

"Why did you react this way to your mission, Sai?" Dom asks in that weirdly soft way of his. His tone implies he already knows the answer, but wants her to say it out loud.

She looks at him for a moment and decides to ask a question in return. "Were you aware that my assignments would eventually include killing?" The words are hard to get out, but she needs to know.

"Of course I knew." It hurts more than she thought it would, until he finishes and adds, "What I didn't know is that Bastian hadn't told you."

"Oh..." Sai sits still for a few moments, running numerous conversations through her head. It wasn't like Bastian deliberately misled her. Nor did he ever tell her exactly what enforcement entailed.

All he'd left her with was the vague sense that eventually

she'd be able to atone for her past and relieve the guilt she lived with every day. Except for the razor rabbit discussion. In his own way, he'd actually asked her if she'd be okay with killing when told to. She'd been the one to read into it what she wanted to hear. But he'd never once lied to her.

"Damn." Sai buries her head in her hands. "Damn. Damn. Damn. Damn." She groans and seriously contemplates bashing her head against the dashboard. Why did he leave things so ambiguous?

"Something the matter?" Dom asks, his tone light.

"Shut up," Sai snaps and immediately feels like a heel for doing so. Bastian told her through omission, in a roundabout way. She should have come straight out and asked him what the rabid bunny reference actually meant.

"That man is a complete ass," she mutters into her hands, rocking herself back and forth to keep the building hysteria at bay.

"I take it you've met Bastian then." Dom fishes the reader out from under his heel.

Sai groans. "Why on earth didn't he just tell me?"

"Bastian has a lot to lose. You'll understand one day." Dom dangles the reader in front of her until she takes it.

"Do I have to? I'm not sure it's safe to understand him."

Dom doesn't correct her.

They pull to a stop just outside UC 22. The vehicle hovers just high enough for Sai to see into the bowels of the city if she looks through her field binoculars. Children play in the brown, sludgy water that trickles from the pipes overhead. The fading chill in the morning air makes the scene resonate pitifully. Memories threaten to assault her, but Sai gulps down the misery and sets her jaw.

The crumbling remnants of what were once the same type of high-towered concrete apartments her family occupied are barely enough to provide crude shelter from the worst of the elements.

She'd heard about the scandal. The builders cut corners when rebuilding after the meteors struck in 2172, wiping most of the habitable coastal settlements out, shattering cities between them, and destroying the ozone and much of the atmosphere.

They rebuilt along the Mid-American strip despite Oklahoma City being a danger zone. When the cost ate into the profits as they reached the outskirts, many of the builders cut corners and used compounds of lesser durability in the outlying blocks of every city.

Watching the children play in the refuse, clutching threadbare garments to their too-thin frames, their hollow cheeks and sunken eyes easily visible, Sai's gut clenches and threatens to make her lose her breakfast.

"Has it always been like this?" she asks quietly.

"Has what been like what? There are a lot of things around us. Your thoughts aren't decipherable at the moment." He speaks fast, moving around the cockpit as he sets things up.

"The cities, the outskirts... Has it always been this decrepit?"

Dom glances out of the windows and back at the camera screens. "Ah," he says softly, "You mean that."

"Yeah." Sai chokes the word out bitterly. "That."

"Not always, but for a very long time. The end of the Psionic Wars left a lot of people without anything."

"Then I guess I was one of the lucky ones..." She watches the scene for a while longer and closes her eyes to take a deep breath. Feeling sorry for herself and others isn't going to help anything. They have several hours of preparation ahead of them before she has to kill the man trying to ruin the lives of millions of people within GNW.

If the dossier is correct, Franklin Jarvs is a character. Older, with an inherent affinity for metal, he's been working on a type of grenade that will react with the adrium used throughout the city and cause it to explode on impact—with devastating range. He isn't quite done with his invention, but it's only a matter of time.

"Why the hell *me*?" Sai mutters to herself before turning around abruptly and glaring at Dom. "That's a damn good question. You're *made* to be the perfect assassin. Why aren't we using you for this?"

Dom blinks at her and shimmers for a moment, allowing his real self to be visible in all its chameleon glory. He stops before Sai gets a headache. "You want me to try to kill someone who's traveling around promoting a compound which reacts with adrium?"

Sai blushes and looks away.

"I didn't realize you disliked me quite that much," he says, his words dry.

"I don't dislike you at all, Dom. I never have. I'm just scared..." More scared than she's ready to admit.

"You can do it. Bastian would have done the mission himself if he didn't have faith in you. He's always been GNW's cleaner. For once, he has someone to share the burden with. It's why he partnered you with me."

"What's boy wonder doing then?" she asks bitterly.

"He's dosing himself with a shot of Shine and sitting in on two days' worth of briefings. Trade convention—weapon manufacturers. People are trying to reintroduce guns, and Bastian isn't the only one who thinks it would be a very bad idea."

"Guns? Are they trying to blow us all up?"

Dom shrugs. "Not entirely sure. I think it's been so long since the cities were established that people forget the reaction between the combustion mechanisms and the filtration agent needed to purge our air."

"He'll be able to convince them, won't he?" Sai pushes down the rising panic in her throat.

"As long as he controls his temper. Another reason for his dose."

"Shine dosing is weird to me." Sai says

"Understandable. Just know it hurts to come down off Shine as your powers essentially reawaken, but he can't afford to be seen as what he is. Though..." Dom looks her up and down critically, flipping switches faster than she can follow. "You'd have the same problem. The more punch your psionics pack, the faster your body will build an immunity to the drug. Unless they overdose you."

"I see."

"Do you?" Dom pauses his flurry of activity and stands in front of her. "Do you really see?"

Sai stands and takes a step back, suddenly hot and penned in. "No, but I probably can't yet, right?" She shakes her head and hugs her arms.

"But you will."

"Great—I'm going to be a murdering, insightful bitch! Just what I always dreamed of." She smiles nervously, her anger depleted.

The time is so close she can smell it. A hysterical giggle starts to rise in her throat and she fights it down, down and away. But it comes back up to the surface after a few moments and pushes past her lips, escaping in what sounds like a soft fart—which only makes her laugh all the more.

Dom stops his work again and looks at her. She can see the impatience in his eyes and it makes her giggle even harder. So hard, in fact, her sides hurt and no coherent words form in her mind or come out of her mouth.

He strides to the medi-kit, just outside the tiny cubicle valiantly impersonating a bathroom, and extracts something from it. Sai can see it through the tears of laughter now pouring from her eyes. She focuses on the object until he reaches out, holds her nose, and squirts something down her throat.

"What the hell!" she splutters amidst fading giggles. At least she didn't cry. There's a warmth spreading its way through her stomach suspiciously like vodka. But the hysterics are gone, and suddenly her legs won't hold her up anymore.

"It's okay, Sai. You needed some sort of release. Laughing is as good as any—it'll make everything easier when the time comes."

She just nods and sits down in a heap on the middle bench. "Mmm this was green before? Did you...How did you..." And the whole vehicle slowly changes. From the holding cells at the back to the pilot panels up the front, a comforting blue seeps through the cabin.

"No way," is the only thing she can think of to say.

"Yes, way," Dom says. "This little beauty is mine." He pats the side of the walls affectionately. His eyes go distant for a few moments. "She was the last gift made for me by my creator. She's attuned to me." He loses the faraway look and focuses back on her. "I call her *Mele*. Short for —"

"Chameleon. Not the fighting style. Got it." She pauses at the surprised laugh from Dom. "You've mentioned her before. Just like you, huh?"

"In more ways than one," he answers softly.

Sai stretches out on the seat, which is far more comfortable than it originally appeared to be, and tries to focus on anything but the near future.

Dom squats down next to her and waits until she opens her eyes and looks at him before he speaks. "I think you should know something."

"Mmm?" she asks.

"If you weren't reluctant about this assignment, I'd think I misjudged you. It's precisely *because* of your reluctance and fear that you are the better choice."

She mulls that over in her head. "I don't quite get how—"

"It's highly unlikely you're going to turn into a rampant glee killer on us."

Sai closes her eyes again. Maybe that *is* a good thing.

"I see them," Dom moves his foot, and the transport opens silently.

Sai follows him out, breathing in the torrid air. Her lungs struggle for a few moments in the approaching twilight. Once the sun sets, the air will ease up. It still won't have the filtered thickness of the cities, but it'll be better. Now she understands why the workers who travel to the steel mills in the distance need oxygen masks.

In the lingering sunlight, the sandy ground appears to hold all the blood the Psionic Wars spilled over twenty years ago. The cold tinge to the air reminds her seasons still exist outside the controlled environment of the cities. They need to work this quickly, or the cold will creep in after the sun sets.

Only the hardiest of trees survive out here—some cactus here and there, a stubborn fir. The cluster of cacti they hide behind is the perfect camouflage, and as she glances back at *Mele*, Sai realizes the importance of the vehicle given the current situation. Just like Dom, she can take on her surroundings and blend, like she was never there.

Sai hefts the blade in her hand, weighing it and frowning. The knife is long and runs down the length of her forearm to her elbow as she grips the simple leather hilt. It feels heavier than it did before, but it could be the shaking of her entire body. "Focus," she says, steeling herself against her conscience screaming to run instead.

"For the good of GNW," she mutters to bolster herself and feels Dom grip her shoulder reassuringly.

Sai reaches out with her mind to locate Franklin amidst his entourage. She scans each person she finds very briefly, not wanting to use up too much of the valuable energy she's going to need to phase. It takes a few attempts before she finds him.

"Bingo." She breathes the word so it's barely more than an exhalation and closes her eyes to follow him with her mind.

Bastian's words come back to her, the warning.

"Lock down your shields. Make sure you don't leave yourself open to hear a dying man's thoughts. Sometimes they can be confusing or psionically trapped. If you're really that morbidly curious, make sure there is no way for them to get a foothold in your mind."

Sai frowns and reinforces her shields twice, just in case, while she continues to track the man. The last thing she wants to do is be drawn into a mind trap.

Dom leads the way to the checkpoint they chose a few hours earlier. It's the only route the man can travel. The plan is to zip in and out, kill the target, and be gone before they notice she's there. In quick, out fast. Clean and clear.

She's not sure what possesses her to do it. Maybe it's the feeling of rebellion against Bastian and his well-worded omissions that roils in her gut, but as she follows Franklin with her mind, she finds herself seeking his thoughts out.

They're jumbled, busy, and boring, but then, he doesn't know he's going to die yet. It's a lot more boring an experiment than she thought and she wishes she'd waited until the cold steel bites into his flesh. She shudders at the image conjured, momentarily scared by her own cold-bloodedness.

Then Franklin passes the point of no return, for him and for her. Dom gives her a gentle push on the shoulder.

Time slows—or, at least, it seems to. She takes three running steps, sure beyond certainty that she can make the jump. It's why she's glad she practiced the hall loop regardless of Bastian's reaction.

One.

"I will not fail," she tells herself, focusing on the point she needs to phase to.

Two.

Upper slash to the right, back and across to the left. She goes over the motions in her head, eyes never leaving the spot. Another second and it'll be time.

Three.

And on.

She phases and comes to rest directly in front of him. Lunging straight in as his eyes are still focusing on her sudden appearance, she executes the first slash. Each piece of skin severs beautifully from the other.

At the end of the first stroke she reverses her hand and drags it back across—just as his blood starts to come to the fore.

For one inherently curious and rebellious moment, she pushes her mind at him—to listen.

The blade completes its second arc, cutting to the bone, and she takes one step before phasing back to where she started.

She angles wide and has to take more steps to phase back to *Mele*, slightly misjudging the distance. She lands on her knees as Franklin's body topples to the ground. She can still see his thoughts, fading rapidly as he tumbles. Then there is nothing.

"Let's go," she says breathlessly as she climbs into the cabin, only now noticing a slight spray of blood has caught the strange black material of her suit. One thing she'll give assassins—they have a much better wardrobe. Sai seats herself on the middle bench to catch her breath and pretend her body isn't shaking.

Dom is already in his pilot's seat, and *Mele* is silent as she lifts into place, the slow underlying thrum gentle on Sai's roiling stomach.

"I think I forgot to breathe..." She gasps for air and looks at her hand still clutching the blade so hard her knuckles are white.

There's barely any blood on it—just some skin hanging on the edge near the handgrip where she must have pushed it in too far.

Laughter bubbles on her lips, but she pushes it down again. There's nothing to laugh at. She just killed a man for wanting to make a difference.

She frowns. He died for trying to make a difference to his own people? What people? Why not...

It happened so fast and flawlessly that it keeps playing over and over in her head. One, two, three—in, two slashes, and she was gone. He didn't understand what hit him. She'd been there a full second at most.

But it took him far longer than that to bleed to death—all of her journey back to the transport. All of it. Another ten seconds of agony and wondering why before he let go of consciousness. There had to be a cleaner way to kill than that.

She clutches her stomach and doubles over on the bench, retching. The words and images in her head won't go away. Maybe next time she should listen to Bastian. Nothing in Franklin's head makes sense; it's all gibberish. There is no evil or sinister intention lurking there. He was proud of his work.

Maybe their information was wrong? Perhaps her mind sift was misleading? She'd only been in his head a few seconds. That certainly wasn't enough to form a valid opinion of a man, was it?

When faced with death, the only regrets Franklin had were not being there to see his work completed, to find his people set free from confinement and exile.

Confinement?

"None of this makes any sense!" She throws herself back and groans, forgetting momentarily that she's straddling the tiny bench in the middle of the transport and falling off the end.

"Sai?" Dom turns his head so fast she thinks he should have popped something. "Are you okay?"

"Forgot where I was."

"Are you okay?" he repeats.

She nods at him, repositioning herself on the floor. "As okay as I can be."

"Do you..." He glances away, and back again. "Would you like to talk?"

"Not yet..." She looks up at him and smiles, tiredly. If she keeps her hands on the ground to support her, she can pretend they're not shaking. "Maybe, when I've had time to sort everything out."

She clambers up from the floor and over to the passenger seat, making sure it's as fully reclined as it can get. Dom is silent next to her, and *Mele* isn't about to be company. Sai stretches her legs as far as they can go, relieved for once to be so short, and tries to sleep.

Every time she's about to doze off, she feels wind in her face and opens her eyes to someone about to cut her throat. Except she doesn't actually open her eyes until they do, and she wakes up in a sweat, panting and clutching her throat.

She gives up on sleep and contents herself with watching the dark sky outside, hoping against hope that the world suddenly turns into sunshine and lollipops so she never has to do something like this—ever—again.

CHAPTER
Twelve

Sai manages to produce her best ever report to hand in to Bastian as they speed back to Central. It's full of tiny details, right down to the countdown and methods used to eliminate the target, with only one teensy omission—the thoughts of the dead man currently running rampant in her head.

If it didn't make her cringe, she'd wish he'd died slower so she could have more answers. It's not that she questions the orders. Her entire life belongs to GNW. She owes them in ways they made very clear throughout her training. She's sure Bastian and Dom would have checked. But Franklin's thoughts won't stop plaguing her.

He was proud of his accomplishments, for both himself and his faction. From what she can gather he was trying to bring an end to the oppression of GNW? To free colleagues?

"Always two sides to a story and all," she mutters to herself as she finishes the last polish on the report and throws it into her backpack while she waits for Dom to guide *Mele* into the city.

"Did you say something to me?"

Sai glares at the back of his head. Bloody super-sensitive hearing. "No."

"Are you sure you're okay?" he asks her for the fifteenth time in the last two hours.

"Yes, I'm okay." There's a constant reminder in her head that she's supposed to be redeeming herself. Supposed to be. Did killing others constitute redemption? Did the ease her knife severed his jugular with count as a good thing?

Her own thoughts mix with Franklin's, making the litany in her head almost unbearable.

"Perfect," she purrs the word out as an idea comes to her.

Dom looks like he's about to say something, but thinks better of it.

Sai starts planning things out in her head. As soon as she gets back to her room, she'll make a list on her personal reader and lock it in. She hasn't done it before, but she'll figure it out.

At least then it's where she can watch it, instead of experiencing the rampant confusion in her mind. At least there it might help her from breaking down like she so badly wants to.

Used to recording things, she should be able to extract most of his last moments, make a list of everything Franklin thought while it's still fresh in her mind. They're so vivid; she can't un-see them. Her planning is interrupted when Dom places a hand on her shoulder and gently shoves her forward.

"We've been parked for three minutes. What are you waiting for?"

She stares at him for a moment, trying to gather her scattered thoughts before stepping out of *Mele*. Sai pats the iridescent vehicle, says thank you, and leans down to kiss the side of the hull. For a moment, she thinks there's warmth to it that wasn't there before, and then it's gone. Maybe *Mele* understands.

Bastian first—then she can get the images out of her head. If only she can keep busy enough not to think about the blood. If only she can keep busy enough so "the incident" stops repeating in her head. If only she can find even a hint of a valid reason why she killed a man left behind in his own memories, maybe the guilt will leave her alone.

Bastian waits for them at his door. She hasn't forgotten his glaring omissions. Her grudge isn't against Dom, but Bastian can go ahead and ingest a pound of Shine for all she cares.

Sai walks past him and drops her backpack to the floor after taking her report out of it. She's knows he'll have a summarized version sitting in front of him, but she's proud of the detailed one. Writing it kept her sane, and if she concentrates on it, maybe she can squeeze out a few more hours of pretending not to be a piece of murdering scum.

"Report?" Bastian holds out his hand to her as he approaches his desk. She hands it to him wordlessly and waits, standing at ease, gaze roaming the office. He scans through the device, lips pursed. Sai isn't sure, but she could swear there are more lines under his eyes than there were a few days ago, and their blue tone seems somewhat muted. He looks more exhausted than she's ever seen him. She waits for him to finish his perusal, trying desperately not to think.

"How do you feel, Sai?"

Bastian doesn't ask the question the way Dom does. He asks it for a reason. He wants to know if she's damaged or if she's clinging to her sanity like he is. Sai can't honestly answer the question. Dom asked because he was worried. Bastian is asking because, if she's broken, he will have to "take care" of her.

"Angry, but fine." It's the most honest answer she can come up with. She's angry at everyone who led to putting her in the position of deliberately taking someone else's life.

But the world is a different place now.

"Anger is okay. Fine—not so much. You need to be able to talk about this. Bottling things up is never good, regardless of what you tell yourself, because in the end it will break you." He sighs, puts the reader down, and walks over to her, placing his hands on her shoulders. "So I'll try this again. How do you feel, Sai?"

His hands are warm, even through the resilient material of her new body armor. She swallows and licks her lips, suddenly parched. Sai looks up and locks eyes with him, choosing her words carefully, her tone tightly controlled.

"You know what? I'm angry! Actually...I am *furious*! Furious at you for lulling me into a false sense of happiness. Furious at anyone for expecting someone like me, with as much baggage as me, to be okay with taking a person's life because I *owe them* my existence. And I am devastated that not only am I expected to do this, but I *can* do this and I'm good at it."

Sai takes a deep breath to calm the anger rising in her throat, threatening to make her scream. She glances at her shoulders, watching them shake. "Get your hands off me. I'm not in the mood to be touched, least of all by you."

Bastian lets go so abruptly she can feel the cold that rushes in to take the place of his hands.

"Don't you feel better?" he asks, no trace of sarcasm in his voice.

"No."

He squares his shoulders, the tension in them obvious. "You will."

"I doubt it." She bends to grab her backpack and slings it over a shoulder. "Will that be all? Or would you like me to lie on your couch and tell you how I felt when Mommy and Daddy Shined themselves into oblivion and forgot they had a child for weeks at a time?"

"No." Bastian takes a step back, his facade up once again.

"Shame. It's not every day someone born to privilege gets the chance to understand what it feels like when your parents' favorite fantasies don't include the life they created together." She turns and leaves, closing the doors gently behind her.

Back in her room, Sai takes a deep breath and leans against the door. If only she could stop the shaking, the shortness of breath. She pulls the uniform off and discards it, cringing at the stiffness where the blood dried on the chest. Not even the hot water washes away the vivid memory.

Sai never cries, and the stream of water makes it easy to keep up the pretense. Even if sobs wrack her frame and leave her throat sore, the water hides it all.

Dry and in bloodless clothes, Sai settles on her bed with her reader and takes a deep breath. Flipping the tablet over, she switches it to receiving mode and creates a locking code triggered by the pattern of her psionic waves.

Recording the images means she'll have to relive them again, have to force some form of coherence into them. The details come far too easily, and the 3-D render only reinforces her consternation. A laboratory complex. A new type of water-purifying tablet. Family and siblings. Then, celebrations back in the lab. A dead dog in a field. Intricate combinations in beakers.

But nowhere, not even once, is there a glimpse of grenades or adrium.

She puts down the tablet for a moment, confused. Had he really developed a technology that would allow acidity to be directly neutralized in water? Had she killed a genius?

Sai pushes the thoughts from her mind and stands up, making her way to the bathroom to wash her puffy eyes and stay awake. She clears her head as best she can and sits down to continue.

The leftover images remain disjointed, scattered, thoughts interspersed through them all. Happy thoughts and sad thoughts, but one prevails over all others: his dying thought.

They'll never escape now. Who will free them?

Nothing in his mind hides a terrifying and deadly secret. Did she kill the wrong man? Where did GNW get this information from?

Her head throbs. The reaction headache in the morning will hurt, and she doesn't have any of Dom's clear little pills to help. But she did manage to retrieve everything she picked out of his head?

Her eyelids droop, but she locks the reader before lying down. As tired as she is, all she can think about is that you can't lie mind-to-mind.

This time she knows it's a dream. The gleam around the edges of her vision and the fact that she's watching herself are a dead giveaway. It's strange seen from this angle. She flies in unobserved, slits a man's throat, and leaves before they react. The scene plays out in her head, over and over.

It's not horrifying in the sense her dreams usually are, but only because she feels so numb. Ice closes over her and holds her in place while she gets used to watching herself kill on repeat. Desensitization at its finest. Her chest constricts and she gasps for air.

Her body jolts awake. Momentarily disoriented, it takes a few moments to realize why she woke up. The knock on her door is faint, but it's definitely there.

"Who's there?" she asks softly as she pads to the door.

"Bastian."

She frowns as she unhitches the latch, wondering if he can already tell the expression on her face. "What do you want?" she asks sulkily as she opens the door a crack.

"Just let us in." He pushes gently and is followed into the room by Dom, who keeps his eyes on the ground.

Sai glances down as she closes the door behind them and pulls on her bathrobe before climbing back onto her bed. "Well?"

Bastian brushes a hand through his hair, an uncharacteristic action she's not seen him do before. "I have your next mission."

Sai blinks and glances out of the window. From the light coming through, it has to be early. "What?" It hasn't even been a day yet. The numbness returns.

Bastian holds up a hand and stops her train of thought. "This is forewarning. Spend a day recuperating, and then a day training before you have to head back out. Ms. Janni needs to see you as well."

"Do we..." Sai stops, not entirely sure how to phrase it. How does she phrase a question that goes against everything she's learned up until now? *Do we trust this source? Are we sure this threat is real?*

So many questions run through her head. Instead of asking them, Sai just wishes she did. "Do we have everything?" If she pushes the color of Franklin's blood to the back of her mind, perhaps she can pretend it never happened.

"Everything you need to know is on there." Bastian nods to the reader Dom is handing to her. "Get to know all about Johnson. Follow the training directions in there."

"Same tactics?" she asks quietly. It feels like her dream, detached from herself. The ice encroaches on her heart painfully. She lowers her eyes and stares blankly at the reader in her hands.

"A variation to keep the element of surprise." Bastian straightens and dusts off his jacket. "Sai?"

She glances up at the sound of her name. Her eyes won't focus for a few seconds and her response is delayed. "Yes?"

"Are you sure there's nothing you want to tell me or ask me?"

Sai pauses for a second and really studies him, wondering if she *can* trust him. "Apart from having killed a man in the blink of an eye?" She shakes her head. "Nope, nothing wrong with me at all. I'm just your perfectly normal ninja teenager. Just the way you like them. All rolled up in obedience."

It's the first time she's ever seen Bastian scowl, but he nods his farewell and heads out of her room without another word.

Dom looks directly at her. "You could give him a break, you know, Sai."

For that one moment she can't breathe, her attention captured by the gold playing back and forth in his eyes.

"He never gives me one." Her voice is breathy and petulant, like the child she no longer is. She can't help it. Every time she's around Bastian, she feels like one. She turns to see Dom pause at the door.

"You have no idea how many breaks you caught when you got him as your mentor. No idea at all. Ask Nimue one day, if you have the guts."

He leaves the room, those words ringing in her ears.

Sai clutches the crossbow she fought valiantly for and stares sightlessly out of *Mele*'s window. The weapon wasn't Bastian's or Dom's first choice, but she stuck to it stubbornly. The proximity to her target in the previous mission was unsettling. Any distance is welcome. Armed with bolts that disintegrate shortly after impact, it's the safest way for her to take out a target close to a city dome.

She pushes down the thoughts telling her to run, asking her why she's doing this. Instead, she concentrates on the dilemma plaguing her since she absorbed some of Franklin's memories and had a chance to sort through his thoughts.

What makes these people her targets? Just because GNW says they have information doesn't make it automatically correct, right? Who is the source? Who is it that decides to end someone's life on the scrap of a rumor?

This time she's determined to make sure she knows. Without a shadow of a doubt. If she's going to kill a man, then she's going to understand why he has to die.

Killing innocent people, even if GNW decides they're in the way, isn't right. Sai takes a deep breath and her knuckles turn white where they clutch the weapon.

She glances around the ship as *Mele*'s color changes and her contours soften. Sai doesn't understand the way the vehicle works, but it's warm and cozy to ride in. It makes her feel safe. Maybe it's because Dom makes her feel safe, too.

Dom appears much more relaxed when he pilots *Mele*. It makes the journey less rigid. For a few hours at a time, Sai can almost forget she's going to take out another target.

"I will not fail. I will succeed. I will not be broken," she mutters to herself and looks out of the small window again. Even though Dom probably heard every word, he doesn't act as though he does.

Mele slows. Though Sai can't see anything beyond the black of night out the windows, she knows they've arrived. She shuts her eyes tightly and, as futile as she knows it is, wishes herself away.

Sai cracks one eye open and sighs at the distinct lack of change in location. She pushes herself out of the passenger seat to help with stationing the transport, but Dom waves her back to her seat.

"I can do this perfectly well on my own. We have a few hours to dawn. I'll wake you in plenty of time."

Sai nods and closes her eyes again, knowing sleep will be painfully elusive but appreciating the chance to rest anyway.

She goes over the assignment in her head. Every placement and step right up to making sure she grasps the victim's direct thoughts and memories before he dies. The crossbow means no need for her to be sprayed by gushing blood this time, and a weapon designed to be untraceable. Not that it matters, since GNW sanctioned the execution themselves.

It's still hard to believe they spared her only to have her take more lives in the future.

The thought makes her nauseous and she sits up to stretch in time to see the first pale rays light up the sky. Heading into winter, the air requires a reduced amount of filtration and the sun's rays aren't as harsh. In its own way, the world outside the cities is wild and dangerous, but beautiful nonetheless.

"Perfect timing," Dom says from behind her. He holds out some water and vitamins for her to take. "You need something and I'm not sure trying to eat food before this is your best bet."

Sai blushes at the vague memory of vomiting a lot on the way back from her first assassination. That has to mean she's still human. "At least I can eat food."

Dom looks at her, face blank. "You realize I *can* eat food too, right?"

"Yeah. Nervous energy. Wanted something witty to come out."

He shrugs. "If that's what you want to call it."

She wonders if there's a smile tugging at his lips or if it's a trick of the rising shadows.

"Are you ready?" he asks softly as she picks up the crossbow, and slings the lightweight quiver onto her back. She pulls the bow up, tests how taut the wire is, and nods, not trusting her voice to come off as steady as she needs it to.

Adrenaline makes her shake in a bad way. It's difficult to calm her nerves. The crossbow has always been her ranged weapon of choice, ever since she attended the training facility. She knows she's good at it. She concentrates on that.

The sun spreads its toxic arms further, tingeing the morning a prophetic crimson. Sai shivers.

She can see the slow-moving party on the horizon, on foot and—if the information in her reader is right—on the way out to their own hidden transport. A few seconds more and she'll have to move. She can barely hear Dom counting down, even though he's right next to her. The world slows again, nothing but seconds. Nothing but the swirling dirt she'll disturb in a moment.

Three.

She hears the number and bends down slightly, ready to run, heart beating fast. Sai reaches out with her thoughts, lightly brushing the approaching people.

Two.

Her mind is already in place, and she syncs herself with Johnson's movements, listening for stray thoughts before her strike. His guards are younger and not psionic, but the man himself seems to have some small ability. The only opening in his thoughts will be on impact.

One.

Sai pushes her frown away and concentrates on breathing as she prepares to launch herself into their path.

Go.

She pushes off, gliding a bit to get her run up and slip into the phase—a beautiful long phase, leaving about a hundred and fifty feet between her and her target.

They've still not noticed her by the time she's cocked the first bolt. Crossbows are more difficult to draw, but the three bolts load in quick succession. If she needs more than three, she's failed anyway.

She sights briefly, her mind still watching them, giving her better coordinates than her eyes alone could ever hope to. She aims with the same aid and fires three times in quick succession.

While the arrows fly, she focuses on him, her curiosity insatiable. There has to be more to this. Just how much has everyone, including Bastian and Dom, kept from her?

As the first bolt hits, his mind flies open. When the second bolt catches him in the chest, every thought he's ever had, every memory he's ever filed away streams across the channel, and straight into the recording centers of her brain.

So much information. Sai stumbles back at the overload, unable to break the link. New and difficult questions bombard her all at once. Her head swims. Her vision snaps. She feels the third bolt thud into his chest as if it were her own, just as the connection severs.

Sai turns, blindly, the need to get back to *Mele* almost a reflex. Tears stream down her face.

She stumbles and throws herself into the return phase with no true direction and barely maintains consciousness as she skids out of the shift without control, tumbling across the harsh red ground until everything goes black around her.

CHAPTER
Thirteen

Bastian glances at his wrist as he heads down to the docking area, concern at Dom's last communication making him antsy. The twists and turns of the corridors afford him time to think about Deign's insistence he take care of fixing the odd blackout situation that seems to be affecting all the dominos. It reflects the general fear of another Damascus incident. The fiasco caused by the Damascus stage of the Domino Project is the reason Mid-Am is now the GNW United Conglomerate, governed by GNW instead of the once democratically elected officials.

"They should be back shortly," Bastian murmurs. The transport won't be long, and from the sounds of it, Dom will be carrying a dead weight with him. He may need help juggling things. Supernaturally strong or not, he can't grow extra limbs.

Bastian knows it for a fact—the scientists tried.

He can't help feeling uneasy. Setting things up was difficult. Johnson wasn't an incapable psionic. Whatever he prepared for her might have been too much. The truth can do that. Seeing what you've believed to be true your entire life exposed for a lie can destroy a person.

Bastian hears the soft hum of Dom's sleek vehicle just as it rounds the corner to dock. The faint breeze as it sets down flutters the hem of his coat. Despite the gravity of the situation, Bastian can't help but smile as *Mele*'s colors adjust back to adrium's natural gold-hued grey.

Sai is the first thing he sees when the door opens. She's paler than he remembers in that black body armor. It doesn't seem to have done its job as well as it should. Parts of adrium-infused fiber have torn away to show rough abrasions. Blood droplets hang onto the fabric. Her dark hair is splayed out over the floor, and she's curled up, defensive even in her sleep. She looks as young as she is and more vulnerable than she should.

Dom moves into sight, and Bastian takes a step back. He's never seen Dom so emotional before. The domino barely even acknowledges him before bending down to scoop Sai up in his arms. He moves slowly, maneuvering her gently out of the vehicle, her head resting against his chest.

"The backpacks are on the passenger seat, Bastian. If you could..."

It's even rarer that Dom tells him what to do. So rare in fact, that Bastian simply does it and follows his friend back to the office.

The doors open soundlessly, allowing Dom and his burden to pass through. Bastian enters last and seals off the room. Once

Sai is safely ensconced in the guest bed, Dom's face relaxes a little, but his stance is tense.

"You okay, Dom?"

His friend focuses on him, colors warring with the usually predominant gold in his eyes while he finds an answer. "I'm not entirely sure. I keep having to fight this lethargy. Like there's something willing me to black out. But I couldn't leave her like that. You should have seen it, Bastian. I'm surprised she's alive."

"Those suits can take a tumble or five. I know, I tested it." Bastian leans against the wall. "How did she get so banged up?"

Dom looks at him and then away for a moment, swallowing visibly before turning back to hold Bastian's gaze. "She went out precisely as planned. The crossbow did the job. I could *feel* the transference of his memories and thoughts. That's how powerful it was. I've never seen one so strong in my life. I think that's what did it." He closes his eyes for a moment and shakes his head. "You know how the domino communication channel appears if you "search' for it?"

Bastian nods.

"Take that, but thicker, more substantial and powerful. It wasn't an option for her. Those memories and all that information slammed into her mind, forced her to receive every detail and experience it all at once."

Bastian winces, not liking that anyone thought this would be a necessary step in her process. "Maybe we should have found another way," he mutters glancing down at the sleeping girl. They need to clean her up. But he knows her well enough to realize she won't appreciate the help or being touched.

"You would have been proud, Bastian." Dom speaks softly and pauses. "Not only did she execute everything perfectly, she managed to keep just enough of her wits about her to get out of there."

"Then how did she..." Bastian's eyes open wide in realization, and he clamps his hand over his mouth just in time to prevent himself from swearing too loudly.

"I'm not sure how fast *you* travel when you phase, but when she came out of it, all she had was momentum. The minute one foot touched down, she had no control. I think she'd already blacked out when she hit the ground. If she'd not been wearing that stuff..."

"She'd be dead." Bastian voices the words Dom doesn't say. He hopes this hasn't broken her. "Now we have to wait for her to wake up and hope the damage doesn't run too deep."

"She wasn't going that fast in the halls. I thought I could catch her when she came out of it, but she traveled farther than anticipated." Dom studies his hands briefly before fixating back on her face.

Bastian glances at his friend and sighs. "You seem a bit worse for wear. I didn't realize that was possible."

Dom tears his gaze away from Sai long enough to smile wryly. "Neither did I. I think there's something wrong with me." Bastian doesn't have the heart to tell him he agrees.

It's a very long night, one Bastian keeps expecting will be interrupted. Ms. Janni trying to hunt her student down, Deign deciding she needs another consultation, or perhaps even Zach needing an outlet. But it's quiet, especially in Sai's case.

For all intents and purposes, she could be fast asleep. The gravel burn all over the left side of her face might have come from falling out of a hovercraft.

Bastian flips through the report. Although Dom's recordkeeping is meticulous, he lacks the individual touches Sai always puts into them. He glances at his watch and nudges Dom.

"Go take care of *Mele*. Sai isn't going anywhere. She'll still be here when you get back, and by the feel of her mind, I doubt she'll be awake."

Dom looks up at him sharply. "You can tell?"

"In a way. She's processing everything. Her mind has shut her body down in order to do that. There's no other way for her to deal with the huge amount of information she received."

"Should have hammered those details out a little better, Bastian. Maybe this wouldn't have happened. Maybe you could have just talked to her."

"If I didn't know better, Dom, I'd say you liked the girl. But that's not possible is it?"

Dom's back stiffens, and he turns to face Bastian. "It's very possible for me to like people. I haven't put up with you all these years because of your charming personality."

Bastian closes his eyes for a second, reinforcing the shields surrounding the room to their strongest possible. "I doubt you could have stopped this. I didn't have time to plan. All I knew was these people volunteered as the decoys, and by using them instead of our real scientists when GNW knew something was up, it was a way to get Sai to see the side of them she'd never believe without a blunt lesson. They brainwash them in the training facility. You know that better than anyone, what with how they treat you when they check you."

His shields waver briefly, and he holds a finger over his mouth in the classic gesture of silence.

"Perhaps. I still just think you could have told her..." Dom mutters, his voice softer than ever. He squares his shoulders and lifts his chin. "I'm going to see to *Mele*," is all he says before leaving the room without a backward glance.

Bastian hears the steel doors with their soft swoosh open and close before he sits down in the chair next to the head of Sai's bed. Holding his shields at their maximum tires him and he lets go.

He looks at Sai, *really* looks at her, and wishes they'd had another option. The choices have never been good—not for him, and not for any Rare. How many did he hear screaming, incoherent, when he went down near the laboratories? How many times did he narrowly escape landing there himself? Both are too many to count.

Maybe she'd see; hopefully she'd understand. It was unheard of for anyone to escape the testing portion of the facility, but they couldn't watch everything all the time. The staff had worn thin over the years. As Rares were drained to fuel the grids, Zach found new ones to replace the used. The more powerful, the better.

Bastian sighs and brushes a few stray hairs away from the mess of blood and flesh on her face. He wonders if he can fix it, just a little to avoid bad scarring, without jolting her mind. The basics are theoretically easy. He leans forward, holding his palm about an inch away from her skin and closes his eyes, focusing.

After a minute or so, he looks at her. Much better. It might even heal properly if she wakes in time to work on the rest. He never got around to telling her that the healing portion of that gift wasn't his forte.

Bastian sits back again and suppresses a yawn. Johnson was the right choice for the decoy. He'd been one of the Rares in the testing facility. One of the batteries to charge the thought suggestion grids with every drop of psionic energy they could tap from him. His mind and body were riddled with damage inflicted on him before he could escape.

And he passed every single memory onto Sai, burning it into her mind. Something a psionic would generally avoid but, in this case, was necessary. Although she'll always know the experience isn't her own, there'll be days she wonders.

Bastian sighs again and lets his mind wander over all the different aspects and possible outcomes to reassure himself that, while painful, this is the best option they have.

A while later the doors click, followed by Dom's sure footsteps. Bastian stands to greet his friend, glancing down at Sai as he does.

He sees her eyes fly open and stare at nothing as her hands reach up toward the ceiling. She opens her mouth and emits the saddest and most painful scream he's ever heard in his life.

Dom arrives in time to see her struggle to sit up. She blinks, her eyes haunted.

Her brow scrunches in confusion, until her gaze rests on Dom, and her shoulders sag in relief. Sai closes her eyes and tears roll down her cheeks. "So..." Her voice hitches and she clenches her jaw visibly. "So much pain... And you!" Sai opens her eyes and looks point-blank at Bastian. "You've known about this all along and done nothing?"

Bastian sighs. "Not done nothing. To be fair, I did tell you about the facility under us. I just didn't give you details or history."

"I don't care about how well you managed to omit something, Bastian!" Her fists ball, and her face flushes. Her voice grates like steel on stone. "You should have told me. I have a right to know what I'm getting myself into, a right to know who I'm serving!" Her tone drops to a whisper. "I have a right to know that I'm being used to kill other people like me." Her eyes scrunch up and the tears flow freely.

Bastian hides the cringe he feels and moves closer, but Dom, his eyes silver for the moment, beats him there.

"Sai, breathe."

She shakes her whole body and pulls away from him. "You don't understand. You didn't see. They... Oh no, is that what they'd do to you? Is that why you dull yourself with Shine? Tell me!"

Sai watches Bastian, obviously waiting for him to answer. He pulls his chair closer and rests his head in his hands. There really is no way to sugarcoat it now. "Got it in one."

"Why don't you leave, go away from here? Fight them! None of them deserve your help." The words tumble over themselves in their hurry to get out her mouth. Her face is flushed, and her breaths come short.

Bastian was expecting a reaction, but not with this much passion. He thinks for a moment, trying to figure out the best way to tell her. A way that might soothe her and help her deal with all the images bombarding her mind, with the things she'll never forget.

"If I don't stay where I am, if I don't continue to work as I have, who will be here doing what I do?" He pauses for a second, double-checking his wards while he waits for the words to sink in. "All you have to do is sort through things. I'm quite certain you'll realize..."

Sai closes her eyes, grips the sheets and Dom's hand, still resting on the cover. Her expression changes to one of surprise, and she lets out a slight exclamation before looking at Bastian again.

"How can you? I thought you were so mean. You've got so much to lose, Bastian. So much to lose. How can you stand this? How can anyone stand this? Why has nothing been done?"

He raises an eyebrow. "You really think I've been doing nothing?"

Sai has the good grace to blush. "I didn't mean it like that." She pauses, and Bastian is relieved to feel some of the hysteria fading, though her eyes dart back and forth while she thinks.

"How long has this been going on? How many people have they ruined this way? And why did you make me kill someone who got out? He managed to escape. How could you let me take his life under their orders when you *knew*?" Her tone is accusatory, and her eyes flare with momentary anger.

Bastian holds a hand out and motions her to wait, to be quiet. "There are things I can't tell you right now. There's only so long I can reinforce my shielding enough to be certain no one can listen. And there are some things that, if you know before you leave, others might pick up on, or you may act on regardless of my advice against it."

"Leaving?" she asks, surprised. "Who on earth says I'm leaving? They need to pay. From the inside—gutted and drained for decades." There's a gleam in her eyes Bastian never hoped to see, and one he's glad isn't aimed at him.

"You'll understand everything soon enough, but for now you must leave."

She gapes at him.

"You're not explaining things correctly, Bastian." Dom pushes himself up and paces for a few seconds before turning back to Sai. "He can't leave to help from the outside. You have an amazing ability to heal not only yourself, but others. What do you think anyone who manages to escape or be rescued from underneath is going to need?"

"Healing?" she answers in a small voice.

"Healing." Dom smiles that strange half-grimace of his and continues. "Not only can you heal, but you're lethal. You can protect. Maybe you can show others how to protect themselves. If Bastian can show you how to recognize different abilities, then you can seek those out and aid their training. Do you understand how important that is?"

"You're kidding, right?" She looks at them both as if she doesn't think they're quite sane. "You do realize I've only just turned seventeen?"

They nod.

"None of these people will listen to me."

"On the contrary," Dom says in a matter-of-fact tone. "They will listen to you because you survived your last test. Do you realize how rare that is? Since the Psionic Wars and the implementation of the Facilities, each location is lucky to have a handful of graduates a year. It's how they thin psionic blood and populate the testing facility."

Sai holds up a hand, her face pale. "Not everyone fails?"

"No, not everyone fails."

She sits there, still, watching her fingers clenched tightly in her lap. "They pull *batteries*," —she spits the word out— "directly from the graduation classes?"

Bastian shifts uncomfortably. "Yes."

"Then how did I get out?" she whispers, clenching her eyes shut.

This time Bastian leans forward and cups her fists in his hands. "You weren't meant to." He watches her swallow as the tears leak out her eyes, before continuing. "But I found you, and I enrolled you and kept tabs on you throughout. I don't attend every graduation."

The moments that pass feel like ages. His neck begins to stiffen in his hunched position before she finally speaks.

"If you hadn't come *that* day, I would have gone to the testing facility, wouldn't I?"

Bastian nods.

"And if you hadn't come to the exam, I wouldn't be here either." She opens those strange, colorless eyes, and a shiver runs down Bastian's spine. The determination practically radiates off her.

"Thank you," she whispers and hugs him fiercely.

Sobs wrack her tiny frame as she hides her head against his shoulder. Bastian glances up at Dom, whose expression is unreadable.

After a few moments, she pulls back, wiping her eyes. "They're kept under here?" Her voice is hesitant.

Dom answers softly. "Kept. Left. Discarded. All three work."

"Leaving takes me to the Exiled? And they can help?"

"They can." Dom pauses for a moment. "We can't afford to give up the benefits we gain by Bastian being here. Since he cannot leave, the logical choice is you."

"Do you come with me?"

Dom shakes his head. "Not yet. There are things I'm still needed here for."

Sai's shoulders slump slightly. "How do I get out?" Her voice is soft and unsure.

Bastian smiles. "I thought you'd never ask. We don't have that long. I'll have to give you brief points and make sure you remember them. Are you sure you're feeling up to it, Sai?"

She nods and clenches her fists.

Bastian runs a hand through his hair as he watches the sun set from his bedroom window. He can hear Sai turning pages of an old text he loaned her. She's determined, horrified, and shocked at what she's learned in such a short period of time.

It's not possible to lie mind-to-mind. She's listed every image she ran across, every experiment Johnson went through, and all the pain endured for the psionic extraction process. All these emotions belonging to a different person cause her pain to take in.

She's stronger than he thought. Bastian smiles and lets himself hope they might have a chance of instigating some change, that maybe his father's untimely death was for a reason. He has so many strings to pull and so much he needs to set up from within. Knowing there'll be backup on the outside is pure relief.

Dom walks into his quarters and stops. Bastian turns to see his friend shaking and his eyes going through a myriad of colors, some Bastian didn't even know existed. He steps back and watches, unsure if he can nudge Dom out of whatever fit he's having.

Then the adrium colors shift and mold to every variation in the room. It's eerie to see just how inhuman Dom actually is. Bastian's grateful he has the foresight to mind-record the incident so Sai can hand it to Mathur for further study and hopefully help stop it.

The rainbowing lasts a full five minutes. It worries Bastian, and he's pretty sure if Dom realizes even half how bad it is, he'll probably be scared, too.

Eventually Dom comes out of it, eyes blinking as he tries to reorient himself. "Dammit."

"You know when that happens then?"

Dom shakes his head. "Not during. Only after." His eyes remain silver, and he taps his ear several times before gold hues rain across his eyes as he reestablishes the tenuous connection with the others. A brief wince furrows his brows, and he stumbles. "If I were a Damascus, I'd say I am malfunctioning. It's odd and is happening to the others as well."

"They're not quite like you, correct?"

"The other dominos? I've never been allowed close enough to study them, but I know it's like they left something out of the mix after Mathur left. They're not as stable, not as 'well built' for want of a better phrase."

"In anyone else, I'd call that conceit." Bastian laughs and steps over to his friend. "You're due for your check-up soon. I'm sure they can fix whatever is wrong."

"Maybe." Dom looks away. "I feel like a part of me has been slipping ever since he left, you know."

"You should go out to see him."

"Not right now. We have more at stake than me." Dom straightens and looks back at Bastian. "Do you think she's ready?"

"No," Bastian answers truthfully. "But I wasn't ready to take on the world when my father died either, and I did it anyway. Sometimes it's not what you are ready to do, but what you can do that matters. Eventually, for Sai, they should end up being the same thing."

"You think she can teach them?"

"Not yet. But by the time I have her ready to leave, she'll be able to identify and seek out any type of psionic." Bastian glances at his watch. "Food will be here soon. I was thinking I'll keep her in my guest quarters for a bit. I think she's too volatile at the moment. If she accidentally comes across Deign in the hall, I can't see it ending nicely."

Dom nods. "You're probably right. The plan is to train her before she has to go out on her next assignment. They're dangerous. She might not come back." His phrasing is obviously to stave off any spikes in interest from anyone choosing to use his connection.

"Got it in one." Bastian wishes it were as easy as Dom makes it sound. Between Deign, Zach, and the rest of GNW, Bastian is starting to wonder if he'll get out of this alive.

Still, if it means they succeed, maybe even death is worth it.

CHAPTER
Fourteen

Sai sits on the floor in Bastian's guest room, staring at the readers in front of her. It aches to look at the pictures. Archaic devices used to strap people down, syringes littering the tables next to them. There's no privacy in the wards or dormitories. In all of the images, they're strapped at the head, neck, shoulders, elbows, hands, pelvis, knees, and ankles. Just to make sure they truly can't get free, their hands and feet are locked into shackles that bind them to the bedframes.

She remembers her parents once watching some old scary movie for entertainment. Apparently Shine could heighten any type of experience for them while they tumbled across the floor accosting each other. Sai shakes her head to clear it of that image and turns back to the remaining ones in front of her.

None of the staff bother to use different veins for injections. The wrists and elbows are ripe with bruising and scabs. With today's tech, an injection should let the skin close behind it and aid its healing. Either it's been done so often to the people that their skin can't obey or else the staff are using abandoned tech.

A tear falls off her cheek and splashes against the screen. Sai rubs it away and leafs through to the next set of photographs. A testing ward, where people are poked and prodded to find their breaking point. She quickly flips through them, trying to suppress the loop of Johnson's memories playing in her head, but there's no relief. The next recorded section shows the psionic-energy extraction process, and Sai shudders with revulsion. Skin pales, bodies convulse, and eyes roll back. Even though she can see them screaming, the sound doesn't come from their mouths, but echoes around in her head instead.

After another few pictures, she pushes the reader away and leans back against the headboard. Maybe, if she crawls underneath the covers and goes to sleep, she'll wake up to a different world where she doesn't have a dead man's painful memories inside her head, where she hasn't lived a lie her entire life.

Taken from scared parents who thought they were sending him to a place that would be better for him, Johnson barely had a chance to know what the normal life he was missing would be like. She clenches her fists at the thought, caught up in the memories as if they're her own.

"Sai?" Bastian pops his head around the divider, interrupting her self-destructive train of thought. "You ready to go over the rules of finding?"

"Seriously?" she asks with disbelief as she pushes herself up off the bed, gingerly favoring her left side. "You call it *finding*? Couldn't come up with anything more original than that?"

He crosses his arms and raises an eyebrow. "I had other things to come up with names for." He leads the way toward the training area.

The rooms are even darker now that she knows their origin. While Sai doesn't completely understand Bastian's position in everything, she does understand that, without him, the Exiled would have one of their major resources cut off. Not to mention removing him allows one less avenue for deliberately misleading leaks to go through. News of her target would never have made it without Bastian.

Their next move will be to fake her death, just as Mathur did years before. She's not sure how she feels about it, even if it's just enough flesh and blood to simulate the remnants of an explosion. Removing the tracker is going to hurt the most.

The one thought she's trying to avoid is leaving Dom behind. He's been there every step of the way, had her back so often she's lost count. Once she leaves, she'll have no one. A fresh start in a sea full of strangers who probably resent her for killing their people. Not that that's a foreign feeling.

She sighs softly and glances up to see Bastian scowling at her.

"Something wrong, Sai?

"Thinking."

"It has to be something major. You've been ignoring me for the last few minutes."

She blinks. "I have?"

"Yeah."

She hugs her chest. "The grid, this thought suggestion thing. I don't understand it."

Bastian shrugs. "The theory was that a content people leads to a content existence. If we can suggest to people's inner thoughts, that there's nothing to complain about, they'll believe they arrived at that decision themselves."

Sai frowns. "Are people really that stupid?"

"Did you believe?"

"What?"

"Did you..." He purses his lips and his brow crinkles for a moment. "Did you take everything you were taught to be the truth?"

"You know I did."

"And did you have any proof, or did you just believe? Like with the razor rabbits."

"They don't count. Their teeth are sharp." She mulls it over in her head. "But I see your point. I was told about them long before I ever encountered one."

Bastian smiles. "So take it one step further. If you weren't told but assumed it was your own thoughts, would you believe it even more?"

Sai blinks as her breath catches in her throat. The horror of it hits her with more force than she anticipated, and she fights the urge to double over and retch. "We have to stop this."

"That's the idea. It's going to be okay." He walks over and places a hand on her head. Despite her hatred for physical contact, it soothes her. She nods at him so he doesn't worry, even if the words do nothing to allay her fears.

"So you understand what you're going to be doing?"

She knows this question has nothing to do with the training but with her leaving the Facilities. "I believe I understand perfectly, Bastian." Her voice sounds mechanical, even to her.

"Good." He smiles one of his rare smiles at her. "Now, let's try this finding, and if you come up with a better name for it, we'll name it that."

The ground is harder than she remembers, like her old bed at home. Her true home, the one where she blew up her parents. Try as anyone might to couch it nicely, the truth was the truth, and there was no escaping it. Part of her would like to think it an accident, but the rest of her knows better.

She turns over to look at the ceiling only to see vines growing through cracks in the cement, and the rest of the roof on a slant upheld by a few precarious concrete beams. Sai moves lightly to the left, making sure not to disturb anything on her way. She half-slides across the angled floor to a doorway and crumbling hall.

Crisscrossing through a maze of concrete walls and arches, her feet finally hit solid ground right next to a large glass pane, half shattered on the dirt. Just beyond it are the remnants of what was once the beautiful botanica. For a moment, she closes her eyes and remembers the welcome solitude and escape she found in that tiny patch of green.

Everything is dead, shriveled in the caustic air. No matter how well they filter, it is never enough for the plants. Someone once mentioned there's a paradise somewhere in Australia, in a place called Tamborine. It remains untarnished and beautiful. Sai recalls laughing at that person. Some lies are harder to believe than others.

Something moves in the corner of her vision, but when she turns toward it, it's gone. Sai frowns and tries again with a bigger show of nonchalance, and this time she sees the creature. Pale and hunched over, it looks like a human who doesn't get enough light. It reaches out to touch her hand and Sai remembers clearly.

Her own memory, lost until now, slams into her and sends her reeling. With everything that happened, she'd forgotten the old woman dressed in pale blue—like the nurses in the images she pulled from Johnson's head.

She'd even forgotten the tempting whispers:

It's okay. We'll make the pain stop. You'll never have to think or remember again.

But footsteps interrupt the woman before she can touch Sai's hand.

Bastian saved her.

She sits up in bed, the sweat on her body mingling with the chill night air. "They almost had me." It doesn't feel real unless she says it out loud. "Almost." She shakes her head, the gratitude swelling inside her as she curls back up in bed, trying to regain some of the warmth.

Regardless of any current butting of heads, she owes Bastian a lot. If helping the Exiled helps him, it's not even a question.

But doubt whispers in her ear whenever the images stop flashing through her mind for a moment. It calls to her, questions her new resolve and scares her.

What if GNW is the victim? What if they've been protecting and *not* using her all along?

And then the dream comes back to her, and Johnson's images slam home. If those aren't the lie, then everything else she was taught has to be. Doesn't it?

The day dawns bright and cheerful, mocking Sai's inner turmoil.

She climbs out of bed, regretful that it'll be her last night in such comfort. It's only been six days since she woke up screaming in it. Amazing how easy it is to form a bond with something inanimate.

Dressing quickly, she tiptoes out of Bastian's quarters and makes her way to the cafeteria. Though she knows Nimue was sent, more than once, by Deign to tap into her thoughts, Sai still feels a sliver of friendship for the girl.

What her mentor demanded of her wasn't her fault. Even less so now that Sai realizes nothing is how she thought. She knows she can't warn the other girl and doesn't have any delusions of saving anyone right now: The operation will be delicate enough just trying to get her out. But saying goodbye in her own way, to the closest thing she's ever had to a friend? That should be possible.

Sai scans the cafeteria as she grabs a squished block of bread and spies Nimue in the corner. She sits with her hair pulled back tightly and her powder pink uniform perfectly pressed. Her pale skin makes the freckles stand out more than usual. Sai thinks she's aged since she last saw her.

"Hey, Nim." Sai takes a seat opposite the other girl and picks at the wrapper.

Nimue looks up slowly and blinks once before a smile spreads on her face. "Sai. They said you were sick."

"Yeah, I was." She turns her face to the right.

Nimue gasps. "Does that hurt?" She reaches out a hand, and Sai shies back.

"Yeah. No touching." Sai smiles to take the edge off the words.

"Sorry." Sadness reaches Nimue's eyes.

Sai hurries to reassure her. "Don't! I didn't really mean it like that. It's still tender."

Nimue smiles, that melancholy tinge still in her expression. "Are you coming back to class?"

Sai almost chokes on her bread, but smiles brightly. "Not this time. I have another assignment. Man, am I going to need your help with schoolwork when I'm done." And she pulls a face for effect. It's not really a lie. She just won't be able to come back for the help.

"Lucky. I get stuck with the boys all the time, and they're no company. My roommate isn't even talkative." Nimue sighs and pushes her food away. "I thought I'd offended you, even after the talk."

For a few moments, Sai watches her before making a decision. "No. You didn't. I just don't deal well with people."

"Good." Nimue sighs in relief. "Can't chase away the one friend I've got."

The words hit Sai harder in the gut than she thought. But she knows there's no way they can take Nimue, too. Not with Deign as her mentor. She pushes back the sudden tears she can feel behind her eyes. "Nope, you can't. Remember I'll always be your friend." And right then, Sai means it.

Nimue laughs. "You sound so serious. Thanks." She grins at Sai. "Been a bit down lately."

"Anything you want to talk about?" Sai asks the question impulsively, surprising even herself.

For a moment, it looks like Nimue might say something, but she shakes her head. "No. It's just training woes. Being in this position... Not everything is like I expected it to be."

A shiver runs down Sai's back as she remembers Dom reminding her how lucky she was to have Bastian. "I know exactly what you mean."

"Good. Sometimes I think I'm going crazy. Sometimes the tension in the air around here is suffocating." Nimue laughs, sounding a little more like herself.

"Heh. I have to go." Sai pushes her chair back, aware her time is running out. But before she leaves, a thought strikes her. "Nim, don't believe everything you hear."

Nimue blinks at her and cocks her head to one side. "I think I can do that."

"I'll see you around."

"See you later, Sai. I'll take notes for you." She winks and goes back to finishing her breakfast.

Sai waves a goodbye, not trusting her voice to speak without giving away the sadness she feels.

Back in the guest room, she tugs two spare body armor suits and squeezes them in the backpack next to her bed. The adrium woven through the material is warm to the touch. Another two pairs of training pants and about six tank tops, pajamas, and a second pair of running shoes follow them in. The side pockets are already stuffed with Shine so Bastian doesn't have to make his usual monthly covert trip. Despite knowing it's not used dangerously there, it still gives her the chills.

Bastian walks into the room without knocking, and she scowls at him, glad she's already pulled her suit into place.

He glances around, patting down the long coat he wears instead of making eye contact. "Ready?"

She sighs. "As ready as I'll ever be. Are you sure I can do this?" *Are you really telling me the truth?*

"I wouldn't have picked you if I thought you couldn't. Dom has a package for you in *Mele*. Make sure to take it with you, please?"

Sai nods and hoists her backpack up, waiting for him to speak again, sure that he wants to.

He opens his mouth, looks around, and finally says, "You have to be careful. I know you can trust Mathur. You can also trust Mason."

"Who's Mason?" She watches the slight twitch in Bastian's fingers, like they want to strum against his coat. He seems nervous.

Bastian's lips draw in a tight line. "Mason is my brother. It's a long story. Suffice it to say I have many reasons to remain in this position, and he's not happy with the risks I take. He can be hot-headed."

"I didn't know you had a brother." Suspicion stirs in her brain, but she quells it. Her gut instinct is to trust Bastian, and it's rarely wrong, even if he seems on edge.

"He's the typical older brother. Bossy." A smile tugs at the corners of his mouth, but it's gone an instant later.

Sai shrugs and tests the backpack position. "I wouldn't know. I never had a sibling."

"It's not all it's cracked up to be. Just someone else to blame for things."

"Can I ask for something?" Sai asks before her courage runs out.

Bastian smiles this time. "Of course."

"Could you please keep an eye on Nimue and the others? It's not her fault. She's not like you imagine. Please?"

Bastian studies her for a moment. "Okay."

Sai scowls. "Not just okay. Keep a real look out for them, especially for her. And figure out a way to help her out of here. This place isn't right for her."

"Okay, and I mean it. I will." He pauses for a moment. "There's one more thing I need you to do for me."

She stops fiddling with the straps and glances up at him.

"I need you to take care of the package Dom has waiting for you. Very good care of it. Make sure it doesn't fall into hands that could damage it or use it for something it's not intended."

She can see he's picking his words more carefully than ever before and frowns, resisting the urge to panic. "Is everything okay, Bastian?"

He nods quickly. "This is important. Promise me this."

"I don't even know if I can protect it, Bastian, you haven't told me what it is." *You never told me anything. How can I trust what I don't know?* The panic rises again, and she takes a deep breath.

"It's an important package. Deliver it to Mason when you get the chance."

Sai opens her mouth to protest, but the determination in Bastian's expression takes her off-guard and she waves a hand. "Sure, with everything else you've given me to do, taking on an extra duty to guard something I have no idea about is easy. Anything else while I'm at it? Want me to get you some kind of paint only available out there in Exiled country because you want to redecorate and no other color will do? I'm sure I can squeeze it in, along with convincing myself I'm not going crazy."

"There's my little spitfire." Bastian looks away for a moment. "You'll do fine, Sai. You're more capable than you think. I've taught you almost everything I know that you can absorb. Hopefully, you can teach others."

She glares at him. He has a way to get under her skin and make her trust him implicitly. "Honestly, I'm not sure how I'm supposed to deal with you, Bastian."

"I get that a lot."

"Are there many healers?" she asks him as they leave the office.

"No, I've told you that."

"You didn't tell me why," she says softly, clouding her voice so only he will hear.

He shrugs. "It's not something highly sought-after in GNW. They use tech for healing. Regardless of how effective the psionic method is, it still relies on a human battery. GNW has other ways to utilize that power."

"Ah..." She pushes down the butterflies in her stomach and the nagging at the base of her skull. Gut. Trust the gut.

"Dom will be with you as far as the...incident. He'll have to be your only contact here for a while, too." Bastian's tone is apologetic, and Sai isn't sure why.

"Sure," she says, barely recognizing her own voice.

"Any questions?" Bastian asks her gently. She shakes her head as they reach the docking bay's doors. Suddenly, Bastian hugs her and slips a tiny device into her hand as he does so, whispering in her ear. "That's an amplifier. If you need me, if you *really* need me, use that to magnify...and you'll find me."

She pulls away, startled by the sudden emotions and annoyed to feel tears in her eyes. "Thank you—for everything."

Sai watches Bastian walk away before she boards *Mele* and stops dead, gaze locked on the slight girl with beautiful, dark, golden brown skin and odd blood-streaked hair curled up on the floor. "What the hell is that?" she asks softly.

"Oh," Dom says, looking around from the front as he lowers the entrance door. "That is Bastian's niece. I believe her name is Ash... Aishke, I think? We need to take her to her father. She wiped out the entire side of her mother's family. I'm pretty sure he'll be fine with that though." Dom grins. "It was a very messy divorce."

Something dawns on Sai, and she stands there gaping at their passenger. "Please tell me we have a real package. Wrapped in synth-paper. Sealed in a prismatic container. Something?"

"Nope—the package is her."

Sai groans. "So I'm playing babysitter *and* hero—great. You do realize I'm going to get both her and I shot, and then Bastian will hate me and everything will have been for nothing and..." She looks around, patting *Mele* for a moment. "Is this secure? Can they hear me? Have I just ruined everything?"

"You realize everything you just thought actually came out of your mouth as a verbal representation of those thoughts, correct?" Dom asks as he begins to maneuver *Mele* out of her parking bay.

"Yes!" Sai snaps while glaring at him.

"To answer your question, you can talk as freely as you like here." He smiles that secretive half-smile, his silver eyes twinkling strangely. "You're safe."

Sai smiles. "I wish that could last forever..." she murmurs and leans forward to rest her head against Dom's cool, smooth shoulder. He feels safe, and she misses him already. Regardless of how much turmoil her head is going through, Dom is precious to her.

She's not entirely sure how long she remains that way, but when she examines the cabin again, their guest still hasn't moved.

"How long has she been out for?" Sai asks.

"About twelve hours. Don't worry. The stuff she got will knock her out for three days. Plenty of time for you to get where you're going, set up shields, and protect her and probably others for when she wakes up."

"That dangerous?" A sinuous voice in the back of her head proposes that perhaps GNW is right to lock away psionics. Sai shudders inwardly.

Dom nods. "For now and unshielded. She never should have tipped past dormant. Even dormants have a spring of power; it's just not accessible or filled unless triggered. Something bad must have gone down there to awaken so late. You'll figure that out when you erect shields on her. Poor thing. Bastian couldn't just leave her there."

"He couldn't leave me there either. For any other reason, making a habit of rescuing young girls would be sort of creepy." Sai sits there for a while, watching the other girl breathe in and out. Sai frowns. "How old is she?"

"Sixteen? Maybe fifteen, almost sixteen? Like I said, she bloomed late."

"Late doesn't even begin to describe it."

Time doesn't pass as quickly as usual for Sai. Her stomach won't stop fluttering and her heart keeps trying to beat out of her chest as the memories spam her mind. "Dom," she says softly, not quite sure she really wants to say the words.

"Mhm?"

"I'll miss you." It feels so final.

He looks over at her, silver eyes bright in the dim light of the transport. "Thank you. That means more than I realized." He pauses and glances back at Aishke before speaking. "I'll miss you, too, and I don't often miss at all."

Sai chuckles, but her heart feels heavy for reasons she doesn't understand. Almost six months at the senior facility and she's leaving. She keeps expecting enforcement cars to sidle up next to *Mele* and pull them over and arrest her for treason, confiscating all the goods she has and imprisoning her, Aishke, and Dom for testing purposes.

No one but civilians pass them, and the journey is uneventful. Sai has to fight the panic she feels when *Mele* comes to rest just outside UC 29.

"This is it," she murmurs and glances at Aishke. "How am I supposed to transport her?"

Dom stands up and fishes a strange set of armor out of the cage. "It's a back harness. We'll clip the backpack to it, too. You don't have to phase for long so you should be able to carry both of you for this. I should be able to erase her out of the footage."

"Great. I suppose I should give you the rest of the evidence, huh?" Sai chose a section of her thigh earlier, but it's a lot more difficult to remove flesh than she thought. Having access to one of Bastian's laser toys certainly helps, but now, with her thigh partially healed again, she needs to provide some more blood. While not completely sure how Dom intends to fake her death with what she gives him, she's perfectly fine with leaving it in his capable hands.

He takes a tool she doesn't recognize out and grips her wrist, somewhat of an apologetic expression on his face as he swipes it over the tracking bracelet under her skin. "You're lucky you didn't get yours at birth. This will hurt, but you'll keep your hand. The flesh needs to look authentic."

She bites down on her lip as the large tweezer-like contraption sends a jolt and a small sear of pain through her arm. Its prongs hook through her skin and into what appears to be a small slot in the bracelet through her skin. Dom grips the thick silver handle and glances at her. "Ready?"

"What—more?" She tries not to laugh as the sweat starts to bead on her brow. Instead she closes her eyes and nods. The sensation when he yanks the band out from under her skin is like fire scraping over stone with enough force to crack it. Her chest heaves, and it's difficult to catch her breath as she opens her eyes, the bloody circle around her wrist flared and painful. She concentrates on it immediately to dull the pain a little before wrapping it in the offered gauze.

Sai just nods and glances at the clock as she pulls her armor back on. Not much time left. On impulse, she walks to where Dom stands checking one of the systems on *Mele* and hugs him. For a few seconds she stays there, not wanting to let go, and knowing she has to. His hands rest against her back and she revels in the first constant in her life: Dom.

Finally, Sai steps back, expression a little sheepish.

"That was nice." Dom smiles his version of a smile at her. "Thank you."

She can tell he means it.

Dawning light has already proven perfect for low visibility. Sai checks her armor and the harness as they wrestle Aishke into it. The girl barely stirs as they finagle the pack onto Sai's back. Aishke is slightly taller than Sai, which makes the harness even more awkward. At least the girl is pretty light, and the harness hoists her up enough that Sai's pretty sure she can phase the short distance.

A faint light shimmers briefly to the north, giving her phasing a destination. Sai looks at Dom and nods, trying not to feel so sad. If she gives into her confused emotions, she'll never leave. She'll end up huddled in a ball in a padded cell or strapped to a lab table.

Instead, she waits for the third light. Waits for the timing so Dom gets the correct footage.

Second light.

Sai starts to bounce on the balls of her feet, getting ready for the jump and used to the increased weight on her back. One day, she will see Bastian again and smack him in the face for saddling her with babysitting duty.

Third light.

She moves out immediately. One step, glide, two—and phase. The first phase feels a little off-center as her burden swings slightly to the left. She adjusts mid-phase and comes out of it only slightly wobbling, immediately rectified in the next step she takes. Two steps, three steps, and phase right into the blast zone, which shakes her as she comes down to take two steps and move on. The pain in her wrist flares up with the proximity of heat from the explosion and is far worse than she anticipated. It throws her equilibrium off as she flies through the third phase. Just one more and she can stop.

The sun starts to crest the horizon, and her body strains under the added exertion. All around her, the strange red sand begins to lose its frosty crust, and she steps through one last time before launching into her fourth and final phase. She overshoots the small group, well-camouflaged by their own technology, and has to jog back. The air stings her lungs. She should have worn a mask.

It feels strange jogging into their camp, specifically set up to mimic an ambush. There's a small tent that flickers in and out of sync with the desert surroundings, sort of like a heat haze. The more realistic the setting, the more authentic Dom's footage will appear. She motions for water and air as she deposits her cargo gently into the makeshift bed they've erected in the center. Inside their tent, it's automatically easier to breathe, and the water is cool, with a mild lemon tang that faintly reminds her of the facilities. Every pair of eyes focuses on her as she sits and sips the water, and the small tent feels crowded. She's never wanted or liked having attention directed at her.

They wait for her to catch her breath. An elderly man at the front of the group with the same square-shaped face as Dom smiles gently.

He steps forward when she stops panting. "I'm Dr. Mathur. Welcome to the Exiled, Sai. We are sorry we had to bring you in the way we did."

She smiles, recognizing him from Johnson's memories, and is overwhelmed by the urge to yawn. Carrying an extra person drained her more than double the usual amount. Every limb is hard to move, her head pounds, and her wrist screams out for soothing. Sai looks up at the kindly old man and smiles. "I think I might need to lie down for a bit."

The last thing she remembers is the world turning upside down before darkness surrounds her.

CHAPTER
Fifteen

Sai blinks her eyes open and focuses on the ceiling with a strange sense of déjà vu. But this ceiling is different and tall. Material drapes it, or rather as she squints a bit to get a better look... Material *is* the ceiling. It appears to be a tent of some kind. Her head hurts. Everything hurts. She's so thirsty she could drink sand.

She sits up abruptly and cries out in pain, immediately searching for her charge. "Aishke?" she speaks—or tries to. All that tumbles from her mouth is a hoarse whisper. Her gaze falls on the bed next to her, and she sighs with relief. Aishke is curled up on the cot in much the same way she was on *Mele*'s floor.

Sai shudders as the pain in her body rears its ugly head.

"You pushed yourself a little hard there, young lady." Mathur's voice is kindly and matches his appearance.

"I didn't realize I'd be taking a passenger..." Her voice trails off, raspy and sore.

Mathur hands her a glass of water. "It is filtered. More so than the water you have had in the cities."

She sips a few times, knowing it's more dangerous to gulp the clear liquid down than to sip it, as much as she might want to. "Do you think they'll look for me?"

Mathur shakes his head. "They should not. My Dom is nothing if not thorough. Will you..." He pauses as guilt and excitement war in his eyes. "Later, after you rest, will you tell me a little of him?"

Sai nods and drinks a few more sips. "Of course."

The older man claps his hands and smiles. He has a jolly smile, and it sends a red blush to his cheeks and a twinkle to his eyes. "Excellent. Now...I have received your delivery. Thank you very much for that risk you took. It will help us at least another month, perhaps a little longer. We may be able to get a little closer to our antidote, but that is a different story. What I need to know, little Sai, is who is this other girl you brought with you, and why is she here?

Sai blinks, unsure how to explain what she barely knows herself. "Bastian said I had a package to deliver to you. This is Aishke—Aishke is Bastian's niece? His brother's daughter? Something like that. Mason?"

Mathur frowns. "Mason is not here. He is at one of the other cities. I am certain he does not have a daughter."

"Oh." Sai pushes down the panic in her stomach at having brought someone with her no one was expecting. What would they do? How would they react?

"Unless it is his ex-wife's adoptive daughter? She could not have her own and adopted a baby girl about two years before she met him. Mason has always loved that girl. That is her?" He eyes the girl with renewed interest.

What Sai thought was blood-streaked blonde hair is just deep red dyed hair. *Mele*'s lighting must have been off. Aishke's build is wiry, and her eyebrows make even her sleeping expression pinched with worry. Her dark skin has a golden sheen, making her look like a statue in the white light. "That's what I was told. I don't think Dom would lie." She half-smiles at that thought.

"No, he does not." Mathur says. "You have risked much to come to us. I am sorry we had to convince you the way we did." His eyes are sad, and then his words sink in.

"You had to convince me the way you did?" She gulps in air, doubt eating at her again. "From what I pulled from Johnson?"

Mathur pats her hand gently. "Bastian did not get opportunity to tell you, then? Franklin and Johnson were decoys."

"Decoys?" That can't mean what she thinks it means.

"We have to protect those of us truly able to change things. We could not 'leak' our real people to GNW, but we could leak decoys."

"Why leak anything at all?" She looks at him in horror, unable to wrap her mind around the thought. Decoys? They were completely innocent. Everything was planned.

"Because GNW knows we have many things in development. As long as we feed them a decoy every now and again, they think they are quelling uprisings. Does not always work, but it makes them feel better. Sometimes they are true targets Bastian has helped smuggle out."

"But - decoys? Bastian has had to kill his friends?" she asks incredulously.

Mathur shrugs. "You could look at it that way, I suppose. But we never send anyone who will not die of some other complication before their natural life would normally end."

Relief floods her for a moment when she realizes what he's saying. "You mean Franklin and Johnson were going to die anyway? I didn't completely murder them?" She hates the hope that floods her tone but wants it more than anything.

"No," Mathur says kindly. "Especially in Johnson's case. He had been ill for years *because* of the facility. For him, this was perfect. He could make sure his memories lived on, giving them to someone who would help do something about treatment that has killed thousands of people over the years." Mathur pauses and takes a drink of water for himself. "You cannot let the propaganda brainwash you. Ever since the Disaster Era, psionics have been born, yes, but we are not a majority. We are working on a method where non-psionics have the ability to protect themselves from thought influence."

Sai nods, determined to understand, but her eyelids keep drooping. "I'm so sorry. I want to hear this, I want to know this, but I can't keep my eyes open."

"I am sorry, my dear, I should have thought." Mathur smiles and pushes her to lie down, covering her with the thin blanket. "Get some rest, because I have a feeling we will need you when Aishke wakes up. Not to mention we have so much more we need to talk about."

The bed is comfortable and lulls her into sleep. For the first time in many nights, Sai relaxes.

When she does wake up, Sai frowns. The ceiling is the same pale type of tent material, but sways like they're moving. Closing her eyes she feels around her, yelping in surprise. She has no idea how they've motorized the medi-tent she's in, but it's definitely no longer stationary.

Sitting up requires a lot more effort than Sai remembers. Merely pushing herself upright smarts her wrist. If she'd had an inkling that she'd be phasing with a passenger, she'd have practiced for it. There's a glass of water on a pristine white nightstand to the right of her, near the pillow. Gratefully she grabs it and swallows its contents, quite certain she should be okay by now.

The cool liquid spreads down her throat and throughout her body like a salve. Whatever the stuff is, she's determined to get a bunch and keep it nearby when she trains.

Sai wriggles her toes, happy to see her legs, while still sore, are working. She swings them off the bed and lets her feet rest on the floor, feeling the tiny vibrations caused by the movement of the room. Aishke's bed is right in front of her, and she frowns at the slumbering girl.

Still asleep, her charge looks peaceful enough. As Sai understands it, Bastian sent her along to the Exiled so Aishke wouldn't end up a battery, tapped for the GNW thought suggestion grid. The girl's eyes flicker while she sleeps.

Bastian and his rescue missions. Sai shakes her head, trying not to miss home too much. She stands, a little wobbly at first, and reaches her arms up to stretch all of her ailing muscles, turning suddenly when she hears a gasp.

A dark-haired woman stands in the doorway, hand over her mouth, a blush rising in her bronzed cheeks. Her long lashes, full lips, and rosy cheeks are slightly juxtaposed with her stocky, strong physique.

"I'm so sorry, ma'am. Mathur sent me to check on you, and I just didn't think you'd be up yet. He said you were injured. I'll bring you a change of clothes if you like." She speaks so fast it's difficult to keep up. Sai blinks and recovers composure just in time to catch her before she goes out the door.

"Excuse me?" Sai asks. "But I'd like to wear the clothes I brought with me." As welcoming as the Exiled appear, Sai misses the protection of her body armor. Just in case.

The woman bows her head quickly and nods as she runs off. Sai moves around the small, far too bright room, stretching as she goes, trying to loosen the tightness of her muscles. Her head still feels fuzzy, but it's much better than the last time she woke up.

"Miss?" The brunette is back with Sai's bulging back-pack and hands it over. "Mr. Mathur said to let you know if there's anything else, to just say."

Sai nods as she pulls clothing and spare shoes out of her bag. "What's your name?" she asks without taking her head out of the bag.

"Iria, miss."

"Please don't do that. Call me Sai. I might not always answer if you call me something different." She pauses for a moment, but the negative whispers have been silent since she woke up.

Iria smiles, and it lights up her whole face in a way that makes Sai warm to her. "Sure, I can manage that, Sai. I look forward to working with you." Iria gives a wave as she heads back out, but Sai mentally follows her progress and notices her stopping just outside the tent to stand guard.

"Interesting," she mutters to herself as she glances around the small room. There's a wash cubicle in the corner. Steam wash. Just like the transports. The controls on the outside of it are a little different, and it appears to be timed.

Four minutes worth of a steam shower is heaven. Her skin feels cleaner than it has in days, and it's easy to dry off, pop her hair up into a ponytail and pull one of her clean suits on. "Finally," she murmurs. "Human again."

Aishke stirs on the bed, and Sai's heart sits in her mouth. She coughs and walks over to her charge, brushing the younger girl's mind and finding with relief that she's still deeply asleep, just not really drugged anymore. She should wake up in a matter of hours. The trace she places on Aishke is light enough to avoid alerting the girl, but will give Sai warning when she starts to wake up.

"Mathur has to be around here somewhere," she mutters and walks to the main door. The movement feels strangely like *Mele*, just a little smoother, and Sai wonders how they do it.

Iria pops her head around the tent flap. "Hi, m—Sai, did you say something?"

Sai narrows her eyes a little, uneasy at the thought of being guarded so closely that even her muttering is audible. "I haven't seen this...vehicle. I have no idea where Mathur is, and I might not have much time once Ash wakes up."

Iria's smile broadens. "You realized it's a vehicle! Nicely done. Most people don't and then get startled when I take them up to the piloting deck."

Sai shrugs. "She feels a bit like *Mele*."

"*Mele*? The transport? I've heard stories about her." Iria chuckles, all her original uncertainty gone. "Follow me, I can give you a quick tour and then take you up to see Mathur."

By the time Iria gets around to leading Sai to Mathur, Sai is completely sure the Exiled are marginally insane. So friendly it's not funny, but definitely insane. They're not really in a vehicle, although she did see a bay with several of them in it. This is a huge, moving town that Iria calls the Mobile.

As far as Sai can tell, it's a large circular dome. The outer layers of the town are living quarters and the infirmary, with some training and meeting areas. It works its way through the layers to the center where the commercial block is.

And it's a true commercial area. There are places to eat, to buy food, to work. Best of all, the very center is home to a greenhouse, far larger than the botanica Sai grew up with. It sits directly beneath a piece of specially treated UV-filtered glass, which allows the sun to help the vegetables grow like they would have before the great disasters.

This Mobile houses over a thousand people, and just like *Mele*, it almost feels alive. The tent-like material encasing the interior hums softly and emanates a warmth Sai didn't expect.

Her footfalls are cushioned by whatever is used to line their walkways. Even though most of the decor is white, it's nothing like the oppressive atmosphere inside the Facilities.

Mathur is in what Iria refers to as the control deck. It sits a little higher than the two-story low dome they ride in. Located right at the front, it allows the navigators an excellent view of where to steer the monstrosity. Sai barely notices when Mathur turns to greet her, so engaged is she by the way the world looks through the visor of the city. She gasps in disbelief at the constantly adapting iridescent colors of the hull.

"Wow." She breathes out the words, not taking her eyes off the view. "It's not what I expected. You use adrium?"

Mathur nods and smiles at her reaction. "In a sense. We use an Adrium-woven net that sort of fills in the blanks as it goes. That is why, unless we are perfectly still, it is not quite camouflage."

"Isn't that dangerous?"

Mathur shrugs. "Not really. When we need full camouflage, we stop. With the sensors, we know with plenty of warning when we need to do that."

Sai smiles and glances back out as the Mobile slowly covers ground. She shades her eyes and starts at the faint flicker in the distance—there one second, gone the next. "There are more?"

"Many more. We are the vanguard of our city. Right now we only have eighteen of these vehicles. Our cities are made up of two or three Mobiles. Provides safer transport. Far better than living like a nomad, although some of our settlements are still stuck out there. This one here..." He pats the wall affectionately. "She is our biggest."

"You built this?"

He nods. "I built this one first, using *Mele*'s plans as a model. Sadly, I can only work so fast, and the components take a while to develop. In a few years, all of our encampments will have Mobiles to carry them."

Sai smiles at him. "I love *Mele*, she's beautiful. This is beautiful." She closes her eyes for a second, startled by the tears that threaten. "How do you know where each other will be if you need help?"

"We meet once every quarter and distribute supplies amongst ourselves, discuss the state of events, and generally have a good time. The Exiled use a specific branding. Once taught our branding system, it is easy to navigate to the meeting places even out here on the plains. For now, let us just say we have our ways."

Sai nods. It's easy to understand that she still needs to earn their trust. The feeling is mutual. She still isn't quite ready to accept everything.

"So..." He looks at Sai expectantly. "What do you think?"

"Of the Mobile?" Sai asks, still watching the passing landscape out the window. She continues without waiting for an answer. "It's breathtaking. I wish I'd had the chance to grow up here, though I probably would have leveled one of these. Such a nicer place to grow up." She shakes her head trying to clear that train of thought. "Sorry, thinking out loud."

Mathur rests a hand on her shoulder. "No, I am sorry. You have been through a lot in your young life, but Bastian was so sure of you, so proud of how far you have come. We all believe in you, because if he says you can do it, we know you can."

Sai can feel the heat rush to her cheeks. No pressure or anything.

"What do you think of the rest of it—us and what we stand for?"

Sai shrugs. "I'm still not one hundred percent certain I know what it is you stand for. But if the people here are the vicious Exiled we get taught to fear and hate? Then it's already a more humane place to be than the UC I grew up in. The world is what we make it, right?" She studies her hands, still clean from the shower and murmurs without really thinking. "Maybe we should make it somewhere people *want* to live."

She looks up at Mathur to smile, but a wave rocks her head and she clutches it, disoriented for a moment. "The trace just activated. Aishke's about to wake up."

Sai arrives at the room on the second wave of her mental alarm. Leaving Aishke to wake alone in a strange place after everything that's happened is probably a very bad idea. If Bastian's instructions are correct, she has three more. Plenty of time to prepare. Sai deconstructs her shields and rebuilds, binding them tighter. She checks over her outer shields and glances up at Mathur and Iria sitting there, waiting eagerly.

"Could you two wait outside for a bit? This might be wiser with fewer people."

Mathur nods, gets up, and motions for Iria to follow him out of the room just as the third wave hits.

Sai wastes no time protecting the door and the entire room. She readies a shield to clamp down on Aishke should the girl wake in a panic and makes sure to sit far enough away that she's not threatening, but close enough that she's there should Aishke break down. It's a tough line to tread, and Sai isn't sure she's got the ingredients right. All she has is theory.

Aishke's eyelashes flutter open to reveal amazing violet irises. Sai blinks to get the bright color out of her head. The girl murmurs unintelligibly, rubs her eyes, and stares at the white ceiling.

Suddenly her expression crumbles as memories hit home, and she curls into a ball toward Sai, rocking herself silently as tears drip onto the pillow. Sai waits patiently so as not to startle her.

"Who..." the girl croaks out, her voice as parched as Sai's had been.

Sai hands her a glass of water before retreating to an unthreatening distance again and answering. "My name is Sai. Your uncle sent you with me to make sure you'd be safe."

At the mention of Bastian, there's relief in Aishke's eyes as she sips the water. "You're sure he meant for me to be safe or so others are safe?" Her tone is bitter.

"Pretty sure he meant *you* to be safe, Aishke." The girl cringes at the sound of her name, but the tension in her shoulders loosens slightly.

"I don't even know where to start..." she whispers, a lost look creeping into her expression.

"It's okay." Sai smiles and means it. "That's sort of why I'm here."

Tentatively, Aishke smiles back, but it only lasts briefly before her eyes glaze over and she starts shaking. Everything in the room shakes, too, and before Sai manages to clamp her shields over the girls mind, she's already sporting a nice cut on her unscarred cheek.

"Great," she mutters as she lays the unconscious girl down on the bed again, and works on making sure she's secured. "Just when you least expect it, right?" She sits on the bed across from Ash, head in her hands. "I have no idea how to deal with someone who just had everything they've ever known taken away." She whispers to the room, hoping it might have some answers for her. But the walls stay silent, like walls usually do. They're not much for talking.

Sai laughs softly, feeling slightly unhinged, but as long as she can remember what her own ordeal was like and how she was helped through it, maybe this will work. Although she's dubious as to whether or not GNW actually helped anything, it's worth a shot.

When Aishke wakes up again, Sai takes her slender fingers and guides them to the girl's temples. "Close your eyes," she tells her. Slowly, so as not to startle the girl into violence, she reaches in and guides Aishke's mind. "Do you see me with you?"

Ash nods.

Sai demonstrates by building shields, showing Ash the areas most important to block off, and how to deconstruct, reconstruct, and fuse the blocks tighter and tighter.

She's not sure how long she spends showing Ash how to fashion a rudimentary shield and how to build it, over time, into a better and stronger one. It's the foundation of everything Sai was ever taught, and until Bastian took her though this different method, she'd never been aware of the fact that the original was lacking. In a way, Aishke is lucky to learn the right way first.

The memories Sai glosses over in Ash's mind are horrifying. No wonder she awoke when she never should have. Pushed through that amount of stress—thinking she was going to die—

it's surprising more dormant carriers of the gene don't explode in such a way. If Johnson taught Sai anything, though, it's to gloss over other's memories, not invite them into her own head.

After a long while, she withdraws from Aishke's mind to find the girl wilting into slumber.

"I did not want to interrupt."

Sai jumps at the voice and turns around to see Mathur standing behind her.

"I am sorry, my dear. I did not mean to make you uneasy." He looks at her apologetically when she stands and helps catch her as she sways precariously. "You sit down on your bed. This is the infirmary, but for tonight, it will do. I have food on the way. It was remiss of me to not offer it earlier. Eat, and rest. Tomorrow you will receive your own quarters, and meet the Council.

CHAPTER
Sixteen

Sai sits bolt upright in bed, shields up, ready to move. She blinks and turns around, certain someone is watching her. Aishke sits in her own bed, watching her.

Sai draws in a very steady breath and smiles. "Morning, Ash. May I call you Ash?"

Ash nods slowly. "You're the one who helped me?"

"Not too clear on yesterday?" Sai asks. The girl shakes her head, a look of mild surprise on her face. "I helped you with your shields."

"Thank you."

Those two words are so heartfelt Sai feels the exhaustion is worth it. "They have a steam shower here if you want to go first. Only on a four-minute timer, so if you want to do your hair, you'll have to be quick." She gestures to the girl's strange pinkish hair, cut to a bob, but with two really long pigtails on either side of her head.

Ash glances around, locates the tiny cubicle, and raises an eyebrow. "That's a shower?" she asks dubiously.

Sai laughs and stands up, happy to find she's not as sore as she assumed she was going to be, but surprised to realize she's still wearing yesterday's suit. "I'll go first then." She grabs her spare and heads for the shower, smiling at Aishke as she walks past.

The clean suit is soft, and Sai shakes her hair out around her shoulders, not caring if the moisture drips down. She walks out of the shower to find Aishke huddled on her bed with her knees up to her chest. Her dark eyes have a strangely tired and haunted look about them. Sai doesn't blame her for trying to pretend, but makes a mental note that she's probably not actually dealing with the situation.

"Someone came for you, for us, I think? I asked them to wait outside." She speaks so softly into her knees, Sai can barely hear her. She's much younger than Sai feels.

"That's okay. I'll go find them."

Aishke reaches her hand out to clutch Sai's good wrist. "Can you wait until I've showered? Please?"

"Of course." Sai watches the girl as she wanders over to the shower and steps in.

Ducking her head through the door flap, Sai catches Iria's eye. "Mornin'." She'd been hoping to find the friendly guide there.

Iria grins from ear to ear. "Morning. Do you want me to tell Mathur you're ready?"

Sai shakes her head in response. "Could you get some clothes for Ash? Her old ones are putrid and should be burned."

Iria nods and runs off, leaving a male guard on duty Sai hasn't met before. Sai nods at him, ducks back inside, and waits for Ash to finish. She doesn't expect Iria to make it back so fast with a set of charcoal-colored training gear. "Thanks."

"For speedy delivery, just call for Iria! Here." She hands a small bag to Sai. "It's got bands in it. They'll deal out your pay and do a few other neat things, like access areas of the Mobile."

"I get paid?" Sai stammers out.

Iria raises an eyebrow and laughs easily. "Of course. I'll dash off and let Mathur know you're almost ready. You have so much to do today!"

She's gone before Sai can blink. "That girl has far too much energy." Sai is pretty sure she hears the other guard at the door snort with laughter.

"Sai?" Ash's voice carries through the room, scared and on edge.

Sai steps back from the flap to be more visible. "I didn't leave. I had them fetch you clothes." She walks up to the cubicle and hands Ash the soft training uniform. "Get dressed. We have a lot to do today. It's worse than school."

Aishke emerges from the cubicle, pulling at the material with a frown. "I've never seen this stuff before, and my mother..." She stops as her voice catches. Tears spill down her face almost immediately.

"Breathe, Ash. Just breathe. You can do it."

The girl listens, breathing in and out in a slow rhythmic pattern. She raises her chin to look at Sai. "Sorry about that. I..."

"I know," Sai says gently, just before Mathur knocks on the doorframe.

When he walks into the room, Aishke positions herself behind Sai and grabs her hand, ineffectively hiding herself. Mathur blinks at Sai, and she shrugs back at him.

"Breakfast and then a meeting," he offers with that strange jovial nature of his, holding out a tray of food much more appetizing in appearance than anything Sai ate back in the cafeteria.

It's enough to coax Aishke into eating.

Sai's fingers appear to have a mind of their own, and more than twice she catches herself twisting her hair so hard it hurts.

"You okay?" Aishke whispers.

Sai shrugs and tries to work the kinks out of her shoulders. "Nervous."

"Why?" Aishke asks, louder this time.

Sai shrugs again, unsure of how to answer. That her stomach is in knots or that she fears they'll laugh at someone her age teaching them anything—neither seems to be a good reason anymore. "I don't like crowds."

"It is not a crowd." Mathur comes to a stop outside a closed door. He motions to the viewing window to the side of it. "See, not a crowd, just some people."

They all seem normal, chatting and laughing, or sitting and staring at the table. Sai lets out a breath she didn't realize she was holding. "Shall we?"

"We shall." Mathur smiles and leads the way into the room.

The walls are more of an off-white than the rest of the Mobile, making it distinctly warmer, more welcoming. The furniture is made of sturdy plastics and steel, although the desktop is fashioned to look like wood.

Mathur clears his throat and motions for Sai and Aishke to take a seat to the left of him. The rest of the room's still-standing occupants settle into their seats, and Iria waves to the girls, her infectious smile bright.

"I would like to give a quick introduction to our newest recruit." A light chuckle spreads around the room, and Sai feels her cheeks get hot at the attention.

"Stand up, please." Mathur makes a flourish with his hands as Sai does so. "This is Sai, delivered into our waiting hands by Bastian. You can sit down now," he half-whispers to her, a twinkle in his eyes.

She does so, able to feel how flaming red her face must be.

"We'll go clockwise around the table. Aishke is Sai's first student. Next we have Trikel Sanien. She's the current overseer of our psionic division." The woman smiles at Sai, relief obvious in her expression.

Mathur continues the introductions. "Next we have James Darson. He heads up defense systems, both human- and machine-operated. Next to him is Doctor Stephen Jeffries."

"I can speak for myself, Mathur." The man's tone is full of disdain, and Sai cringes involuntarily. "I've told you my feelings on the matter, and she should know them, too."

Mathur sighs and looks away. "We have talked about this."

"No, you talked and didn't listen." Jeffries crosses his arms and turns to Sai, his eyes trying to strip her soul bare. She shivers while she waits for him to speak. "I'll be watching you.

Regardless of what Bastian might think you are? I won't believe you're not a plant by GNW to infiltrate our ranks until you prove me wrong."

Sai blinks at him, and suddenly isn't sure herself. If they've been mind-controlling everyone, doesn't it stand to reason they could be controlling her, too? She clears her throat and pushes the thought to the back of her mind. "I trust Bastian."

Jeffries snorts derisively and looks away, terminating the conversation.

"Next is me!" Iria pipes up, her exuberance overriding the previous man's affect. "But you know me already, most people do."

"Hard not to." Trikel smiles at Iria briefly. That small interaction is enough to calm the butterflies turning somersaults in Sai's stomach.

Iria grins. "Mason isn't here today, or he'd be sitting up there with Mathur."

Sai pats Aishke on the hand when she feels the girl stiffen at her stepfather's name, and Mathur steps in smoothly before Iria can run off with the conversation some more.

"Next to Iria is Kayde Thaniel. She is our resident genius. The antidote for non-psionics, which should eventually help them to withstand mind suggestion is her brainchild."

"Antidote?" Sai clenches her fists to keep her voice from shaking. "Bastian mentioned it, but I don't quite understand."

This time Kayde clears her throat. Her voice is a warm alto. "The Shine Bastian—and this time you—bring us isn't generally used for what you think. We don't have Shine addicts in the way you're used to. The only people who use it here are those not amenable to their psionic abilities."

"They might not want their abilities, but it's not like they're out of control." Sai crosses her arms and bites her lip, still trying to grasp her new situation.

"True." Kayde cocks her head to one side, her shoulder length blonde hair swishing as she continues, "The rest of it is used to ascertain the properties and break down the components so I can better learn to reverse the effect it has on non-psionics..."

"Oh!" Sai interrupts, "You're trying to harness a way to protect them from the thought manipulation they're currently subjected to."

"Mind suggestion, thought-coercion, maniacally manipulating the populace into complacent drones..." Kayde grins, but the smile doesn't reach her eyes. She holds up a hand as Sai opens her mouth to speak, stalling it. "This cure isn't a fix-all; it's just a stop-gap measure. Depending on how the Facilities have their grids cast, if they push with enough reserve power, even dormant psionic genes won't hold up against thought-coercion."

Sai tries to swallow the sudden lump in her throat. "Yeah, I know."

"I told you she knew more than she should." Jeffries smirks at her, and Sai clamps down on the immediate retort lingering on her tongue.

Mathur claps his hands together. "Enough! Now we all know each other, yes?" His smile beams around the table, daring people to gainsay him. No one speaks up, not even Jeffries. "Excellent. Now, we can move onto business. I will answer any questions afterward. Some of us have limited time."

Sai nods and settles back to observe.

"Sai's role here will be to assist Trikel in the stages of voluntary psionics development. She will scout for, as well as see if we have any Rares capable of training to the level of Sai and Bastian. I will ask that everyone cooperate with her. Any questions?" The old man pointedly glares at Jeffries.

It's all Sai can do to stop her arm raising, even though the ones she wants the most are the things she feels the need to ask Jeffries.

"Great." Mathur opens an old-fashioned folder and pulls out a strange, long flat reader. "Then we will move on now. We are gearing up and getting ready to put the assault plan into action. I would like to hear from everyone as to where you are for your stage of the infiltration plan."

Darson clears his throat. His voice booms across the table, a perfect accompaniment to his stature. "I have fourteen scouting groups ready to go once Mason gives the word, not to mention twenty-five sets of reinforcements. My men are ready when the plan is."

"Ebony won't be ready in time. We'll have no way to mitigate their net's impact yet, so they won't remember any of it in a couple of days." Kayde taps a stylus against her reader without looking up. "I can't contribute much to this assault, but I will tap their surveillance and record it all for posterity, as well as a few other little tricks I should be able to hammer out. We have time, yes?"

Mathur smiles grimly. "We have as much time as Sai needs to get her pupils ready."

It's not the first time Sai understands the beauty of the facade taught to her by Bastian. Behind it she can be scared, while showing everyone else she's as prepared as they think she is.

She waits until they're back in the medical wing before she lets the meeting get to her. "Sure. Of course, it's extremely simple. Even though we don't trust you, we'll let you train every psionic among us to overthrow the stranglehold GNW has on the citizens of the UC." She throws herself down on her bed and wishes she hadn't, because it's definitely not as soft as she'd thought.

"You know..." Aishke ventures timidly. "That's not exactly what they said, Sai."

"Really? That's precisely what it sounded like in my head," Sai grumbles, still pushing down on her panic.

Aishke pauses. "My family would call you melodramatic. You're overreacting."

"Sit down. I'm not about to bite." Sai sits up and puts her head in her hands, weary after listening to people drone on for hours, debating procedures and tactics to infiltrate Central and then telling her how much of a relief it was to have her there, even if Jeffries rarely stopped glaring at her. "How did they say it then?" she asks, her voice tired.

"Really?"

Sai laughs. "Really."

"Okay" Aishke sits down and closes her eyes for a moment. When she opens her mouth to speak, it's her voice that comes out, but Trikel's exact phrasing.

"I'll need to work out a strategy with Sai before I can give my report. I'm quite certain with Bastian's training behind her, we'll have something worked out by the end of the week. I'm confident that between us, we'll find the best way."

Sai gapes at Ash. "I guess that is a little different."

Aishke smiles, encouraged, and starts to speak again, and this time, she's completely herself. "It's not just different. You feel victimized. I understand it, but you can't let Jeffries get to you. Bastian wouldn't have sent you or put me in your care if he didn't believe in you. Give yourself credit."

Sai lies back again. "I guess I'm a bit panicked."

"And maybe a bit overwhelmed?"

She raises an eyebrow. "You're an eloquent little thing."

Aishke shrugs. "I'm my mother's child." Her bottom lip trembles and for a moment moisture wells in her eyes, but she blinks it back and continues. "No matter what she did or didn't allow on her own premises, she was still my mother, and my family was something to be proud of. Not anymore, though. I've ruined that forever."

"I don't think you've ruined anything, Ash."

"And I don't think you have any right to doubt Bastian's judgment," Aishke returns slyly. When Sai goes to protest, she holds up her hand. "I feel brave right now, so let me speak. If they're not busy duping people who don't understand or are scared of psionics into committing themselves or others to this 'better' institution, GNW is busy pulling in the stronger psionics as soon as their powers awaken. You and everyone here have a chance to change that. To make it better, to take back what GNW has taken from everyone."

Ash takes a deep breath and looks Sai directly in the eyes. "I didn't know this either. Not until I woke, not until I realized the gravity of the situation here. They need you, or someone like you, to make this possible. Have a little faith in yourself."

Sai feels pricks of heat behind her eyes and blinks away potential tears. "You're far too young to be so wise."

Aishke blushes and laughs softly. "I may have cheated."

"Cheated?" Sai cocks her head to one side. "How do you mean cheated?"

"I may or may not have heard my dad give my uncle almost exactly the same advice when I was very young."

Sai laughs. "And you remember it?"

Ash's grin is impish. "People hate conversations with me. I never forget them."

"I'll have to keep that in mind." Sai reaches over and squeezes Aishke's hands. "Thank you. I'll have to keep those words in my pocket and take them out when I'm particularly down. This isn't going to be easy."

"Nothing worth doing ever is."

"Mason?"

Ash shakes her head and her eyes mist over. "No, my mom."

Sai leans back again and studies her first official pupil. "One day, I'll tell you my story. It takes some time to tell, but I hope it'll help when I do."

"What about now?" Ash's eyes look haunted again.

"It's not a good story for now. For either of us."

"Okay." Just like that, Ash drops the subject and turns to the side-table next to her bed. "So you get paid then?"

Sai shrugs. "Apparently. I don't quite understand this currency thing."

Ash raises an eyebrow at her. "You've not had money before?"

"My parents didn't have any that wasn't used for Shine, and GNW pays in: you're allowed to live. I didn't grow up in a wealthy environment."

The other girl's expression is strange, and she chooses her words carefully, her eyes never leaving Sai's face. "Despite everything, I think I was luckier."

"Maybe." Sai smiles tightly and stands, retrieving the bag in one quick movement. It's a small soft pouch. Money earned is credited to the identification bands which allow both her and Ash access throughout the Exiled Mobiles. She digs in and tosses Aishke's to her, putting her own around her uninjured wrist. It fastens tight and attaches itself to her skin, not quite burrowing beneath, but camouflaging to it. She shivers at their similarity to the GNW tracking bracelets. If they want them removed, they'll probably have to go see Kayde.

"I'm going to get changed, and then I'll go get us some food?"

Ash suppresses a yawn. "I'm tired."

"Nice timing," Sai laughs and dives into the small storage cupboard to grab out a change of clothes.

She pulls on a training suit, with clean underwear and a tank top, and heads back out of her room. Aishke seems to have fallen asleep her bed, curled up in a ball with her hair over one eye, so Sai tries to be quiet as she exits the room.

"Sai!"

Only to have it spoiled with Iria waiting there. "Hey, Iria."

"Are you okay?"

"Yeah, Aishke is napping."

"Sorry!" Even Iria's soft voice isn't very soft. But it's bright and cheery and improves Sai's mood. "I thought I'd wait for you and see if you were going to do any shopping or wanted to find an apartment. There's a great two-bedroom near the center." Iria smiles and leads the way. "Apartment first?"

Sai pauses for a moment. "Yeah. I have to take food back to Aishke."

"Excellent. This way!" Iria is quick and weaves around the corridors easily. They venture toward the meeting rooms and then past them and off to the left. Sai can see what looks like a gathering area surrounded by little booths open out from one of the exits and strains to see more. She almost bumps into the now-stationary Iria.

"Here we are!"

Sai pokes her head inside the open door. It's simple. A small living room with two loveseats and a coffee-table in front of a kitchen with a table and two chairs. She walks in a few steps past the couches to see a hall with a bath directly in front of her and a room on either side.

"Like it?" Iria's voice is softer than usual, but when Sai glances up, the smile is still as big.

"Mind if I take a peek?"

Iria shakes her head, and Sai walks into the room on the left. It's patterned in blues. The closet is to the right of the bed, while a side table is on the left. She opens the doors to the wardrobe and lets out a low whistle. Eight suits of body armor hang inside, along with several sleek black training suits like Aishke's grey one. Not to mention underwear, T-shirts, and tank tops in the three drawers. Several pairs of training shoes adorn the floor of the closet.

Suddenly, Sai feels very lucky, despite the fear Jeffries instilled nagging at the back of her mind. The body armor is a cut above what she wore back at the facility, too. She brushes her fingers over the material. It's stronger, more supple. With a sigh, she shuts the wardrobe, and walks back out.

Iria is leaning against the main door. "So?"

"It's perfect." Sai smiles this time, fighting back a yawn. "But now I need food."

"Good. I'll have Kayde set this as your locks." Iria pushes herself away from the door. "We can go grab food, and I'll bring Aishke back here."

"Sure." Sai walks with her toward the center. The booths appear to be little stores. At first they seem uniform, but there are subtle differences in decorations which allow each shop a distinct appearance. Iria leads her over to one with fresh salads and fruits behind a counter.

"Hydroponically grown," Iria offers as Sai helplessly tries to pick something. "Try something simple. We'll take two salads, please. Just the house special."

"That'll be twenty-six credits," the woman behind the counter says.

Sai glances at the almost invisible band around her wrist and, with Iria's help, finally figures it out. She passes her wrist over the sensor on the counter and feels a faint click. "Thanks," she adds hurriedly as they leave the stand.

"There's a place for everyone somewhere, Sai. You just have to be open enough to finding it."

"Doesn't seem like Jeffries wants me to."

Iria studies her for a moment, her tone more gentle than usual when she speaks. "One dissenting voice doesn't mean anything. Forget him and just be you."

"What's with everyone giving me wisdom today?" Sai says, a little hotter than she intends. "Sorry, I'm just..."

"Overwhelmed? Confused? Lost?"

Sai nods.

"A lot of us are, but we're doing what we know in our hearts is right. Sleep on it and see how you feel tomorrow." Iria hugs her quick enough that Sai can't react. "I'll go fetch your starving roommate, and if you need me, just call."

And she's running down a corridor before Sai can blink.

CHAPTER
Seventeen

"She's what?" Deign doesn't raise her voice. She doesn't even blink. Only her jaw tightens, almost imperceptibly.

Bastian almost takes an involuntary step back, but checks himself in time. Dom is to his left, staring evenly at the GNW chairwoman. One thing Bastian's learned in the years he's known Deign: her anger simmers in a quiet, white rage.

"She's dead." Dom's voice is devoid of any of the emotions he's exhibited over the years Bastian's known him. Perfectly hollow and inhuman.

"How?" The skin under Deign's left eye twitches ever so slightly.

"They knew we were coming. An explosion was planned. I didn't sense it until she was halfway in, and by then, it was too late to stop her." Dom's voice echoes through the office.

Deign glances down at the reader in her hands, gripping it so hard her knuckles are almost transparent. They watch her as she views the very convincing footage for a third time.

"How did this happen?"

Glass shatters as the reader flies through Deign's once-delicate desk. Those screens cost a fortune to build and will cost more to replace.

"Well?" Her tone lowers to a whisper as she stands, hands on hips, facing Bastian.

"I can speak now?" He knows it's foolish, but it's irresistible.

"Bastian," she grinds out, the warning clear.

"We hear the information, which means others will be aware of it, too, Deign. Your sources have never been from infiltrators, always from plans overheard in places our own staff don't frequent." He pauses for a moment to let the words sink in. "It's not necessarily those who gather information for you, but perhaps the delivery of said information itself."

She mulls it over, her eyes never leaving his face. Deign has never been a stupid woman, but her pride often gets in the way of good judgment. On occasion, Bastian counts on it. "They'll pay for this, Bastian. I need you to see to that."

"Security is Zach and Markus's responsibility, Deign."

She waves his words away, already processing some other angle. "Of course. Of course. That's beside the point. We'll get them another way—your sort of way." Her eyes gleam briefly with something close to glee. "It's probably a good thing."

"A good thing." Bastian shakes his head slowly. "A good thing they killed the one potential protégé I've had in the last few years?"

"Oh no, Bastian." Deign laughs for the first time since hearing the news. There's no warmth in the sound at all. "They wasted a precious resource and funds I can't even begin to calculate without sitting down to do so. The rebuilding of that block in UC 17, the hospitalization fees for her and her victims, her schooling, training... Oh, yes, they've squandered one of the potentially largest investments GNW has made in a long time. Her assignments hadn't even scratched the cost of her existence yet."

"Then why is this a good thing?"

"Because at least you had her to send. Just think what might have happened if they'd killed you." Deign shakes her head. "No. It's a harsh financial loss, and one I fully intend to extract from them, but at least it wasn't you."

Bastian nods to acknowledge the backhanded compliment, not sure he can trust himself to speak.

Deign glances at the clock, and scowls as she realizes it's shattered along with the rest of her desk. "That *is* a bother." She sighs and turns back to Bastian a bright smile on her face. "Be a gem and ask Harlow to commission me a new desk. It's about time I got one anyway."

"Of course." Bastian forces the words out and gladly takes his leave, Dom following in his wake.

"That went well," Dom says dryly when they're out of earshot.

Bastian raises an eyebrow. "Depends on your definition of well."

"The footage was convincing." Dom shrugs. "There's really nothing else to it."

"She even showed us her sunny side."

Dom grins. "Do you want me to head down to Harlow and catch up later?"

"I'd better do that myself. Tag along? I'd prefer to have you with me when I 'inspect' the testing facility." The mere thought of it gives Bastian a bad taste in his mouth. "You have a calming effect on me. Maybe I won't kill all the doctors on the spot."

"I'll make sure of it."

Harlow's offices are on the ground floor, a huge see-through box in the middle of the cavernous concrete hall. Its walls are made from conductive glass, just like Deign's former desk. Anything from any camera in any part of the entire region can be viewed on all of the glass surfaces. Expensive, but worth it.

"What do you want, Bastian?" She pushes back thick strands of brown hair and adjusts her gaze to look at him, a flicker of color grazing her eyes as the implants switch into standby. "I'm a little busy today."

"You always are, Harlow. Deign needs a new desk."

The security chief stops short, her finger comically elongating a docking bay feed. "She what?"

"She may or may not have accidentally flung a reader through it?"

Harlow lets out a soft groan. "She'll be the death of us all one day. This equipment isn't as cheap as it once was. We keep losing our damn bioengineers. It'll take a while."

"You tell her. I'm not a messenger." As Harlow opens her mouth to protest, Bastian continues. "Unless you want to visit the testing facility in my place?"

Harlow grimaces. "I'll let her know."

"Great." Bastian smiles at her. She's one of the only members of the board he actually likes. "See you at the next meeting."

She smiles absently and waves him away, her attention already shifted to another task.

It's easier to face the trip down to the basement with company. "I didn't think you'd make it back in time, and I've been putting this off longer than I should," Bastian says quietly as the lift takes them down past the normal levels of operation.

"It was a relatively simple operation. There was no need for me to stay afterward." Dom's eyes follow the ticking of the floors as they delve deeper. "You'd think humans could teleport by now."

He says it so softly, Bastian barely hears it. "What?"

"Centuries ago, lifts were like this. Not exactly, but similar in style and structure. They've barely been refined at all."

Bastian shrugs. "Sometimes there's only so much you can do."

"Sai hates small spaces."

Bastian steps through the doors into a dimly lit corridor. "I know," he murmurs as he gets his bearings. The lights to the left flicker as they valiantly try to illuminate the path to the equally unstable exit sign. It's the lights on the right that give off a constant, dull glow. A nurses' station is situated halfway down the corridor, and the lighting gives the crisp white uniforms a yellow tinge.

Two women stand at the desk, chatting with each other, oblivious to the men approaching them. Bastian clears his throat to get their attention. One of them drops the clipboard she's holding with a gasp, and hurriedly retrieves it from the ground.

"Excuse me," he says softly.

The women watch each other, eyes darting back and forth

between Bastian and Dom. The blonde standing on the outside of the counter straightens her back and smiles tentatively. "Did you have an appointment, sir?"

"How remiss of me." Bastian doesn't smile back. "I'm Bastian. Here for inspection."

The blonde visibly gulps, but squares her jaw. "I'm Marlena. This is Farah. We weren't informed you'd be here today. I apologize."

"That's perfectly fine." Bastian softens his tone just enough to make the girl relax and recalls where he's seen her. "I decided a surprise visit might be in order for my first one."

Marlena's gaze drifts again to Dom and her lips move, but she purses them and nods instead.

"This is Domino 12." It's fun to watch the reaction people give when they realize Dom is a domino. Their faces usually cycle through a myriad of emotions before settling on mild fear. Marlena is different.

She nods again and smiles the same tentative smile, directly at Dom. "It's an honor to have the prototype visit us. I've never seen you before, but we have many dominos who serve on guard duty down here."

"Of course," Bastian murmurs. "I'd like to undertake that inspection now."

"I'll be your guide." She smiles brilliantly. "Please follow me."

Bastian wonders what on earth possessed the girl to get a job secreted away in the bowels of GNW. Then again, it's not necessarily a person's choice that gets them anything these days.

They pass a few rooms, each one with a closed door and dust on the handles. Marlena pauses and takes the first corridor to the left. There are no doors in this area, just open arches with multiple rows of beds in the twilight beyond.

Marlena stops to the side of one of the openings. "I'll wait here for you, sir, if you'd like to take a look around."

Bastian nods, not letting on how relieved he is that she won't be following them around closely. There are things they need to accomplish without a guide. Dom follows him as they enter the first room on the left.

It reminds Bastian of a morgue, with bodies lying on flat metal beds, covered by cloth. Death and Shine linger in the air, its potency having long since stripped the bodies of their former strength. Like an alcoholic too wasted to think for themselves, unable to kick the disease, all that's left are husks of the humans they once were. As soon as the dregs of their psionics are drained, these occupants will be left with the stench of rotting flesh and feces to torture them until they die.

Soft illumination is embedded into the walls, and the room isn't lit so much as glows. The low noises Bastian originally thought to be the hum of machinery prove to be the groans and whimpers of the room's residents. He frowns and nods at Dom, who exits the room again. They need plans of this area. With no blueprints available in print or digital form, Dom's memory is the next best thing.

Bastian walks farther in. Every bed is filled. Though it's difficult to tell from the doorway, the patients are bound, secured by their wrists, ankles, and midsections so they can barely move. In some cases the manacles have bitten into their skin and left reddish-brown smears stark against the white sheets. Tracking bracelets hang limply against flesh that tries valiantly to constrain it to the too-thin wrists.

He stops several beds into the ward and takes in every nuance of the confinement. Patient 12089, as notated on his chart, has an unmoving metal band securing his head. GNW has always had a penchant for numbers.

Bastian clenches and opens his fists numerous times to stay the anger boiling inside. The misery in 12089's eyes synchronizes with his surroundings. Like so many times before in his life, Bastian reaches in with his mind and grips the man's heart, holding his gaze. Patient 12089 smiles, and the relief reaches his eyes as Bastian wrenches the valves from the heart and brings the man peace.

Their thoughts clamor at his mind, feeble and desperate, and Bastian squeezes his eyes shut to reinforce his shields. He can't put all of them out of their misery. It'll arouse suspicion and leave him drained.

A hand rests against his back, its weight familiar and welcome.

"This is inhuman." Dom's tone is soft, only loud enough to reach Bastian's ears.

Bastian nods, unable to trust his voice from shaking like the rest of his body. He waits for a moment, and steadies himself before speaking. "Are the rest of the rooms off the other side of the corridor the same?"

Dom nods. "Some aren't completely full."

"Small mercies." Even to his own ears, Bastian's voice sounds bitter. "You'd think they could leave them with some dignity and put them out of their misery instead of draining every last drop."

Dom is quiet for a couple of steps. "If you're not careful when you dose, you could disarm yourself completely. You'd think great things about them if you weren't able to access your own defenses."

Bastian bites back all the heated comments that come to mind. "I'm not stupid enough to overstep my own limits. I do what's needed."

Marlena stands where they left her, twisting her hair around her fingers in a way that echoes Sai. She smiles brightly as they approach. "Do you have any questions, sir?"

"Do you like working here, Marlena?"

Marlena stops and stares at Bastian, her hair and fingers stationary. "Not all of us get to choose our careers, sir. This is a job, and now my father has passed, I get more than a token of what I earn. I'm sure there are worse things I could do to earn a living." She looks down at her feet, and her face flushes, visible even in this poor lighting. "I'm sorry to be so bold, sir."

"Please, be bold." Bastian takes a step closer, making sure to keep the anger out of his voice.

"I won't lose my job?" she asks, her blue eyes brim with tears.

"Never."

"They scream. Sometimes I hear them when I'm asleep at home." She laughs nervously. "I know it's supposed to be voluntary committal, but I didn't sign on to learn the ropes of a mental institution. My father volunteered me into medical service to pay off his debts. I've been here since I was fourteen. Six years now." She takes a deep breath. "It could be worse. I know. I could have to clean the retirement rooms..."

"Retirement rooms?" Bastian asks.

"The ones in this corridor. Where they put those who're ready to die." Her skin pales, and a tear creeps down her cheek. "We don't talk about it. We all value our jobs, sir. We need them. But sometimes I wonder if some of these people are voluntary in the way I was when I was fourteen."

"Maybe some of them are, Marlena." He looks at her a moment. "How does that make you feel?"

"Sad." She pauses and speaks even softer. "Even luckier, that I wasn't born like them. I could have drawn that straw."

"Like them?"

"Cursed with the gene..." Her voice trails off.

Bastian probes her mind gently for a moment and smiles sadly. "You are fortunate." He doesn't tell her how lucky she is. Her psionic abilities, while minuscule, are definitely there, but not strong enough for Zach to latch onto. "Can we proceed with the rest of the tour?"

"Sure!" She brightens up again and wipes her hand over her cheek. "Follow me," she says as they head back to the main corridor.

He's fairly certain her tone is less exuberant than before.

Marlena leads them back into the main walkway and down again halfway, toward the other exit. She stops just inside the next corridor and motions with her hand toward several doors which start about halfway down the hall. "I don't have rounds in the actual testing facility today. If it's okay, I'll stay here."

"Thank you." Bastian smiles briefly at her to put her at ease. "We'll be back shortly."

As they venture farther in, a domino guards each door. A pulsating array of color ripples across their human forms, dizzying in effect. "Your brethren." Bastian smiles as he speaks.

Dom glances at him, his lips curling into a half-scowl before he schools his face.

Bastian nods at the guards—who barely acknowledge him, but salute Dom—and steps into the first room. He takes a deep breath and wishes he hadn't. Shine fumes permeate the area. It's larger than he thought, more of a waiting section, which branches off to four other decently-sized rooms.

He reaches over and grabs a mask off the ledge by the door. The last thing he needs in here is to be hazy about what he remembers. With any Shine in his system, access to his psionics is tapered, but if the dose is high enough, it's non-existent.

Each room appears to have one occupant strapped to a metal slab in much the same way as those in the retirement section, but with two exceptions. Their slabs rotate and tilt, allowing excellent access to the patient. There's still some fight left in these people. Still something left to drain.

The glass panes in the walls and doors make viewing easy and give better access to the area Bastian and Dom find themselves in. It's an observation room. Bastian pushes his anger aside and cracks his neck to release the tension.

At least this area doesn't smell of death and decay. It reeks of Shine and disinfectant instead.

And then the scream hits him, rebounds off his shields, and echoes through his head. Bastian stumbles back a step, only to be steadied by Dom.

"You okay?" Dom asks, his brows furrowed.

"No, I... Shh." Bastian closes his eyes to track the echo and opens them again to rest on the far left room. The man inside is hooked to a huge machine, and the mental scream is so loud Bastian wonders how it doesn't bother anyone else. But the occupants of the other rooms appear to be in their own dire straits.

The attendants, unlike Marlena, seem to have no psionic talent whatsoever.

"It was loud, Bastian, but surely you expected it in here?" Dom asks quietly.

"I should have, but I didn't." Bastian shakes his head and strengthens his shields again.

"I'll be back shortly. Will you be okay?"

"Go, Dom. I'm fine." Bastian waves his friend away, shields clamped tightly around his body. But for a twist of fate, it could be him in one of those rooms. Or Sai. Or Mason. Or Aishke. So many people escaped. Far too many haven't.

He takes a deep breath as he crosses the corridor to enter yet another viewing room. The other areas hold the same arrangement. There are older patients, younger patients, and even a child.

The boy sits, strapped to a chair, his eyes wide open, tears falling down his face as the three people in the room take blood samples while injecting different substances into him. From the scarring on the child's arms, some of those injections have burned his veins.

He must be a new arrival. There is no draining pipe hooked up to him yet. The brief glimpse Bastian takes of his mind shows nothing there but pain. Coherent thought and cognitive processes are no longer an option. The child is ruined.

Some are stronger than others.

Between the rest of the viewing rooms and their exhibits, Bastian fights the urge to be sick. His stomach clenches and he retches a few times, glad he decided not to eat before the visit.

Dom joins him in the last one. "Took longer than expected. The others rarely see me." He adds.

Bastian nods, exhausted from clamping down on his shields. "Let's go. I've seen what I needed to."

Dom glances at him for a moment. "Why did you let her talk you into this?"

Bastian walks back the way they came. "Deign doesn't exactly take no for an answer."

Marlena is still waiting for them, but her face doesn't break into a smile this time. Instead, she seems relieved.

"You don't like this area?" Dom asks, and Bastian is grateful for the reprieve.

"I don't like the pain in there. It's so obvious it's tangible. Each nurse only pulls one shift a week in the lab. I had mine two days ago." She smiles tightly. "Was there anything else you'd like to see, sir?"

Bastian shakes his head, but reaches out and grabs her arm after she takes a few steps. Marlena flinches involuntarily, her eyes fearful as she looks up at him. He releases her.

"It's okay. I wanted to reassure you nothing you told me will be repeated. I sincerely wanted to know about the working conditions here, and I'd like to thank you."

Her answering smile is genuine. "Thank you, sir. The stories about you don't do you justice."

Bastian laughs. "Perhaps, but some of them serve a purpose." He winks at her briefly. "I'll put in a good word for you," he adds as they begin walking again.

"Oh?"

"Maybe we can get you a bit of a raise."

"Sir, that would be wonderful." Her smile has almost returned to the wattage it was at the beginning.

They arrive at the nurses' station, and she rests against the counter.

"Thank you, Marlena. We will see you soon." Bastian turns

on his heel and heads to the elevator with, Dom close behind. He waits until they're out of earshot, and whispers, "A raise is the least we can do. When the time comes, we're getting her out of here."

Usually Bastian likes the view out his window, but today, it feels confining. GNW advertisements gleam back at him from below, taunting him with cloying slogans and computer-generated smiles.

"Are you done yet?" he asks Dom, impatient.

Dom looks up from the sketch he's creating on Bastian's desk. "If you keep asking me every two minutes, I never will be. Would *you* like to do this?"

Bastian sighs. "No."

"Then, please, let me."

Sometimes Bastian can't tell if Dom's faint sarcasm is deliberate or not. It's not ten minutes later when Dom taps him on the shoulder with a piece of rolled up old paper a few feet long.

"You drew them up old-style?" Bastian arches an eyebrow, impressed.

"That I did." Dom waits for Bastian to spread them over the desk. They're huge, but the exits and ducts are very clearly defined. Far more than Bastian saw on their visit.

He twists them this way and that and frowns. "You've been down in the testing facility without me, haven't you? Why didn't you say so?"

Dom grins. "You never asked." His expression sobers before

he continues, switching back to that smooth and glossy stone-like appearance he and his counterparts share. "There are just some things you need to see for yourself."

"True." Bastian purses his lips. "Sometimes I take your humanity for granted and forget you generally avoid people."

"I'll take that as a compliment. All I need to do is blend. When it works, anyway. Born to blend in, I guess you could say."

"Nice." Bastian laughs and then quiets for a few seconds while they study the prints before them. "The fact this research facility isn't operating at full capacity gives me some hope. Maybe more of the populace is learning to accept and deal with psionics in their families. Maybe Zach has lost his sense. Maybe more are escaping to the Exiled than we realize."

"I believe there are more facilities," Dom says quietly.

"What?"

"I believe there are more facilities than just the one beneath us. During my excursions, I found reference to more than one location. Add to that sheer population numbers, and there's no way the people beneath us are enough to fuel the grids to cover all the UCs. There are no specifics, though, so I'm not certain."

Bastian sighs and rubs at his temples. "It's okay. Let's see if we can break down the defenses for long enough to get in there quickly and save those we can. We won't be able to rescue any of those in the retirement wing. It's not possible. They'll need relief instead." His stomach clenches at the thought.

Dom nods. "One thing at a time."

Bastian watches his friend closely and sees an occasional flux of gold in his eyes, the tremor that runs through his left arm. "Are you doing okay, Dom?" Dom hesitates, and so Bastian pushes the question. "I mean it. Tell me. Don't think about it from the point of being what you are. Think of me as the friend I'd like to think I've become. How are you holding up?"

"I don't know," he whispers.

It's the first time since he's known the domino that Bastian has ever heard him sound close to being scared.

"I just don't know," Dom repeats. "I black out more frequently. At first they were random, every now and again... But lately they happen weekly and now almost daily. The thing is, I'm not one of the worst affected. I can feel it in the others, too. We might not exactly share thoughts, but we share..." He struggles to find the words. "We share concepts in their broader sense. One of them is complete and utter confusion. I've never felt so..."

"Scared?" Bastian supplies softly.

Dom nods. "Scared is probably a good word for it. If Mathur were here..." He looks away abruptly. "He's getting old, though, I don't want him to get caught. He deserves better than that."

"We'll figure something out, Dom. Try to hold on a few months. Can you do that?"

Dom actually laughs. It's an oddly pleasant sound, tinged with an echo of sadness. "I'm trying harder than you can imagine, and I'll keep trying. If everything goes to plan, I'll get to see him again." Dom goes back to studying the blueprint. A smile ghosts across his face, and he speaks softly. "Sai, too."

Bastian isn't sure what wakes him, but since he rarely sleeps, all interruptions are annoying. He gets out of bed, catches a shin on the bedside table, and bites his tongue to keep from crying out in case the person visiting at midnight isn't a welcome guest. Since his mental-alarms didn't go off, it's doubtful, though.

With a wave of his hand, he switches the lights on. He's never been a fan of the voice-activated programs. They went through a phase of needing to be reset every time he got a cold.

There's another noise, and something thuds lightly against the wall to his room. Bastian frowns and decides to be vocal. "Who's there?"

He thinks he hears something, but whether it's an answer or not, he can't be sure. Bastian starts to move toward the entrance to his private quarters, intent on making it to the wall and checking around the corner. He barely reacts in time to avoid stepping on Dom, whose body flickers through so many different dark shades that he almost blends in with the floor. Bastian bends down and frowns.

"Bastian..." the domino croaks. He's hard to look at and even more difficult to understand. His eyes flicker in and out of gold and silver, with swirls of color attacking in between.

"Bastian," he repeats, this time stronger.

"It's okay, Dom. I'm here. I heard you." Bastian has no idea what to do and reaches out to take Dom's fingers. If Dom can't partially move on his own, there's no way Bastian has the strength to drag him to the bed. When the adrium isn't directly fired by some form of electricity, its real weight takes over. Fit though Bastian is, he's not that strong.

Frustrated, he grips his friend's fingers tighter. "Stay, with me Dom."

There's a frighteningly long pause before Dom croaks out his answer with an oddly metallic clang. "Can't go anywhere right now..."

The predicament almost brings a tear to Bastian's eye. "Tell me what to do, Dom? I don't know how to help you."

By this time, Bastian is sitting on the floor, half-cradling Dom against his side.

"A minute... More energy... "Dom starts to push himself up with tremendous effort, while constantly strobing. "Bed. Now."

Bastian needs no further encouragement and guides him. Dom falls sideways onto the bed. It creaks loudly in protest at the mass of weight, and Bastian thanks technology for beds made out of sterner stuff than the pine of old.

"Bastian." Dom's voice rasps like the grating of a knife being sharpened.

"What?"

"I don't think I'm okay anymore..."

Bastian chuckles. It's easier than crying. "You can move past a person faster than the eye can see, but you had to make me drag you here."

It's hard to tell if there's amusement in Dom's eyes, or if they're just chaotic.

"I have no idea how to help you." Bastian tries to keep his tone light for Dom's benefit.

Dom's eyes dim for a moment before flaring bright red and settling back to gold. "For now, this is good. Help me seal? I want to come back whole. Please?"

Bastian closes his eyes and nods, trying to stave off the memory. Over ten years ago, when he was still a child, Dom had a relapse. They'd done what they called a reset of his synaptic connections, the ones fusing his human components to the adrium parasite that made up the bulk of his body. In hindsight, they probably didn't realize or care that it would reset him.

It took over a year to undo their clumsy work and provided a huge setback in Dom's progress. Bastian refuses to let it happen again. "I'll make sure we can retrieve you. Let me in?"

"Promise you'll keep a look out for the others. They're not dealing well with this." Bastian nods as Dom's eyes close and the barrier to his mind relaxes.

Dom's mind is a dark place. He has vague implanted memories of everything that went wrong with the previous eleven domino attempts, not to mention the Hounds and Damascus. Visual images of the complete cycle of incubations to produce not only his predecessors but himself as well. Everything imprinted into one, safe part of his mind by Mathur. The vault where Dom locks himself away, too.

Usually, Dom does it, but right now his concentration is unreliable. Before the techs come calling, Dom will need to be what they expect. Despite their hopes for an invincible defense in the dominos, GNW wasn't seeking to create a sentient race. They neither want nor expect him to evolve.

Bastian works on gathering everything where it needs to be. Dominos' psionics are beautiful, elegant almost. Despite their human origins, they're a complete contrast to the whirlwind of disarray in a human mind. Bastian seals everything into the vault and locks the door with the trigger word. He smiles as he chooses it.

Sai.

CHAPTER
Eighteen

Sai stands in the training hall, ignoring the material of her suit as it clings to her back. Regardless of any technological advancement, physical exertion still causes sweat. She moves her head from side to side in order to pop her neck and lets the relief wash over her as she does.

James Darson is demanding, and Sai's muscles ache, despite the week of training now under her belt. More than once, it's reminded her of training under Ms. Genna, only more difficult. A few more minutes and she'll have the training hall to herself for her own psionic students.

Her own students.

What a strange concept. She reaches up and stretches slowly, feeling her back crack and ease the stiffness. Mornings are filled with meetings or physical training. Mostly training right now since Mason still hasn't made it back to their Mobile.

Sai tilts her head back and gulps down the soft-tasting water. Mathur mentioned they treat it to replenish electrolytes as well as destroy bacteria. She closes her eyes and feels it rush down her throat and into her body. The Mobile is so peaceful. It's easy to forget they're preparing to invade the GNW testing facility.

"Sai?"

She cracks one eye open. "Why're you waiting at the door?"

Aishke shrugs. "You looked busy?"

Sai laughs. "Try again."

Aishke crosses her arms and glares for a moment, allowing a glimpse of the rebellious teen she must have been back home. But it fades quickly, leaving the usual unsure girl in its wake. "I don't want to do this."

"There's nothing to worry about, Ash." Sai softens her tone and suppresses the urge to sigh. "I've cleared this afternoon for you." She doesn't add that she had to reschedule three of the classes for after dinner. Ash doesn't need that kind of pressure.

"All afternoon then?" Aishke's expression wars between pleased and scared. Finally a small smile emerges, and Sai claims a silent victory.

"We'll start small. I promise." Sai grins and walks over.

"You're sure I can phase?"

Sai blinks. "You're a Rare, so I assume you can phase. Bastian can, I can..."

Aishke glances around, her eyes blinking nervously. "Can the domino?"

"Dom is an exception to every rule."

"He can't?"

"Dom can do pretty much anything." Sai pushes down the pang of sadness in her gut and blames it on a lunch eaten too quickly. "Stop changing the subject. You have to learn this. More lives than yours may depend on it one day."

Ash nods reluctantly.

"Excellent. Watch me. I'll do it as slowly as I can. You'll try afterward, and eventually it'll click." It goes to reason that what worked when Bastian taught her refinements to her technique should work for others.

Sai breathes in and counts to three. She takes two steps instead of her usual run and phases. It feels slower, and the distance is a fraction of what she usually travels.

Aishke's face scrunches into a frown, and she shakes her head.

Sai repeats the process three more times and figures out how to slow it more each time. After the fourth example, she hears Aishke gasp and looks over to see an expression of triumph. "You just sort of...will yourself to that point. Got it?"

"I think so."

"Then show me. Phase to me." Sai stands a short distance away and crosses her arms.

Every attempt ends up with Aishke jogging over to her.

"I don't get it!" Ash clenches her fists and scowls.

"We'll try it again, but this time you can see with me. Here." Sai takes Aishke's hand and touches it to her own temple to show the girl what part of her mind helps her visualize the sequence. "Can you hold the contact?"

Ash nods.

"Stay with me," she says softly. It's not often she relinquishes any of her shielding, but Aishke needs more than a visual. Sai repeats her demonstration from earlier another four times.

Ash sighs. "I'll try again."

Sai waits, arms crossed, resisting the urge to tap her foot, when suddenly she's propelled forward and crashes into Aishke, sending them both sprawling. Her shields slam back into place immediately, and she can feel the mental yelp from Ash despite the thick walls separating their minds.

"What was that?"

"I don't know!" Aishke balls her fists and blinks her eyes, but a tear escapes nonetheless.

Sai takes a deep breath. "I'm sorry I slammed my shields up, but it startled me. Do you think you can do that again?"

"I don't *know* what I did." The younger girl sounds miserable.

"Can you try?"

Ash nods her head glumly, and Sai returns to where she was. For a few minutes they stand there, motionless except for the grimaces on Aishke's face as she exerts herself to no avail.

"It's no use. Maybe it was something else." She sits down with a plop, pigtails in disarray.

"Something else?" Sai murmurs to herself. The shields. "Stand up." She manages to take the sting off the words just before they slip out. "I'm going to lower my shields like they were the first time. Will you try then?"

"If you don't snap them and give me a headache again," Ash says sullenly as she pushes herself up.

Sai nods and braces herself.

A moment later, they're both sprawled on the floor again and Sai blinks in shock. "Wow." It's the only word she can think of. Ash can't phase. She can pull. It might be useful. Sai isn't sure how since all of her own training involves keeping her distance from opponents, but she'll think of something.

"Don't get too excited." Ash dusts herself off as she stands back up. "If your shields aren't down, all I can do is look constipated."

A snort of laughter escapes Sai before she can clamp down on it. "Well..." She recovers her composure quickly. "We'll just have to work on that, won't we?"

"Whatever you say, boss," Aishke says with a hint of a smile.

So far Mondays have proved to be the most hectic day of the week around the Mobile. Sai climbs up to the navigation deck in order to give Mathur a rundown on her schedule and progress only to find the room filled with many more than the handful of people it takes to navigate the giant transport. There's tension in the room that usually isn't there, and Sai frowns, trying to determine the cause.

Usually the full briefing with the rest of the department heads takes place after Sai has briefed Mathur. But this time Kayde, Trikel, Darson, and Jeffries are all there, huddled together. The urgency in their tones as she walks into the room isn't lost on Sai, despite the silence that falls as they notice her presence.

She tries to catch their eyes, but everyone but Jeffries avoids her gaze. Finally she puts her hands on her hips and scowls. "What aren't you telling me?"

Mathur attempts a smile but fails. Alarm bells go off in Sai's head. The old man is usually easygoing, mostly jovial. Something must be seriously wrong, but she can't begin to fathom what it is. Unless of course...

"Is Bastian okay?" she whispers, not sure she wants to know the answer as her stomach threatens to heave.

"Bastian is fine." Mathur shakes his head, the sadness still evident in his eyes. "Let us go get some breakfast."

Jeffries's silence impacts her more than anything else. It has to be bad if he's not grilling her. Sai shakes her head. "I've already eaten," she murmurs.

"Then humor this old man." He takes her gently by the arm and leads her out of the room and down the steep stairs.

Her heart beats faster. She follows Mathur down to one of the small cafés, where he sits in the back.

"Just tell me." She glances at her watch. "Darson's training session starts in forty-five minutes. I don't have time."

"In the early hours of this morning, we learned via communications from Bastian that something is wrong with my Dom. With Twelve." Mathur takes a deep breath, his thin fingers clenched.

"Dom? Wait." Sai sits down. "Dom doesn't get sick. He told me that himself." But the memory is there. Of Dom and the strange blackouts; of Dom and the loss of form control; of Dom rainbowing.

"I said there is something wrong with him. He does not get sick by our standards."

"But he isn't his normal self."

"No." Mathur shakes his head for emphasis. "He's not even aware of himself at this point in time. Everything about him is dormant."

Sai blinks rapidly at the unexpected heat behind her eyes. Being emotional isn't going to help Dom. "Can you fix him?" The hitch to her voice surprises her.

Mathur shakes his head. "Not from this distance, and I cannot risk a trip into Central right now."

"I promised I'd see him again, Mathur." Her voice comes out raspy, and she reaches for the glass of water on the table, unsure of when it was delivered.

"He is not dying, Sai. Bastian assures me it is nothing like that. You have to understand that when I left, they tweaked him. They did things they probably thought were improvements but that I know are not. GNW does not quite understand Domino 12, and so far this has helped keep him safe and away from their machinations."

"What?" Sai shakes her head. "You're not making sense."

"Dom is the prototype. The others are copies. If I were still there, I could fix them."

"Fix them? The others are broken, too?"

"I did not tell you that?" Mathur smiles softly. "I thought I did. Forgive me. They began to fall into dormancy shortly after Twelve."

"And you can fix them?"

"If I could get them to me, though it will take time to fix them all, I am certain I can do it."

"Then how do we get them here?"

"It is not that easy, Sai."

"No." Sai stands, rocking the table. "Dammit, Mathur. It has to be that easy. You need to fix him. You need to fix *them*."

Mathur raises an eyebrow. "For now, the people who work in my old laboratory can patch Dom up. This should be enough for the others to find the foothold they need to function again. It will also give us enough time to figure out a solution."

Sai sits down again and stares at her hands. It's far easier to fuel herself with anger than to be calm and try to deal with the roiling of her gut. Fixing him later isn't enough. He needs to be whole now. "Is he in danger?"

"Elements of him are in danger, but eventually he will be fine."

"If you're trying to be reassuring, you suck at it," Sai murmurs, suppressing a yawn.

"Perhaps. You will have to forgive me, yes?" Mathur's eyes sparkle for a moment, some of his usual self returning just briefly.

"I'll forgive you when you fix him." Sai allows a small smile in return.

"There is one thing, though." He pauses as she yawns again, ignoring her demand. "The timetable for our operation has been moved. With the dominos' current situation, we have little choice."

"Moved? How much time does 'moved' mean?" Sai sits up straight, suddenly suspicious.

"A month or so." Mathur shrugs.

"It'll be the dead of winter. We can't travel like that."

"On the contrary, winter will make it easier." He puts a hand on her arm as she's about to protest and shakes his head. "It is okay, Sai. We will be ready. You will be ready. And together we will do what needs to be done."

"Easy for you to say," she mutters and glares at him for good measure.

Aishke falls to the ground, tears streaming down her face.

Sai feels like a monster. "You can do this, Ash," she says in what she hopes is a soothing tone. The girl isn't used to work, period. Sai has to remind herself it's not Aishke's fault. "I'm sorry for being so harsh, but if I'm not, you might die when we get to Central."

Ash's tears stop, and she looks up through one of her disarrayed pigtails. "Die?" Her bottom lip trembles. "I don't want to die."

"Then punch through my shields. It's only three layers, and I know you can do it." Sai's been waiting for it to happen all afternoon, but isn't prepared for when it does. The shattering hits her hard, and the tug of displacement as Ash pulls her forward unsettles her stomach. Sai's shields slam up as she dry heaves a few times.

"Sai!" Aishke's glare is accusatory. "You promised you wouldn't do that!" She rubs her temples, her brows furrowed.

"Sorry. Didn't expect you to punch through immediately." Sai glances at her watch. They've been at it for hours. It was going to be another late night, but at least it was worth it.

"I don't want to die, Sai," Ash says softly, her fists clenched at her side.

"Everyone dies eventually, Ash."

"Maybe, but the longer I can prevent it from happening, the better."

Sai picks herself up off the floor and uses dusting herself off as an excuse to mull over Aishke's words. "We're not invincible, Ash, no one is."

"Dom is. Bastian always said Dom is."

Sai shakes her head. "Dom isn't, and he's different. He doesn't count." Even as much as she'd like him to. "Do you remember how you punched through?"

Ash nods, her expression determined. "Every little bit."

"Good." Sai walks back a few steps and braces herself. "Try four layers. This time, I'm ready."

The punch doesn't knock her off her feet, but the tug almost succeeds. Sai finds it hard to breathe after the initial displacement. "Good," she gasps out. "Knocks the wind out of you."

Ash grins. "I can break through more shields, right?"

Sai shrugs. "I'm just guiding you here. This is your thing. But I'm quite sure you can improve."

"You know it's not a game, right?"

Sai and Aishke whip around to see Iria leaning against the doorway, her arms crossed and that familiar grin on her face.

Ash scowls. "It's never been a game."

"Just checking." Iria pushes off from the doorway and meets them in the middle. "When do I get to fight, boss?"

Sai takes a deep breath. "We've been over this. Your defensive capabilities are far beyond your offensive."

"I can be the best damn shield you've ever had." Iria grins, and Sai finds herself grinning in response. The girl's good humor is infectious.

"Now who's treating it like a game?" Ash mutters and kicks her jacket off the ground and into her hand. "I'll see you later, Sai."

"I'll be late."

"I know," Aishke says softly as the door closes behind her.

"What's with her?"

"Probably you." Sai pulls her own jacket on, suddenly feeling a chill. She slams her shields back into full force, disliking the vulnerability without them, and notices a shadow at the door.

Jeffries. It's not the first time she's noticed him spying on her.

There's no smile on Iria's face when she breaks the silence, not even a hint. "Either me or the fact that she's not the child we're all treating her like and realizes she may actually have to kill or be killed when the time comes to storm Central."

Sai shakes her head. "No. She's no child, and she understands death more intimately than I think anyone realizes." She glances at Iria and grins. "You, on the other hand, still need work."

Iria rubs her hands together. "I thought you might have given up on me. What with the constant rescheduling."

"Aishke is not only volatile, but that abyss of power she has makes her a Rare as well. She has priority. But you? A shield? I'm not sure how far we can push that."

Iria nods. "I've had some time to kill lately. And I think..." She hesitates and smiles, almost shyly. "I can extend my shielding to cover others. It takes effort, but in a pinch..."

Sai smiles, realizing how easy it is to be around someone who's genuine. "Show me."

Iria furrows her brow in concentration and reaches visibly. At the same time, Sai can feel something stretching over her and draping down. She closes her eyes and probes tentatively. It's definitely not perfect, but a lot better than she expected. There are thinner and thicker areas, and the ends don't quite hit the floor. The shield becomes frayed the longer Iria holds it, but there is definite potential and a way to protect multiple people at once.

"Drop it," she says and opens her eyes when Iria does so. The brunette is sweating profusely, but the pride in her eyes is obvious.

"This is probably going to be more work than you wanted. There are some shield-strengthening exercises I want to give you. I used them to protect my room from prying minds back at the facility. If you practice these once in the morning and once at night, you shouldn't get too exhausted. In a week, we'll work on your reaction time. With some luck, I think you can do this."

Iria beams. "I knew it."

"It's not the answer to everything, Iria," Sai cautions her.

"Not that." Iria shakes her head impatiently. "I knew you were a leader."

"Come again?"

"Regardless of how you see yourself, people look up to you. Anyone who realizes how hard it is to break the hold on your mind the GNW fosters from the first day you come under their care. You're a leader, Sai. Thank you for choosing to help."

Sai blinks and wants to refute the words. She's still not sure GNW doesn't have some sort of hook in her, aren't playing tricks on her themselves. "Without Bastian, I'd be dead. Thank him." She glances at her watch again. "I have another student in a few minutes."

Iria shrugs. "Bastian isn't here, and you are. You're a good person. You are defining yourself here and now, by your actions. Don't pay any attention to Jeffries."

The panic rising in her throat constricts her chest, and Sai has to breathe deeply to keep from letting it consume her.

People's lives depend on her, even if she thinks they shouldn't. Anything less than her best just isn't an option.

"How goes the list?" Kayde Thaniel pops her head around the door to the meeting room and grins.

Sai pinches the bridge of her nose and shakes her head, putting down the reader in her hand. "It goes."

"That doesn't sound encouraging, oh fearless leader," she says as she sits down.

"You're the second person in the last two days to tell me I'm a leader. I'm just here to help."

Kayde shrugs her shoulders. "Okay. That doesn't sound like the almighty helper, then."

Sai laughs. "Fine. You win."

"What's got you discouraged?" she asks softly.

"Everything." She sighs and leans forward to rest her head on the cool glass of the table. "I got the impression we were like an infestation."

"By we, you mean psionics?"

Sai nods. "They always taught us isolation was for our own good. To protect us and others. To harness our abilities and use them to benefit the people of the GNW United Conglomerate. But this list..." She lifts her head up and peers at the reader again, like it might bite her. "This list is so much shorter than I imagined. Given the size of the Exiled population, I thought the list would be so much larger."

"What number were you?"

Sai stiffens. "What?"

"What number were you? In your intake year."

"52," she murmurs and closes her eyes. The designation always makes her feel less than human.

"You realize that's fifty-two people in your intake year. Some older, some younger, depending on their awakening. That's only about fifteen hundred people every year. In twenty-nine cities, Sai. And then there are the exams, and the facility that powers the grid."

Sai nods. She still has nightmares. "Four people. Four in my year passed."

"Out of fifty-two?"

"Maybe more? I don't remember hearing a number higher than me."

"So maybe 150 people make it into the workforce. That's a low success rate. And those are the psionics they allowed to live. They're the ones they chose to invest in training. There are less of us because of GNW, but there were never overwhelming amounts of us to begin with." She stretches her arms back behind her head and grins. "I mean, think about it. Meteors crash, kill the atmosphere, and shortly thereafter psionics start appearing. Even breeding like rabbits, we couldn't be everywhere yet. The epidemic they've always treated us as? Never remotely existed."

CHAPTER
Nineteen

Running late to her meeting, Sai rips open the door to reveal a tall, dark-haired man eerily similar to Bastian. His blue eyes crinkle, and a somewhat delicate mouth opens in a big smile. He's a bit bulkier than his brother, but even the olive tone of their skin is perfectly matched.

"Sai, I presume?"

Sai extends a hand and glances back toward Aishke's room. "It's good to finally meet you, Mason."

"Thank you for taking Ash in, taking care of her. I don't have the time to give to her right now, but hopefully I'll be around more soon."

"She'll like that." Sai smiles sadly. Ash isn't going to be happy, but with the looming infiltration planned, there's not much they can do. She's about to call out when Mason places his hand briefly on hers. "Sorry. Please come in."

He looks around, brushing down his uniform in a way eerily similar to his sibling. "Does my brother still think he can save everyone?" he asks softly.

"I don't think Bastian knows any other way. He'll keep saving everyone until he can't anymore," she answers as she walks to Aishke's door. "He doesn't smile much."

Mason sighs, and his shoulders sag a bit. "He's a bit obsessed. Sarah's death left him angry and determined."

"Sarah?"

"Our mother." Mason hesitates for a moment as Sai knocks.

"Aishke? You have a visitor."

"What?" Ash comes out of her room, pulling her strange hair into pigtails, and stops. "Mason?" she whispers before leaping to hug him.

Sai backs out quietly and runs to the meeting, hoping Mason won't be late.

The huge center area of the Mobile is cleared out for the gathering. Anyone who wants to attend is welcome to come and listen, and for this, many people have gathered. Some clasp hands in hearty handshakes and hugs, clapping each other on the back. Others stick to themselves, their expressions somber and concerned.

Regardless of how comfortable the Exiled have managed to make their lives, many of them left people behind. Sai has Johnson's memories, and failing that, leaving Bastian, Nimue, and Dom hurt more than she likes to admit.

Everything people in the United Conglomerate are taught is just another lie on top of an older one. GNW justifies it, and the people accept it because they have no other choice. With patients from the testing labs fueling the mind-suggestion grid, and

301

weaker psionics unwittingly syphoning that strength to enforce false contentment, justice is too nice a word. Sai clenches her fists to calm herself.

The sheer number of people surrounding her is daunting. She inches away and leans against one of the supports, as far as she can get from the throng without leaving.

"You're either scared of crowds, scared of speaking, or both." Iria pops up right next to her, the usual smile in place. "We're in the last days of the countdown, you know? In a few days we could be in there, getting our people out and letting the world know just what GNW is."

Sai steps back and studies the girl she's come to think of as a friend. "You're far too eager to seek revenge. Killing someone, deliberately or not, is something you'll live with forever. You'll wake up dreaming about it, screaming about it." She runs a hand through her hair, trying to forget her own nightmares. "We should get in, cause confusion, grab what we came for, and leave. Too much bloodshed will turn those people against us forever, and stop them wanting to join us in what we're fighting to achieve. If we do this smart, it'll work. There are different types of freedom."

Silence greets her when she stops speaking, and Iria winks at her. Sai lowers her head and scuffs her foot against the ground, the flush in her cheeks hot and irritating.

"She's right, you know." Mathur smiles as he walks past her and pats her on the shoulder. All eyes refocus on him and Sai lets the tension melt away. With her eyes on the floor, she catches a glimpse of his leg as his pants sway and frowns.

She knows what they're about to discuss, and thanks to Mathur's timely intervention, it's easy to slink away unnoticed.

Suddenly, she has something to do.

Sai pokes around until she finds Mathur's living quarters. It makes sense for them to be close to the navigation deck. She slumps down the wall to the floor and waits for him to get back.

The meeting runs long, enough for thousands of questions to assault her mind. She sighs and drops her head into her hands. Everything would be much simpler if her entire life hadn't been built on a lie.

"Sai?" Mathur asks from the end of the hall.

She pushes herself up and dusts off her pants. "Sorry, I didn't want to stay."

"You missed Mason's speech." He grins at her as he unlocks the door.

"If he's anything like his brother, I can imagine it well enough."

Mathur laughs and motions for her to enter the cluttered but cozy apartment. She sits down on his couch, much more comfortable than her own, and gets right to the point. "I have questions about a lot of things. But first, I didn't know you had an adrium leg."

Mathur smiles fondly. "I do. Limb loss replacement was the first viable use found for the compound. Highly expensive at first, but extremely effective. Once we could reproduce it, it became more affordable. Why?"

She ignores his question. "How did they find out it worked like that?"

"An extraction accident. The electronic pulses that go

through our bodies were enough to ignite the slumbering parasite in the metal. Until then, we thought the meteors simply contained a metallic compound. The meteors themselves never showed any sign of parasitic activity. Through further experimentation, we learned it reacts to electronic fields. And voila." He pulls the leg of his trousers up a bit to show the shiny metal.

"You don't camouflage. Why not?"

He shrugs. "It is a minimal replacement. There is no need for it to respond to my brain commands, just simply fill in the hole that was there."

She takes a deep breath. "Is that why you made Dom?"

He hands her a cup of tea before sitting in the recliner across from her and sipping out of his own cup, infuriatingly slow, brow creased in thought. "I did not build the dominos as you know them. I only created mine—Dom. At first I created him because I needed to see how far this adrium fusion with psionic DNA could go—what could it offer and how could it benefit us. That, and I always knew the Damascus were wrong."

"Why?"

"Because they were too much machine, and the alien personality came to the fore with no conscience. It swallowed what humanity it had and became driven by a single-minded motivation to survive."

"I thought you said adrium is a parasite. Doesn't it need something living to survive?"

"It needs electricity to give it life. That is all. Machines run on power as well, and there is no humanity to temper the alien hunger for destruction." He sighs, a light flush to his cheeks. "My directions were to create a weapon. The ultimate weapon.

Duty to GNW demanded compliance."

"But Dom is so...so human."

"He is not just twelve because I had some whimsy and decided hey, I like the number twelve, my dear. He is the twelfth in the line of attempts at creating what he is. My first attempt survived a measly eleven minutes, but it was more than I had hoped for. Dominos do not grow; they are incubated at full size for months and it takes a long time to mature. But the first three I made had varying rates of immediate failure. They ranged from eleven minutes to three days."

Mathur sighs, his eyes downcast, before continuing. "By the time it got to that stage, GNW was very interested in my experiments, a lot more than they should have been, or than I should have let them be. I fixed the incubation problem only to find the synaptic fusion with the adrium wasn't holding up. The adrium was too heavy. By the eighth, I finally had it and number eight lived for six whole months."

"Nine and ten could not harness the ability to shift. It literally drove them crazy. Eleven? All I can say about him is, he was close, but not perfect and his light went out at just over twelve months. I spent the next six months perfecting everything theoretically before I incubated Dom."

He smiles triumphantly. "And I was right. He was human enough to adapt and was so in tune with his adrium body that it was beautiful. Able to camouflage himself at the drop of a hat, alter appearances. He could run; lift a transport. I had lived every little boy's dream, Sai!" His eyes sparkle as he speaks. "Guess what I did?"

"What?" she asks, caught up in his nostalgia.

"I created a superhero! He was, or he could be. And do you

know why the dominos they created in my absence are inferior to my boy, to the closest thing I have ever had to a son?"

Sai just shakes her head.

"Has Bastian ever told you what my psionic strength is?"

Sai blinks at the quick change of subject. "Everyone is taught that. You're a healer, like me."

"Exactly. While the instructions I left with the facility when I 'died' are technically correct in every aspect of their creation, Dom was created and nurtured with the use of my ability. The new versions will never be the same unless I can work with them, and even then, it is doubtful."

"Is that why he's ill? Is he blocking the other dominos out?"

Mathur nods. "He was not meant to communicate with their wavelengths. They are all slightly out of sync with each other, and even more so with him. He can open and maintain a communication line with them, and they have been using up his strength bit by bit to keep themselves whole."

"You see..." He pats her hand. "It is a failsafe. His brain has shut itself down so it does not have to deal with the interference coming from the others. Even if they have damaged him again, Bastian can help restore Dom's mind with the trigger word. A reboot is not what you think. Usually, without his direct consent, it cannot be performed. He is not a Damascus, not a machine. It is an invasive cleaning of his adrium and human junctions. It takes a while and can cause temporary amnesia."

"As long as we get the others and fix them, we can save them all?"

"It is very possible." Mathur looks at her for a second, a frown at the edge of his smile. "Did I answer all your questions?"

"Why don't people know?"

"Sometimes, people do not like the truth. He is strong. He is *almost* invincible. People do not need to fear him more than they already do."

Sai blinks down at her teacup.

"Can I ask you a question, Sai?" His tone is serious, his eyes intense.

She nods in response.

"How do you feel about Dom?"

Taken a little aback by the question, Sai mulls it over and feels the heat rise in her cheeks. "I miss him," she says simply.

Sai suits up in her room, admiring the blending capacity of the adrium-woven material. Nothing like the dominos, but it resembles a dense liquid as it makes contacts with her skin. She walks out to find Aishke standing there only half-finished. "Here," she tucks Aishke's collar under and to the side, and presses down until the clasp hits. "Like that. Sometimes it can be tricky."

Finally, she hands Ash the long blade the girl has been practicing with. "It's no use against a crossbow, but if you can't tell one's coming, then you're doing something wrong."

Ash nods. "I wish I wasn't shaking. I wish I could be as brave as you." Her violet eyes look panicked and scared.

"I'm not at all brave. I'd like nothing more than to run away and find somewhere no one has ever heard of GNW. But I don't want to regret anything in life. There's right and wrong, and the wrong needs to stop. It's as easy as pretending you're brave and just doing it, okay?"

Aishke nods again.

"Good. You keep that knife, and stay close to me. Don't be a hero unless it's an easy catch. We have work to do. Got it?"

"Got it." Ash grins nervously.

"You're brave, remember?"

"Got it, sir!" This time her smile is genuine.

It's not long before they join Mathur on the navigation deck. Sai twists her hair, hoping it'll stop her teeth from chattering. *In and out, just in and out,* she tells herself. No casualties. Get the drugs, get what prisoners they can, and get out of there. Strike hard at their core, and let the whole world know the truth—even if they don't remember it for long.

Mathur's usual smile is absent, replaced by a frown that tugs down strangely at the corners of his lips. He catches Sai's attention and motions her over. "We have a problem. The other dominos are functioning outside their usual parameters. I thought we had more time."

"No dominos guarding the lab will be a plus, but will they help us or them?"

"There is no telling. Though Dom has had his reset, Bastian informs us the trigger is not working."

"Dom doesn't have a trigger." Sai almost laughs, but stops at Mathur's expression.

He shakes his head. "Trigger word. For when they reset him—to help him keep the advancements he has made since his creation. A way to seal off his experiences, his memory, himself essentially."

Sai blanches. "He doesn't remember me?"

"He does not remember anything right now. It should slowly come back to him, but for now, he is in his original state until we figure out what is blocking his trigger." Mathur's tone is kind, but that's not what Sai needs.

She sighs and pinches the bridge of her nose. "We'll deal with the dominos if and when they try to run interference. Focus on rescuing those we can. Take all of the Shine we can get our hands on so the grids can only tap into already drained reserves. It's not a Damascus-level malfunction, is it?"

"Not even possible. They are suffering a loss of self, rampant confusion."

"So, as far as we know, they're not dangerous, just having an identity crisis."

Mathur raises his eyebrows. "In a manner of speaking."

"Like I said, then—everything to plan unless something interrupts us."

"We have received the blueprints of Central from Bastian. What it amounts to: Dom and Bastian think there is more than one facility for this type of...research."

Sai swallows and keeps her eyes on him.

"We need this trip to count."

"Will Bastian be coming back with us?"

Mathur shakes his head and Sai feels a moment of irritation. He looks at her apologetically. "I am sorry, little one. We need him on the inside to chip away. Help us take them down from the inside out."

She laughs and pushes down the flare of emotion Bastian's stubbornness conjures. "That's fine. We've got this." The bravado sits strangely, an awkward pretense she hopes will become reality.

"Now, for the serious business." Mathur pauses. "Iria wants to go with you."

Sai blinks. "She can't. Her offensive abilities are practically nonexistent, and her response times are too slow. I can't take someone with me who may be more of a detriment than a benefit."

"I'm glad you said that." Mathur seems relieved. "I will let her know that the answer is still negative."

"If everything goes smoothly, maybe she can help me do the final perimeter sweep. Maybe," Sai says grudgingly.

"Oh! Thank you, Sai." Iria darts out from behind Mathur and practically strangles her in a tight hug.

Disentangling herself, Sai glares at her. "It's not a promise. It's a maybe. If we start losing people, I don't want you to be one of them." By the end of the speech, Sai's voice is barely audible, but Iria nods, smile shining regardless.

"You got it, boss!" She salutes and runs off before Sai can say anything else.

"I'm going to regret this, aren't I?" Sai suddenly feels cold. Everything is piling up and her gut clenches in that tense way she knows isn't good.

Mathur shakes his head. "Never have regrets, Sai. It ruins your life." His eyes take on a shadow for a fraction of time, and then it's gone. He looks down at her and places a gentle hand on her shoulder, reminiscent of Dom. It's strangely comforting as he points out of the massive window in front of them. "Do you see it?" he whispers to her.

She squints at first, but then she sees it, on the horizon: Central's tall buildings, with the sun glinting off their woven protection.

Their destination. Their target.

Sai stands on the ground underneath the Mobile, frowning at the slim pieces of metal currently supporting it. She's glad they're usually on the move and not resting on the flimsy-looking poles. The sun is sinking in the sky, and the chilly air makes her shiver involuntarily.

Aishke taps her on the shoulder. "You okay?"

"Mhm?" Sai keeps her eyes on the disappearing sun. "I should be asking you that question."

"You're not much older than me, are you, Sai?" Aishke's expression is thoughtful.

"Not much older at all. Why?"

"I just..." Ash squares her shoulders and stamps one foot. "I need to learn to depend on myself and help you, not hinder you."

Sai smiles. "You'll do fine. I think you'll surprise yourself. Just no heroics, okay?"

Aishke nods and returns the smile.

"Am I interrupting something?" Kayde's eyes sparkle, but she's easily amused if Sai is any judge.

"No."

She grins. "Reporting for duty, ma'am."

"Cut the crap, Kayde. If everyone starts pulling this, I'm quitting before we go in." Sai fumbles in the pocket of her suit, frowning until she finds the small reader they engineered to fit her forearm and straps it into place. Kayde's bright blue eyes always feel like they're boring into her soul. She frowns at the reader, as if it can change that. "Besides, you're technically not coming in with us."

"Spoil all my fun." The grin is firmly affixed on her face, but no longer reaches her eyes.

"You sure you're up for this?" Sai jokes, trying to alleviate the tension around them. Kayde may be irritating sometimes, but everyone is too stressed.

"I can take Harlow on with my eyes closed." She winks, and Sai laughs.

"Just make sure you do. There's no second take to show the world."

"Sure thing, boss."

"Stop that," she says automatically and inserts the earpiece, shaking her head as it molds to fit. "I'm not sure I like this route, but at least we have a guide."

"Who's guiding?" Aishke asks.

"We're taking Mason—or he's taking us."

Aishke frowns.

"I believe his words were: I want to hit Deign where it hurts." Sai glances at Aishke who's fighting a giggle. Much better.

"Are you talking about me?" Mason says, suddenly behind her. Too quiet. It's a good thing he's on their side.

"Talking about my team, Mr. Mason, sir!" Sai glances at her watch as the sun dips further, and she tries to ignore the persistent uneasiness tingling down her spine. It won't be so bad once they're on the move. They're so close to the city walls, she wants to reach out and touch them.

She can see the advertisements that play inside the domes as they flicker in and out, in a twisted reverse rendition. They're not meant to be seen that way. It's too easy to remember how normal she once found them.

Mason is their tunnel system guide. Sai isn't sure she wants to know how the tunnels got put into the city or why, but what was used to sneak Bastian and Shine out, can be used to sneak the Exiled in.

There are several exits, including one out into the type of block Sai grew up in. Everyone they can reach will be given a chance to get out.

Two full teams and her own are ready to pour into the facility itself. Sai takes a deep breath and closes her eyes, throwing out her hope and wishing for someone to catch onto it and make it true.

The adrium net overlaying the Mobiles highlights the red in the last of the sunlight. It's deceptive in its camouflaged state. Even in its engineered form, the parasite is beautiful.

Mason nudges her. "Focus, Sai. We're in countdown mode." His words are stern but gentle, and she chides herself for getting distracted. Plenty of time for that later. She refuses to wonder if there'll actually *be* a later.

The sun finally hits the horizon, and Mathur directs the scouts to take out Central's guards in the vicinity. They don't have to wait long. The blending abilities of body armor go a long way in the twilight.

Mason gives the signal to move to the hidden entrance. The words echo through their earpieces. They move out in double-time, two across, Mason and Sai at the lead. She steels herself and squeezes Aishke's hand as she reaches out for her, giving her the assurance they both need. It takes a five-minute jog to get to the tunnel entrance and inside.

There's no turning back now.

CHAPTER
Twenty

Bastian makes his way down the corridors toward the meeting room. The sun hasn't sunk beneath the horizon yet, and stray rays of light bleed through the halls. He pauses to make a comment and corrects himself just in time. It's been hard to get used to Dom's absence over the last few weeks, but there's been more than enough to concentrate on.

He squares his shoulders and sobers his expression before stepping into the corridor leading to the room. He's not the last to arrive at tonight's meeting. Deign tends to call them at differing times to keep people from getting complacent, while reinforcing that she is, indeed, in charge. Bastian glances around the room with feigned indifference. It's not where he wants to be right now, but it'll do.

Deign grasps his hand and shakes it, eyeing his gloves with distaste. "You never trust me, do you?"

"When have you ever known me to trust anyone?" He raises an eyebrow and watches her flush at the words. Sometimes it's all too easy pretending to be something he's not, with a slight twist on the truth.

Zach eyes them both warily as he enters the room.

"Hey, Zach." The fondness in Bastian's tone isn't forced. No matter what, Zach will always be the first friend he had.

"Good evening, Deign."

She barely glances at him. "Hello, Zacharai."

Zach scowls at the use of his full name.

Bastian has to stop himself from laughing at them both. His nerves are acting up in anticipation, and his head feels a little ditzy considering he had to dull with Shine. It takes a while longer for everyone to arrive, greet each other, and get seated.

Deign stands and fake-smiles at everyone. "Let's get down to business."

She's always loved the sound of her own voice, so Bastian settles down to listen. The lights flicker. He schools his face and waits.

Deign glances at the lights and frowns but continues on. "As you're all aware, the outer blocks of the United Conglomerate are largely populated by those less fortunate." The words carry a faintly mocking disdain. "Due to an unavoidable rise in illegal Shine distribution, the circle of poverty is creeping closer to the city centers." She pauses enough for her words to sink in, and Bastian grips the arms of his chair to stop from jumping up and smacking her in the face. "We need to get them away from the working sector of the cities—through any means necessary."

The mumbling around the table disperses as the intercom flares to life.

"What is it, Frances?" She waves a hand over a section of the table to activate her side of the security's intercom.

"Ma'am, we seem to have lost our connection to the labs with the power surge just now."

Deign sighs. "Doesn't this usually happen? Isn't this just one of the power outages?"

There's a pause on the other end. "It's off-schedule," Frances admits, "but does occasionally happen."

"Then don't bother me again until you *know* something is wrong. We're in the middle of a meeting," Deign snaps, her tone cold.

"Yes, ma'am." Frances cuts out.

Just before Deign can start speaking again, the lights flicker off.

Harlow clears her throat as the lights come back on. "I need to get down to the security station."

Deign raises an eyebrow. "Seriously? Can't you just open that fiddly little thing in your hand, or blink your eyes, and control it from here?"

"Not if the main systems require attention. It's not that simple."

Deign waves her away. "Go with her, Bastian," she says just before the intercom starts buzzing with white noise. "Go! Before this drives me insane."

The intercom falls silent, and one security image flickers over the wall behind them. It only shows one brief shot. Just one moment of people there and then not.

Deign pales at the image and frantically pushes part of the screen on her desk. "Get that feed back *right now*, Harlow."

"On my way." Harlow grabs her things and throws Bastian a long-suffering look before they head out of the door.

Bastian schools his face into an expression of shock as he hears Deign start her tirade in the room behind them. "I thought we were supposed to have backup systems..." is all he hears before the door shuts.

The facility is on a yellow alert. Guards stand at attention—or, at least, those who aren't running around trying to be somewhere. Harlow's heels clip the marble crisply as they make their way to her security haven.

Bastian didn't expect to be sent to the security center with Harlow, but he's not one to look a gift horse in the mouth either. There are few better places he could have intentionally situated himself, especially after the monitor glitch.

Harlow's brow furrows as the security system she designed herself scans her for access. Once inside the center, she activates numerous desktops and wall displays to provide an alarmingly well-illuminated picture of the current events.

"I should come down here more often." Bastian is careful to only lean against the doorway. The other surfaces of the office are far too delicate to bear the weight. "You've made some changes." Changes he realizes he should have noted the last time he visited her. Even a short while ago would have given them the heads up they needed.

Harlow shakes her head. "I've had to be busy. Deign doesn't make this job easy. She has so much paranoia I need to prove incorrect, not to mention actual individuals trying to utilize that paranoia to their own benefit..." Harlow pauses, shaking her head as she types things too fast for Bastian to follow. "If I didn't want to make sure my father's work was continued properly, I probably wouldn't put up with her crap."

Bastian shifts his weight, not quite sure how to play this new bit of information. Surely he can use it to his advantage. He notices the panic in her expression as she realized who she's said what to.

"I..." She pauses, her lips slightly parted, brow pinched.

"What? I'm interested in seeing where it was this image came from so I can let Deign know if we have a situation."

Harlow smiles tightly. "Thank you." She flips through several screens, a frown forming on her face. "I can't find anything," she says finally, throwing up her hands in exasperation.

"Nothing?" Bastian frowns. Surely Kayde managed to pull it off.

"I can't find any evidence of infiltration, not from any specified location. It's more like a flash of something someone might have wanted us to see? It's used an override code not even I can crack. Wait a second..." She bends over the desk, hands flying over different portions of the surface. She glances up at Bastian fearfully.

"What is it?" he asks, unsure of what Kayde is playing with. Technically, the plan allowed her a lot of leeway.

"I think I'm being set up. That's Deign's code, Bastian. I don't know it. I can't even access it, but the system recognizes it as Deign's signature."

Bastian scowls to cover the laughter he feels in his throat. "Doesn't Deign need to trigger her own code with a personal scan?"

Harlow nods slowly.

"Then something's malfunctioning in the system. It's not you—I've been with you the entire time."

Harlow seems surprised. "You'll vouch for me?"

"Definitely. Not many people argue with me." Harlow isn't one of the bad guys. His mind races as he tries to figure out how to protect her, and still aide the Exiled as planned.

Kayde already has everything under control; the next step is to make sure it stays that way. If Harlow remains in the control booth, that's going to get tricky. Bastian grabs her hand and drags her back outside, hoping his assumption is correct. "We need to get back to Deign."

"No, Bastian, I need to stop this. She'll have me killed!" There's genuine panic in her voice, her hysteria very real.

"Harlow! Think a moment. If I leave you here to report to Deign while the systems are down, not even my most convincing argument is going to save you."

She pales as her determination sags.

"If you come with me, then you've never been out of my sight. Someone has her codes or access to her DNA scans, and it's not you and it's not me. If you're with me, she can hardly refute that, right?"

Harlow nods, the color creeping slowly back into her complexion.

"Excellent. Then follow me."

With any luck, Kayde's outdone herself and tapped through the electronic barriers to be able to hear the whole conversation. He hears the door click behind them with a finality that makes him smile. No one will get past Kayde's failsafes and into the control booth anytime soon.

Frances is talking to Deign in hushed tones when they get back upstairs. Deign pushes him none too gently aside when she sees Bastian and Harlow reenter the room.

"What have you done?" Deign's voice is silky and soft—a sure danger sign. "I'm waiting, Harlow."

Bastian steps between them. "Actually, Deign, it's what have *you* done? How has someone got a hold of your codes, your scans?"

Deign shakes her head and takes a step back. "What are you talking about? No one has my master scan but me."

"In that case..." Bastian crosses his arms. "What are you playing at? Because it's those codes blocking us from everything, and it's your bio scan now barring us from the system controls."

Deign's eyes dart wildly between him and Harlow. "She's behind this—all of it!"

"Then I must be, too, because I've been with her since before all this began and she couldn't reverse what's been set in motion."

Deign narrows her eyes. "You can reverse this with time and get the security back online, correct?"

Harlow nods. "I'm not sure how long it's going to take."

"Frances said they've swept along outside and down through the facility. So far there's nothing to report. It looks like it's a malfunction or that someone got creative with that brief image. Still, I want to be sure, so his men are sweeping again. Take the time you need, but don't let it take too long. I want the grid reserves, the batteries, and the Shine labs back online. Sooner than later. Clear?"

"Crystal." Harlow bows and dives to her meeting room workstation to start tackling access to the control booth again. Bastian breathes softly, glad one crisis is averted.

"Bastian."

"Yes?"

"If there are people in this facility, I expect you to get rid of them. I don't care who you need to take with you. I don't care how bloody it gets. Clean it up and make this go away. We have far too important work to do to let someone come in here, sabotage my security systems with my code, and think they can get away with it."

Bastian nods, his stomach clenching in response. Deign likes to get her way, and if something interferes with it, she needs it gone.

She steps closer to him, using her height to her full advantage, and locks her eyes on his. "Do you understand? I don't care if this is some lab techs having fun and trying to overcome boredom. They need to disappear. This all needs to disappear. I don't like bad days, Bastian. Do I make myself clear?"

There's a weight to her words, a psionic pressure at his temples. Deign's projections, when angry, can be lethal. He nods, glad he only took a small dose of Shine. "Perfectly."

Deign smiles and pats him on the shoulder as the sudden tension surrounding him dissipates. "Good. Now we just need to figure out what the hell is going on. On top of the domino incident recently, it feels like someone is out to get me. Only that's perfectly stupid, isn't it, Bastian?"

Again, he nods, a chill gripping his chest. Whether she knows what it is or not is irrelevant. Deign clearly knows something and isn't about to let it or him go unless she has to. That's the problem with doing his job so well; it's not the first time Deign has used him for her own personal security.

Usually he doesn't care, but right now that's not where he wants to be.

"Fine," he says instead of arguing and turns to the guard. "Frances, take your men and do another sweep of the facility, just to be safe. I know you've done it once, but do it again."

Frances smiles tightly and nods. "Understood perfectly, sir." He turns on his heel and the tension in his shoulders reduces visibly. Deign has that effect on people.

"If he comes back with an all-clear, we can shut down the yellow alert," Bastian says to Deign.

She scowls at him and grabs his hand. "If he doesn't, *you're* sweeping the facility and taking anyone out of place down with you."

Bastian grins grimly. "As you wish," he says, glad for the hundredth time that he chooses to cover his skin when she's around.

It's been pitch black outside the windows for the last thirty-odd minutes. Bastian glances at his wrist, while pretending to pour over the reports Harlow is going through, trying to track down the culprit.

So far, Deign is certain it's a prank, which allows Bastian some leeway, but soon she's going to realize it's not. About when

Frances doesn't return from scouting, or when the feeds fully shut down and begin looping their content, and definitely when the alarm sounds, though he's fairly certain she'll catch onto it before then.

Her pride doesn't get in the way of her brain for too long. Deign scowls as she pulls over Lourd's wrist and glances at the man's watch. "Bastian."

As he stands up, the screens flicker on, back to their usual display of empty halls. Except this time he knows they're on a loop, and in about twenty minutes, so will everyone else. When not one guard patrol has passed any of them, everything is going to hit the fan.

Bastian plans to be gone by then.

"What?" he asks, just this side of impatient as he comes to stand next to her.

"You need to take a couple of guards and go down to check where Frances is."

Bastian waves a hand, dismissive of her concern. "Frances is a big boy, Deign. He'll radio in soon."

"It's not up for debate."

"It's Davis's lab. Shouldn't he go down and take care of it?"

Deign hesitates. "He's bringing me a failsafe, just in case."

"In case? I thought I was your failsafe," he almost jokes. Failsafe doesn't sound like a good thing.

She taps her foot with exasperation. "Not in that way. A just-in-case method."

"Deign, don't you think you're being a little paranoid? We often have grid-outs. This isn't all that different."

"But we don't have them for this long without fixing them."

Bastian shrugs, attempting to minimize her panic. For the sake of the Exiled operation, he needs to make sure she doesn't overreact too soon. "What is this failsafe?"

"Domino," she answers simply.

"The dominos aren't functioning within normal parameters, Deign," he cautions, though he's already sure she doesn't mean just any domino.

She laughs. "Not them. The prototype appears to be recovering well. He'll be on standby should I need to send anyone out after you."

"I can handle this," Bastian says, just the right amount of disdain for her disbelief in him coloring his tone. But inside he's churning. Sending out Dom right now could be disastrous. His memories still haven't returned, and neither has his humanity. Right now he's running on pure programming, with the urges of the parasite unchecked.

"I'll go run your errands to make you feel better." He grins at Deign and motions to two of the guards by the door. "I'll take Filip and Jones with me."

"Don't humor me, Bastian. Do what I pay you for," Deign says softly before turning and effectively dismissing him.

Bastian doesn't look back. Harlow is as safe as he can get her, and right now he needs to try and make it past Kayde's fortifications to the lower level of the facility to warn Mason and Sai of what's coming their way. If nothing else, he needs to make sure they get Marlena out and away from that hellhole.

CHAPTER
Twenty-One

Sai takes a deep breath and tries to imagine herself not squashed into a tunnel with a crowd of people. "Let me guess," she murmurs to Mason. "You hadn't filled out so much last time you went through here?"

He laughs. "Pretty much."

The claustrophobia is hard to drown out, and the air feels so thick, it's difficult to breathe. She closes her eyes and tries not to imagine the front collapsing and blocking the way out.

"Our first stop is the Shine labs." Mason's words rip her out of her delusional nightmare.

She glances at her watch, synchronized with every member of their assault team. "We have seventeen minutes to get there. Will we make it?" She bites her lip.

"You have to," Kayde's voice says in their ears. "I may or may not have accidentally triggered an alarm and alerted everyone in Central to a potential breach."

"Fantastic," Sai mutters under her breath, momentarily distracted. They proceed down a ways, shuffling steadily toward their goal.

"Out through here." Mason motions her ahead of him into a dark room.

She can smell stale beer and peanuts. A woman stands on the other side of an elongated room and nods to acknowledge Mason. She's holding a trap door open. Mason directs the tail end of the troops to leave through the main entrance to the tavern, and start their end of the assignment in the dingy blocks of the city. They need to reach everyone.

"How are you, Mary? Where's Garr?" Mason asks as he drops down the short jump into the tunnel, barely tall enough for him to stand in. He motions for Sai and the rest to follow him as he moves to help the old woman hold the door open from below, while the rest file into the corridor.

"Garr's keeping watch. Things will be much better after tonight." The woman smiles and gently urges Sai along into the tiny, death-trap-like space.

A few minutes later they're all shuffling through another tunnel. "Who was that? Who is Garr?" It's easier to ask questions than to think about phobias.

"Mary knew our mother," he says, lips tight, looking straight ahead. "And Garr... Well, Garr is a long story. Get Bastian to tell you sometime."

Sai makes yet another mental note.

Several minutes later, another group splits off and heads toward the residential blocks of Central. Two sets of operatives deployed, and now it's her turn.

Finally the cramped and dingy path ends. They stop at the exit and glance at their watches.

"In a minute, the camera system in the Shine labs will go down." Kayde's voice is loud and clear through the ear piece. "It'll remain down for thirty minutes only, by which time you need to be out of there."

Sai keeps telling herself to breathe.

Kayde continues her briefing. "The power outage will disable most of the locks, under which different variations of pure Shine are secured. You are go in five...four...three...two...one..."

Mason motions them all forward as the whir of the cameras powering down starts. Swiftly and silently, they move as one down the left-hand corridor. "Here." He motions for different teams to each take a separate door.

"Some workers might be lingering. Not everyone in Central relishes going home. Make sure you take everything you can get your hands on and make it snappy. The less they have to work with, the more precarious the drained reserves become. We have twenty-five minutes. I want three minutes of safety to get back to the entrance area for our TV debut. Talk to people. Don't stab first and ask questions later, okay?" The soldiers nod. "Finish with one room, move onto the next."

Sai, Aishke, and two of the soldiers she only knows by sight separate off into their own groups. While she now understands the importance of Shine for the Exiled to develop Ebony and to, at least temporarily, inhibit the storage of drained psionics, it doesn't make the retrieval any easier for her.

If it were up to her, she'd douse it all with degrading chemicals.

GNW has become complacent. They may have halted the Damascus with their pulse device, but their once-infamous control over pharmaceutical security has grown lax.

In the third room she checks, Sai comes across a man huddled against a tiny glass-doored fridge. In fact, he's hugging it. He holds a button alarm in one hand, frantically pushing it, tears coursing down his face.

He mutters repetitively, eyes clenched shut. "You can't have this. You can't take this."

"Sorry," Sai says as the soldiers pry him away from the fridge. "But we have to take it all."

"They'll kill me," the GNW employee stutters. "I'm the only one on my shift with access to the source. If it's gone and I'm here, they'll kill me." His eyes are wide with fear.

Sai pauses, perplexed by the fridge and its contents, not to mention the suicidal employee. Not only is the refrigerator lock still powered, but it's also locked with an old-fashioned padlock. Her watch beeps. They have four minutes until they need to head back. She thinks quickly. "I don't have much time. If you can help us open this, we can save you. Do you have the key?"

He holds it out, hands shaking.

"We're going to knock you out now and take you with us. At least this way, you won't die. Deal?"

His eyes light up for a second, and he holds his hand up just in time to stop the hit. "It needs to be refrigerated. Take one of the bags next to the machine. The black one is the best one. Don't let it heat up more than 4 Celsius. Ice blocks are in the bottom drawer." He closes his eyes and cringes in anticipation.

"Thank you," Sai says, surprised and slightly suspicious, but she's running out of time and motions to the men with her to knock him out and tie him up. "We'll leave him at the entrance point." She fumbles with the keys, trying not to think how easily metal like this would bend to Dom's will.

"Let me do that?" Mason takes the keys from her and works magic on the locks. "We need to head back now. Hurry up." He squints through the glass door as it opens and deposits the contents into the black bag. "Is this what I think it is?"

Aishke carefully piles ice around it, and Sai shrugs. "Something about the source and if we took it and left him here and it was gone, he'd be killed."

Mason blinks at the information, and pauses before responding. "He's right. If this is Shine's source, they can't create the purity levels they need for psionic extraction without it." Glancing at his watch, he calls out. "Move back to the entry point!"

They make it just in time to stow the people they'd found on their trip. All of them had opted to escape. Maybe the employee retirement plan at GNW wasn't very promising.

The power comes back on, whirring to life. There's a distant sound of fighting, and for the first time in a long time, Sai actually notices the mantra.

For your own safety, please do not leave your designated areas. Report any unauthorized personnel immediately. Remember, the future of GNW depends on you.

She cringes at the sound, and Mason ushers everyone back into the hall and holds his hand up on his watch. "Synchronize! You know the time limit, you know the goal." He turns to Sai and grabs her gently by the shoulders. "Can you do this?"

Sai fights down the urge to giggle nervously. "I don't know."

"You have to. No one wants to see me up there; I'm not memorable. You know what you need to say?"

"After a while, they won't remember me anyway."

He shakes his head. "For now, but we're working on that. Do you know what to say?"

Sai nods, still fighting off the nerves and wondering if her voice will transmit as shaky as she feels.

"When that light turns blue, you speak. You need to enunciate or it'll pick up too much static, understand?"

Sai nods again and clears her throat. Once they're on camera, everyone will see her, everyone will recognize her. She's not sure that's a good thing. The light shines and she takes a deep breath. It's now or never.

"GNW United Conglomerate."

She pauses, using the time to gather the courage she needs to complete the speech.

"I'm not sure what you remember or think about people born with the psionic gene. But I know some of you might believe you've sent loved ones whose powers awoke to a better place. We are here to show you, to prove to you, that you haven't. We are here to show you what really happens to those people."

She pauses again to let the impact sink in. Though, for now, the people will only remember it for a short time—Kayde is recording it for posterity.

"You don't send them to a hospital or a psychiatric ward. Nor does enrolling in one of the Training Facilities guarantee them the chance to live. What it does is ensure their power levels are tested, and if deemed strong enough, they are relocated to the testing facility. Those thought unnecessary are destroyed."

She takes a deep breath to steady herself. "This testing facility's primary use is to extract all of their psionic energy to power the grid that controls us all. To find the best extraction methods, they are tortured and put through pain you can't imagine. The people here are used as batteries for the grid that makes your contentment possible. The only escape for a patient here was death. Until now."

Sai pauses to blink the budding tears away. "This program is all about control. Controlling what we all see, hear, and believe. Controlling how you react to their activities. GNW has no one's interests at heart but their own. And though you may not remember this tomorrow, once they reboot the grids, you can see it now."

She turns and jogs down the right hall, the map of this place burned into her memory. She adjusts the earpiece she's wearing. Kayde said she'd let her know if her control was in danger of being shut down.

Her voice in Sai's ear grounds her, giving her the reassurance she needs. "All sunshine and roses. Lifts are good to go."

She nods grimly, and watches as her team files into the elevators before getting in herself.

Sai steps out of the elevator, already shaken from being piled into a small container of doom. Getting out will be easier as the service elevators are accessible from this level. At least they're larger boxes of doom.

She closes her eyes and envisions the corridors the way the recording showed. A shiver creeps down her spine. Sure of the way in, she heads down the lit corridor, nodding to the first camera she sees with more confidence than she feels in her tightly knotted stomach. No dominos in sight. In a way, it's a relief.

There's a welcome desk, with two nurses huddled behind it. They look like children playing at hide-and-seek.

With a sigh of exasperation, Aishke leans over the counter. "We can see you, you know."

"We're not going to hurt you." Sai smiles at them, resisting the urge to smash them against a wall and scream into their faces. Why would they work here, knowing the pain and suffering that goes on? She counts to ten far too quickly in her head and attempts another smile. "If you could help us, we'd really appreciate it."

Sai can smell the Shine. It's not sealed up tightly enough down here. It's in every breath, in every gust of air. "Masks!" she calls, glad she remembered the warnings Bastian gave. One of the nurses, a pretty blonde thing, crawls out from behind the desk, a determined look on her face.

"What do you need help with?" Her lips tremble, but she holds fast.

"Listen..." Sai reads the nametag. "Marlena, is it?"

The girl nods.

"Do you know? That these people aren't here voluntarily?"

Marlena nods, her face pale. A tear runs down her cheek.

"Will you help us?"

"I can take you," she whispers.

"Marlena, don't listen to them. They're trying to fool you with lies!" comes a muffled voice from behind the counter.

"Shut up, Tawny." Marlena struggles to keep her voice even and plants her hands on her hips with determination. "Follow me. You probably don't have much time."

The march down the hall feels like any other type of hospital, but it's not. Moans echo through the halls and the occasional sob can be heard. Whimpering backs the other sounds like an accompaniment.

"It's too late for the doctors and aides to be here. My shift is over in two hours when the night crew is due in." Marlena's shaking, and Sai bets there are tears dripping down her face. "I never wanted to be here," she murmurs quietly.

With a few quick strides, Sai catches up to her. "It's okay. We can take it from here once we know which corridors to go down. I need the retirement wings and the testing sections. Then you should go and sit back up with Tawny. When we're ready to leave, we can take you with us, if you like."

Marlena looks up, her face smeared with tears. "I'd like that," she whispers. "I've taken part in enough of this."

They reach the first junction, and Marlena indicates the hallways on either side of her. "Down each of these is a retirement wing. There are three rooms in each." Tears drip down her face again, but she clears her throat and continues. "The testing sections—" and her face expresses distaste as they walk farther down the main corridor "—are further down. Until a couple of days ago, dominos guarded them. Now there are just regular guards." She lowers her voice and points. "It's that junction, just there."

There's a scuffle behind them, followed by a thud.

"Sai!" Aishke screams behind her. "Move!"

Sai dives for cover, instinctively pulling Marlena with her. They land uncomfortably against the concrete wall as a rain of crossbow bolts fly past them. They're sitting ducks in this hall.

She looks over at Mason, whose men drop to the ground and provide cover. Marlena starts to crumble to the ground, her back sliding against the white-washed concrete leaving a bright red trail.

"Um..." Her hand rests on a bolt in her left shoulder. "I think they got me."

Sai kneels next to the woman and snaps the feathers off. One hard yank of the tip, and the bolt is out, punctuated by a scream from Marlena. There's no time to be delicate.

Sai exerts power into the wound, knitting the muscle back together and leaving a volatile scab in its place. All in a matter of seconds. Getting beaten up regularly on missions helped hone her healing abilities. "I have work to do. As we move in, go to the previous junction and hide there. We'll come for you."

Her eyes are big and scared, but she nods.

"Sai!" Mason calls loudly. "We can't let them gain this advantage. We don't have enough time."

Sai nods and dismisses Marlena. She's done all she can possibly do right now. Turning to Aishke, she grabs the girl by the shoulders. "You sure you're up to this?"

Aishke nods grimly in response.

"Remember," she says. "For now, disabling them is our preferred choice."

They move two steps to the side so they can see their targets. "Take the one in the front, Ash. On four, break his shields. He has them up."

Aishke blanches. "What if he has too many up?" Her tone is tinged with panic and her strange eyes are abnormally large.

Sai keeps her voice hushed, trusting that the noise of the action around them will drown out her words on camera. "You've broken through nine of mine and Bastian taught me. Not them. You can do this."

Ash nods in return and squares her jaw.

"On four."

They feel like the longest four seconds of her life.

Three.

Everyone is covering them, shooting valuable ammo at the hiding enforcers.

Two.

She clenches her muscles. There will be no steps this time.

One.

She hears Marlena whimpering in the background and feels the team putting the retirees out of their misery.

"Go," she whispers and phases into a man, elbowing him under his jaw. He opens his eyes wide before his head slams into the wall and he drops to the ground. Sai barely notices how startled the other shooter is as Aishke punches through his shields and pulls him to her, letting a couple of the guys around her take him down.

Four left. Sai ignores the flash of doubt gnawing at her. She lunges to the right, drawing her arm in close to execute a swift a punch into the next man's solar plexus. He stumbles, and she rounds with a kick to the head. She slides down to balance the ball of her foot on the wall before launching into a spin straight into the next girl, who barely avoids the hit and stumbles back.

Sai dives to the side, narrowly avoiding her opponent's jab, and crouches to sweep her legs from underneath her. Once on the floor, one quick punch to her temple knocks her out. At least, Sai hopes it wasn't too hard a hit.

Something sharp hits her thigh, but she seals the pain off to deal with later and continues on. Two more to go. She can't afford to fade yet. They're at the end of the hall, too far away to run to without assured death for herself.

Sai takes two steps, phases, and comes in again with an elbow, missing the chin and hitting his neck. She feels his windpipe strain as his head snaps back and pulls a fraction of the psionic reinforcement from under her skin. His neck almost snapped. She lets him crumple to the ground and barely avoids the other opponent about to strike her from behind. It's so close she feels the gap the knife opens in the side of her suit, where the armor is weakest.

GNW troops play dirty. Had it really been her bright idea to try and keep their enemies from suffering casualties? She twists around to face the last opponent just in time to see Mason punch the girl in the back of the head. Her eyes cross before she falls to the floor, limp.

"Thanks," Sai gasps out, clutching her side and suddenly realizing there's a crossbow bolt sticking out of her leg. She lets herself slide to the ground as the rest of the crew rush around to get their attackers tied up. None appear to be dead, merely unconscious. A few broken bones and definitely wounded pride, but alive nevertheless.

Mason flexes his fingers, blocking her from the cameras. "Don't make me do that again."

"Sure thing. I'll get right on that." She concentrates on the wound. It takes a few moments to yank the arrowhead from her leg, and biting down only muffles her scream. She's lucky these bolts don't have barbs.

Sai peeks out from behind Mason and waves at the camera, forcing a smile to her face. "Don't worry about me. Worry about the people forced to live down here." And she gestures at the doors in the hallway.

"I'm fine," she whispers to Mason. "Where's Ash?"

"Here." The girl's face is pale as she approaches them. "I'm here," she says, a little stronger this time, and sits down next to Sai.

Mason nods and directs his men into the remaining sections to take care of anyone else who might be in there and want to play hero. "Nice workmanship," Sai says through the pain as she studies the remnants of the arrowhead. It's a lot easier to knit herself back together than it is others.

A minute later, she gingerly tests her leg for strength and nods her head with relief. "Are you okay, Ash?" she asks as she slides the blade back into the sheath, very glad she hasn't had to use it yet.

"A little tired," the girl says.

"Sai?" There's a crackle in her earpiece. "Sai?"

She presses against her ear and answers. "I hear you."

Kayde sounds relieved as she lets out a sigh. "We have news of another facility. Can you check it out if I send coordinates to your reader?"

"Facility? Near here?" Sai frowns. "I can't reach another city today. I'm not even sure I can reach it in this city. Contrary to popular belief, phasing is not a different word for flying."

She hears muffled laughter on the other end. "Same city. Outskirts. Well hidden in the rubble. Are you hurt?"

"I'm fine. Did you get the draining room footage?"

"Yeah."

Sai is relieved, but frowns at the news of another facility. Definitely not out of character for GNW, but still odd. "I'll take some people with me and scout it out once I've made sure things are done down here."

"I'll send the information."

The crackling in her ear cuts out.

"Can I come?" Aishke asks her as they head into the first section.

"No." Sai holds her hand up to prevent an argument. "You're exhausted. How many shields did you punch through?"

"Fourteen," Ash answers, crossing her arms and glaring at Sai. "But his were sloppy!"

"It was a long pull, and a lot of energy. What're we going to do if we get halfway back and I have to carry you the rest of the way? You know how much energy that will cost me, don't you?"

Ash nods her head reluctantly.

"Good, then that's settled." Sai focuses on the cage-rooms containing people who've experienced far too much pain. "Mason, let me know when we're clear," she says softly, glad they didn't make her go with them into the testing rooms. She has enough of those memories in her head to last her a lifetime, even if they're not hers.

Sai's heart lurches when she hears his voice, but she schools her expression into one of distaste, holding Aishke back with a cautionary hand.

"Don't forget. This is being broadcast. Don't make us look worse than we already do." She can hear him mumble to his entourage. His voice is quiet, commanding, and completely Bastian. He walks with an assurance to his stride Sai knows all too well.

Suddenly Mason is beside her, a nasty grin on his face. "Looky who we have here."

Sai holds Aishke back. "Remember, Mason. No deaths. You can punch him, though," she says through clenched teeth. If this were a real fight, she knows Bastian would beat Mason, but right now, it's all for the cameras.

"Where has the scared little lamb gone?" Bastian mocks her. "There's no getting out of here for you."

Sai sees the flicker of recognition when he spies Marlena slumped off in the corner, but it's gone as quick as it appeared.

She phases in to the guard on his left without a countdown, just as Bastian gapes at Aishke punching through the shields of the guard to his right and dragging her away. If it weren't such a dire situation, Sai would laugh.

She ducks around, pushing her fatigue away, and aims several quick punches at different pressure points to make short work of her target. Sai turns to where Bastian grapples with Mason.

The fight is a dirty one, so no one will think twice if she steps in to help. As she grips him by the collar, he grabs her wrist and pulls her in with both hands, whispering into her ear. "Make sure Marlena gets out. And watch out for Dom. He's dangerous right now. Make this convincing."

Mason grins like he's having fun, and he probably is. With a nice upper hook and a push of his own psionic power so focused Sai can feel it, Mason sends Bastian flying into a wall. His head clips the stone before he slumps to the ground.

Sai takes a second to reach out and make sure he's still breathing before they head off to make their exit, trying not to worry about Bastian's message.

CHAPTER
Twenty-Two

They make their way to the far end of the testing facility. Sai stops short as she hears synchronized footsteps approaching them. She ignores the pain in her leg as she crouches in waiting, but can't keep the surprise off her face when she sees the source of the sound.

A line of six dominos stands in front of her. All very similar, but each uniquely different, and none of them her Dom. These are his clones, his brothers, sisters, siblings—whatever you want to call them. But they are not him. She pushes down a sudden swell of disappointment.

"You are her." One of them speaks. The clang of her voice grates as it echoes through the hall. She steps forward and looks at Sai, before bending to one knee in a bow.

Sai can't help the snort of laughter that escapes her, but they don't appear to take offense at it. "I'm Sai," she states, not entirely sure what they're talking about. If she can keep them occupied long enough, Mason and the rest can start the long trek out.

The domino rises off one knee, and the others close in formation. There's a small golden thirty-five embedded in the metal of the adrium on her left-hand shoulder. "He always thought of you as her."

Sai takes a step back, shaking her head. "He?"

Thirty-Five face flashes through colors and steps closer. "Twelve. Always trusts you."

Sai shivers, and not from the cold. "What do you want?" she asks, modulating her tone and dismissing Mason with a motion of her hand as he waits to see if she needs his help.

"We haven't heard from Twelve in weeks." She pauses, as if searching for vocabulary, her head cocked to one side. "Sometimes he isn't there, but then he always is. We've been waiting, but he isn't back. Now there is you."

"You've been waiting down here?"

Thirty-Five nods.

"Waiting for me?"

"Waiting for Twelve, but he is not here, and you are." She reaches out a hand, before drawing it back. "We are breaking. Something isn't right." Her voice is sad and metallic. The resonance almost makes Sai cry.

"Go with them," she says impulsively, pointing to the mass of patients being ushered out. "Help them get out and then we can help you."

Thirty-Five nods again. "We help you. You help us. We find Twelve."

Sai shakes her head. "I don't know where he is, but this will help. A lot."

Thirty-Five bows her head and moves down the corridor, the others flanking her eerily. As they approach the rest of the group, more dominos filter out of uninhabited hallways. Mason looks up at Sai, startled, and she nods as she brings up the rear.

"Let them help." Sai fights the urge to sit down on the floor, and instead leads Aishke with her through the throng of people slowly making their way to the elevators and out to the safety of the tunnels. "I have to make one last trip. Kayde's tip. Are you okay getting them out?"

Mason nods, and she knows the escape route is well off-camera. She walks out of the corridor and into the limelight. "Our presentation is almost over. We hope you're empowered by this little revelation." She gestures to the guards who're sitting wide-eyed, trying to loosen their bindings.

"In a few hours this will be over, and tickets out of here will be on hold." She lowers her voice. "If this scares you and you no longer want to let lies control you, find one of our patrols, and we'll take you with us, while you're able to think for yourself."

She reaches up and puts a hand over the camera—the signal for Kayde to cut the transmission, but to keep the grid offline for several more hours—then hurries back the way the others headed. Catching up with Mason, she slows down. He carries an exhausted Aishke easily as he walks.

"Do you think it worked?" he asks her.

"I hope so, or Bastian is up the creek." She runs a blood-caked hand through her dirty hair and sighs. "I have to duck out up ahead a bit. I only have a few hours to scout this out and maybe retrieve some more people."

Mason nods. "We'll be fine."

They enter the tunnels from a wider section, and a lean ball of energy barrels into her. "Sai!"

"Iria." Sai smiles. "I thought I told you not to come to the front lines."

"We're the retrieval team. That's not front lines!"

She glares at the older girl and shrugs. "Fine. Whatever."

Sai turns back to Mason as they file through the tunnels. "What's the news? How're the reactions?"

Mason shrugs. "GNW is still scrambling to organize. They're going to erase that broadcast and hunt it down. With their suggestion grids cast over the entire population, this will fade into the memory they choose."

"But Kayde is working on that, right?"

"She can work more efficiently now. You got the Holy Grail, you know."

"What?" She shakes her head, trying to piece together a team in her head.

"That specially stored Shine you secured. With that, Kayde will be able to produce Ebony much easier, and they'll never be able to reproduce the pure Shine they need for extraction. That stuff is the original invention."

"Surely they have a recipe somewhere?"

He shakes his head. "Nope, for all the dickish things in the world my grandfather did, he destroyed any other way to recreate the drug before senility completely over took him."

Sai feels the color drain from her face. "Your grandfather created that crap?"

Mason nods, his own expression grave. "It's not something we're proud of. You have to remember that GNW was initially a pharmaceutical company, trying to give those affected since the meteors the option so their abilities didn't change their lives. I know it's hard to believe, but like many other things, the road to Shine is paved with good intentions."

She swallows several times to make sure she doesn't snap, and decides to change the subject. "Will they get back safely? Have we started getting them to the medic ship? Are Jeffries and Vaneska holding up well enough?"

Iria laughs. "It's going better than expected. Almost feels too good to be true. Jeffries still hates you though."

"Not surprised." Something nags at her in the back of her mind. "How're we schedule-wise?"

Mason glances at his watch. "Just over three hours in."

"Sai." Kayde's voice is loud in her ear and makes her jump.

"Yes," she snaps back. "Sorry, you startled me."

She can hear her laughing. "I should be able to maintain a few more hours of their system. Don't worry—just get back before the sun compromises my connection and the safety of your team."

Sai nods her, forgetting for a moment that she can't see. "Excellent," she says instead and hears the connection phase out.

"Truth be told, Mason, I'd prefer for us to be moving away under the cover of dark in case the light heralds the returning of their brains." She pauses for a moment, cringing as she asks, "Casualties?"

"Three," Iria answers, her tone subdued. "A few dozen are injured, but they'll be fine. She takes a deep breath and sighs. "We lost a few, including Trikel."

Despite only knowing the woman for a short time, her death hurts. Right now, there's no time for grief. Pushing it aside as they arrive at the exit junction she needs, Sai clears her throat. "Iria, come with me. Mason, can I take the two men you sent in with me today?"

"You mean Ethan and Panel?"

"Apparently."

"You need to get better with names." He motions for the men to join them and Sai smiles.

"Adding it to the list. We'll see you in a few hours." As they set off in a steady jog, Sai tries to ignore her unease.

In the end, Mason sends another man to accompany them. Ethan, Panel, and Deacon. Sai is quite certain the extra protection is for Iria, but given her own limp, she might be kidding herself. She highly doubts anything will come of the visit anyway.

"Thanks," Iria says as they exit the tunnel in the outskirts of the city. Her fresh smile falls as she looks around them. "People live here?"

Sai nods, feeling equally as disgusted. "I used to live like this." There's pain in her voice at the memory. Memories of her parents before she collapsed Block 63 make her eyes sting.

"Oh." Iria's voice is softer now, and a faint pink suffuses her mocha skin. "I didn't realize."

Sai concentrates on being careful in this area and ignores Iria's discomfort. She can hear people off in different directions. Screams here and there, the occasional thud of something falling. The worst sounds are those in the corners of the buildings, in the alleyways they pass. The ones doped up, staring at the ceiling of the city, imagining it to be the most perfect place on earth as their brains melt into some sort of goo that barely holds their bodies together.

The effect of Shine on non-psionics makes bile rise in her throat. She glances at Iria, relieved to see it makes someone else feel the same way.

Sai forces herself to focus. It would be so easy to relax and go home. Because that's what her little apartment in the Mobile is—a true home. The first she's ever had. But dubious as it might be, what if there are people here she can save? What if she can give someone else a chance at a home? Everyone deserves a life free from destitution.

She glances at her reader to double-check and frowns. The area looks deserted. But that would discourage people from settling there, which is probably what such a facility would want. Sai pushes out her senses and finds nothing at all, not even an absence of something, which would indicate a hidden lab.

Panel, Deacon, and Ethan fan out, crouched low, weapons at the ready. There's one tall building off to her left, just outside the bare lots. It would make sense that she isn't picking up anything if the facility is underground, just like the other one.

"This way." She motions the rest of her team over to the building. It's badly maintained, but none of it is crumbling yet. Sai frowns.

They move silently, even Iria. It's good to know her friend understands when to shut up. There are three elevators on the right side of the building. That area is well-lit, in contrast to the rest of the structure, but Sai is still wary and her companions' facial expressions echo her own concern.

She walks over to test the exit door down, but the handle is locked and won't budge when she tries to force it. They can't use the emergency staircases to navigate below. Swallowing her hatred for elevators, Sai pushes the button to call one up.

A jolt runs through the supports as the mechanism springs to life, noticeable even through the concrete beneath her feet. The elevator opens to reveal a spacious interior and no troops to fire on them at will. Even with all five of them inside, Sai feels less panicked than she thought she would.

Just as Iria leans forward to hit the close door button, Sai sees something move out the corner of her eye, followed by a sharp, resounding snap.

Everything moves in slow motion. Sai extends her shields around the group and shoves them out of the elevator with the power of a phase, but her energy flags. She slams hard against the cold cement floor at a diagonal angle, one knee on the edge of the doorframe, the other one farther in. The hands reaching for her move sluggishly; her own fingers find no foothold to pull herself forward.

"Sai!" Iria's scream echoes in Sai's head.

There's a blur in front of her, and she feels herself pulled away from the door as excruciating pain rips through her body. She can't feel anything except exploding agony that pulls dark edges around her vision.

"Sai!"

The voice rips her momentarily away from the focus of pain. "Dom?"

"I didn't mean to, Sai. I wasn't me." His words stumble over each other, and his eyes radiate every color of the spectrum.

Pain bleeds back into her mind, and she reaches up a hand to touch the smooth surface of his face as he pulls her into his lap. "It's okay Dom, we got it. We saved them."

Even to her own ears, her words are slurred. But it's okay because she made a difference, and Dom is there after all. Dom and his safe arms. Dom and the hum of his adrium psionics as it infuses her.

She can hear the others murmuring and panicking as she drifts in and out of consciousness, but the only voice she wants to hear soothes her with hurried words.

"Lend me your talent, Sai," Dom coaxes her, and she hears the strain in his voice. "Just lend me the talent. I have the energy."

And it's Dom, so she lets him in, as her head swirls with dizziness. Slowly the pain recedes and her weakness steadies.

Sai isn't sure if she's dreaming or not when she feels herself lifted onto a stretcher. Nor is she sure of how much time has passed. The faint light deep down tugs at her, but she doesn't have the energy to respond.

All that feels certain is the lukewarm touch of Dom's adrium hand as he strokes her hair back from her face, murmuring words she can't define. While the hum of his psionics lulls her to sleep, one thought echoes in her mind:

I will not be broken.

Acknowledgments

A lot of people helped me get to this stage of my career, as well as shaping this book into what it is today.

First and foremost, I have to thank Jami Nord—her unwavering belief in me, her staunch constructive criticism, and her relentless perfectionism. Without it, I wouldn't be here, and I probably wouldn't be writing. And to Owen, whose keen eyes make my fight scenes beautiful.

To Trevor, for letting me pursue my dreams, and to Kami, for being an amazing driving force, even though she never understands why I have to work when she goes to sleep.

To my papilie, for his ability to be constructively critical even though he has a father's pride, and to mumskins, for giving me a love of reading from before I can remember.

To my first-round readers for tearing things apart: Kylie, Quentin, Jai, Anthony, Heather J. and Heather C. To the final round of readers, for nitpicking me into the ground: Becca, papilie, and hubs. And then there was Jude—thank you for believing when no one else did.

To my CPs who encourage gently, while critiquing ruthlessly and supporting me all the way: Brenda, Andrew P. and Heather R.

To my dear friend Carrie Ann, who held my hand every time I panicked and showed me better ways to achieve my ends. And to Caitlin for calming my fears about interior design.

To my amazing cover artist, Sean, and his pure talent and ability to transfer my vision to the cover. Also to Becca again, for being meticulous and amazing in her nitpicking of all the final details.

And thank you to Julia E, Louise, Brianna, Kendra, and all of my street team.

To my amazing friend Margaret, who said yes to helping me and took it so much further.

Thank you to everyone who has cheered me on and helped me bring Sai, Domino, and Bastian into the world

About the Author

KT Hanna has a love for words so extreme, a single word can spark entire worlds.

Born in Australia, she met her husband in a computer game, moved to the U.S.A. and went into culture shock. Bonus? Not as many creatures specifically out to kill you.

When she's not writing, she freelance edits for Chimera Editing, interns for a NYC Agency, and chases her daughter, husband, corgi, and cat. No, she doesn't sleep. She is entirely powered by the number 2, caffeine, and beef jerky.

Chameleon is her first book. You can find out more on KT's website, kthanna.com.

Hybrid (The Domino Project #2) Excerpt

Coming November 2015

CHAPTER ONE

"Why is he different?"

He hears the sounds and tries to give them meaning. His eyes are heavy and unwieldy, but when he manages to open them, an array of colors assault his mind.

"Domino." The word is so soft, almost reverent. He looks in the direction of the speaker and after much concentration defines a man with grey beginning to creep into his hairline and a kind smile. Not sure why it's kind, he knows it is.

"Domino." He attempts to mimic the word, but the sound that escapes his own mouth is harsh and metallic, and he cringes in response.

But the man chuckles and moves forward, placing fingers gently against his throat. A slight hum of warmth enters the system, and he blinks back and tries again.

"Domino."

"Much better." The man claps his hands together, tears dripping from one eye. "I am Mathur."

The Domino cocks his head to one side, still trying to puzzle out the strange surroundings he's in and his innate understanding of everything around him. "I am Domino?" The sound feels different in his mouth now he knows it relates to him.

Mathur nods. "You are my Dom. And I think, this time, you worked."

"Worked?"

The woman over at the desk chuckles, her tone melodic compared to the older man's. Silver weaves its way deftly through her hair, defined in a plait down her back. It makes her seem older than she looks. "We've been trying to make you for a long time." Her tone is almost wistful and Dom frowns.

"Why?"

Mathur blinks at him and for a few moments no one has an answer. "Because we believed we could."

"Belief?" Dom closes his eyes for a few moments, running the concept over in his mind. A mind that, while his, feels foreign and new, yet older and knowing. "Because you wanted to prove yourselves right?"

For a minute Mathur just looks at him, a strange red hue momentarily shadowing his face. "Maybe because we could is not always the best reason, eh?" He smiles kindly, but there's something else Dom doesn't understand behind those eyes. Something distinctly sad.

The man turns and gestures to the woman. "This is Garr."

Dom inclines his head and tries to move, but finds restraints in place. "Am I not supposed to move?"

"Ah, yes," Mathur hurries to his side, the smile back in place, and unbuckles the thick straps. "I did not expect you to wake so soon."

Dom thinks he likes the smile. It's used to put people at ease, but his own face doesn't seem to want to stretch in the right way and he knows, without looking, that his mimicry of it has failed.

"Am I alone?" he asks, unsure of where the question comes from.

"For now." And he believes the man, because after all, why would he create only one Domino and then leave it all alone.

Dom stands next to Bastian, trying to battle the strange tide of emotion in him. The tide he didn't even know he had.

"Can you walk now?" he asks, after his newfound friend breathes easier.

Bastian shakes his head, and even that motion looks uncertain. The gangly teen breathes rapidly, his pupils dilated, and the confident smirk that usually underlies every word he speaks is gone. "No, not yet. Let me sit a while." The words are gasped and he looks pale and ill. Awakening will do that.

"Did it work?" Dom asks.

"I think we'd have visitors if it hadn't." The human boy grins weakly. "Thanks again. I thought the shine would work, but..."

"It dulls the powers, not the awakening moment." Dom shrugs. "You needed a shield."

Bastian watches him for a moment, so long that it makes Dom glare back at him.

"Mathur left you alone."

Dom swallows his surprise and shrugs awkwardly. "Technically."

Dom blinks at his surroundings, at Sai's piercingly pale eyes caught in that one moment of the elevator's suspension. Memories and thoughts come crashing back to him in a split second and he reacts, trying to pull her out in time. But he doesn't make it, and the pain that floods her system is tangible to him.

Even with her healing ability trying to staunch the flow and seal the wound, trying to save her life is almost impossible. He has the energy, the power, but not the experience. This was his fault, but it was also their fault. All those people who thought they knew what it was Mathur and Garr had achieved. The people who'd screwed with his head.

Sai feels so light in his arms, with most of her legs gone. Her pale face is clammy and the dark hair sticks to her skin. Still, she looks up at him, vaguely aware, recognition in her eyes. No judgment in her expression, not yet.

So he holds her, and talks to her, and exerts more of his power to make sure she survives.

Because if there's one thing she's taught him, it's that he doesn't want to be alone.

A faint beeping permeates her consciousness. Sai tries to ask it to stop, because thinking is so difficult, but the words won't form. Her heavy eyelids fight the desire to wake fully.

Fog shrouds her mind and she knows instinctively that something is very wrong, but what it is escapes her.

The refusal of her mind to focus hits Sai in the stomach with a heavy fluttering of leathery wings. She pushes against the murk shrouding her brain. One moment of clarity hits her before the pain takes over and she loses consciousness again.

The haze begins to lift and Sai finds herself waking differently this time. The beeps, though still irritating, are easier to define as infirmary machinery. Instead, she focuses on the whispered voices barely audible over the backdrop of sound.

"How are her vitals?" Mathur's voice sounds weary.

"Steady." The answer is curt and clipped, and though familiar to Sai, she can't quite place it.

"Then the fusion worked?" Dom's voice is clear in her memory, but beleaguered by an inflection uncharacteristic to him.

"It worked."

Sai breathes deeply, calming herself, trying to tone down the images dancing in her head. The fear of small places, crushed by too many people plays in her mind over and over. Machines keep their staccato beat to the movie in her brain. They become more erratic and alerts echo through the room, but she doesn't pay them attention.

Sai finally succeeds in opening her eyes. The room is blindingly white and she blinks several times to focus through the pain. Every part of her hurts, but her legs most of all. They're like fire and ice clashing on her skin. As if she can feel every sinew, every nerve...

"Sai?" Dom leans over her, his smooth brow furrowed.

"Dom?" she crocks out, squinting just a little. "Dom?" she asks again after clearing her throat and forcing her eyes to focus.

"Did I?" It's more of an effort to speak than she realized. "Did I hurt people again?" she asks, surprised to feel a tear run down her cheek at the thought.

"No." Dom swallows visibly and looks away. "You saved people."

"Then why?" Sai asks as she struggles to sit up and gasps in pain.

The audible snap as they waited for the doors to close. The split second decision to phase push the others out. Dom suddenly there and apologizing. The look in his eyes. Her giving him permission to use her talent.

And the pain. So much pain.

She averts her eyes, anger and bewilderment at war in her mind, and clenches her fists.

The beeping of the machines around her is the only sound in the room.

The pain in her legs makes sense now, and she's loathe to look and see they're no longer there. Phantom pain is something she's heard of, but never truly believed existed. When some part of the body can't be replaced, the brain sometimes makes do with what it has and won't forget the missing section.

"Damn." Her whisper croaks a little again, her throat still too dry, but she pushes the words out anyway. "It was you, Dom?" her voice cracks on his name and the tears flow.

"Sai, I..." Dom's shoulders sag.

Sai turns her head away, tears streaming down her face to soak in the pillow. She can hear footsteps leave the room. How could he not deny it? How did he dare be there?

But after all, hadn't he also saved her, a tiny voice whispers in the back of her mind. And she knows that's right too. Confusion doesn't even begin to describe the pain in her chest and the thoughts in her head.

Her ability to help the Exiled is gone. There will be no redemption now. Her parents were right. She's useless.

The door swooshes closed and she pushes with her mind, checking for privacy only to realize Dom is the only one who left.

Her chest constricts and she opens her eyes to stare at the tented ceiling.

"Talk to us." Mathur's accent is as lulling as ever. Tempting even.

But Sai just shakes her head, feeling for once like the child she never had the chance to be: vulnerable, alone and scared.

Mason moves around to the other side, flanking her. "Sai, will you listen to what we have to say? There are things you need to understand."

She nods.

"I'll keep it brief." Mason pauses. "Dom's trigger was set incorrectly. In his haste to set it in time, Bastian emphasized the trigger on your appearance and not your name. It was only when Dom saw you that his trigger unlocked. Although he was supposed to kill you, he truly did save you."

"Saved me?" Sai almost spits the word out. "I'll be useless for the rest of my life." He face crumbles and the tears pour out despite her best efforts. "Just let me sleep."

Mason sighs and shrugs his shoulders. "You have to listen to Mathur first."

She rolls her head back over and locates the old man. He feels like the father she never had. "What?" the word comes out sullenly instead of with the combative force she intended, but there's no energy left to draw on.

Mathur smiles gently at her. "You will be okay, Sai."

She blinks a few times, wondering if he's finally gone senile. "I distinctly remember the pain. No legs is no mobility."

"But Sai," and he pulls up his trouser leg to reveal the iridescent metal of his prosthetic limb. "You have legs."

Sai blinks at him and tries to level herself up to look at her own body, but everything hurts and her arms give way.

"Careful. You have been out of it for a while. You are going to need to regain some of your strength before we work on anything else." Mathur pushes her back down and pats her head. "Even if you lost everything Sai, you will still be the same person. Nothing will ever change how much you have helped everyone."

Tears threaten to take over again, but Sai gulps them back. "This will work?" she asks suspicion waring with fear and hope.

Mathur chuckles. "If you get rest and do not let yourself get too worked up? Definitely. You will be capable of more than you imagine. But you must promise me this one thing."

"What?" Sai asks warily.

"Consider what Mason said true. That Dom had no real choice in the matter until he saw you and triggered himself. If it was anyone's fault, then it was mine. I left that failsafe there and made the reset possible."

"I'll try." With the confusion and anger warring inside her, it's the best she can offer.

"It is enough for now. I simply ask that you do try." Mathur smiles and her and moves to the door. "Sleep a bit, you need your rest."

His request is easier said than done. All Sai sees as she lies there looking at the ceiling is the elevator the second before it falls. On repeat.

11894991R00214

Printed in Great Britain
by Amazon.co.uk, Ltd.,
Marston Gate.